SNOW X DWIGHT

DAMSELS OF DISTRESS

DAKOTA KROUT

MOUNTAINDALE
PRESS

To my sister Brianna, a well-adjusted chiropractor, and the only member of my family I would march into war with.

CHAPTER
ONE

"I CAN'T *BELIEVE* they're letting us go on our own!" Rose squealed just as the carriage rattled over the last of the cobblestones and settled onto a quieter dirt path. "There it is, the farthest we've ever been away from home without our parents."

Snow turned away from the window, smiling brightly at her twin sister. "Can you think of a better birthday present than *not* being surrounded on all sides by people we barely know?"

"I mean, we're going to have to be back on our birthday *proper*." Rose half-shrugged, though she flung her hand in the air to show how little it mattered at that moment. "Wouldn't want to waste any time getting our *Advanced* Class, now would we?"

It was the first time they'd been allowed to journey out to their mother's cottage on their own, as the trip had always been a family event held over the autumn equinox, which also happened to be their birthdays. 'Alone' may have been a bit of a stretch, as a half-dozen royal knights rode along behind the princesses' carriage. As their father always warned them: hope has soft edges; daggers do not.

Even so, their usual minders—stuffy maids obsessed with etiquette—had been left behind, giving the girls a chance for a genuine vacation. After their fourteenth birthday, they would need to resume their studies in kingdom management and focus on advancing their newly granted skills as swiftly as possible.

Whether each became the queen of their own kingdom or a neighboring one, it was essential that they were prepared to take on those responsibilities, something the maids they had left behind never allowed them to go so much as a day without hearing.

"Speaking of skills…" Rose leaned in conspiratorially. "Am I wrong in thinking you had a hand in *convincing* them to let us go? Not two weeks ago, father all but forbade this adventure."

Snow's laugh was a soft, delicate thing as she shook her head. "You know I wouldn't do that, Rose! We must have just impressed them over the last few weeks, or perhaps they're planning a surprise of some kind and need us out of the way. Besides, with the way father's been acting, I'd been under the assumption *you* had something to do with the trip coming together."

Thanks to her sister's reminder, Snow glanced down at the details of her system-granted Basic Class and skills. Trailing her right index finger across the inseam of her left arm, she silently read the golden words that wrote themselves out on her pale skin.

Basic Class: Darling Princess
Basic Skill: Precocious Command: Level 10/10.
Having been raised as a princess, one who cares deeply about those under her care, you [Perfectly] understand the body language of others around you who are not using skills or magical effects to specifically hide these physical reactions.

Through various means, such as pleading, showcasing diligence, or demonstrating scholarly behavior, you can [Perfectly] persuade people to fulfill your requests. This skill [Perfectly] enhances your ability to gauge moods and personalities, allowing you to tailor your approach for maximum effect. Whether it's convincing courtiers to support your initiatives or inspiring your subjects with your dedication, Precocious Command makes you [Perfectly] adept at navigating complex social dynamics.

Advanced Skill: Aura of Innocence: Level 6/10.
Aura of Innocence grants you an enchanting presence, making you exude an air of purity, kindness, and sincerity, [Considerably] amplifying your natural charm. When speaking in a heartfelt manner, your true thoughts on the issue will be [Considerably] felt by those you are speaking with. If your words and meaning are in alignment, the resistance of those around you will soften, making them [Considerably] more receptive to your words.

Aura of Innocence also has a unique effect of attracting small animals. Birds, rabbits, and other gentle creatures find [Considerable] comfort in your presence, often gathering around you in a serene display of trust and affection.

Requirement to advance: Over the course of three consecutive meals, eat only what you gather for yourself. Two-thirds of your intake must be meat.

"As if I could get away with something like that," Rose shot her twin and exaggerated pout. "Not after Mother started ordering customized magical items to alert them if they were being 'affected by an outside source'. Seriously, you think keeping someone in a good mood for a couple days would be a positive thing—they acted like I had tried to melt his brain or something."

"I kind of understood what they were getting at," Snow carefully stated, not wanting to make her sister think she was siding with her parents *too* much. "Maintaining the exact same mood for so long just isn't natural. Who knows what sort of long-term effect that could have on someone?"

Rose only shrugged, dismissing the familiar argument out of hand. Snow could only return to looking out the window, though her thoughts stayed on her twin. They were as different from each other as night was from day, with Snow being soft, quiet, and helpful, while Rose was outgoing and always ready to have an adventure—or pick a fight. Even their class and skills seemed to be two halves of a whole, though the system seemed to have mixed up who should have what.

Snow was given the ability to persuade and convince others through her words and deeds, whereas Rose could directly alter and impact their mood. Given her less-exuberant nature, Snow's skills had grown slower than her sister's, but Rose's rampant usage had caused... issues. People were always second guessing themselves around the younger of the two twins, wondering if how they were feeling at the moment was natural or not.

At least with Snow's power, they were able to hear her arguments and come to a decision on their own, as they were only more *likely* to be swayed. As her mother had always cautioned her, even when her ability to be more convincing had been *Perfected*, that didn't mean she'd always get her way. In fact, even when she had good reasons, great ideas, and *knew* she was in the right, people would likely disagree or refuse, based on their own deeply held ideals.

The companionable silence continued until the smallish home finally came into view, nestled along a riverbank, multi-colored stone walls bathed in the soft autumn light. Snow's mind settled as she breathed in the peace that always filled her when arriving at the cottage. This wasn't *just* their family retreat, but a way for them to get away from the pressures of court and act like an actual family—at least once a year. "Haa... lots of good memories here, right, Rose?"

"Yeah. Hey, what do you think the chances are of getting

one of the knights to practice with me? Even if we *are* going to be away from the training grounds for the next week, that doesn't mean I have to let the others get ahead of me." Rose's hand almost unconsciously reached for the sheathed sword propped up next to her in the carriage. "I think I've just about figured out how to fight someone to a standstill by making them feel like they want to give up."

"Better than inciting them to extreme violence when they're supposed to be teaching you." Snow ruefully chuckled as she pushed open the carriage door. "Can we take at least a couple of days and just, you know, *relax*? Maybe we can go to the nearby village and see what they've been working on. I bet I could convince Mother to host a fair here, if I bring back some samples of their wares."

"Hey! It's not easy to push an emotion on someone when *I'm* not feeling it," Rose protested as she popped out and stretched on the manicured lawn. "Same as you, right? If you don't believe what you're saying, it's a lot harder to make them go along with you. When I'm fighting, it's *exciting*. Convincing someone to be so bored with the fight they just give up in the middle of it...? I think that's going to be enough to push me into *Mastery*."

"*Mastery*? Isn't that level nine?" Snow hadn't thought her sister was that much more advanced than her, but they had stopped discussing exact levels years ago, when she started to fall behind. "I'm only at *Considerable*, level six, with my Advanced Skill. That's incredible, Rose!"

Clearly uncomfortable, her strawberry-blonde-haired twin glanced away, not meeting Snow's eyes. "Yeah, thanks. It's a lot of fun to test out. Want to go fishing while they unload? Or something?"

Instead of denying her sister, as she'd clearly expected, Snow thought it over and agreed. While she wouldn't say it aloud, the raven-haired teen had truly been shocked at how far behind she'd fallen in skill level—and immediately resolved to make up the difference. "Yeah… I think I wouldn't mind fish for dinner, and… maybe breakfast and lunch tomorrow."

"Fish for three meals in a-" Rose cut off, wincing in understanding as she realized what was happening. They tended to talk about most things, and the requirement for Snow's skill to increase a level had been the same for nearly half a year. The sweet young lady simply didn't have it in her to sing for her supper, to have the small animals that flocked to listen to her voice get slain, gutted, and plucked, only to appear on her plate later that day. "Fish, huh? Yeah. I can eat that for a day or two. Whatever you think sounds good."

"Thanks." Snow flushed slightly, even if she didn't *quite* understand why she was feeling so embarrassed. Setting up next to the slow, lazy river flowing next to the cottage, the twins spent the rest of the morning quietly fishing. As the lunch hour came around, a servant spread out a small picnic beside them before leaving them to enjoy the perfect day.

Leaves colored in vibrant hues drifted from the trees, painting the ground or floating away if they landed in the water. The sun cast a soft, warm light over everything, and soon Snow felt her eyes grow heavy as she soaked in the silence. Letting out a long, happy sigh, she started to drift away, only to sit bolt upright, sputtering furiously as she was splashed by the large fish Rose had yanked from the water.

"I *got* one!" Seeing her twin succeed always put a smile on Snow's face, but also drove home that she'd once *again* stopped before succeeding. As Rose put the fish on a string and dropped it back in the water to keep it fresh, Snow lifted her own line and took a deep breath.

"Want to see my fish call?" Rose glanced over curiously as Snow's eyes twinkled with mischief. "*Here,* fishy, fishy, fishy! You know you want to take the bait!"

"Oh look." Rose rolled her eyes dramatically. "It's the exact same as her duck, deer, and rabbit call. Let me guess, it's going to be just as effective-"

Splash!

Snow yanked on her pole as it bent under the weight of a fish, laughing with excitement as she reeled it in. After a brief fight, she lifted it out of the water and turned to her sister. "Works every time."

Ro~oar.

Before they could banter any further, a guttural, animalistic bellow filled their ears. They pushed themselves to their feet, looking frantically for the source of the sound, even as they prepared to run. They found it at the same moment: across the river, a man was running toward them, clutching a large sack in his hand as a truly gargantuan bear closed in on him from behind.

"Abyss!" Rose belted out. "*Run*, sir!"

"This way! The cottage has wards to keep out dangerous entities!" Snow shouted as she waved her arms above her head. "Swim! You only need to make it to shore!"

Yet the man ignored them, save for flashing a cocky grin as he dropped his sack and turned back to face the beast closing in on him. A gleaming dagger appeared in his hand, and he swiped at the creature with full confidence that he'd be able to take it down.

The bear slid to a stop just before the blade would have bit into its side, pushing itself up into a standing position and letting out another fearsome roar. Rose watched the interaction with rapt attention, even as Snow desperately shouted for the knights to come and help the man. There was no reply, and the older twin wasn't about to run off and leave the man to fend for himself.

After searching along the ground, she grabbed a large stick and started toward the water's edge, only for her sister to grab her shoulders and pull her back. "Rose, what are you doing? He needs help!"

"Are you kidding? If anyone needs help, it's the *bear!*" Her twin's words caused Snow to look at the pitched battle once more, and her jaw dropped at the amount of blood coating the bear's fur, the volume increasing every second. The man was barely shorter than the animal he was fighting and was clearly highly skilled with his blade. Even so, in terms of raw strength, he was desperately outmatched. He ducked under a swinging paw, coming up and kicking at the bear's chest in an attempt to knock it over, only to fall on his back when the bear didn't budge.

Snow's shriek died on her lips as he rolled to the side, avoiding the bear's follow-up lunge. Not wasting a moment, the man grabbed his sack and threw himself off the riverbank, plunging into the water with the beast close behind. Now having a use for the long stick she had grabbed, Snow rushed into the shallows and shoved it forward, both twins yanking on it as the man gripped the other end. The bear let out a deep grunt of frustration as his prey was pulled away, going still and watching the man as he slowly drifted downriver.

"Ha-*haa*!" The man got to his feet, knee-deep in the shallows, and shook off the river water like a dog before smiling brightly at the twins and striking a heroic pose. "That bear won't soon forget a brush with *Gasteel*! Thank you for your assistance, though it certainly wasn't necessary. Oh, fish! Fantastic, I've a real hankering for a victory dinner after my usual morning bear wrestling session."

Reaching down, he grabbed the string their catches were on, cutting through it with his dagger in a single motion. Rose stepped forward and tried to grab it back, but he avoided her grasping hand simply by turning and watching the bear float away. Still, the fiery young princess wasn't about to let him do as he pleased. "Hey! That's *our* fish. Are you really going to steal from us right after we saved your life?"

"You did *nothing* of the sort," Gasteel scoffed incredulously, finally taking his eyes off the bear and looking at the furious young woman in amusement. "Consider this payment for getting to see *me* in action from so close. I'll finish that creature off later. Truth be told, it's a real menace. Natural bears don't act so intelligently; would you believe it set an ambush for me?"

"Did you steal *its* fish, too?" Rose ground out around clenched teeth.

Snow realized the situation was devolving, so she put a hand on her sister's arm, fully pulling her back onto shore. "Sir, I don't know where you came from, but if you're hungry, you are welcome to share in our catch. I'll have the servants start a fire so you can dry your clothes and get on your way."

"On my way?" Hefting his waterlogged sack, Gasteel showed a smile with too many teeth as he waded through the water, a dark glint in his eye. "But I see a perfectly acceptable house I can use as a base right there. If I'm going to be doing the locals the favor of removing this man-eating bear, the very least they could do is host Ba... they can host Gasteel, bravest and most handsome-"

Thrummm.

A wave of power shook the air as the man attempted to step on to shore, smacking him back into the water as though he'd been hit by a swinging battering ram. His belongings went flying, mostly landing in the water, though a blanket rolled onto the ground near the girls. The twins dropped to the ground and let out a startled, quickly cut-off scream. They covered their ears until the sound faded, only slowly looking up and around to see what had happened as knights came rushing from the house.

When they arrived and heard what the princesses had to say, each of them drew their weapons and began searching along the shore for the vanished Gasteel. Snow looked at Rose, not a hint of levity in her expression. "He activated the wards by trying to step onto our land... what does that mean? I thought it was only supposed to keep dangerous beasts away."

"Given his manners, I'm not shocked it considered him an

animal." Rose kicked at the bundled blanket. The material unfurled as it rolled closer to the river, revealing a strange, onyx-black totem. Both of them went silent as a dark, malevolent feeling radiated outward from bear-shaped carving. "What... is *that?*"

"Whatever it is, we need to get rid of it." Snow stepped forward, the sensation of wrongness increasing as she intentionally drew closer to the item. "It's-"

*Ro~oar." Their chins lifted, gazes traveling across the water to land on a sopping wet bear, river water still raining off of it. Strangely enough, the sound it made was... plaintive? Snow stared at the ursine creature, which sat back on its haunches and pressed its front paws together as though pleading with them.

"Did that man *actually* steal something from you?" Snow muttered the words, and to her surprise, the creature nodded as if it could understand her. After glancing at her twin for confirmation that she'd seen the same thing, the older of the twins pointed at the statue, "Is this yours? Do you want it?"

The bear nodded several times, letting out several soft *chuffs*. Rose shook her head. "This is clearly some kind of evil magical item. Should we really be handing it over to an intelligent beast? Doesn't the very fact that it can understand us mean it's at least an *Awakened* Beast? What if this is what it needs in order to become a true monster?"

"I don't think that's what this is." Snow stated slowly, picking up her long stick and using it to adjust the blanket, then push the totem onto it. "After seeing the kind of person the bear was chasing, I kind of want to give it the benefit of the doubt?"

"Really, Snow?" Rose twitched her head back and forth. "Just because one person is bad doesn't mean the other creature is *good.*"

"I may not know the *best* thing to do, so all I can do is hope I'm doing the next *right* thing." Snow crouched next to one side of the blanket. "Can you grab the other side? I think we can slingshot this across the river if we work together."

"Hope has soft edges; *daggers* do not," Rose grumbled even as she complied. Grasping the other corners of the blanket, they pulled it taut and launched the totem across the river.

The bear caught the foul item between its paws in a very human-like motion, letting out a deep bellow of rage and excitement as it *chomped* down on the glassy-smooth surface. A thick black miasma exploded out of the shattered statue, surrounding the bear for a brief few moments before blowing away in the wind....

... leaving behind a young man covered in thin, still-bleeding cuts.

TWO

"*Yaaaah!*" The muscled teenager across the river jumped in the air, pumping his fist. "I'm me again!"

"What." Rose spoke for both of the twins as they stared at the solo celebration. Somehow, he heard the dry, shocked statement and turned to face them, immediately shifting into a courtly bow.

"Thank you for saving me from that curse!" he practically shouted at the ground he was now nearly parallel with. "I've been stuck as a bear for over a year, and that maniac has been hunting me for nearly six months. I admit, I was starting to lose myself. Had I stayed in that form much longer, I may have been trapped permanently."

"How... were you a bear?" When Snow finally managed to speak, pure incredulity filled her voice. "Curses can *transform* you into-?"

The man popped upright, seemingly bubbling with energy as he rushed to the water's edge. "Give me a moment, I can *bear*-ly hear you! Ha!"

Moments later, he was in the water, swimming powerfully toward the twins. Reaching the shallows, he waded closer... and stepped onto shore with no sign of the wards activating.

Snow felt unexpectedly relieved and allowed herself to relax slightly as the grinning young man restarted his tale.

"It's so nice to finally be able to *speak* again." Seeing how his rescuers shied away slightly, he lifted his hands to signal 'friend', staying rooted in place as he recounted, "My kingdom came under attack from a coven of Witches and their minions. They made off with several of our most precious treasures, and we mobilized after them. During the chase, my father and brothers fell back upon seeing their dark powers, but I failed to heed the warnings."

His eyes went distant, seeming to relive the tale even as he told it. The tips of his fingers brushed against his arm, drawing Snow's eyes to where a faint, raised scar puckered his skin. Seeing the pain on his face, she spoke up before he could continue further. "You don't need to say more. We can help you get back and-"

"No, please, I don't mind. There's a type of healing to be had in sharing one's sorrows—especially since my tribulations have come to a close." Even as he spoke, he offered her a warm smile of thankfulness. "I would gladly accept whatever help you could offer in returning me to my home. I've traveled... I don't even know how far. My supplies are gone. Not to mention, the food I was able to eat as an animal would not sustain me now, and..."

He glanced down, flushing suddenly before letting out a relieved sigh. "It seems my clothes have transformed with me, thank the system. I had completely forgotten to worry that they wouldn't survive the curse."

"Yeah, that would've been... unfortunate," Rose agreed with a shudder. "You have a name, or should we keep thinking of you as 'that guy that was a bear just now'?"

Snow rolled her eyes for her sister's benefit even as the young man quickly introduced himself. "Dwight Charmant, Duke of Artek. Or, presumptive Duke, so long as nothing unfortunate has befallen my brother, Crown Prince Charmant

Charmant the Second. Err… also, assuming my father has not declared me dead and raised another to my position."

"Your father's alive, Duke *singular* Charmant?" Rose questioned him without pause, getting a nod in reply, "You look to be about… what, fifteen? Then you're not a duke *yet*; you're a prince."

"Duke," he stated with a touch of steel in his voice. "The only way I become a prince is if my brother has been felled, and I would never wish an ill fate on him."

"Well, Duke Charmant, please allow us to offer you hospitality," Snow declared firmly upon seeing her now-guest begin to shiver as the excitement of his rescue wore off, and the chill from the river set in. "I'm looking forward to hearing the rest of your troubles, but let's not add to them by allowing you to catch your death. Besides, when's the last time you had a hot meal?"

"Too-" He cleared his throat and looked away, his jaw working as he bit clamped down on his outsized emotional response. When he spoke again, his voice was raw. "Too long. It would mean the world to me to dine with you… both. To be treated like a person again."

"Then come, let us away." Snow pulled her sister along, still not perfectly comfortable with the man claiming to be foreign royalty.

The twins hurried to the door of the cottage just as the royal knights returned, their search for Gasteel unsuccessful. After a quick introduction and explanation, the knights looked at Dwight with less suspicion—not *no* suspicion, but less—and he was shown to a room to be dressed in warm and dry clothes. When he rejoined the gathering, there were several additional curious people listening in as he continued his story.

"I ranged far afield, doggedly pursuing the Witches, who had robbed our vault. Apparently, my hunt brought them no end of annoyance, as they were unable to settle in and celebrate their successful raid. In the end, one of them threw a brew in the air, shattering it with an incantation and bathing me in a dark energy. Just before it coated me, I activated my skill and took the attack in my second form-"

"Ah!" Sir Upp, the royal knight who had been charged with Snow's safety since she was a baby, snapped his fingers in excitement as he made a connection. "I *have* heard of your kingdom! By the system, Prince Charmant... you're a long way from home."

Completely unconcerned with the interruption, the young man leaned forward eagerly. "How distant is a 'long way'? I traveled as an animal would, but with the boundless, endless stamina of humanity."

"The Kingdom of Artek is in the northernmost parts of the continent, two years' travel by carriage if there are no delays whatsoever," Sir Upp enthusiastically explained, not at all bothered by how Dwight's face fell at the information. "You took a direct strike from a Witch and were only inconvenienced? It speaks well of your powers to be able to resist her dark influence."

The royal knight turned to address the twin princesses. "The royal family is known to have a powerful bloodline gained in the distant past by a Dire Ursa, who ascended to Monstrous status, only to turn away from its base desires and walk the path of a *Hero* after it gained intelligence—becoming essentially the best of human in all ways that matter. Princess, those of royal blood are rumored to be able to transform into bears, are powerful combatants, and have potent resistances to most ill effects."

"Princess?" Dwight perked up at the casual mention by the knight. "One of you is a princess? I had assumed you were both from some noble family, but this makes expressing my gratitude much easier!"

Leaping to his feet, he shifted into a deep bow once more, "Princess, you who have saved my life, please accept my formal offer of engagement. While I may not be from the largest kingdom on the continent, we are powerful and wealthy."

"Wow." Rose leaned back in her chair. "Can you believe it? You do something nice for someone, and they try to ruin your life in return?"

"Rose!" Snow hissed in shock at her sister's jest, but the blonde powered on without concern.

"Tell me this, Dwight. Which one of us is the princess? Who are you proposing to right now?" The princess leaned forward, glaring at the older boy. "How are you able to stand there with a straight face and announce the first thing that crosses your mind like that? I understand you've been away from other people for a long time, but right now, I think you should *feel ashamed*."

The duke stumbled away, his eyes rolling in his head as a wave of intense emotion washed over him, forcibly wiping the smile off his face. "No insult was intended, I swear! I'm simply attempting to honor the life debt I owe-"

"Stop it." Snow shot to her feet, pulling her sister's chair back away from the table and breaking her concentration. "Look at him! He's shaking worse than when he broke a curse and immediately swam across the river. It's been less than an hour since he managed to return to his current form. Can we *please* give him some grace? If not, would you at least tell me what's the *matter* with you?"

"He's trying to *separate* us!" Rose shouted at her sister, going pale as she realized her sister's passive persuasion had caused her to blurt out her real thoughts. Even so, she didn't stop herself from speaking, "You heard what Sir Upp just said! Dwight's kingdom is two *years'* travel by carriage. You're going to be queen here someday. What if our parents actually *accepted* his outlandish proposal? Do you *want* me that far away from you?"

Completely taken aback by her sister's outburst, Snow

hesitated for a long moment before leaning forward and wrapping her arms around the outraged twin. "Of course I don't want us to be that far apart. But why in the world do you think *I'm* going to be queen? I'm two and a half minutes older than you are; that doesn't matter when choosing the line of succession. You're powerful, you can fight, and your skills are growing. Not to mention…"

"Oh, don't say it." Rose huffed as she saw a familiar pain in her sister's eyes.

"You know it's true." Snow overrode her sister in a quiet tone. "What kingdom would accept a queen who only has *Epic* skills like I do? With five modifiers, you have a *Legendary* skill set and are the clear choice to be the next sovereign. I'm completely fine with that, as it means I'll be able to live a happy life and support you in the background."

"You're legitimately a born, system-approved diplomat." Rose groaned uncomfortably, pushing her sister away. "I can't believe you think you won't be able to take the crown because you have 'only' Epic skills."

"Four modifiers means I have less versatility." Snow shrugged nonchalantly. "It's just a fact. Our neighbors would see us as weakened, and even if I have a better chance of talking people into an alliance… those are just words. Kingdoms *respect* strength."

"Look, let's not… discuss such private matters in the open like this." Rose turned to look at the duke, who had remained silent since her outburst. "My apologies, Duke Charmant. I tend to feel deeply, as I'm sure you realized by now."

"Yes. If what you caused me to feel was even a fraction of your true passion… that is far beyond my standard, um…" The duke stammered, trying to figure out how to remain polite after being subjected to her skills. "That depth of emotion may chase me, but it has never before managed to engulf me."

"Poetic way to reveal your shallow ability to feel-" Rose bit off her retaliatory remark as Snow gave her a *look*. "My, uh, *apologies* once again. It's been a… trying day. Please, we've interrupted you so many times. Tell your story?"

"Ah. Yes. Certainly." Dwight furrowed his brow, his expression clearing as he remembered what he'd been saying, though he spoke with a hint less enthusiasm than he had been. "Just before the foul attack of the Witch landed, I transformed, using my bloodline's Class Skill. Instead of doing… whatever it was supposed to do, the cursed fluid wrapped around me, partially cutting me off from the system by removing my ability to return to my human form."

The duke paused for a heartbeat, his face clouding, "From how my horse was rendered to glue, I can only assume the effects of the vile brew were meant to be far deadlier. Ah… Snowflake. You'll be missed."

"Snowflake… melted?" Snow gulped at the vivid image his story conjured in her mind, hoping it wasn't a portent of her own future. "Yet you were merely trapped? That must be *some* magical resistance. How did you know to seek out the totem which reversed its effects?"

"Instead of dissipating, or washing off, after the fluid took effect, it came together and formed that totem." Dwight grunted in frustration, "The Witches took it with them, telling me they would be sending a hunter to show me 'how it felt'. I was meant to fight him to the death to reverse this curse, but he was far too skilled. Even when my last-ditch ambush went all but perfectly, the hunter would have at *least* escaped except… well, you know the rest."

"You're safe now, lad!" Sir Upp boisterously stated, slapping a hand on Dwight's shoulder and gently shaking him. "I'll send a couple of my men back to the palace with you to explain your situation. I'm certain they'll send you home in style. We should be off soon; otherwise it'll be too dark to-"

"I cannot rest here?" Dwight's face fell slightly as Sir Upp shook his head firmly.

"Certainly not! It would be *completely* improper for you to stay under the same roof as the princesses." The knight pulled his hand away, a slight suction pulling at Dwight's shoulder as he did so. "Apologies, I seem to be a bit sticky."

"But why?" Dwight glanced at the hand in question with no small amount of concern in his eyes.

"Sorry you lost a year to being a bear, Duke Charmant," Rose casually called, calmer now that she knew this interloper would be moving along shortly. "I'm glad we could help you."

"It's not all bad." Dwight turned back to the twins, looking between them. "So, you are *both* princesses of this kingdom? How fascinating. Oh, when I say it's not all bad, being a bear was... surprisingly pleasant when I wasn't being hunted. Beyond giving me a deep grudge against Witches—never a bad thing—the situation provided fantastic growth for my skills. In fact, I will gain access to my Breakthrough Skill upon reaching a Class Shrine."

"Congratulations! That's quite the achievement." Snow grasped his offer of an olive branch, turning the conversation to more pleasant topics.

Yet, the meal could only last so long, and soon a pair of knights were flanking the duke as he walked toward a prepared horse. Pulling himself on with the ease of someone who had long hours of training with large animals, he looked at the twins and raised a hand. "I shall not forget my promise nor the debt I owe you. Before I sojourn home, I will surely take the time to repeat my offer to the king and queen. Farewell, and I hope to see you again someday."

"Farewell, Duke Charmant," Snow called cheerfully.

"Four years at the minimum, if his journey has no delays," Rose commented under her breath, "Glad we could help the guy, but we're never seeing *him* again. Good riddance."

The rest of the week they had at the cottage passed slowly and uneventfully compared to the first day. Each day spent together allowed the twins to relax further, speaking on their dreams and plans for the future. Still, time relentlessly marched forward, and soon they had returned to their carriage and were making the trip back to the capital city.

"At least *one* of us managed to use our time productively." Rose poked at Snow as the raven-haired princess glanced happily at her left arm. Even with as relaxed as the last few days had been, Snow had managed to make more progress than she had in the previous six months.

Skill increase! Aura of Innocence [Level 6 (Considerable) → Level 7 (Proficient)]!

Requirement to advance to level 8: Mediate a peace talk between feuding groups commanding immense power, calming tensions on both sides.

Their journey home lasted two full days, and they managed to arrive at the capital, the port city of Deckbett, on the eve of their birthday. From there, it was only an hour through the forest and up the mountain to reach the palace just outside the city. As they clamored out of the carriage, ready to rush in and learn how Dwight had been received, their father stepped out to greet them.

"Welcome home, Snow. Rose." The excitement the twins had been feeling melted away as they took in the dark rings under his eyes, his haggard appearance, and the general air of despair surrounding him.

"Father-?" Snow began, only for Rose to interject.

"What's happened? What's the matter?"

The king ran a hand through his hair, letting out a deep sigh. "I had hoped your return would be a joyous occasion. Unfortunately... I do not have good news to share. A few weeks ago, your mother, the queen, was struck by a severe illness. We didn't want to scare you, but unfortunately... the healers and alchemists have been unable to find a curative which will restore her. She's resting now, but-"

Without waiting for another word, Rose dashed into the palace.

"-she doesn't have long," the tired man finished sadly.

"Father… why would you send us away?" Snow inquired as she stepped forward and pulled him into an embrace. Hot tears trickled down her hair as the king quietly allowed his feelings to spill over, soon joined by hers. They parted slightly and began walking toward the queen's chambers.

"We had hoped that this would all be taken care of, and you wouldn't have to worry for her." His words rang hollow, but there just wasn't more he could offer. "Don't allow yourself to fall into despair. We have the best people in the kingdom searching for a cure…"

"…She's going to be *fine*."

CHAPTER

THREE

THE WOMAN PLAYING her lute at the queen's funeral wove the most entrancing, heart-wrenching music Snow had ever had the misfortune of hearing. Even through her grief, she couldn't help but shoot glances toward the lutenist. The performer wore a solemn expression, the entirety of her attention on ensuring there wasn't a dry eye during the parade down from the palace, through the port city, and to the wharves.

Not one shop was open, as every citizen had been given the day off to mourn the loss of the queen. It was an eerie experience for Snow, walking past thousands of people silently stone-faced, staring at the procession. Only the creaking wheels of the caravan, the hooves clattering off cobblestone, and the ever-present music coming from the singular source broke the silence. Somewhat uncomprehendingly, the fourteen-year-old princess watched as the still form of her mother was loaded onto a small, ornate ship.

Thousands of flowers filled the air, everyone near the water doing their best to coat the ship as it was pushed off and away for the final voyage of their lost monarch.

Many landed on the boat, and a sweet scent filled the air

as they flew. Finally, as the wind caught in the small sails, one final flower bloomed, arcing into the air higher than the rest. Only after a long moment did the oddity break through Snow's stupor, just in time for the flaming arrow to land with *Perfect* placement on the oil-soaked ship. A wash of fire raced across the entire contraption, consuming the craft down to the water line in mere moments.

Snow barely remembered the ride back up the mountain to the palace, numbly staring at her left arm to read and re-read the class and skill she'd unlocked only months—yet a life-time—ago. Her rededication to improving her skills and maximizing opportunities had waned greatly as it had become ever-more clear that no cure to the mysterious ailment plaguing her mother would be found in time. Still, the queen had expressed great excitement at her renewed commitment, so Snow had tried as hard as possible, anything to keep her mother smiling one moment longer.

Advanced Class: Influencer
Basic Skill: Influential Aura: Level 3/10.
Influential Aura subtly yet powerfully affects those around you, [Rudimentarily] influencing their thoughts in a positive or negative manner using Influence as a currency. You are able to [Rudimentarily] sway opinions, inspire action, and guide decisions with a variable cost.

Influencing people in ways contrary to their desires will cost additional Influence, while moving them in ways aligned with their own goals will give an influence discount of [30%], increasing to a maximum of a 100% discount. Use caution, as leading others toward goals not in their best interests will slowly push you toward darker powers.
Your Influence is gained at a rate of ([3]*total followers/10) per day, with a minimum of 1.
Current number of followers: 14
Influence: 252/825

Requirement to advance to level 4: Collect and maintain a minimum of 825 influence for 24 hours. 0/1.

There were so many aspects of her skill she didn't understand, but Snow's mother had taken many of her waking hours to guide her daughter. So many of the numbers on her arm fluctuated frequently, with the number of followers increasing or fading away with seemingly no rhyme or reason. There had even been a terrifying morning Snow had woken up to see that her total number of followers had dropped to zero, which had instantly removed all of the 'Influence' she had been saving.

After careful consideration, they'd decided the loss had occurred because Snow hadn't gone out and maintained her relationships with those who had begun to listen to her. Holing up in her room and trying to save up for the next level had generated the opposite of her intended effect, leading to a brand-new mantra she and her mother had come up with together.

"It may not be easy, but it is simple." Snow wiped away a tear as she softly repeated the words her mother had driven deep into her mind over the last few months—bound and determined to put her quiet and less outgoing daughter on the path to success. "Who likes to leave their comfortable areas and seek out the company of others at all times? Pushing myself to do better is not easy… but it is simple."

At that moment, the carriage jolted to a halt, and she and Rose silently followed their father out, plodding to the doors of the palace.

The twins nearly ran into the king as he came to a sudden stop, and Snow looked on in confusion as he slowly turned and stared back at the lutenist still softly strumming on her instrument. His tired voice echoed out, the notes fading away as he spoke. "You. Never before have I had such a terrible day, and even so, I was able to recognize your *Mastery* of your instrument. I don't have much happiness in me right now, and I know I'm not alone. We could all use some music in our lives over the next few days… might I be able to extend an invitation for you to stay a while longer?"

"It would be my honor, *my* King." The woman spoke in a soft voice. Even as she bowed low, her fingers never fully stopped, playing chord after chord. "I will happily stay as long as you wish."

"Good." As the king turned away, resuming the slow march to resume his duties, Snow blinked in confusion at the small orb clipped onto his belt, which was shimmering with an effervescent light. It was beautiful, yet Snow was almost certain that meant something… *bad…*

The music increased in volume as the king entered the palace, and Snow glanced back at the stunningly beautiful woman following along, now playing a slightly more jaunty tune. It was still appropriate for the occasion, yet not actively pulling tears from the eyes of those gathered. The princess smiled gratefully at the musician, though the expression passed quickly. "What's your name?"

"I simply go by Kat, Your Highness," came the demure answer. "Please don't worry about me; I'll try to remain in the background as you go about your day."

Snow agreed immediately, bobbing her head in acknowledgment before following through the doors of the palace after her father. The remainder of the day passed in a blur. Before she knew it, the princess was laying in bed, staring at the ceiling without being able to fall into the warm embrace of sleep. Just as she was about to give up on resting through the night, music flowed through her window, swiftly lulling her into slumber.

Upon waking, the young woman was filled with energy, focus, and a reignited drive. She hurried out of her room after dressing for the day, nearly running into her sister. Rose managed to grab her, swinging them around so both would remain on their feet. "Snow! What are you *doing?*"

"I've got an Epic skill to advance, and sitting in my room all day moping around isn't going to help me improve." Snow firmly answered, brushing off her sister's hands and marching down the hallway.

"Advance?" Rose ran after her, sliding into Snow's path and staring her sister down. "What do you mean, 'moping'? Our mother's funeral was *yesterday*, Snow. Taking time to grieve is not only expected, it is *necessary*. You can't tell me you're ready to just jump back into regular life already... right?"

"It feels..." Snow paused before answering, a small frown quirking her lips downward. Shaking off the strange dichotomy in her mind, she pushed past her sister. "Maybe I just slept well, Rose. Look... I'm not *happy* right now, but... we all knew this was coming and did our best to make peace with it. I've been in mourning for months. How long should I hide away so you can feel my response is appropriate? I can't imagine our neighboring kingdoms are going to sit back and wait to exploit our resources so we can compose ourselves."

Leaving her sister behind, Snow went down to the throne room to have a discussion with her father on hiring a tutor. With her mother now gone, she had no one to guide her on increasing her influence. Even if it *was* a niche skill, the Crown Princess shouldn't have to flail around in the dark hoping to stumble upon an answer. Pushing past the knights standing guard, Snow went still as she watched a bizarre scene play out.

"Your Highness, all I'm asking for is a small stay for my village on our taxes. I'm not-"

The king held up his hand, the peasant woman kneeling in front of him biting off her words as she bowed her head. "I fully understand your predicament. The loss of your town's granary to a fire is enough to starve all of you. Adding a tax on top of your losses would be a crushing blow. I'll send you home with…"

"Your Highness," another voice cut in, a quiet reprimand in her tone. Snow's jaw dropped as the lutenist, Kat, directly interrupted the king as he was issuing a decree. "You are a wise and kind ruler, this is something that's known throughout your kingdom. If I may, do we have any evidence of this woman's *claims*? I wouldn't want your gentle nature to be used against you in these trying times."

"*Claims?*" The peasant woman's head jerked up, a thunderous expression on her face as she lifted her small child slightly. Snow's eyes took in slight marring on the youngster's face, the telltale sign of painful burns sprinkled across his neck. "I lost my husband in the fire, and my son has been burned and needs healing if he's ever going to be able to speak above a whisper. We've lost everything, and what little we have left needs to be put into healing and rebuilding. Otherwise, we'll surely starve, and our village won't last the winter."

"Either no tax this year or no tax ever." The king nodded solemnly, his eyes flicking over to Snow, who stood silhouetted in the doorway. "Ah, perfect timing. You have been learning the basics of investment theory. Tell me, daughter, how would you handle this situation?"

"It's just as you say, Father." Snow slowly stepped farther into the room, confused as to why the musician hadn't been *harshly* reprimanded for her interjection. Such an offense had often led to sleeping in the stocks in the past. The king was just, and he was fair, but he was also *not* to be trifled with. "If we do not take care of our people when times are hard, we will never be able to thrive due to their efforts when they get back on their feet."

"Just so."

"Yet, taxes are not *negotiable*, are they?" Kat spoke up once more, and Snow's jaw nearly hit the floor as the king turned to look at her, patiently waiting for an answer instead of having her escorted from the room. "If they are, I'm certain everyone from the archduke on down would be rushing here to plead their case to the crown."

"Hmm." Snow's father rubbed at his beard. "That *is* true as well. Yet, a hard-working citizen of my kingdom does not have the same sort of obligations as the nobility. Mercy is *always* affordable, and you cannot get blood from a stone. If they have nothing to give, pushing them harder would make me a tyrant."

"If that's the case, why not solve two issues with one simple act?" Kat volunteered, nervously strumming on her instrument as the knights protecting the king started to become agitated at her frequent interruptions. "I might be able to offer a solution, if it were not… too bold of me."

"I think we're past that point," the king wryly stated, breaking some of the tension in the room. His knights calmed down slightly, though their hands remained on the pommel of their swords. "Please, feel free to offer your insight. How do we collect our tax while also helping our citizens?"

"Give them all a better life," Kat offered easily, nodding at the young child the peasant woman was clutching to her chest. "Without the granary, food for their village will be hard to come by, expensive, or at least extremely laborious to produce. Instead of wasting their money on expensive healing-"

"*Wasting?*" The mother's outburst caused Snow to flinch. For some reason, the princess had nearly forgotten the supplicant herself would likely want to weigh in on the situation. "The healers we've already seen tell me he has lung damage. Without medicine and healing, he'll never-"

"Speak above a whisper. Yes, I heard you the *first* time." Kat snapped at the interruption, brushing her hand to the side as if shooing away a fly. "Frankly, that sounds like the perfect palace servant. I recommend you let us buy him."

"*Buy* him?" The peasant gasped at the thought. "My son is not for *sale!*"

"Let *us* buy him?" Snow murmured in confusion. "Who is 'us'?"

"Ugh, I misspoke. No one's trying to *buy* him, I meant *raise* him. Let the palace buy him a better life, raised to be a servant for the royals themselves." Kat cocked her head to the side in annoyance. "He will have guaranteed food and shelter. He won't need to suffer through whatever tasks your town would otherwise have him take on. He will receive training and education, landing a career and living a life others are forced to compete for. You no longer need to pay for him, and the king still receives his tax—though in this case, sustaining the lad, not to mention his training, will *cost* his majesty coin over the long haul."

The woman's jaw worked silently, clearly wanting to immediately refuse, but her mind forced the words to stay inside as she thought over the offer. She looked down at her son, who looked back at her with pleading eyes, then back to the king. "Your Majesty. If... if this is your will, I'd be honored for my son to live a life I could never give him on my own."

Things progressed quickly after that point, yet Snow remained unmoving the entire time. The boy was accepted into the service of the king, the town was granted tax clemency for the next few years, and Kat was looked at in a new light...

...especially by the king.

CHAPTER
FOUR

Snow cried out as her foot came down at an odd angle, the protruding root twisting her ankle and sending her tumbling to the ground as she ran through the dark forest near the base of the mountain. Breathing heavily, she pushed herself back to her feet, glancing behind herself and up at the palace, which had been her home for her entire life. The princess held still for a few, trembling moments, utterly *certain* she was about to be set upon by her evil stepmother's Huntsmen, thanks to her careless shout of pain and surprise.

But the night remained just as dark and lonely as it had since she began her escape. Snow glanced down at her slippered feet, not for the first time debating whether it would be better to just leave them behind. They'd been dyed various shades of brown and green by her off-road travel; even *one* of those stains would've had her casting them into the fire not a day previously. Allowing the wasteful thought to pass, the princess began moving once more, reminding herself that even the most minimal protection for her feet was better than going barefoot.

"Rose…" Snow whimpered as she moved around yet another tree that seemed to have come out of nowhere in the mist. "Why couldn't *you* have been the one to escape? You were the one who resisted her control, who figured out what was going on. Why didn't you escape when you had the chance?"

Ever since Snow's mother's funeral, Kat had slowly been sinking her claws into the political center of the kingdom, making it impossible for those closest to the king to see her for what she truly was.

Looking back on the last years, it was clear now to the princess that she hadn't been acting like herself. Ignoring the tragedies plaguing the kingdom, how those royal guards most loyal to the royal family vanished, the king's uncharacteristic empty eyes... and all of the shining baubles her mother had once demanded be placed throughout the castle... magical items which glowed in warning when someone's mind was being tampered with.

They'd been shining so much they had begun bursting recently, the final straw for Rose to try and get through to her sister.

The fiery princess's words had somehow finally managed to pierce through the haze around Snow's mind, probably because she had spoken with feeling, using her class to peel through the layers of bewitchment and release Snow's captive emotions. Even now, the words echoed through Snow's mind, practically burned there from the sheer amount of power used to free her.

"—she's been controlling him and us for years! Snow... she's a *Witch*!"

Snow let out a *hiss* of pain as she caught herself against the rough bark of a tree. The stinging scrape against her forearm was a shocking reminder of how unprepared she was for this sudden escape. She was sixteen now and hadn't left the palace since her fourteenth birthday, but for one unfortunate trip to the ocean. For years, she'd never so much as walked through the manicured palace gardens without an escort and had remained holed up in her room for the majority of that time. It hadn't even seemed strange, since she'd been entirely focused on understanding, exploring, and leveling her skills.

"Fat lot of good *that* did me," Snow bitterly spat, glancing down at where she could look at her status if she so chose. "I can only grow in power and influence by interacting with people. How did she manage to make me so... *tame?*"

A distant snap of a twig made Snow freeze, her breath catching in her throat as her wide blue eyes tried and failed to pierce the veil of night shrouding the forest. Unable to see anything, she began moving once more, calves protesting each uneven step. Her self-flagellation came out as a muted whisper as fear caused her to increase her caution. "If the *Huntsmen* are out for me already, I'm as good as caught... or worse. If I stay still, they *will* come and find me."

Queen Kat had been building a private, elite force within the palace, taking the best of the royal knights and returning with gloomy abominations hidden behind cloaks and steel masks. While Snow wasn't certain what had been done to the men, she knew they were unswervingly loyal to the new queen and enhanced beyond the realm of any person who hadn't been directly granted physical-based classes and skills from the system.

All of them. Dozens, hundreds... more? All seemed to have the same enhancements, though at the cost of their system-granted skills. It was unnatural and stirred a deep revulsion in her, now that her mind was freed.

Snow distantly remembered watching the Huntsmen spar against the royal knights: dominating them with ease, sometimes going so far as defeating a trio of the highly trained warriors on their lonesome. They were able to move incredibly quickly, contort into strange positions, and each of their attacks contained the entirety of their strength. They had no fear of pain or death, to the point she would've called them *berserkers,* were it not for their calculating actions during combat.

Not... *all* of them came out that way. There'd been a few instances where whatever the queen had done to them generated *side effects.* Those few had been sent out on 'missions', their loyalty still unquestioned, but the queen being unable to control them well enough to trust them near herself. Snow recalled having walked in on more than one grisly scene where one of these deranged Huntsmen had been at the epicenter of a disaster. At the time, she had simply accepted the situation, calmly going back to her room when instructed to do so.

As more and more of her memories lost the haze that had been separating her from demanding action, Snow began to push her current discomfort to the side. Thinking back to her sister—who had forced Snow out the gates and drawn a sword to hold off the knights intent on dragging them back—her bright red lips pressed into a firm line, and her eyes narrowed in determination. "Rose... I'm coming back for you. I swear, I will *not* leave you there to be the puppet of that... that *Witch* Queen."

She dashed her tears away, leaving a smear of dirt behind on her cheeks. Snow crouched slightly, pushing forward through the forest and doing her best to keep her mind on her current predicament. Even with as tame as the forest between the palace and the city was, there was no guarantee she would run into *no* danger. She couldn't go back, she couldn't afford to stop, and so the only way out was forward.

An hour passed, then two. False dawn began to light the sky, barely noticeable through the thick canopy of leaves above her head. Despite her earlier determination, the princess was on the verge of collapse. Her muscles were aching, a deep burn in her lungs seemed to promise she wasn't just tired, but *injured,* and blisters had formed between each of her toes and all along her heels where the rough ground had chafed through the thin material of her slippers. "How did I get so weak? No… how did I *let* myself get this weak? Maybe I could just take a *little* nap?"

As far as she could remember, Snow had never pulled an all-nighter. She'd always been able to fall asleep easily, and over the last couple of years had been sleeping more and more frequently. Now, this extended period of wakefulness felt like absolute torture. Blinking heavily, she continued plodding forward, stumbling once only finding herself resting against a tree. Her eyes drifted ever-so-slowly closed…

Only to fly open in terror as the image of Queen Kat bursting out of the palace and grabbing her sister appeared on the dark backdrop of her eyelids. The queen's beauty, her flawless looks, had been nowhere to be found. Her pale skin was blotchy and uneven, marred by marks as if skunks had gnawed on her or vultures had been pecking at a corpse. Her teeth were flawed and broken, diseased gums revealed as a wide smile stretched across her face.

Even with the Witch holding onto her directly, Rose hadn't begged for her life. Instead she had simply looked back at Snow, using her skills to fill her twin with unimaginable fear, causing her to turn and run like the wind down the mountain and into the forest.

"I understand why you did it, but if I'm going to be seeing that every time I'm drifting off to sleep, I'm going to blame you for my life-long insomnia," Snow grumbled half-heartedly as she thought of her sister. "How did a Witch like *that* manage to fool everyone for so long?"

Now that she was more than half awake, the princess rolled her shoulders and grimaced as she felt the grime caked onto her skin, but nonetheless started moving once more.

Pushing some low-hanging branches out of her path, Snow found herself blinking as a flood of sunlight suddenly washed over her. As her eyes adjusted, she could make out the edge of the port city not far from the tree line, and a surge of relief gushed into her. All thoughts of sleep fled immediately and as she rushed out onto the open plain around the city, and she internally swore to spend as little time in forests as possible.

Even though it had seemed to be *right there*, it still took nearly three-quarters of an hour for Snow to circle the city enough to find an entryway. She hustled up to the gate, a bright smile on her face, only to have it falter as the guards gave her a once-over and began chuckling.

"What happened to *you*?" the first called out as she got closer. "Sleepwalking? Did you awaken some uncontrollable teleportation skill? Spell went awry?"

"Nah, clearly that's the *princess*," the second called, and Snow froze in shock, her jaw dropping at being recognized so easily. "Obviously someone finally decided to do something about the crippling taxes the king has imposed and threw everyone off the mountain. They've been living so lavishly that she must've hit the ground and *bounced*!"

Snow glanced down at her ruined sleepwear, completely failing to understand their jokes. If anything, *she* was closer to starvation than they were. Long years of being all but confined to her room had led to her skin being as pale as her namesake, and any definition in her muscles had long since fled. If she looked at her abdomen, she would be able to individually count each of her ribs—she'd been nearly knocked over by a stiff wind several times through the night. "Good morrow to you, fine gentlemen. I seem to have need of entry to... the city."

It was only as she was speaking that Snow realized she didn't know the name of the port city, having simply called it as such since she was a child. The first guard rolled his eyes and simply waved her through. "Welcome to Deckbett, the jewel of the kingdom. Good thing your shoes are already ruined; I wouldn't recommend putting on any new ones until you're back where the air is fresh."

Snow didn't know what to say, simply nodding as if she

understood, and entered the city. Immediately, her hands flew to cover her face as the foul stench of humanity slammed into her olfactory organ. "By the *system*! What happened here?"

She had visited the city several times in her youth, touring enough of it that hiding degradation on this scale would have been nigh-impossible. Sewage flowed through the center of the street, trickling at a snail's pace down the incline and toward the ocean far below. Trash was piled wherever the wind couldn't reach, and somehow *she* was the cleanest person in eyeshot *after* having spent a night wandering through a dark, muddy forest. Unexpectedly, the answer came from behind her as the second, less sarcastic guard spoke up.

"The money the king used to allocate to his cities to keep them pristine has been diverted toward other... projects... as of late." The man spoke heavily, a sharp, bitter edge to his tone that showed he had once been proud of his king and country, only to have lost his faith in them.

"Don't wander into any dark places here, lass. People have started vanishing like flies on the web. It might be treason to say it out loud, but there's also been a sudden surge in the *Huntsmen* population."

CHAPTER
FIVE

AFTER THANKING the guards for their help, and receiving a warm smile in return from the jaded yet surprisingly kind men, an unfamiliar sensation tickled the crook of Snow's elbow. Glancing down, she saw a tiny line of text appear and vanish, nearly fast enough for her to think she had imagined it.

Current number of followers: 2.

It had been so long since she'd interacted with others that the feel of her skills activating caught her completely by surprise. Still, upon seeing the first indication of positive change, a bright smile appeared on her tired face. Not entirely certain where she should be going, or even what she should do now that she was once more around people, Snow began walking cautiously through the city, carefully picking her way around the worst of the filth.

"I've escaped the queen—for now—but I have no way to stop her or rescue Rose. How… or perhaps a better question is, who do I speak with to gather enough people to rid the kingdom of that Witch?" Having no better options, the princess followed the slimy trail downhill, moving barely faster than the runniest of the sludge racing to the edge of the ocean. As she got closer, more people came out onto the street, and by the time the sun was fully above the horizon, the princess was being jostled back and forth by the dense crowds.

She tried keeping her breathing calm, easier as she was actively choosing to breathe only through her mouth, but Snow found herself shaking with something akin to nervousness at the sight of so many people. Having been in near isolation for so long, the press of humanity was strange and intimidating. People were yelling everywhere around her; whether it was trying to sell their wares, calling out to friends, or even a few people who looked like they were about to take out their anger on each other.

Even though it was intense and put her on edge, Snow had to keep reminding herself that this was a *good* thing. The more people moving around, the less conspicuous one lost teenager was. She was just another person going about her day, dodging across foul puddles, or carefully watching for pickpockets—not that she had any coin to her name. As soon as she had the thought, Snow realized that didn't *have* to be true. "You know… I bet I could convince some of those people in the stalls to give me some breakfast. Maybe even a few coins to get me started."

A merry tune played on a pipe sprang from one of the shops, catching her attention and somehow making the food smell even *better*. Her stomach gave a plaintive wamble, and Snow drifted closer, eyeing the vendor playing his pipes and selling grilled skewers that didn't look *too* much like rat meat. It wasn't stealing if they willingly gave her things, right?

"Yeah. I'm the princess, the kingdom is being controlled by a Witch, the least my people could do is help me stay strong as I try to take it back. What payment? Isn't having a queen who takes care of them and doesn't let them live in filth like this payment enough?"

Another step closer, and suddenly a strange man was right in front of her. "*Fre~esh* fish!"

"Uhm." Snow blinked rapidly as if coming out of daze. "No thank you? I'm just trying to get at the-"

"Fish!" The man wiggled a still-gasping halibut at her. "You're a hungry-looking young aristocrat, don't see many of those! Look at this, fish is good for the heart. Come over to my stall, I'll make sure you have enough energy for the whole day. I've got fried fish, smoked fish, even *raw* fish, if you're one of those people that likes it on gemstone rice."

"No, I'm really thinking I'll just take-" Snow took a deep, annoyed breath through her nose as the man stepped in her way again, swinging the fish toward her and splattering her with droplets of water.

"Look, lady. No one with coin on them looks like you do right now." Suddenly the fishmonger was speaking in a low tone. "I see you angling toward ol' Pieder Pipers Skewer Shop, but I guarantee you those are *sewer skewers*, if you catch my drift. Yeah? Besides… from the captivated look on your face, I don't fancy your chances of not vanishing into the night if you make yourself known to him."

"What?" Suddenly cautious, Snow narrowed her eyes and stepped away from the softly speaking man. Her recent conversation with the guard flitted into the forefront of her thoughts, "Is he-?"

"Let's just say he's been doing a little *too* well for himself in recent months." The pushy salesman quietly shooed her farther away. "Some of us have started to notice a little pattern we aren't so happy about. One day he's getting rats to follow him out of town, loading them up onto a ship setting sail for foreign waters instead of just drowning 'em, the next day he's bragging about earning a new skill. Not long after that, people eating at his shop all on their lonesome end up not coming back into the area no more."

"Is he working for the qu-" A fish-slime-coated finger

pressed against her lips, cutting off her treasonous gasp. She backed away, sputtering as she tried to get the salty taste out of her mouth. "*Nasty*!"

"Better than having no tongue to taste with." The man nodded to the side, drawing Snow's attention to a pair of dark-cloaked men wandering through the crowd, noticeable by the wide distance everyone tried to give them. "The Huntsmen don't take such statements lightly. Here... take this. It's not much, but it's filling, and I'm not going to offer you up on a silver platter, like some."

An oily cloth wrapped around what Snow could only assume was fish was pressed into her hands, and the man stepped around to the side to block her view of the slowly approaching threat. Pulling the package close to her chest, Snow studied the man's face, solemnly vowing, "I'll never forget your help this day. I will make sure to repay your kindness in some way."

"No problem, princess," the man whispered, shooting her a wink when her eyes went wide. "I don't know how or why you're out here on your own, but by the state you're in, I can't imagine you're in a rush to get back home. If you're looking for help, I'd recommend going to where they sent off your mother. People down there remember what life was like back then, and you might find some friends who would go out of their way to help you. Now, if you'll excuse me..."

The canny look in his eyes faded, and his jaw slackened as he spun around, hoisting the no-longer-struggling catch of the day. "*Fre~esh* fish! Get your not-so-fishy fish here! We catch 'em, you eat 'em!"

Hurrying away from the food stalls, Snow berated herself for getting caught in a musical trap *again*. Strangely enough, she found herself soon surrounded by dozens of people hurrying away alongside her. The princess realized they were looking back even more than she was, each of them eyeing the roaming

Huntsmen with caution and no small amount of fear. Her fear that she'd look out of place being so nervous faded away, and she allowed herself to glance around as much as she desired.

The third time she looked back, Snow nearly gagged in fear as she locked eyes with the taller of the two Huntsmen, knowing in that instant he had recognized her. The *thing* began to crouch, as if preparing to spring after her, only for the hubbub of the area to fall silent as a massive scream-sneeze drowned everything else out.

"HaaAAH-*Chooo!*"

People all up and down the road flinched away as fluid filled the air, practically erupting from... the man who'd given Snow breakfast and a warning. The fishmonger seemed to have been caught equally off guard, and as a second sneeze rocked him, his wares went flying, his fish leaving his hands to slap directly into the Huntsman's face. Snow didn't see what happened after that, turning and running down the road alongside half a dozen other people.

"He threw something at a Huntsman! There's going to be a bloodbath!"

"Let's get out of here, I'm not getting caught up in this."

"What could make someone fall apart like that? You think he's sick?"

"Uh, *yeah.* I think I saw a part of his lung come out of his nose!"

Not knowing where else to go, Snow continued along the winding cobblestone, drawing ever closer to the sea. Eventually, she'd left the Huntsmen far behind. Another painful rumble in her gut decided her, and she stopped to pull the string holding the waxed canvas together. An entire smoked fish was revealed, ready and perfectly prepared for her to nibble on. Though she was extremely hungry, the princess only picked at the fare, unsure when she would be able to convince another person to give her food—especially now that she had learned that some of the locals were likely to be hidden agents for the queen.

Carefully wrapping the remainder, Snow licked her lips, only then realizing how thirsty the salty meat had made her. Looking around, she saw a woman standing near the road next to a cow tied to a post, a crude drawing of a milk bucket leaning against the wall beside her. Seeing that no one else was near her at the moment, and the woman was wearing a warm smile, the escaped princess stepped closer, ready to run the *instant* she heard music. "Pardon me, Goodwife. I seem to be lost…"

"Goodwife? Now *there's* some nostalgia for me." The lady cheerfully laughed, wiping a strand of hair out of her face as she took in Snow's bedraggled state. "Have I gotten so old? I suppose I should be glad you aren't calling me spinster or hag!"

"I…! I meant no offense-" Snow stuttered, falling silent as her words were waved away.

"So *formal*. Don't worry your pretty little head. It's just that *my* mother used to be called 'Goodwife'. Usually, I hear 'Goody' these days. Just strange how things change over time, isn't it?" Perhaps realizing that she was rambling, the lady held out a hand. "I suppose that means you could call me Goody Spriggins. I'm at your service, can I offer you some milk?"

"That would be delightful. I am… I don't think I've ever been this thirsty." Snow lay her hand in the outstretched palm, patiently waiting for Goody to kiss the back of her hand. Instead, all she got was a strange look as her limp hand was given a firm shake.

"Sure. Have a sip." Pulling out a ladle, Goody poured a small cup of milk into a cup and handed it to Snow, who greedily slurped it down. "Ahh… probably should've collected up front, but that'll be a copper. You… ah. I see by the sudden fearful look in your eye that you don't have any coin. No, don't worry, that's on me. As I said, I should've collected up front. Not going to make you give it back now, am I?"

"Sorry…" Snow replied weakly, trying not to sink in on herself as she offered a sheepish smile.

Grumbling softly to herself, the woman cast a glance over Snow, "Tell you what, maybe you do me a small favor, and I'll give you more the next time I see you? If I recall correctly, you said you were lost? Noble district is that-a-way, heart of the city is down yonder, and if you're looking for a boat… just keep on the road until the nightsoil splashes into the water. Then take a right."

Opening her mouth to thank her unintended host, Snow's words faltered as Goody snapped her fingers. "Right, the favor! My boy ran off down the hill, left me all alone up here to handle the milking and the customers. If you run into a tow-headed lad with a crooked smile and mischievous eyes, that's Jack. Tell Jack to get back. He went off track, I'm not gonna stay here all day and pick up his slack."

Instead of trying to speak over the loquacious lady, Snow simply nodded vigorously and backed away, rejoining the traffic on the road and aiming toward the water. Thoughts began spinning through her head as she tried to make any kind of simple plan to get through the *day*, let alone her end goal of freeing her sister. The princess clenched her fists and growled at herself in frustration. "How am I supposed to influence people if I can't even muster up the courage to speak over them? I can't get a word in edgewise around here!"

Back at the palace, whenever she had spoken to someone, they would stop whatever they were doing and listen carefully, only speaking if they required clarification to her words. "How do people live like this? Do they not take turns speaking? It's like… like they don't care what other people have to say. My skills are doing *nothing* to help me out here."

Glancing at her arm in frustration, Snow trailed her index

finger down the inseam of her left arm, only for her eyes to
nearly pop out of their sockets at the change she found there.

Current number of followers: 31.

"*What*? How?" Tapping at her arm as if the system had
somehow glitched for the first time in recorded history, the
princess waited for the inflated number to fall away. "I've
barely spoken to anyone, I've done nothing but be rescued and
given food and drink. How could I *possibly* have influenced
more people in this amount of time than I've ever managed at
once before?"

Nearly wanting to pull her hair out in frustration over the
unanswerable questions, Snow walked until she finally reached
the water's edge. When the wind washed over her, for the first
time since she'd entered the port city, it was filled with a clean
if somewhat salty scent. Taking a deep breath, she took a
moment to simply stand there and appreciate *not* gagging on
the ambient stench.

"Hey there!" A chipper voice entered her ears, and Snow
cautiously turned to look at a golden-haired boy standing with
his hands on his hips, a gap-tooth smile wide on his face.
"Don't mean to bother you, but… you gonna eat that?"

"My fish? The only food I have with me?" Snow snorted
softly as the boy shrugged, his smile unwavering. "Yes. Yes, I
do indeed have plans to eat this later. Wait a moment… are
you Jack?"

"Aha! I see my magnificence precedes me." Jack swept into
a bow, nearly falling flat on his face as the loose cobblestone
beneath him shifted. Standing straight once more, he looked
into Snow's eyes, a question forming in his own. "Yet, I've
never seen you in the area before. How did you…?"

"Your mother was looking for you." Snow chuckled as his
face blanched. "Something about leaving her to both milk the
cow and sell the milk?"

"Pah. Yeah, right. I've never *once* seen her make a sale." Jack let out a soft groan. "I forgot she was planning on selling today. Usually she tells me before taking Milky-white to the market. Thanks for the warning; I'd best get up there before she runs out of milk to give away to random passersby."

"Hey, as one of those random people, I appreciate the drink." Snow could only shrug as he shook his head at her.

"Taking our milk and not even offering me a bite of fish. Shame." His tilted grin took any sting out of the words, and Jack took another look at her. "What's someone like you doing in Reste, anyway? You look pretty fancy under that mud; you're clearly not from here."

"Just take the fish, Jack. *Abyss*. Now, what do you mean? This is Deckbett, isn't it?" Snow began looking around uncomfortably, wondering if she'd somehow walked through a magical transporter while lost in the city. After a moment of concern, her tired eyes landed on the palace at the top of the mountain positioned grandly above the city. "Yeah, Deckbett. I'm sure of it."

"Yeah, but you're out of the main city. We're in the low quarters, if you know what I mean. We'd be the slums, if those didn't somehow catch fire and burn to the ground about a year ago. Nice open shorefront now, with a bunch of properties getting built up now the squatters are outta the way."

As the young man talked, Snow felt her heart sinking. Before she could ask what happened to the people who had called this place home, Jack pressed on, "Anyway, you know Deckbett means 'quilt'? 'Reste' means 'scraps'. That's pretty much what this part of town is. You know, the scraps of the city where the only people here are the ones that *have* to be here? Just strange to meet a high noble like you in a place like this."

"How does everyone immediately know I'm a noble?" Snow hadn't wanted to ask anyone before now, but she wasn't too worried about some eleven-year-old turning her in for a reward.

"Really? Even if those clothes are as dirty as mine, I could still buy three or four cows if I sold them off. Maybe five, if I washed 'em first." Jack raised an eyebrow as the princess grimaced. "Then there's *that*. Every single thing you're thinking is right there on your face, plain to see. You've been talking more than I have, even if you don't know it. Oh, and when you *actually* speak? Feels like you're treating every word like a little gem you're trying to put in just the right spot."

"You take after your mother, don't you?" Snow grumbled softly, getting a laugh in reply. Despite herself, she couldn't help but grin at his infectious exuberance. "Look, if you go up this road, stay on the right side, and you can't help but find Goodwife Spriggans."

"Exactly! There you go again, using all that formal talk." Jack waved at her, starting up the road as he called over his shoulder, "You wanna blend in? Swap out those clothes, and just let the words out as fast as you can. Don't think, just talk!"

"Thank you for the advice, but no thank you!" Snow replied, turning and walking along the shoreline. Taking a deep breath, she began trying to pick out where someone might go to get on a boat headed to a not-so-distant shore.

"There's way more people than I expected in the world... is taking the palace back going to be harder than I thought?"

CHAPTER
SIX

APPROACHING the wharves of Deckbett was nearly as intimidating as walking into the city itself. Seemingly endless rows of warehouses stretched into the distance, filled with a massive crowd of people bustling to and fro loading or unloading enormous ships. As Snow drew closer to the area, the cacophonous sounds of the district slammed into her: waves crashing against the shore, ropes of the ships creaking as the tide attempted to pull them out to sea, sails snapping in the wind as they were blown back and forth.

Beyond the constant ambient noise, the teeming crowd of dock workers, merchants, and guards seemed to be doing their best to shout over each other at all times, offering direction, planning routes, or simply barking at each other as they tried not to smash into someone while hurrying about their business. The scents of the area reached the princess immediately after she started to process the sounds, the pungent aromas of fish—both fresh and rotting—tar for waterproofing the ships, brine, and the ever-present stench of unwashed bodies combining into a collage that left her head swimming.

"I should have kept walking along the shore," Snow's low voice was lost in the din of the area, and she found herself nearly having to shout to hear herself think. "I gave myself five minutes of breathing room. Maybe I should have allowed myself a proper rest? Maybe I should... *no*. The easy choice is almost *always* the wrong one. I need to start getting used to doing uncomfortable things. Otherwise, I might as well get on one of these boats and sail away, leaving my sister to fend for herself."

Steeling herself, the princess pushed forward into the sensory extravaganza. Dodging around burly men, she rushed along the patchwork cobblestone, surprised at how this area smelled better than the residential neighborhoods higher up. The road had layers of gravel and sawdust poured over it to provide traction, and on the rare occasion she saw someone slip, the fall was quickly followed by a group of boys rushing over and dumping buckets of the gritty material on whatever had slicked the area. "This is... a very well-run operation. How many people are hired just to keep *other* people from getting hurt?"

As she got farther into the mix, the princess realized that what had seemed to be absolute chaos from the outside was actually a well-ordered logistical dream. No one—except for her—got in anyone else's way, each of them seeming to know exactly where they should be going and what pace they should set so as to not run into someone crossing their path. At one point, she saw a group of four heaving men carrying an enormous load, moving fast enough that she was *certain* they were going to run into a stack of crates in the middle of the road. Just as she was about to call out a warning, the barrier was hoisted upward with a pulley system at the last second, swung onto a ship where laborers immediately began breaking down the pallet of goods.

"This is so... efficient. Everyone is moving so fast; how am I ever supposed to find someone to help me?" Taking a deep breath, she began searching the faces of the crowd, a challenge in itself, since each individual moved quickly, weaving in and out of the teeming masses. Soon her gaze came to rest on a man with a stern expression, moving slower than the rest as his gaze darted among the workers. For some reason feeling terribly embarrassed and uncomfortable, she hurried over and tapped the weathered man on the shoulder.

He glanced at her in surprise, his intense stare sweeping over her before returning to her face. "I've no open positions, unless you have a class that makes you far stronger than you appear. If you're looking to hire some laborers, you should-"

"Please pardon my intrusion, but I'm looking for someone who can help me." Trusting her *Perfected* Precocious Command skill, which was whispering that she had absolutely picked out someone who had a higher position than the laborers, Snow allowed her Aura of Innocence skill to guide her into adjusting her stance and opening up her body language. The difference was immediate, as the foreman paused a moment longer, then turned to face her directly.

"It looks like you've been having a rough day, lass." Seemingly losing an internal argument, he looked around, pointed at someone, and gestured for them to come over. "If you were robbed, there's nothing I can do about it, but I'll have Lloyd bring you over to the guards. They can at least take your statement and get you home safe."

"No! That is, that's not the kind of help I'm looking for. Thank you, though, you clearly have good character to be so concerned about me." Snow flashed him a brilliant smile, and the agitation on his face melted slightly. "I'm looking for someone who can help me with a very large, long-term, potentially dangerous project. If I had to go into negotiations like that... who would you recommend I speak with?"

His left eyebrow quirked upward, and just as he opened his mouth to speak, the man's head whipped to the side and he shoved a finger at someone carrying three crates stacked atop each other. "Set that down immediately! You put the heavy one in the middle, and the top is filled with fragile goods. You can make it another twenty steps at best before you're going to cause it to fall. Lloyd, I don't need you here, go help him figure out how to carry things."

"That kid's worked here for almost three years, you'd think he'd have wrapped his head around it by now," the foreman softly grumbled as he turned back to Snow. "I don't have the ability to negotiate or get you on the schedule; you've gotta go talk to someone else."

"Who might that someone else be, if you don't mind?"

"Look, lady, I don't have all day to chatter-"

"I know! But this is really important, I *promise*."

Her Aura of Innocence reinforced the sincerity in her words, and the man clenched his teeth before quickly launching into an explanation. "Look around you. Everyone you see is a laborer, which is the foundation of our workforce. They load and unload, doing maintenance and other physical tasks. I'm a dockhand foreman, I make sure things are moved safely and efficiently—you're getting in the way of that."

"I know, I'm-"

"Don't be sorry, just don't make me explain myself twice," he spoke on, maintaining his measured tone. "There's three people I can think of who can help you. A 'crane operator' is going to be able to give you a few more minutes than I can, and should be able to direct you to a 'tally clerk'. *They* will be able to get you in touch with a 'warehouse keeper', who should be able to assess your order and see if it'll require direct negotiation. If you've something dangerous going on, go speak to one of the bully boys over there and get them to introduce you to their shift supervisor or the wharf constable. Now, I need you to go do other things, or I'm going to make you stay to take responsibility when things start breaking."

Current number of followers: 41.

Influence combo! Directly convince a supervisor in charge of at least 10

people to focus on you three times, without damaging their productivity.
Influence +10!

The sudden burst of messages from the system felt like a trio of feathers tickling against her skin, distracting the princess just long enough for the foreman to walk away, already seeming to have forgotten their conversation as he barked at another dockhand. Snow didn't mind, as she'd gotten a lead and learned something new about her skill. "I can gain influence even without having to wait for it to refill? So... doing influential things will give me currency directly? The system called that a 'combo'; is it repeatable?"

Her next approach was clumsy, as she needed to move faster than a walk but slower than a jog to keep up with a focused laborer coming off the dock while carrying a barrel on each shoulder. "Pardon me! I'm looking for a crane operator or a-"

The man jerked his chin up and to the side, rolling his eyes as he pushed past her. For a moment, the princess thought he'd simply ignored her, but, when she followed the direction he'd indicated, she saw a towering crane looming over the warehouse. Resisting the urge to slap her forehead at how obvious her intended destination was, Snow instead rushed over to the base of the simple machine, where half a dozen men were being directed to spin large wheels attached to the permanent emplacement.

Though she tried to remain patient, the slow-moving machine seemed to require instructions from the operator every few seconds, and Snow couldn't find a good time to interrupt. She got closer, trying to get his attention a few times, only to have him wave her off in annoyance. Finally, he called out to his workers, and they stepped away from their positions, obvious looks of relief on their faces. Only then did the crane operator turn to her, a hint of curiosity breaking through his annoyance as he looked at her filthy yet obviously high-end clothing.

"You've got about five minutes until that cargo crate is unloaded, what do ya need? I'll warn you, if you're here trying to sell me something, I might stuff you in a pickling barrel. I don't get many long breaks, and I treasure my short ones." Not allowing her to get a word out, the man simply allowed words to pour out of his mouth. "Normally this would be my bathroom break, but I don't mind holding it another little while as long as you've something interesting to say. No? Just going to stand there gaping at me like a fish pulled out of the ocean? Both of ya get that same exact look of surprise on your face, not going to lie-"

"Sir!" Snow finally belted out, interrupting the operator even though it went against all of her etiquette lessons to do so. "I was told you could direct me to a tally clerk? If that's the best you can do, it's fine, but I was hoping to skip to the top of the chain if at all possible. I have a large, long-term, danger-ous, but *profitable* task I need to negotiate."

"Dangerous and profitable, you say?" The operator shrugged as he brought his fingers to his chin and began twisting his short beard back and forth. "You sure you don't want to go and find some mercenaries?"

"I can't afford mercenaries right now; this is… too long-term for that." Snow picked her words carefully, not sure how much detail she should be allowing out into the public sphere.

"Sure, sure. I can get you to a tally clerk. But… if it's as good as you say," the operator leaned closer, a fervent look in his eye. "I can get you past the clerk, right to a warehouse keeper. If it's even better than you're letting on, why, I could get you in touch with a shipwright supervisor or even a harbor pilot!"

"They could help me with a long-term project?" Snow questioned uncertainly, her head swimming from the unfamiliar terms. "I need someone who can approve a whole bunch of different things."

"You need repairs or maintenance of ships? No? Probably not the shipwright supervisor then. Hmm." The operator looked up, his eyes twinkling and excited. "You trying to leave, or bring in your own ships? You have a fleet somewhere?"

"That's..." the princess hesitated, not wanting to lie. In *theory*, she was someone who could command their naval fleet, but she would never get approval from her father, or her father's wife. Snow snorted softly, realizing that even in her own mind, she couldn't bear to think of Queen Kat even as her stepmother. "I will not be directing ships, as far as I'm aware."

"Well then, the tally clerk is about as far up as I can send you. Without more information, I'm not going to put my name behind an introduction to the *wharfmaster*," the operator scoffed even as he said the words. "You look like a proper landlubber, so, uh, the wharfmaster is in charge of the overall operations around here. Ship schedules, berth assignments, coordinating with merchants, and the like."

Snow's gaze sharpened at the mention of someone even higher up the hierarchy, beginning to despair at ever following the proper chain of command to its end. "Wharfmaster is the highest authority around here? No one else they report to?"

"Well, of course there's someone else he reports to!" the operator stated, though his attention was drawn back to his machine as one of his men let out a sharp whistle. "Whoops, looks like I'm needed back on the-"

"*Who?*" Snow demanded, unable to allow this chatterbox to escape without filling in the last piece of information she needed. "*Tell me.* Who does the wharfmaster report to?"

"I wouldn't go so far as to say he reports to... ah, you're not after a whole bunch of history here, are you? Faction dynamics and all that? Well, that's too bad, it's quite the interesting topic." The operator grinned as Snow leaned in, her eyes practically staring daggers in him. "Ah, don't get your knickers in a twist. I'm just jesting with ya. Everyone around here reports to their individual guild, and the guild reports to the guildmasters."

"Who do the guildmasters report to?" Snow found herself asking, even as internally she wanted to be done with this conversation.

"Only to their members and the crown." The operator's voice sounded strained, and Snow felt a strange emptiness swish in her gut. She nodded at the man, and he blinked rapidly before returning to his tasks with aplomb.

Influence: -12. New total: 2.

"Did I just *make* him talk?" Another unpleasant feeling swirled through her, though this one was far more natural than the loss of her power source: guilt. "I did, didn't I? I influenced him to keep speaking, even when he needed to get back to work. But... it didn't feel any different than regular conversation. Except when... when I *ordered* him to speak?"

Various emotions and concerns collided in her mind, and she watched the team work the simple machine for a short while as she tried to reconcile her thoughts. Eventually, Snow turned away, knowing there was nothing else she could do. An apology would require her to explain her power set, which even *she* didn't fully understand. She couldn't pay him for his troubles, couldn't offer to work off the debt she felt she'd accrued.

No, Snow could only remember this moment, how terrible and intrusive it made her feel, and make sure it didn't happen again. With a clear goal in mind and her bitter emotions tamped down, she began walking past the warehouses, drawing ever closer to completing her new goal: trying to get a meeting with a sympathetic guildmaster.

CHAPTER
SEVEN

As THE DAY passed all too quickly, Snow began to piece together the complex web of people governing the wharves. Although she'd managed to learn the name of her destination, almost no one had information on where such high-ranking individuals as the guildmasters themselves could be found. She went from operators to managers, bounced between warehouse keepers, only to find herself having to repeat the process with the bully boys of the 'Shield and Truncheon Association': the guild in charge of offering protection to warehouses and escorts for high-value goods.

"This is like trying to put together a puzzle with missing pieces, using a drawing of a picture which *kind of* shows what the final product should look like." The princess's voice was dull and enervated as she walked to yet another warehouse on aching legs. She paused and leaned against a crate for a long moment to stretch her throbbing muscles. Taking a few deep breaths, she forced herself to stand upright, using the back of her hand to dash the sweat from her brow before setting off once more.

Turning a corner as she got past yet another storage site, her eyes locked on an old man lounging near the entrance to a warehouse with a bright blue door. She approached him as quickly as her legs let her move, watching as his relaxed demeanor shifted to only *appearing* relaxed. Her *Perfected* Precocious Command skill allowed her to read his body language with such precision that it felt as if he were all but shouting 'I absolutely do not want anyone to know what was happening in the building behind me'.

"Can I help you find somewhere *else* to be, lass?" His green eyes twinkled above the massive, bushy, gray-streaked mustache parked just north of his lips. "This part of the city isn't really open for exploring, if you know what I mean."

Snow offered him a small, tired smile. "I hope my questions brought me to the right place, then. You look like someone who knows what's going on; might I trouble you for some advice?"

"Advice, she says? From me? You must be truly desperate." The man chuckled softly, his sharp eyes appraising her as he spoke. "I think there's nothing for you to do here, except leave."

Snow played along, pretending to turn back the way she had come, only to begin walking with purpose toward the warehouse entrance. "Well, that's unfortunate. Because I'm pretty sure I need to be walking through that beautiful blue door behind you, if I want to meet with the guild leader of the-"

"Oh... I truly didn't want to have to warn you off like *this*." The man was on his feet in front of her, a thick cudgel held to the side. He'd moved in an instant to cut off her path, and it didn't escape Snow's notice that he stood a head and a half taller than her, and nearly twice as wide. "Pretty ladies such as yourself should know better than to barge into dangerous areas like this without a proper escort."

"Finding a team to keep me safe is part of why I'm here." Snow carefully and delicately stated, swallowing the dryness from her mouth as she spotted flecks of dried blood in the whorls of the knotted length of wood. "I have business that *must* be discussed directly with the guildmaster of the Shield and Truncheon Association. If… if I'm not mistaken, he's here today."

"Sorry to have to turn you away, but SATA isn't taking on new clients until tomorrow." Seeing Snow's dejected expression, the man lifted his offhand and ran it over the back of his head. "Don't look at me like that. It's not my fault your desires and my profession are at odds right now. I could offer you a small protection detail until tomorrow, if you wish. Instead of the major protection you might be here to discuss, you can get a SATA-light squad, which will circle around you until your meeting?"

"It… it has to be today. It has to be now." Snow glanced at her arm, where a shiny gold '50' stood proudly as her new total current Influence. She had carefully replicated each combo she discovered, and over the course of the day had managed to scrape together only this much of her social capital. Looking up, she met the man's eyes and took a deep breath. "I am also sorry about this. I need you to stand aside. *Now*."

Snow felt as though she'd been punched in the gut as her skill attempted to enact her will on the man in front of her by influencing him to follow her orders. The accumulated power drained out of her, yet the man showed no indication he was going to listen. To her great relief, just before the last of her influence was spent, the mustachioed man blinked rapidly, and swayed as if dazed. The princess darted around him, rushing toward the door and throwing it open even as he let out a strangled shout, followed by an explosive sneeze.

"*Haah-choo!*"

Rushing through the open area, Snow searched around desperately for the person in charge of the guild, but no matter where she looked, the princess only saw people going about their business as usual. Near the back of the warehouse, there was a sectioned-off block which was likely to be the office area, so she rushed toward it as the guard entered the building behind her, letting out one massive sneeze after another.

"Did I make him spill *pepper* on himself, or something?" Snow's half-starved, petite form allowed her to slip through stacks of crates, barely evading the grasp of the guard hot on her trail as he was forced to go over or around. She threw herself recklessly in front of people moving boxes and barrels, *anything* to stay ahead of her pursuer.

Finally, the door was right in front of her. Slapping the handle down, she lowered her shoulder and rammed the thick wooden barrier, falling into the room and sliding a few feet before managing to scramble into a standing position once more. When she finally did, Snow looked around, her mind requiring a few moments to catch up with what she was seeing.

Seven people sat around a round table, each of them looking directly at the sudden intruder in their midst. At least, she assumed they were looking directly at her. Each of those seated wore an ornamental, face-and-identity-hiding mask. A different design was carved, painted, or embossed on the otherwise plain surfaces, creating a simple facial expression.

Behind each of those seated at the table stood two or three people with less impressive versions of each of the masks, though they were clearly affiliated with those seated—likely trusted guards or the like. The first to move was an enormously muscled man at the table. Ever so slowly, he got to his feet, the red frown and two simple slashes indicating angry eyes painted on his mask perfectly fitting his ogre-esque form. A deep voice resonated out from behind the wooden disguise.

"How in the *abyss* did this child manage to barge into the room?" There was no anger in the words, only cold resolve; which for some reason was *twice* as frightening to the princess.

"*E~easy* there, Grumpy," another voice spoke out, this one

from behind a lacquer mask. The features on this were exaggerated, a tiny mouth with puffy cheeks and huge black eyes with panda smudge of red paint drawn around them. "My lookouts got us the warning in time. She hasn't seen our faces, so there's no need to get all… drastic."

"Perhaps we can seek answers before action?" a wizened voice slowly drawled out from a mask made of thick layers of cloth. This one was shaped to resemble the face of a pangolin, with the long nose draping over the speaker's mouth to give them additional breathing room. "Child, why have you intruded on our meeting? What we speak of today is not for the faint of heart and could have disastrous implications not only for us and for you, but the greater citizenry, if you were to spread what we are discussing."

"The more the merrier, I always say!" A disbelieving chuckle erupted from an enormously fat man, his face hidden behind a mask clearly made of electrum. His 'eyes' were shaped into gleeful crescents, and a smiling mouth with gemstone dimples literally gleamed at her. "If we are going to hang, we might as well drag everyone down with us."

"*We* would all hang, you… zey would have to *behead*, Happy." A thickly accented voice sounded out of a nondescript man, muffled slightly by the monkey-faced half-mask he wore. Unlike the others, this man didn't hide the upper portion of his face, instead covering only his nose, lips, and jawline.

'Happy' looked at his contemporary with what might've been shock, though his disguise ensured Snow was left guessing based on his body language alone. "Whatever could you mean by that? I'd proudly hang next to you, my dear Dopey! We're in this together '-til the end. As in life, such is death."

"No, Happy. I am saying they wouldn't want to scour the kingdom just to find a rope strong enough to hold you aloft." Dopey explained clearly, his eyes narrowed as he looked at

Happy in confusion, uncertain if the man were intentionally misunderstanding him. "We'd all die. That is the only certainty. On that note, I'm sure I have something here that would erase her memory of this day. Instead of having to give her over to our *Grumpy* friend to… manage."

"I'm not here to cause you problems or get you killed." Snow took a step back, only to run into a warm wall. Course hair tickled the top of her head as she looked up, the glance revealing an angry man with a furiously twitching mustache staring down at her. "Sorry about… all that."

"There I was, trying to save you from yourself." He didn't sound mad… just disappointed. As if he'd resigned himself to her fate.

Snow whipped her head around and immediately began explaining to the figures at the table, "I don't know who any of you are, but if someone could just point me to the guild-master of… SATA, was it? I'll forget I saw any of you, I promise!"

"Yes." Dopey pulled a small bottle from the recesses of his cloak. "You will."

"Hold…" The pangolin-faced man called out, suspicion laced throughout his voice. "I know you… it couldn't be. *Princess Snow Weiss*? How are you here? No one has seen you in years."

"Prinzessin Schneewittchen? Oh, no, no, *no*." Dopey reached back and pulled the hood of his cloak up, covering the top half of his head as a susurration swept through the room. Not only the attendants, but those at the table murmured to those adjacent to them.

Snow jumped at the opportunity to unload some of the burden she'd been carrying. "I escaped from the palace last night and have been seeking help ever since. That's why… that's what brought me here to you."

"Escaped? What do you mean escaped? What has

happened?" The wizened voice pressed her, fear evident in his tone.

"The king probably finally decided to put a tax on his daughters as well. Gotta squeeze every last copper out of *everyone*, not just the destitute." The person who spoke this time had been silent until this point, but as he gained the attention of those in the room, he leaned back and put his feet on the table. A mandolin appeared in his hands, and he strummed it carelessly as he spoke. "Go on, tell us… what's the matter with you?"

As soon as the first note had reached her ears, Snow had clapped her hands over her ears, dropping into a standing fetal position as she waited for his magical music to fade away. Those at the table exchanged concerned glances, but it was Grumpy who motioned at the mustachioed man to pull the princess to her feet. She struggled with all her pitiful might against him, "*Please*! I'm *trying* to tell you everything, you don't need to tamper with my thoughts!"

"I'm… I'm just trying to create some dramatic mood music to go with the moment!" the man with the mandolin sputtered. His mask was nearly the opposite of Dopey's, with the nose, mouth and chin carved out to allow sound to pass freely. Everything above the tip of his nose was covered, the eye holes being large black ovals—as though he were perpetually surprised. "I don't have any abilities that can tamper with your mind… directly."

"Clearly there is a plot we are unaware of." The final person at the table leaned forward, his voice a gravelly whisper from behind a solid steel plate adorned with three straight lines carved horizontally to represent his eyes and mouth. Snow nearly fainted as he studied her. In all things but the horizontal lines of his mask—the usual were vertical—he looked *exactly* like one of the queen's Huntsmen. "Be at peace, princess. None of us wish to cause you harm."

"I do wish to remove her memory of this… *chance encounter*, and harm may be an unavoidable side effect." Dopey contradicted immediately, wiggling the bottle back and forth and looking around to seek support. When no one agreed with him, he shrugged and tucked the bottle away. "*Fine*. First we hear what she has to say, *zen* we make a decision."

"Please." Fearfully staring at the surprised-looking musician at the table, Snow bobbed her head as the others looked to her impatiently. "I just need to find the guildmaster of-"

"The Shield and Truncheon Association. Yeah, you found me." Grumpy butted in irritably. "You also found a *whole* lot more than you were looking for, princess. Start talking."

Eyes going wide with realization, Snow looked around the room. Now that she wasn't utterly terrified, her skills started filling in key details she'd been missing. Those at the table, though tense, didn't seem terribly concerned over her presence. Their body language spoke of those with immense power and comfort with wielding it. People like this didn't need to wear disguises, not unless they were planning on doing something… something that someone even *more* powerful than them would hunt them for if they knew about.

Barely believing what her skills were telling her, Snow breathily stated, "You're discussing… *treason?*"

"Time to bottle those memories! Shh, now… I pull the corky-cork, and the mem-mems go bye-bye!" Dopey abruptly stood, reaching into his pockets.

Everyone in the room suddenly went very still as the princess wiped away a tear, barely managing to finish her thought through a broken sob.

"Thank the *system*."

CHAPTER
EIGHT

It took a while, but after realizing there was no leaving the room with her memories intact, at least not without getting these people on her side, Snow eventually decided she had no choice but to trust them with the truth. Alongside some coaxing from the pangolin-masked man—who went by the alias 'Doc'—Snow managed to explain the entirety of the situation: from her mother's death to how the palace had been undermined and silently stolen.

The dimly lit room hummed with silent tension as Snow waited for someone else to speak after her tale had been told. Her heart began hammering in her chest as the eyes of the guild leaders and their attendants, veiled as they were behind their masks, began to bore into her. As the weight of their scrutiny continued to press down on her, Snow's eyes went wide as she realized she had no proof to offer to these power-houses who seemed to control every sector of the kingdom—or at least the city.

Eventually, it was Doc who spoke up, indicating to the princess that even at this gathering of peers, he held some additional sway over the others. He gestured to the table. "I think you should take a seat, young princess. We need to have a... a long *talk*, shall we say, about what you just said."

Feeling an odd twinge of dread, as though she'd been caught misbehaving or lying—though she had spoken only the truth—Snow sank into a chair and gripped at the armrests as though they would help her hold her ground. Doc reached up to his face, fingers bumping against his mask. He seemed surprised at the barrier, and Snow's skills whispered to her that he must be someone who wore spectacles and regularly adjusted them. When he spoke, the man's voice was tired and strained, as though he were about to give her some terrible news.

"Do you even realize the risks you've taken this night, Your Highness? The true danger of the game you are playing, unwitting or not?" At Doc's words, Snow's brows furrowed indignantly.

"I've spoken nothing but the truth, and... I understand I've given you perhaps too much trust for our first meeting, but..." here she paused and looked pointedly at the mustachioed man still pacing in front of the doorway. "What choice did I have? Either I explain my situation, or I may not see tomorrow or remember today. I suppose now I learn if my trust was well-placed?"

"No guile, this one." Sleepy's raspy whisper echoed against his steel mask. He chuckled softly, settling into his chair even as Snow flushed, her hands leaving her arm rests to clinch together beneath the table. "If we let her go off on her own, she'll be dead in a week or captured within a day."

"Ah, come on." The perpetually surprised masked-man spoke up on her behalf, his defensive body language indicating that he felt somewhat responsible for the princess's intensely fearful breakdown. She noticed his mandolin was nowhere to be seen, and found herself appreciating the man more as he continued speaking in a rich baritone. "Look at her upbringing. How could she possibly learn to be a two-faced snake like most of the nobles we have dealings with? She's so… pure."

"Like freshly fallen powder on a mountainside." Dopey chimed in with his thick accent. "The problem with being so clean, so 'pure' as you put it, is that even a single speck of dirt added to the mix will stand out. Then, that will be the only thing *anyone* focuses on. No one sees the field of sparkling ice crystals; they only shy away from the yellow patch."

"Gross." Snow's mutter returned the group's attention to her. "Even so, isn't that a *good* thing? Did you want me to fabricate a story or lie to you? Why would I, when the truth is so much more compelling?"

"You should thank the system that you managed to barge into this room." Doc's disapproving *tut* cut through her rising temper. He gestured toward the as yet unnamed musician. "Bashful, would you be so kind as to enlighten her?"

"*Jolie fille*," the surprised-faced mask caught the light as Bashful leaned forward, staring directly into Snow's eyes. "Let me explain in plain terms how close to ruin you've truly come. The best outcome you could've hoped for was being mistaken for a spy and losing the trust of all those around you. They *may* not have retaliated, thinking you would perhaps have material support from the queen if they raised a hand against you. But even if they had driven a knife into your heart, if your story is true, that would still have been better than the alternative."

"Which is…?" Snow whispered the words through suddenly-dry lips.

"They *believe* you." Bashful whispered back at her, his words utterly captivating. "If they were agents of the queen, they might have turned you in for a reward. If they weren't… think of the lives that would've been lost as the people of Deckbett raised their fists against the crown and marched on the palace as they staged a coup. Even beyond the royal knights, who at least have *some* semblance of care for the citizens, I tell you true… I've seen the Huntsmen in action far more often than I ever wished. Even *one* survivor left to spread the tale would have been a surprising outcome."

The room once more fell silent as Snow felt the weight of his words settle on her shoulders. Her tired mind tried to pick out a path that wouldn't lead to the outcomes Bashful had just plainly laid out. But now that she was aware of the possibility, the princess had to admit everything he'd stated was not just possible, but *probable*. "What am I supposed to do, Bashful? A Witch has taken the kingdom from within. She holds my father and sister hostage. I *must* stop her."

"Which is why it is so good that *this* is the room you walked into tonight," the huge man, Happy, cheerfully called to her through his gemstone-studded electrum mask. "It so happens we were just discussing our next goals for the upcoming years. All of our attempts at convincing the crown to lower our taxes back to the reasonable rate they were less than two years ago have fallen on deaf ears. We were about to try something more, hmm, *drastic*, and now the figurehead we needed in order to get the people to rally has come to us instead!"

"You are getting ahead of yourself, Happy," Doc stated in a warning tone, raising a hand to stop further conversation. "Princess, luckily for you, we believe what has been spoken tonight. You may very well have saved us by stopping us from trying to make an appeal to the better nature of a *Witch*. Luckily, now that we know the truth, we will not simply be washing our necks to allow a clean cut to fall upon it. But… do you now understand my concerns? The chaos such an accusation, true or not, could cause?"

Grumpy butted in, "Think beyond the possibility of a slaughter. If she's as powerful as it seems, thereby making the fight seem hopeless from the start, how could you expect effective people to rally to your side?"

The pangolin mask wove side to side, cutting off Snow's

immediate retort, "I think, and I *believe* I speak for all of us, that we will rally to your cause. But as you are now, exactly as Happy blurted out, you're only good to us as a figurehead. Is that what you want? Would you like us to convince the kingdom to rise up against the current monarchy, with your role simply being someone we pointed at who could integrate into the kingdom's ward structure and therefore take the throne without magical backlash?"

"Is-" Snow tossed her head back and forth in denial. "-is there any other option? I have nothing to give, nothing to contribute. I don't want to be a pawn, I want to be…"

"The Queen?" the as-of-yet unnamed man in the lacquer mask spoke up, continuing the chess analogy even as Snow blinked in surprise as she suddenly remembered he was at the table with them. For some strange reason, she had *misplaced* him in her thoughts. "I can see that. Are you sure that's what you want? From what the betting pools have been saying, your sister might be better suited to the role."

"If she's a better fit, I'd give her the position in a heart-beat," Snow firmly stated, not missing the subtle nods the others gave each other at her words. "But until I know what she wants, I need to act under the assumption that she's a hostage. If acting as the queen is what is needed… I'll do it."

"Thank you for your insight, Sneezy. Now, Princess, if you want to be a queen, and not just a figurehead we move around the board…" Doc started leadingly, leaving space for the others to chime in.

"You need to be more cunning." Bashful melodiously murmured.

Grumpy grunted garrulously, "Not to mention less weak."

"Able to bring people to your cause!" Happy hopped in hotly. "Ooh, I have so many *ideas*!"

Dopey ducked down, shrugging as the others impatiently awaited his input, "Willing to do what it takes to win."

"Able to find the right people and put them in the right

places without the Witch catching on." Sneezy shot a searching stare at the young woman, tapped at where his nose was under his mask, then pointed at her knowingly. "Also, more aware of your surroundings."

"Be able to resist her dark influence." Sleepy stated sinisterly. Something about his words caused Snow's brow to furrow, as if she had missed something, but she lost that thought as Doc abruptly clapped his hands.

"Less *afraid*." Somehow Snow could tell that he was gently smiling at her under his pangolin mask. "After all, everyone wants to follow someone who is confident they will succeed. Now, how will we make all of this happen? Tell me, Princess, beyond your birthright, what does your class allow you to bring to this fight?"

Snow was still reeling from the abrupt shift in conversation, but gratefully latched on to the lifeline Doc had thrown her. "I only have my Advanced Class unlocked, and my skill is to influence the people around me. But it's... broken? No, that's not the right word, it doesn't seem to be under my control? Not unless I force it, but then I am taking away people's agency. I don't want to use... I don't know, dark powers?"

"But what if they would allow you to *win*?" Dopey's exasperated question was waved off by Doc, who tilted his head slightly in confusion.

"Broken, you say? In what way?"

"It's not working how it should. I'm able to use it, but not in any kind of cohesive way. I've only been able to find a few things that work, then I try to repeat them as much as possible." Snow grimaced, struggling to articulate the problems she was having. "Ever since entering the city, it seems like my skills are much weaker, but somehow reach more people. Trying to get one person, to do any *one* specific thing, is *incredibly* draining."

Extending his hand, Doc motioned for her to do the same. "I'd like to take a look, if I may."

"At what?" Snow reached out and clasped his left hand with her own, only then realizing what he meant. Eyes going wide, she tried to pull back her hand, only for him to hold on with a firm grip. "You want to see my *status*? That's incredibly inappropriate!"

"Your Highness," the man spoke gently, yet firmly. "I'm a *healer*. This is what I do, and I swear to you that the details of your status will go no further than those in this room, *if that's* what you wish. To me, this is no different than standard practice when diagnosing an issue. Please… you've begun to trust me. I will *not* break that trust. Let me help you?"

Her eyes darted back and forth as she studied the mask in front of her, hoping her skills would give her a better understanding on how truthful he was being. When she pulled on her hand once more, he allowed her to withdraw, giving her enough space to take a deep breath and think. After a moment, she inhaled through her nose, swiped her right index finger along the inside of her arm, and offered her hand back to Doc while looking anywhere but at him.

He took her hand and leaned forward, eyes scanning over the displayed classes and skills as they wrote themselves out, only to vanish moments later. "Oh. Oh, I see. Yes, that would certainly change things, now wouldn't it? By the way, have you noticed you have a new skill level waiting to be viewed?"

The understanding in his voice caused Snow to glance over, wondering what he was seeing that she could not. "What do you mean?"

Skill increase! Aura of Innocence [Level 7 (Considerable) → Level 8 (Extensive)]!

Requirement to advance to level 9: Turn a combat situation around by redirecting the efforts of the combatants attacking you back on their leader.

"May I have your permission to speak out loud about your class and skills?" Doc waited until Snow reluctantly nodded, then waited even more until she did so *firmly*. "You see, your Basic Class is 'Darling Princess'. Though you've reached Perfection in Precocious Command, you have not done so with Aura of Innocence. Your Advanced Class is 'Influencer', with a second area of effect skill, Influential Aura."

Raising his hand, the man gently cleared his throat before explaining himself, "You are in a very unique situation. Your skill set is deeply tied to your very identity as an influential *princess*. At the palace, your commands had additional strength on everyone around you, because of who and where you *were*. Now that you have fled the palace and set yourself against the legal queen, you can no longer be considered a 'lawful' princess of the realm."

Snow sucked in a sharp breath of air, but Doc's next, gentle words allowed her to slowly control herself, while also subtly reinforcing how she needed to think of herself as more than a princess. "You mustn't see this as a disadvantage... *Snow*. It's an opportunity to progress in a way that does not continue to tie you more deeply to the palace. As you already noticed, the impact of your words has lessened significantly, but you've already begun to grow in a new direction. This works well for us, as we will need someone with a broad, firm foundation of power to lead us."

The fallen princess blushed as his words resonated with her. For the very first time since her escape, she felt the barest glimmer of hope that she might be able to succeed.

"Gentlemen, I suggest we scatter to the winds and reconvene upon the morrow with strategies to help our newfound rebel queen fulfill the duties required of her." Doc turned and bowed fractionally toward the young woman. "As you have saved us from making a grave error and putting our lives on the line, I feel compelled to return the favor."

As the people in the room stood and began making their

way toward the doors, Snow tried to think of what to say to them, but could only think of a question. "Wait! What do I call you?"

"I suppose we never did proper introductions, did we? I'm *Bashful*, this is-"

"No, not that..." Snow shook her head, thoughts fuzzy from sleepiness and swirling emotions. "This group. All of you are guildmasters, correct? How should I refer to you, collectively?"

"You shouldn't," Grumpy shot back. "The less people who know we are interacting, even if you couldn't describe our faces, the less risk we have."

"Usually we just go by 'the seven guildmasters' when we're on the wharves," Happy called over. "Despite appearances, sometimes we're not overly fancy."

"The name, it is too long," Dopey muttered. "Does not roll off the tongue. Bad mouth feel."

"The seven guildmasters of the wharves." Snow pondered out loud, voice thick now that the adrenaline of their initial contact was fading away. "The seven of the wharves. The seven... D'wharves."

"Perfect." Bashful heartily chuckled, inciting Happy to join in as well. "Look at us, the Rebel Queen Snow Weiss and her seven of D'wharves."

CHAPTER
NINE

CRASH!

Snow jolted upright, nearly falling out of the small cot tucked away in the corner of the warehouse office. As she stumbled to her feet, for a long few moments the princess was too disoriented to recognize where she was. No light came from outside, as her host, Grumpy, had deemed it an unacceptable risk for the princess to sleep in a room with a window where 'anyone could peek in and find her'.

Heavy footfalls against the creaky wooden floor echoed in the otherwise silent space, and she pressed herself against the shuddering wall while staring at the door with wide eyes.

"Sorry about that!" a jovial voice rang out as Happy kicked the door open, sending bright daylight pouring in and leaving his expansive form silhouetted in the frame. Moments after Snow relaxed and started allowing her eyes to adjust to the light, the fragrant scent of freshly baked bread made her nose twitch, and her eyes focused on the stack of plates the huge man was carrying. "However, I foresaw your host forgetting about the simple pleasures in life, such as food *other* than dried jerky, and thought I might take the opportunity to build some good will!"

"I… thank you, Happy." Snow rushed forward, pulling some of the plates off of his wobbling stack to make sure he didn't drop anything. Setting them on the table, she hurried back to offer additional help, but he simply squeezed past her and began arranging the different dishes. "What was that crash? Did someone fall, or-"

"Stop worrying about other things, at least for a little while!" Happy casually fluttered his hand at her concerns. "Abyss, that's the motto, the very *creed* I live my life and run my businesses by. It's made me successful beyond the wildest dreams of my most ardent detractors; why change things now?"

The princess remained standing awkwardly as the masked man lifted the covers off the food, revealing a mountain of muffins, pain au chocolate, platters of exotic fruits, sausages, bacon, and an oversized skillet of scrambled eggs with shredded cheese melted in. She gawked at the display—even at the palace she'd never seen such an extravagant breakfast. Each time Happy's bulk blocked her view, the feast seemed to extend out further, until the entire table was practically creaking under the weight of it all.

"Where is it all coming from?" She hurried around the guildmaster, hands half-raised to catch whatever was about to fall. But as Snow looked over the spread, she realized all of it had been perfectly positioned to cover the entirety of the table without going over. Only as she glanced up did Snow realize Happy had already seated himself and was pulling on a bib large enough that she could wear it as an apron.

"It's just what I do, my future queen." The man chortled with a slightly wicked wink. "When I find something that brings someone joy, I'm able to multiply it. You like food? Why not have a buffet? The taste of strong drink? Why not an entire cask of the best mixed drinks? Beautiful… *ahem*. We'll discuss the details of all of my businesses another time. But, let's just say I'm in the business of *luxury* goods. *All* of the businesses in that category."

"What are you the guildmaster of... exactly?" Only now that she'd gotten a half-decent night's sleep—having only been awoken once, by a nightmare of her sister shouting at her—and was able to think clearly and rationally, did Snow realize she didn't know anything about her erstwhile allies. Happy simply shrugged, gesturing frantically at her to begin eating.

Sitting somewhat cautiously, she pulled out a sausage and bit into its casing, her eyes nearly rolling back at the bouquet of flavors and hot grease rolling across her taste buds. "I... pardon my poor manners; I didn't realize how hungry I was."

Happy put his palms together and clapped the tips of his fingers in excitement as Snow tucked into the food, hungrily devouring everything in reach until her stomach was groaning in pain from the effort of keeping it contained. "Feel better? You should! Only a few things in life are guaranteed to bring you happiness no matter how often you do them. *Those* are the things my guild represents. Gambling, restaurants, and a few other, ah, *relaxation* houses I'm sure you'd have no interest in hearing about. Oh! I nearly forgot about our newest members, the luxury bath house industry joined—every last one of them throughout the kingdom."

"That's..." Snow covered her mouth as a small *burp* escaped her lips. "That's an extensive list. I can't imagine how much impact you have on the lives of-"

"How much *influence* we have on them." Happy's eyes gleamed through his eye holes, as bright as the electrum of his mask. "Oh, yes. *Influence* indeed. Something I am well aware you have a vested interest in exploring. I may not be able to sing a song or create lasting illusions like Bashful, heal ailments and wounds like Doc, or notice every last little detail like my good friend Sneezy. But, I could go to any of them and buy *exclusivity* to their services. Being able to have whatever you want, whenever you want it, and stop others from having the same... should the need arise? Top. Tier. *Influence.* Coin is power, my Rebel Queen."

"Are you... teaching me?" Snow looked around the room, but her eyes eventually returned to the shimmering electrum mask barely covering the corpulent face of the man seated at the other end of the table. "I don't have any money right now, so I'm not certain how I can earn this lesson."

"No, no." Happy flapped both of his hands at her, the motion continuing for a few moments as he silently contemplated what to say next. "We all had a meeting this morning and shared our opinions on who should train you, and on what. You see, Snow, none of us work for free. I'm here to open negotiations. But, as they say, good relationships are formed when your stomach is full, your mind is rested, and... well, those are the only two parts of the saying you need to be concerned with."

"I *do* feel much better now that I've had some sleep and such a lovely breaking of my fast. Thank you for your consideration, Happy." Snow went to stand, planning to sweep into a curtsy as well to show her gratefulness, but the guildmaster was having none of it.

"Sit, *sit*! I'm simply a well-to-do merchant. I've no need of your formalities, no matter how well-practiced they are." Chuckling, he patted his own stomach. "Plus, were you to stand, 'etiquette' would demand I do the same. I'd truly rather let my meal digest in peace."

Snow looked down at the table, shocked to find that all the food up to three quarters of the way across the table from Happy had vanished. She hadn't even seen him move his mask aside, and had no idea when he had managed such a feat. Sinking into her chair, she watched expectantly as Happy tapped the tip of his index finger against his mask, a soft *chime* echoing out each time he did so.

"Princess, as you say, you have no money... right now." Happy tilted his head slightly to the side, and beneath the jovial mask he wore, she saw how sharp his eyes had become. "Because of this, I have nothing to teach you. All of my influence comes from investments, compound interest, and aggregate success. Instead, I will be the one funding both your training as well as the rebellion you'll be leading. Since it is my coin, and you are therefore considered my investment, I'm sure you can see why negotiations are mine to handle."

"I can." Snow didn't particularly care for how he was laying out his thoughts, but so far as she could tell, nothing he said was untrue.

"Superb!" Happy wiggled in his seat excitedly as he leaned forward. "Here's what I'm proposing. I need to recoup my initial investment, not to mention getting a return on it. When you retake the throne, all I ask in return is…"

The man paused for dramatic effect, giving Snow just enough time to think over what she could offer him in the future. Land, varying ranks of noble titles, access to kingdom trade routes that had been blocked off for the use of the crown only.

"…a reduction in the tax rate of my businesses to two and a half percent for twenty-five years, beginning immediately upon your retaking of the throne."

The princess waited a few heartbeats, but Happy had finished speaking. Trying to control her face, she cleared her throat and leaned forward, "is that all?"

"That would save me coin enough to make my current wealth look like a beggar's belongings by comparison." Happy sternly stated, for some reason glowering at her… or perhaps more accurately at the small smile on her face. "You're not going to actually *accept* that, are you?"

"Should I not? I'll have my kingdom back, the queen will be deposed, why shouldn't you get something wonderful out of it as well?"

"Perhaps I *do* have something to teach you, after all." Happy snorted good-naturedly. "What I just gave you is something we in the business world call an 'extreme lowball offer'. It is frankly ridiculous terms that benefit *me* immensely, while doing the bare minimum for *you*. Let me be frank, if I allowed you to swear to these terms, and you retook the throne *tomorrow*... in a year, the kingdom would collapse into civil war."

Completely stricken by the revelation, Snow failed to answer before Happy gently explained, "Currently, my businesses have a luxury tax which comes to a total of forty-one percent of our total income. My guild represents *every* luxury-specific business in the entire kingdom... which means-"

"How much of the kingdom is run by the tax money we get from you?" Snow managed to whisper out, realizing she'd nearly doomed her kingdom by failing to ask even the simplest of questions.

"I don't want to say *all* of it, but... at least *most* of it is funded by the taxes my guild collects and pays on behalf of our members." A wicked giggle bubbled up out of his throat, high-pitched enough to make Snow feel uncomfortable hearing it coming from such a huge man. "Your first true lesson, then. When you are given an offer, *never* say yes unless you know exactly what the value you are giving up represents."

"Never take the first offer?" Snow questioned him, confusion filling her eyes as he shook his head.

"Oh, no. When you're working with someone who values their reputation above all else, it's likely that their best offer *will* be the first offer." Happy spread his hands to the side. "But if you don't know what you are giving up, how will you ever know if it's a good deal or not? You don't know what you don't know. But as soon as you have your first offer, you'll be able to compare it to the second, and the third. Very quickly you will come to understand who values you and what you can offer, versus those who would make an offer just to get you under their thumb."

"I see…" Quite crestfallen, Snow offered a sad smile to her first teacher. "I don't know what to offer you."

"Two and a half percent… *off* of the tax rate, from before the new queen took over." Happy cheerfully stated, and Snow heaved a deep sigh of relief, feeling as though air had only just returned to the room. "That would be more than fair for my services."

"You don't say?" The corners of Snow's lips quirked up. "In that case, one and a half percent off the previous rate. I'm happy to offer you a fair rate. *More* than fair means I am taking away from the well-being of my kingdom."

"*Ha!*" Happy slapped the table, causing plates, pans, and cast iron skillets to bounce into the air before clattering back to the wooden surface. "At least no one can say you're not a fast learner. Let's discuss."

By the time they'd settled on one-point-nine-one percent off of the rate, Snow was nearly ready to eat lunch. Happy sat back, exaggeratedly wiping the back of his hand over his glistening forehead and swatting away beads of sweat. Neither of them had gotten exactly what they wanted, but Snow had the faintest inkling that was the hallmark of a successful negotiation.

"With that settled…" the princess took a deep breath, preparing herself for the trials that lay ahead. "How soon can you muster up the funds needed to march on the palace? Three days? No more than two weeks, certainly?"

Happy had just raised a glass to the lips of his face mask, but at her words began choking on the liquid and sprayed an excessive amount of liquid into the air, where it caught the light and formed a rainbow before dissipating. "Two *weeks*? You can't-"

Catching his breath, the guildmaster shook his head and tried again, in a low tone. "Snow… perhaps you still don't understand the monumental effort that will go into a successful coup against the queen? Especially when she is a powerful Witch, on top of having access to the resources of the kingdom and control of the king—who is connected to the ward structure governing the entire land by right of rule and bloodline? The training you need alone... a year if you prove to be a fantastic study who puts everything she has into learning everything she can, every waking moment. But more likely two or even three."

"*Years*?" Snow yelped, on her feet in an instant, her hands slapping onto the table as she leaned toward the guildmaster. "You can't possibly ask me to accept that! A Witch has taken over the kingdom, is holding my family hostage, and you're telling me we are *not* storming the castle as soon as possible?"

"Us and what army?" Happy carefully inquired of her. "Do you remember any of what we spoke on last night? An untrained mob five times the size of the royal guard would be cut down to the last."

"The people you represent! Who all of you represent! If each of you called on your members-"

"Even if we did so, and each of them called on three more people..." Happy hijacked the tirade, "Then we'd have a lot of angry people. Not much else. We need to gather them, yes, but we also need time to train and outfit them. Do you want to lead a rebellion or become a *martyr*?"

"The Witch grows stronger as we wait," Snow pointed out angrily. "Rose is still trapped-"

"Do you know why it is so *hard* to keep nobles alive?" a third voice cut through the rising tension as Grumpy stepped into the room. "It's because none of you ever seem to realize that everyone has their own motivations for doing things. You lock eyes on your goal and rush toward it, never expecting the knife in your back. I have a message for you, Princess."

"For... me? From *who*?" Snow blinked rapidly as her argument was cut down.

"Your sister, Princess Rose."

For a long moment, Snow thought the man-shaped wall of

rippling muscle moving toward her was playing a cruel joke. But as he handed her the missive, her pupils shook as she recognized her twin's handwriting on the scrap of parchment.

Confined to the castle. Forgotten for now. Mother's artifact being polished. Run, Snow. Never be caught. -RW.

After reading the note three times, she read it out loud, prompted by Happy clearing his throat expectantly. Upon doing so, the room fell silent, the cryptic words hanging heavy in the air. "Why would she mention Mother's artifacts? That makes no sense."

"She thinks you'll remember something specific, which would take too much time and space to write on a scrap she managed to smuggle out." Grumpy calmly walked her through his reasoning, having obviously known the contents of the note and came prepared with questions. "It's going to be something magical. Not the kingdom's, but your mother's specifically."

"That's why it doesn't make sense." Snow's lips twisted in a moue of distaste. "Mother had few of her own things, the palace provided everything. What she *did* bring in from before her marriage was certainly not magical, and nothing that would need to be polished... the jewelry would be taken care of by the servants, but... oh."

"I don't like the sound of *that*." Grumpy shifted uncomfortably as Snow did the same. "Out with it."

"It's possible *Kat* now has my mother's locket." The princess tapped on the table as she tried to decide how concerned she should be at the moment. "It's a powerful artifact that, when opened, allows the user to scry nearly anywhere within the kingdom. It's tuned to the wards, and it was never intended for... only the bloodline of my mother should be able to use it, and Rose would never willingly do so."

"Tell me the risks, so I can start planning on how to mitigate them." Grumpy demanded with a deep sigh. "Abyssal magic, intruding into the lives of law-abiding, tax-paying citizens."

"Unless Rose decides to help her with a clear mind and conscience, whatever she looks at will not give her a clear view. Still," Snow tried to recall the exact details of the locket. "The locket is shaped like a golden apple when closed. When opened, it will expand into a large mirror. When someone speaks about the person looking into it, specifically when they say their name or title, they'll be able to scry what is happening in that area. Details will be nearly impossible, but large things like landmarks in the surroundings will be at least recognizable. If someone were to strike a fatal blow on the person wearing it, the locket will save them... once."

"The more someone speaks about the viewer, the more clear it gets, I'm guessing?" Grumpy grumbled in frustration as Snow bobbed her head in acknowledgment. "Perfect. Well, all I'm hearing is it's time for you to get on the road and not stop moving until you're on your way back to the castle at the head of a disciplined fighting force. Grab a sandwich, splash some water on your face, and get moving."

Snow tried to get a word in edgewise, but the powerful man shook his head and motioned for her to follow him. "Bashful is already waiting, which is lucky for all of us. Our timetable for getting you out of here just got moved *way* up."

CHAPTER
TEN

"Sɪʀ Gʀᴜᴍᴘʏ, we don't even know for certain if my guess about my mother's mirror is accurate or not!" Snow huffed and puffed as she half-jogged behind the enormous brute of a man, a grimace on her face as she held her overstuffed stomach. "Is there really such call to rush?"

"You want to spend a few more days with Happy? Tell you what. Why not just make it a week? You'll hang out here, and maybe in a month or so, you'll feel like getting up and going off to train. A year from now, you might even make it to the door," the guildmaster scoffed, glaring over his shoulder toward the room they had exited.

"Here's the truth, Princess. With Happy, ambition melts into contentment before you even notice. He has a way of making people content with what, where, and *who* they are. For most people, well, there's nothing wrong with that. But for you? Are you gonna go do what it takes to save this kingdom, or are you *content*?"

"I... see." Snow followed his gaze with a complicated expression, a pang in her heart reaching out through her body. "It was just nice to be around someone who gave without expectations. He seemed to care so much, and I've missed being cared for. He seemed to genuinely love life…"

She trailed off, and Grumpy snorted in agitation as he pushed the door in the side of the warehouse open and cautiously peeked around before motioning her forward. "Without *expectations*, she says. Pah! Something interesting to think about on your journey, then. Being happy is perfectly fine; it leads to increased productivity and innovation over time. A *long* period of time. But Happy is who he *is*. What he *offers* is different. His skills push happiness taken to the extreme. Absolute hedonism. Nothing pushes someone to complacency faster than too much of a good thing."

"Too much of a good thing?" Snow stepped out the door, taking shallow breaths as her overfilled stomach twinged yet again. "I may have a *small* idea of what you mean by that. He just kept making food appear. It was so *good*."

"Complacency is the seed of ruin, Princess. First, it withers the resolve of a man—that is, of any person—then it rots the foundation of nations. Resting too long in comfort is inviting the weight of the world to collapse through the roof you've allowed to rot over your head." A carriage rattled around the corner, and Grumpy nodded at it in greeting. "We've decided to start with Bashful's plan and get you out of the city to strengthen your talents on the move. Joining a troop of his bards will give you the cover you need, and more importantly, access to the ears of the people."

"So, I'm to leave the shadow of the palace, for who knows how long? All in the *vain* hope I will be able to return one day and *perhaps* eke out a victory?" Snow's voice was small as the carriage came to a halt, quiet enough that she was surprised to receive an answer from inside the covered conveyance.

"Trust me, Snow." The melodious voice of Bashful caressed her ears as the door opened invitingly. "There are none better than my people for bringing your ability to capture hearts and minds to *Perfection*. Though, if you just so happen to be completely unteachable, well… the best plan is always the one that keeps you alive. Now, in you pop!"

Behind her, the door of the warehouse firmly popped into place, the scraping of metal on wood signifying that it had been barred from the other side. With nowhere to go but forward, Snow stepped into the carriage and was guided onto a plush seat moments before the horses started forward, and the carriage jolted into motion. For the next few moments, she allowed herself to get used to the swaying and the clatter of wheels on cobblestones.

Finally, unable to weather the intense stare boring into her from the opposite seat, she broke the silence. "Tell me, guild-master Bashful. How did you come by such an interesting name?"

Bashful smiled, his lips on full view under the mask of perpetual surprise he wore. "I'd sing you the entire tale, but something tells me you'd rather I simply explained."

"Music and I have a… complicated history," Snow carefully replied, knowing he had witnessed her near breakdown the night before. "*Queen* Kat controls people through her music. Not to mention, I ran into someone doing nearly the same thing in the city."

"Oh? Someone in the city playing music to lure unsuspecting youngsters in? Tell me more."

Suddenly Bashful was *very* interested in what she had to say, and the surprised princess gave a swift accounting of the man selling meat skewers and playing on his pipes. After she finished her explanation, Bashful sat back and swirled his hands around each other, clasping them together before opening them to reveal a small white bird. Carefully opening the door of the moving carriage, he tossed the creature outside, and it swiftly flapped away.

"Consider this piper no longer a *factor* in this city, Princess." The heat in his voice made Snow blink, sinking back into her chair and painting a smile on her face in hopes his wrath wouldn't turn on her. "He will be examined and removed. Your testimony is all *I* require, yet my people will make sure to do their due diligence. No one uses music to harm others and gets away with it. Music is meant to bring joy, to give an escape from the harsh realities of life. Not compound them, nor be used to ensnare the innocent."

Finding herself immediately liking the man as he finished his righteous tirade, Snow relaxed slightly. "Um… now I *really* have no idea how you got your name. You certainly don't seem shy in the slightest. If I may ask, what guild do you lead that allows you to so effectively, err, 'remove' people?"

"Yes! We had been having a conversation before I so rudely turned it toward my own ends." Bashful reflexively reached for a large pouch, only for his fingers to halt midair and slowly return to his lap, palms facing upward to show they were empty. "As I'm sure you can understand, none of us use our real names. If our true identities were known, we'd be constantly swimming upstream against the unending river of requests. For money, for jobs, for charity. Worse, those of us who have families would be putting them in constant danger, and we would never know a true friend again. I'm known as Bashful…"

He paused, lifting his hand above his head, palm toward his face, and bringing it down until his hand stopped in front of his chest. Wherever his limb passed, his appearance shifted, until Snow was staring in awe at a nondescript dockworker. Each time she blinked, his features shifted slightly, and all attempts to stare at him were met with failure—a different face ever awaiting her when her eyes reopened.

"…Because I never allow anyone to know what I truly look like." There was a wide smile on his face as he sat for a few heartbeats and allowed Snow to squintingly appraise him again and again. "I'm able to impart my skills onto items, such as these masks, and use my abilities to make myself and the other guildmasters unrecognizable, even to each other. As to my guild… would you care to take a guess?"

"Assassins?" Snow rasped out, her eyes darting to the door as she did so.

Bashful tutted softly, shaking his head at her. "Nothing so monumental or dark, Princess. All of us represent legitimate businesses, well… six of us do. No, that is, *five* of us."

Snow scooched closer to the door, a motion not missed by the guildmaster, who decided to stop playing his guessing games. "I am, in essence, the highest-ranked performance agent in the kingdom. My people are bards, troubadours, roving carnival employees, jesters, jugglers, and entertainment of all sorts not confined to a structure—which would intrude on Happy's domain."

"Yet you can casually eliminate a random stall owner?" the princess pointed out with an arched brow.

"Well, I wouldn't say the performance industry *isn't* cutthroat. Sometimes that just so happens to be more literal than others." Bashful shrugged at his traveling companion's uneasy expression. "In an attempt at full transparency, we are also an information brokerage. Because we move around the kingdom, we are able to monitor the events and happenings within our borders and beyond."

"You're a spy network, then?"

"If you want to distill all of our efforts down to one demeaning phrase, I suppose that would be one you could apply to it," Bashful replied with an easy smile. "*Knowledge,* dear princess, is the most potent weapon of all, when you're looking to the future. Still, if you're in a fight, a dagger works wonders. Now, since you didn't ask, I will volunteer the information. We are on our way to Drienhurst, a small city known for vibrant art, and of course, its bards. One of my most advanced troupes is awaiting us there, truly the best and brightest I've ever trained. They'll help you learn the tools of their trades, which I'm sure you understand the importance of... yes?"

Snow blinked as she tried to absorb the deluge of information, allowing her lips to part as she searched for an answer. "I need to learn how to stay on the move to avoid being a sitting duck, and... convince people to join me in our eventual rebellion?"

"We have a few days together; I suppose they will be spent learning," Bashful muttered with a rueful smile. "It is obvious you have only lived in the palace, if this simple subterfuge is beyond you. No, do not be so crestfallen, Princess! Innocence is a gift, and I *am* sorry I need to be the one to tear off the pretty packaging of life."

Shifting in his seat, his back upright, chest forward, Bashful began to speak once more. As he did, Snow unconsciously responded, shifting her own position to a receptive, studious pose. "You are thinking *too* far into the future. First, you must begin to understand what it is that convinces people to listen to you. A troupe of bards can get into places no one else can. Some places no one deemed sane would *choose* to go. Think of it like this, Snow. Entertainment is a universal need. Can you imagine a world with no music, laughter, no escape from the daily requirements to keep yourself fed, clothed, and housed?"

As he snapped his fingers, tiny sparks of light danced up from his fingertips, spinning into the shape of tiny animals that ran across his palms. This elicited a startled laugh from the princess, who leaned closer just in time for the creatures to flare and vanish. Her smile faded quickly, and Snow turned her eyes upward, meeting Bashful's. "But I'm not a bard, I don't have the class, nor the skills. How could I-?"

"I don't mean *system* skills, Princess." Bashful grinned at her confusion. "Think of all of the ways I've been communicating with you over the last short while. Even when I'm not speaking, or when I'm overloading you with words, my meaning is coming across clearly because of how I am holding myself. When you were worried, I allowed my hands to be open, my body itself communicating that I was a friend. When I needed you to focus, I held myself as a teacher would. Certainly there are those who have the ability to do this better than even I, especially when bolstered by the system, but I have spent a lifetime studying how to apply myself."

He leaned forward, an illusory eyebrow appearing on his mask just so he could arch it at her. "Would you like to learn?"

"I *would*." Snow startled even herself by latching onto the idea of personal instruction so vigorously. "Now that you point it out, my skills were even telling me what you did as you were doing it. Yet I didn't *listen*! I… I *need* to be able to do that, don't I?"

"Exactly right." Bashful tapped on his nose then pointed at her. "Learning with my people, you'll hear gossip and rumors you'd never be able to encounter as a princess surrounded by a retinue. You'll learn to spread your own messages in parables, as well as, *yes*, in songs and music. That is one phobia I simply cannot allow you to continue living with. By the end of your time among us, you'll be able to spread the seed of change, you'll know your people's secrets, their hopes and fears. Each of the ideas you plant will grow into movements and eventually into the great harvest: a rebellion against the Witch you so desperately crave."

"The rebellion the kingdom needs," Snow rebutted firmly, coming back to her senses and leaning away from the guildmaster. "Trust me when I say I have no interest in leading a rebellion. It's just that the other option is so much worse."

"Which is why we agreed to assist you in the first place." Bashful knowingly nodded along with her words. "But the key to all of this is learning to *influence* people naturally. Get them to do what you want without any expenditure of your own power, allowing it to accumulate until you truly need to use it."

"Influence people, without them realizing it, for free, without having to impact their minds?" The princess bobbed her head in acquiescence. "Where do we start?"

"You and I will continue our conversation. Correct me if I'm wrong, but you can already read body language *Perfectly* thanks to your first skill, yes?" Getting a positive response, Bashful bore down, "Then all we need to do is take your ability to read people and apply it to your *actions*. If you know what I'm trying to get across when I do *this-*"

Barely moving, hardly even breathing, Bashful's lips quirked ever so slightly, a half-smile paired with ever so slightly raised eyebrows, and Snow's skill immediately informed her he was looking at her with a mix of skepticism and amusement, as though he found her attempts at understanding him amusing but didn't fully trust or believe that she would truly be able to codify the information.

Then she was looking at a blank mask once more, shocked at how intensely he'd been able to convey the complex meaning.

"-Then you should be able to mirror it and use such expressions on your own." Bashful started to laugh, a low, melodious rumble. "Even before that, I suppose we might need to work on *not* showing every thought on your face right when it goes through your head. It's great for earning trust, bad for negotiations and most other aspects of life. No one likes someone without self-control to be in a position of power over them, after all."

When he finished speaking, Snow let out a long, slow breath. "It's going to be a busy few days, isn't it?"

"Oh, yes." Bashful's teeth flashed in the bright morning light coming through the window slits as they trundled along. "Isn't this *fun*? I love a captive audience."

CHAPTER
ELEVEN

Snow slid bonelessly out of the opening of the carriage as they stopped at the tavern in Drienhurst, feeling nearly as tired as she had during her flight from the palace. Dark rings under her eyes showcased her commitment to learning from the guildmaster, but she would be the first to admit the need for a break to absorb the ceaseless information she'd been offered.

Bashful poked his head out after her, a smile playing on his lips. "Are you *certain* you wouldn't like to circle the town another time or two? It's a rare thing for me to have such a dedicated student."

"*Uhhnng.*"

"Such eloquence! Vivacity!" Bashful dryly replied, waving toward the door of the tavern. "Ah well, we all have different levels of talent in different subjects. Go, get some sleep. Tomorrow you'll be meeting Ted, Ned, and Zed, and they'll teach you everything else you need to know. Singing, storytelling, tumbling, and juggling!"

"Not juggling. Please, I don't want to be someone who can juggle."

"You're obviously too tired to know what you're saying." Bashful breezily waved away her groaning. "Being quick with your hands is an invaluable skill. Just as tumbling is about more than acrobatics; it's escaping bindings, navigating locked and trapped rooms, or even just moving in ways others won't predict. Abyss, I nearly forgot costuming! Disguise! At some point, you will need to learn to be someone else. Until then, you can simply play the part."

"I can never tell if you are being serious or speaking in metaphors," the princess shot back at him tiredly as she strolled toward the door. "I think 'Chatty' would have been a better name for you than Bashful, but either way... I truly do thank you for your tutelage. You've given me a lot to think about."

"It was fun for me, as well." Bashful paused as he reached for the handle of the carriage door. "I tell you true, you are a better student than even *you* may have expected yourself to be."

Unwilling to think too hard about his words, as everything the guildmaster of information gathering seemed to have multiple meanings, Snow simply walked into the building and moved to the counter. After taking one look at her, the proprietor of the tavern tossed her a key and silently pointed her to the stairs.

"Room three. I'll make sure to keep breakfast warm for you tomorrow. Sleep in. We heard you rode in with the guildmaster; you're going to need the rest."

"Everyone knows about him? It wasn't just me that made him act like that?"

"He could talk the ear off a stone statue," the man stated solemnly, no hint of humor on his face. "Truth is, he's phenomenal at what he does. No one else even comes close. Also true, it's practically impossible to spend any length of time around him."

"He said he had students, though?" Snow was swaying on her feet, indignation the only thing keeping her awake at this point. "That means he had to teach them, right?"

"Small doses, lady. That's the trick. Small doses." Then she was shooed away, and the princess gratefully went to her room, locking the door behind her before collapsing on the bed and knowing no more.

"—SHE's been controlling him, and us, for years! Snow... she's a *Witch*!"

The muffled sounds of a busy tavern woke her up the next day, freeing her from the recurring nightmare she'd had ever since Rose freed her.

A quick glance out of her window informed the princess that the day was nearly half over already. Led out of her room by the smell of hearty stew and the rumbling of her stomach, Snow quietly chose an unoccupied bench and sat down, looking around hopefully. Luckily for her, only moments later, a bowl of thick, steaming stew was unceremoniously plopped in front of her. Even before she could thank the server, he had hurried on.

Halfway through her meal, the bench next to Snow creaked as someone sat down, just as another person swung their leg over the bench on the opposite side of the table. Cautiously glancing between the two of them, Snow's suspicious stare was defeated by the beaming smiles on the faces of her uninvited guests.

"Hi there, trainee! I'm Ted!

"I'm Zed," the man seated next to her happily chimed in, only for Ted to take over the conversation once more.

"Tell me, is it true?" Ted leaned in, his voice dropping conspiratorially as his head bobbed up and down as if already agreeing with himself. "Are you really like *us*? One of Bashful's students?"

"Uh-"

"They say you rode here in a carriage, just the two of you, for nearly a week," Zed spoke in an awestruck whisper. "How is your brain not just *mush* at this point? I did one day a week for a year, and I swore I'd never go back."

"I alternated with him." Ted swallowed hard, a haunted look in his eyes as he turned to stare into the distance. "There's no better source of information... but the survival rate is truly daunting."

"No, we don't mean people actually died." Zed casually patted Snow on the shoulder, making her blink in surprise. Casual touch wasn't something she, as a princess, was used to receiving. "Just that the turnover rate is ninety-nine percent per month when he decides to allow someone to shadow him. One hundred people go in, one person manages to make it to the next session."

"But... he said so many nice things about the two of you!" Snow couldn't believe what she was hearing. "Bashful thinks you are the best students he's ever had; do you know how *many* times he said that?"

"Seven," both of them replied instantly, causing Snow to go silent in surprise. Furrowing her brow, she thought back over the last few days and realized the duo were exactly correct.

"How-?"

"It's one of his patented teaching methods," Zed explained happily. "He calls it 'serving the seventh subconscious'. By repeating something seven times, at least one in seven people will remember it forever. He really, truly wanted you to know how much he liked us-"

"What a nice old man," Ted jokingly interjected.

"-so he made sure to bring it up seven times over the

course of your journey." Zed finished off as Ted sneaked his spoon into Snow's bowl, stealing a bite of stew for himself. "Now, when your brain isn't as terribly bruised, the two of us are going to take over and give you a casual, but much more hands-on version of the training. Shouldn't take more than a few months to get you up to snuff."

Snow winced at his casual statement but didn't disagree, as she had resigned herself to this being a lengthy process. Just then, a third person joined them, likely Ned, going by the list of names Bashful had attempted to drive into her skull.

"Hello, Princess Snow." Ned stated with such casual ease that the others didn't register the title for a moment. Then, both Zed and Ted shot to their feet, eyes wide as they dropped into overly formal bowing positions. "Little late for that, isn't it, boys?"

"Ned!" Zed hissed at the third member of their party. "What are you doing?"

"What are *you* doing?" Ned shot back with a scoff. "To me, it looks like you're going out of your way to alert everyone in town that the escaped princess is right here. Why not just collect the bounty for yourselves at this point?"

With stricken expressions on their faces, Zed and Ted shot into an upright position, looked around wildly, then gave up and dropped back to the benches. Ned reached forward and tapped on the table, drawing Snow's gaze over to his dark, solemn eyes. "From what I understand, beyond the need for *discretion*, the highest priority is going to be working with you to create a parable or a song, something catchy that'll spread among the people and leave them receptive to your message in the future."

"A song? How will that make people open to fighting against the Wi—the tyrant queen?" Snow bit her lip, frustrated that she'd nearly revealed the queen's dark secret in their first conversation, so soon after having been warned off of doing so by the guildmasters.

"Really?" Zed looked at her with a tilted head. "Your Highness, a message of change can reweave the very fabric of people's reality!"

"You can inspire huge groups of people at once to see the world differently and prepare them for being receptive to… *anything.*" Ted finished Zed's thought, and both men nodded sagely at the other.

"From what I hear, when *you* tell it, when *you* believe it, the message will become unstoppable." Ned stared knowingly at Snow, who flushed slightly when she realized some of the details of her skills had been passed on. Even though she had permitted it, exact knowledge of other people's skills were typically reserved for incredibly close family or serious suitors at the absolute maximum. "So that's the main item on the agenda we're going to work on with you. In essence, we're not only teaching you the ropes, but crafting the narrative. With the right story, and the right bard singing it, the kingdom will rise for you."

"But… what do I say?" Without her realizing it, Ted had fully purloined her stew and was eating it slowly, watching the drama unfold in front of him with wide eyes.

"A story of heroes and villains, something that will endure even after you retake the throne. Something that'll inspire loyalty and belief. When people look back on what we do here, together, they'll sing along, even *centuries* from now." Ned finally sat back, taking a deep breath and releasing the intensity with which he'd been speaking in a long, steady sigh. "But that's well down the road, isn't it? First, I'm told the first thing you want to learn is how to juggle?"

"*Bashful,*" Snow ground out with faux anger in her voice. "Is it just me, or is he just a… a *turd* to everyone?"

There was a moment of stunned silence as the jaws of the others at the table dropped, even this gentle indecency going against the vision they'd painted in their minds of the delicate waif sitting among them. Then all three of the men burst into laughter, gently reaching over and nudging Snow with closed fists to show their admiration.

"It's everyone, I swear it!" Zed managed to choke out around his laughter.

Eventually, they all calmed down, and Snow showed a tentative smile to the group. "Thank you all for agreeing to help me… I just, I don't know what I'm supposed to do. Everything seems to be changing so fast."

"Ah, yes. Change." Zed spoke with deep nostalgia in his voice.

Ted cocked his head to the side, raising his chin at his companion. "Change? You mean the thing only wet babies like?"

"That's the one." Ned joined in, causing Snow to roll her eyes at their well-practiced antics. "Well, color us surprised! Now, I think it would be best for us to travel, learning on the move, in a fast-paced, hands-on environment. Also… perhaps we alter your look as we do so?"

Reaching into a satchel, the bard dropped a parchment on the table with a good likeness of Snow's face, as well as a reward for her safe return. "As you can see, the kingdom is already searching for you, and no one's happy at how many *Huntsmen* have been mobilized. They're knocking on doors, searching through carts, and generally making a dangerous nuisance of themselves. Not nearly as much as we'd expect, as she didn't tell the kingdom you're the princess, just someone they're looking for. Speculation *abounds*."

"I think she could pull off blonde. Thoughts?" Zed leaned back, hand cupping his chin as he stared at the pale princess. "Hmm… perhaps if we let her catch some sun while we're out and about. Otherwise, she'd be completely washed out."

"If we shave her and dress her in baggy clothes-" Ted started to offer, only to hold his hands up and surrender as Snow glared him down. "Never mind. Any help from Bashful on this?"

"I have a hair tie for her that will shift her eye coloration to blue and make her teeth a bit less white." Ned pulled out a leather strap, passing it over to the princess now that he'd been reminded. "Anything more than that'll have to be a physical alteration, as too much magic will draw the eye instead of diverting it."

"Subtlety is the spell that lasts the longest," Ted muttered, echoed moments later by the other two bards. Seeing Snow's questioning glance, the man shrugged. "Just another one of Bashful's little nuggets of wisdom."

"No, I like it." Snow repeated the words herself, tasting them on her tongue. "I think that's the key lesson I should be trying to learn under Bashful's tutelage, right?"

"It's a good one, if nothing else." Ned stood up, gesturing for the others to follow along. "Until you get a good handle on the paints, as well as ways to adjust your posture and stride, and, hmm, a selection of clothes to quickly change into and out of, we can take care of your disguise. It just makes it a bit… *tricky*, if someone trained to find inconsistencies is on the hunt for you."

On the way to the door, Snow looked to the side, catching her reflection in the gleaming pans hanging over the opening between the kitchen and dining area. To her surprise, the woman looking back at her was a blue-eyed brunette with a tan complexion and dull, dry lips. "Ned?"

"Each of us are at least *Masters* of some sort of illusion." Zed quietly explained to her, taking her by the elbow and leading the group out of the door. "We can't do anything about your voice, so take care who you speak with outside of our little club."

"Ha!" Ted's sharp chuckle made the others look at him questioningly, but the man only shook his head and gestured up and down at Snow. "Sorry, I'm just glad we decided against trying to dress her up as a man. The best illusion in the world wouldn't hide that fancy highborn *sway* you walk with. You're going to throw your hip out by the time you're thirty if you keep on with that."

"You-!" Snow flushed bright red even through the illusion, even her ears going crimson as she tried to storm away, only for her companions to begin laughing and nodding along with Ted. "-are so *uncouth*!"

CHAPTER
TWELVE

UPON LEAVING THE TAVERN, the quartet had approached a wagon, but Snow had been stopped just before she could clamor inside.

"How will you ever learn to walk like one of us if you don't *walk*?" Zed playfully questioned her, yet even with as insincere as he'd sounded, he *had* insisted she walk alongside the wagon as they did.

Thus began the most difficult journey of her life... so far. Although the princess knew she wasn't as physically inclined as her sister, she'd never once thought that simply *walking* would be the most demanding thing she had ever done in her life.

The road itself was punishing, being uneven and made from whatever local materials best suited the purpose. Just as she would get used to marching along a dirt path, it would shift to gravel, which always seemed to skitter out from under her feet no matter how carefully she plodded along. They hadn't even traveled two hours before the uneven paths had left Snow's ankles throbbing, and the straps of her borrowed pack had dug grooves into her shoulders.

Even so, she refused to allow herself to complain, especially when she noticed how full the packs were that the others carried, how they handled the terrain without difficulty. With her vision tunneling, Snow focused on the burn in her thighs as she forced herself to walk uphill with the stubborn determination of someone who had no other choice—only to nearly collapse as Ted caught her and gently directed her to a fallen tree.

"Sit here, Princess. You're doing great… for someone who's never walked more than the length of a banquet hall."

Snow rolled her eyes at him, breaking out in a grin despite herself. The others quickly and efficiently made camp, and she tore into the food they handed over, barely tasting it before it was down. Her fingers felt thick and clumsy as she tried to pull her bedroll off her pack, needing to be helped by the ever-patient Ned in order to have a place to sleep for the night. As soon as she lay down, she was once again asleep…

…only to be roused by quiet voices the next morning.

Not wanting to interrupt the conversation, Snow remained still and quiet as they prepared breakfast. Zed's voice faded in, and she stiffened as she realized they were discussing *her*. "-surprised she lasted that long yesterday. Do you see how little food she can eat?"

"All but starved to death," Ted solemnly agreed. "Are you sure she can't get in the wagon?"

"Doc's orders." Ned sighed softly, and Snow had to force herself to remain still as she felt the weight of their glances fall on her. "As much food as she can eat, as often as possible, and only light exercise and stretching until she starts to regain some muscle. That's one of the reasons she's with us for the first part of her training. Imagine how those ex-soldiers under Grumpy would be acting when she couldn't lift so much as a short sword."

Not wanting to eavesdrop, and not certain how she should be feeling about what she had already overheard, Snow began to stir as though she were only just now waking up. The conversation died off, and she sat up, her gaze meeting three smiling faces as Ned handed over a plate with an enormous mountain of eggs and thick cut of bacon. No... the princess frowned at the plate, their conversation fresh in her mind, and realized *perhaps* two scrambled eggs and a single slice of bacon wasn't all *that* much food.

"Morning, bards." The words came out thick, but luckily the excuse of having just woken up covered the swirl of emotion she was feeling in her gut instead of hunger.

"Right back at you, Princess." Zed chipperly called from across the campfire. "How are you feeling today? We've got some salve from Doc to help with any blisters. It'll heal them right up but leave the skin toughened behind. Fantastic stuff for newbies getting out on the road for the first time."

Snow nearly hurt her neck, she nodded so quickly. Soon she was slathering the jelly-like substance over her feet, ankles, and shoulders where her pack had rubbed the skin raw. Immediately she felt a sense of relief as the potent, obviously magical-in-origin substance regenerated the tiny wounds. "I can't believe how much damage walking for only a few hours did to me. Look at this! Even my hands had blisters on them where I was trying to pull the pack forward and relieve my shoulders."

The other three exchanged knowing glances, and Snow felt a hint of embarrassment for having listened in on their private conversation. Ned adjusted his position as the smoke from the fire began drifting toward him and waited patiently for her to finish her breakfast before speaking. "We're going to keep traveling today, but before then, we're going to practice working with your voice. Telling tales and singing for hours at a time will leave you raw and in need of recovery unless you have some training and practice."

"Isn't it just talking, but making it all kind of run together?" Snow teased the man, grateful for the change in topic. "That's what Bashful told me, after all."

"He has a knack for simplifying complex things and overcomplicating simple things." Ted snorted at the reminder of their mutual instructor. "This morning, we're going to start with *scales*."

Ned began explaining the process and had her run through the easy warm-ups while Ted and Zed offered contradictory advice.

"Do you want your throat to be as raw as your feet were just now? Project from your diaphragm!" Ted stepped close and poked his index finger into a space just below her ribs. "If you're not feeling the vibration here, you're doing it wrong. Stronger! More air!"

"No, not like that!" Zed countered immediately as Snow tried to follow Ted's advice. "You're not training to become a town crier, but a singer, a storyteller! Modulation is the key! Don't just belt it out, adjust, sometimes make us lean in to hear you. If people are curious enough, they'll follow the soft parts as well as the loud ones."

Snow looked to Ned for help, but he shook his head at her and nodded at the others as they nitpicked her attempts over and again. "A half step up, a half step down..."

"I think scales focus too much on technical nonsense," Ted chimed in as Snow worked to focus on the person who was *supposed* to be instructing her and ignore the others. "*Emotion* is what matters to me. If you can't make me feel what you're singing, I might as well be going off to bed."

Snow's voice faltered as the mention of passing along emotion reminded her of her trapped sister, but she tried her best to recover and stay on pitch as Ned moved her through the scales over and over. An hour later, her head was swimming, the sound of her own voice grated on her ears, and her throat felt raw enough to bleed.

"What is wrong with these birds? I've never seen ducks swoop at people before!" Zed slapped at the waterfowl, getting his hand nibbled for his troubles.

"My skills," Snow rasped out. "Singing makes animals flock to me."

"We can use that." Only then did Ned hold up a hand. "Good work, trainee. Remember, this is the easy part. You're only learning the basics right now, and it's going to be a long time before you've got it all down."

"Great voice for it, though." Zed commented, obviously trying to bolster her spirits.

Ted nudged Zed. "At the start, at least. By the end there, she was sounding pretty-"

"Pack it up," Ned interrupted before Zed could finish teasing the princess, who was gulping down water to fix her parched throat. "We've got a long way to go before we get to our first town and lots to practice before we get up on stage. *All* of us."

The glance he sent at Snow sent a thrill of nervousness through her, but between her aching body and her sore throat, her nerves for the stage fright passed quickly.

Days began to pass in a grueling blur.

Though she tried to push herself to her limits, Snow found herself frequently being guided to a tree stump, a large rock, or even just a pack set on the ground so she could take a breather. At first, she was frustrated with what she considered to be the bards babying her. Yet, as the days turned into a week, and they had only managed to cross a few dozen miles, she realized how badly she needed the conditioning. Snow held her peace, ate as much food as she could stomach, and threw herself into any opportunity for training the bards offered.

They sang as they strolled, practiced when they paused, and engaged in eating at every opportunity. At the end of the first week, Ned pulled out his instrument as they settled for the evening and carefully watched the princess as he gently strummed it. "Tomorrow we'll reach our first stop, and music is a large part of our process. Are you going to be able-"

"Thank you for your concern, Ned." Snow met his eyes directly. "Don't change things because of me. I need to figure *all* of this out. I'm ready."

Morning came quickly, and just after breakfast, they managed to enter a lively market village perched along the banks of a slow moving river. Snow looked around in wonder at the simple buildings, the people in well-worn yet cared for clothing, and the bustling trade going on along the riverbank. Small boats glided across the water, crates brimming with vegetables were passed from shore to deck or vice versa, and groups of children ran along the dirt streets, screaming with excitement as they chased some ball or other group.

"First impressions?" Zed gently elbowed Snow to get her moving again.

"It seems... nice. Doesn't stink like Deckbett, at least." Snow began moving forward once more, her eyes drinking in the sheer *life* the town exuded.

"The farther you get from the palace, the better things get." Ted smiled at her sadly. "Didn't used to be that way, but things change quickly."

"That they do." Ned interrupted their morose spiral, gesturing to a small raised platform. "Looks like they didn't tear down from the last time we were here. Nice to know they liked us enough to keep the stage as a permanent fixture. Let's get to work."

Ted walked closer to the stage, casually leaned against a post, and began strumming a cheerful tune to lift the spirits of everyone within earshot.

"Look at how, with minimal effort, and asking for no investment on their end, he gets people to acknowledge him. Anyone passing by will spread the word that there are bards back in town, and the gossip will make sure everyone knows within the hour." Snow was pulled along with Ned, who took the opportunity to point out how the others began drawing interest, masterfully explaining the reasoning and intent behind each of their choices. "Turn your eyes to Zed, if you can find him."

The princess looked around, figuring it would be easy to pick the redhead out of the sparse people mulling about. Eventually, Ned had to point their companion out—Zed was deep in conversation with a group of children, surrounded on all sides as his deft fingers twisted cloth into puppets to dance with the melody Ted was strumming out. Soon, the cloth puppets popped into the air, intermixing with colorful balls as the man began juggling.

"Get the children excited for a show, send them home to tell their parents to come and be a part of it?" Snow murmured to Ned, who nodded approvingly as she made the intuitive leap. "You all seem to know exactly what you're doing... how do I get there?"

"Just keep doing exactly what you're doing now. Watch, learn, participate." Ned gently patted her on the shoulder. "You're a quick study and naturally quite observant. For the next few hours, just watch. Stay fresh for when we get you on stage this evening."

Songs and acrobatic shows followed over the lunch hour, drawing large crowds of people taking their midday rest. None of the bards seemed to mind the intense sunlight beaming down on them, not even seeming to break into a sweat as they threw themselves into their work. The crowd thinned shortly after they wrapped up an impressive set, promising to remain for the rest of the day.

Snow followed the trio, eyes shining with excitement as they proudly slipped behind a building... and practically deflated, sinking to the ground groaning and panting for air. Her jaw fell open as they began stuffing food into their mouths, sucking on their water skins as though they were dying of thirst. "By the system, what happened? Are you well?"

"Takes a *lot* of effort to make all this look effortless, Snow,"

Ted managed around a mouthful of meat bun. "Gotta get it just right. Make it *magical*, ya know?"

"Hold on... were you using illusions to hide your sweat? Your pallor?" The princess's mind spun with interest as she thought of dozens of areas in her past, and in the future, where such minor enhancements would make a huge impact. "That's absolutely *brilliant.* I would have thought you'd use your skills for larger and more showy things, but-"

"Food first, talk later." Zed tossed her a bun. "You probably don't even realize how drained you are after having stood in the sun as long as we did. Eat up!"

They rested until the dinner hour, and as the sun began to sink on the horizon, Snow listened as the three men wove their magic yet again. This time, it was inside the local tavern. No longer did they choose exuberant songs or puppets, but instead tales of heroes and villains. Snow was utterly enraptured as Zed's voice dipped and rose, pulling the room into the stories with his exaggerated expressions earning laughter at just the right moments.

Ted punctuated the story at various points, flying into acrobatic motions to act out Zed's words, while Ned, the quietest of the trio, ended the story with solemn warnings, his words drifting and lingering in the air like the smoke from a dying fire.

As they stood, and the packed tavern erupted into applause, Snow came back to herself with a sinking feeling—realizing she'd gotten caught up in the story instead of studying how they told it, how they worked the crowd.

Ned noted her panic-stricken face and simply winked at her, banishing much of her concern... only to send it soaring at his next words. "Ladies and gentlemen, gather round, for our trainee-apprentice-newbie first timer's very first debut! Try not to laugh too much at her stammering, she's already proving her bravery simply by taking the stage. Tonight, she tells a tale of intrigue, mystery... and defiance!"

As Snow got to her feet, sparks of light erupted around her, swooping into the air and bursting into flame, smoke pouring down around her in interlocking waves to add an air of intensity to her movements—and to hide her adrenaline-induced shaking.

Choking down the nervousness and first hints of actual bile that had risen in her throat when she looked over the sea of faces, Snow reminded herself that these people didn't know who she was, that they didn't have to like what she had to say. Here, she wasn't just a princess. If she did terribly, they would only boo her off stage.

For some reason, that was a comforting thought. "They don't have to love me. So… if they do, they *actually* do."

Taking a deep breath, and remembering what she'd been learning over the last week, Snow took control of her wavering voice and began. "Once upon a time…"

"*Boo!*" came a drunken voice from the back of the room. "A children's tale?"

The voice cut off with an awkward *squawk* followed by a meaty *slap* ringing through the room. "Don't you get us kicked outta here again. I swear I'll-"

"*Once upon a time.*" Snow started firmly, near *angrily*. This time, she received no comments from the peanut gallery. "There was a royal king of the nixies, shapeshifting water spirits, who was kind to all of his subjects. He and his wife did their very best for their subjects, trying to help each of them find happiness, and their kingdom thrived…"

THIRTEEN

"-So THE UNDERWATER KINGDOM found peace once more, each of the citizens returning to their homes after working together to restore justice to the kingdom. Each of them found themselves bound in friendship and camaraderie, their neighbors no longer faceless people, but blood brothers and sisters they'd give their life to defend. Never again would they allow evil to rule their land."

Snow finished her story with a flourish, the beautiful images and illusions conjured by the bards fading away and swirling around her as though she were caught in a whirlpool. Then the twinkling lights faded away, and the tavern filled with polite applause that died just as fast, as everyone returned to their food and drink. Feeling slightly dissatisfied, she rejoined the others and sat down, feeling immensely emotionally spent.

"They hated it."

"They didn't *hate* it, Snow." Zed snorted into his drink at the unexpected statement. "It just so happens you went after all the other masterfully performing, seasoned bards."

"Yeah, probably should've had you start with the kids outside. Easier audience." Ted pointed out thoughtfully. "You did well for your first time. Don't take anything away from this except that."

"You all literally had to rescue me from getting thrown out of the building by making illusions appear around me to give details of the story I was telling." Snow continued her brutal self-assessment. "Don't forget that I can perfectly read their body language. No one kept listening because *I* captivated them."

"You can read the room perfectly, yet you *didn't* adjust your storytelling style one whit?" Ned's incredulous voice made the other three wince, two in sympathy, while the princess practically smacked herself in the face in realization. "Hmm. Well. We all need to practice, and all of us started where you did. Don't forget to use your advantages in the future, and don't worry… you get to try again tomorrow."

"I think they might riot," Snow grumbled, causing the others to chuckle softly.

Zed patiently patted her on the shoulder. "Don't worry, Snow. Tomorrow we'll be at another town downriver. They won't know how bad you are until you *show* them."

"*Thanks.*" Her voice practically dripped with sarcasm as she showed an exaggerated eye roll. "Any tips on getting better *before* then?"

"Just remember," Ted smiled warmly at her. "This isn't about *Perfection*. You don't have the skills to be a high-level bard. What you're here to do is create *connection*. Just like Ned said, read the room. Speak to them how they want to be spoken *to*. You'll get this. Gentlemen, what other thoughts would you like to offer?"

The conversation devolved into a detailed breakdown of what she *had* done well and what she had definitely *not* done well. Unfortunately for her, the second half of the list was much more extensive than the first.

After her embarrassing debut, the next days and weeks began to blur together, an exhausting cycle of learning, traveling, and performing. Each day began with stretching exercises Ned, Ted, and Zed insisted were crucial to building the flexibility she needed for tumbling routines. It wasn't long before her stiff, untrained body proved them correct. Her muscles screamed in protest each time she stretched too far, and the blisters which formed on her hands, elbows, knees and feet fought heroically against the healing balm she applied religiously.

Breakfasts were spent regaining energy, gulping down as much food and drink as she could manage, then followed immediately by beginning their daily trek toward the next town they would frequent. Ted drilled her relentlessly in vocal modulation as they walked, her voice often left cracking and raw after multiple hours of practice.

As a silver lining, when she sang, her Aura of Innocence caused many small animals to flock to them as they traveled. The creatures cheerfully basked in her presence, and now that her instructors were aware of the effect, they took advantage of the ample opportunities to restock their travel rations with fresh meat.

Mid-afternoon was the next rest, once more feasting on hearty, nutrient-dense foods such as roasted rabbit. Zed summed up their dining routine with a simple phrase, 'Breakfast like a queen, lunch like a princess, dinner like a beggar.'

Snow quickly began to realize they ate as much as they could in the morning, mainly because they were uncertain what the day would hold and needed every bit of energy possible. Their late lunch followed a similar trend, and the final meal of the day often went completely uneaten, as they spent the time singing and telling tales until late into the night. When they *did* manage to eat, it was often an exceedingly light meal, so they wouldn't be too full to go through their practiced routines.

On the rare evenings they didn't have a performance, Snow's hours belonged to Ted, who helped emphasize the importance of captivating an audience through physical presence and body language. It mainly boiled down to him helping her directly act and react in real time based on his own reactions, forcing her to use her Perfect skill to adjust.

After one particularly grueling session, Snow snapped at the bard in frustration, "Ted! I know I'm getting it wrong. I'm *trying*! Can you please show me a little love here, I'm doing the best I can."

The bard stared at her serenely, waiting a few moments before taking a deep breath and stating, "This is *not* your best, Snow. I understand you're tired, but this is when you need to train the hardest. When we're exhausted, barely cognizant, we fall to our lowest level. If you haven't gotten the hang of making this happen while absolutely out of it, you haven't truly mastered what we're trying to teach you."

"*Mastered?* I'm-"

"Yes, I understand, you don't have acting skills from the system." Ted motioned with his hand, indicating she should begin once more. "Doesn't mean you shouldn't truly give it your all. Remember, we are here to help you make changes, not excuses. If we had all the time in the world, I would train you like a standard bard. Years and *years* of careful patient effort."

"But we don't." Snow let out a soft sigh, her shoulders sagging as she was once more reminded of the goal she'd set for herself. "Thank you, Ted."

"What for, princess?"

"For caring about me enough that you push me harder and tell me when I'm wrong." Snow offered a sad smile. "I know this can't be easy for you; I see the pain in your eyes when you push me to the brink. Please, I hope you know I need it, and it is the right thing to do."

Completely flustered, Ted leaned forward, eyes going watery as he opened his mouth-

"Success." Immediately, Snow shifted her posture, going

from sad and broken to triumphant in an instant, a smug smile on her face as Ted blinked in confusion for a few long moments. "You know, I think I'm getting the hang of this."

Zed started slowly clapping, swiftly followed by Ned, who laughed at Ted's stricken expression. Snow bowed to the small audience and sent a wink at the beet-red man. "Hey, don't blame me for this. You guys are teaching me everything I know, so you can only blame yourselves for being such great instructors."

At the end of each night, Snow collapsed onto her bed roll, too tired to think about anything at all.

As the seasons changed, she caught her reflection in a frozen puddle and inspected the changes that had taken hold. Feeling at her arms, she grasped lean muscle instead of the soft frailty she'd carried since her escape from the palace. Her legs were the same, travel-hardened and filled out thanks to consistent, healthy meals. The princess hadn't even noticed how much further they'd managed to travel each day as her endurance increased, not to mention how she was able to last through longer performances without exhausting herself or losing her voice.

Her happy chattering with her friends about how they'd managed to transform her health came to an abrupt halt as the foursome rounded a bend in the road and found themselves face-to-face with a handful of men wearing cloth bandanas over the lower half of their faces. Snow continued forward a few steps, only to have Ned wrap an arm around her and pull her roughly back, moving to shield her with his body as the remaining members of their group fell back to flank her.

Knives appeared in their hands as if by magic, the bards armed to the teeth in a flash.

"None of that, now." The highwayman in the center of the opposing group called out, gathering their attention and all but proclaiming himself the leader of the bandits. "We've got more on the side of the road, arrows aimed at your hearts. You're going to hand over your packs, your weapons, and go on your merry way. Otherwise, we'll take the goods off your bodies and leave the rest for the critters in the area to clean up."

Bluff. Fear. **Hunger**. *Weakness. Desperation.*

Snow's skills began whispering furiously into her mind. She could tell instantly that the bandit was lying—they were alone on the road, and by the trembling in their hands, the shaking at their knees, these were not practiced thieves. More than likely, they were simply the most recent victims of the queen.

*Protect at **all** costs. Slay threat. Exit area. Patience.*

At the same time, the princess saw how seriously her friends-turned-protectors were taking the bravado, and by the slight distortion around Zed, she assumed he had left behind a false image of himself and was already circling the group.

"Everybody stop!" Snow was nearly as confused as everyone else when the words erupted from her mouth. She stepped forward, pushing Ned's protective arm to the side and ignoring his sharp hiss to stay back. "There's no need for any of this. You need to get out of the way, or you're going to get hurt. I don't want that for you."

"You got a death wish, lady?" The bandit leader's eyes narrowed at her suspiciously. "What're you playing at?"

"I would very much like to remain alive, and I'm assuming you would as well." Snow kept her tone measured and calm, yet laced with an undercurrent of authority she'd been practicing for weeks. "It's just such a shame if we all walked away from this poorer than when we arrived, when it's so easy to enrich each other's lives."

Clearly intrigued, but unwilling to lower his guard, the bandit glanced at his fellows, then back to her. "Gotta eat to live, gotta steal to eat. The king has made it *all* too clear there's

no way for us all to get along. Sorry, lady. That means somebody's gotta get hurt."

"Does it, though? Look at us. We are traveling bards.
Does it look like we have money and valuables? If you rob us,
you gain what? A lute? Handmade pipes? Threadbear
tunics?"

"Someone might pay for them," the man stated with a
heavy sigh, lifting a heavy longbow up and drawing an arrow
from his quiver. He nocked it to the string, but didn't yet pull it
back. "I don't want to hurt you. Truly I don't. Leave your
things, don't fight us for them, and I pinky swear we'll allow
you to leave unharmed."

The air suddenly felt like molasses as Snow breathed in
sharply, the golden light of the system wrapping around the
man's hands as the world itself acknowledged his oath. Even
as the tension in the air ramped up, she felt a burden lift off
her as the system turned its attention away from their situation. "Wouldn't you say that's a heavy oath for an archer?
Don't you need your pinkies?"

"Not as much as you might think." The man gently pulled
back on his bowstring, using only his index, middle, and ring
finger. "Now… please?"

"Might I make you *one* last offer?" the princess tried again,
shifting her tone slightly to wheedle him. "You are clearly
someone honorable, and I can tell none of you are excited
about the prospect of hurting others. What if I could help you
gain something more valuable than maybe gaining a copper
or two for our rough-spun goods?"

The bandit didn't say a word but lifted an eyebrow to indicate interest. At least, that's what Snow's skills whispered to
her. She pushed on. "Reputation. We're bards! What would
happen if we spread word that this road, and this forest, are
controlled by a group of men who don't just take, but also…
protect? Have honor? We are clearly not wealthy; letting us go
will not burden you in the slightest. But when someone with

money comes along, and you rob them, are you going to keep everything for yourself?"

"Of course not. Some of us have families, and our village was all but burnt to the ground by some failed experiment of the queen." The bandit spat, the motion mirrored by the others. His bowstring relaxed slightly, and the man glanced between his compatriots for confirmation before speaking once more. "Go on. How does this help us? Reputation doesn't put food on the table."

"So you rob from the rich and give to the poor." Snow put her hands together, then dropped them forward to point at the would-be thief. "People around here will respond to that, offering you food and shelter when you need it, while the rich will put up less of a fight, knowing they will walk away with their lives even if their goods have been lifted from them. You and your merry men here could start an entire underground society in the forest. All of this could start as early as *today*."

"Robbin' the rich, huh?" The man heaved a sigh and pulled his arrow away. "Fine. Look, I didn't want to have to do this. None of us do. Just go on your way, and... I don't know."

"First, let's have a meal together," Snow firmly asserted, sending a sharp look at Ned when he grumbled under his breath. "Our treat. Do you have a fire nearby?"

Over the next hour, as Ted and Zed made a stew out of their supplies, Ned and Snow worked with the bandits to figure out how they could brand themselves to begin gener-ating a reputation for being peaceable, honorable thieves. As soon as their meal ended, the bards hustled out of the area, ready to tell tales of Robin Hood and his band of merry men.

"That... was the bravest, most foolish thing I've ever seen," Ned informed Snow as they crested a hill, relaxing in relief at the small village laid out below them. "You just turned highwaymen into the protectors of your people with nothing but words."

"If I hadn't seen you craft that story right in front of my

eyes, I'd have never believed it. If that wasn't worthy of you being called a real bard, I don't know what is." Zed chimed in with no small amount of awe in his voice.

"I'd even call it quite *Proficient*." Ted's voice carried a hint of sadness in it as he exchanged glances with the others. Snow looked between them, unable to ascertain the underlying meaning of his words, even with her Perfected skill in reading people. "Let's get down there and have a hot meal."

"Snow…" Ned started softly, only for Zed to nudge him as he moved past.

"Later, Ned," the bard all but whispered, leading the group down the hill. Snow stared at each of them with growing concern as they worked to look anywhere but at her.

CHAPTER

FOURTEEN

"It's time, Snow."

The princess looked up from her bowl of stew, eyes filled with questions as Ted spoke, while the others remained conspicuously silent. "Time for *what*, now?"

"For the world to see you as a princess once more," the bard explained with pain in his voice. Two weeks had passed since their encounter with the highwaymen, and the entire journey, they had pressed hard, only stopping in smaller towns if they happened to be along the path.

When they'd walked into Thalfanghein, the second largest city in the entire kingdom, Snow had understood *something* was happening. "Tonight, you'll be performing as yourself and spreading the first seeds of your overarching plan."

Snow's chin dropped, her eyes on the ground as she responded in a low voice. "From there… what happens?"

"You'll be moving on to your next training," Ned broke in, the quiet authority in his voice informing her there was no room for argument. "Over the last months, you've toured many of the smaller towns, gotten an idea of the layout of your king-dom, and learned how to hold an audience's attention. There's only so much we can offer you, unless you stay on with us or a nearly permanent basis. Even then, it would just be refining what you've already learned. To be completely honest-"

"-You're well on your way already." Zed took over without pause as Ned trailed off. "All of the core principles of what we've been attempting to teach you, you've soaked up like a towel being dropped in a river. From here, it's just practice, practice, practice. Day after day, all this princess needs to do is practice, practice, *practice*. I've never seen someone more willing to throw themselves into their studies like you. I'm certain you won't let us down."

Before the princess could speak, Ted chimed in, "Don't worry, we're going to be out there helping you along. Divide and conquer, as the sages tell us. From here, we will scatter like the four winds across the world, singing and spreading your story. On the day of reckoning, as you march on the castle, look to the west to see me leading a contingent of people toward you, while singing a happy tune."

"To the north, you'll first find Ned," stated Zed.

"From the south will march Zed," insisted Ned. "He'll be trailing behind, gathering the people teetering on if they should join or not."

"Which means you look to the East to find me." Ted reached over to pat Snow. "I don't know where you're going tonight, but… you will be missed."

"I'll miss you most of all… Ed." Snow swallowed the lump in her throat, banishing her pain behind a bright smile as the others looked at her with ever-so-slight confusion.

"Was that Z-Ed?"

"N-Ed?"

"T-Ed?"

"It *absolutely* was." Snow pushed her bowl away, getting to her feet and walking toward the stage. Behind her, she could hear the men arguing softly about who she had been speaking to, and chuckled softly.

After months on the road, practicing each and every day in front of a live audience or not, Snow had become adept at performing on stage. With one quick sweep of the crowd to ensure there weren't any Huntsmen in attendance, she hopped up and took a deep breath, beginning by singing a soft, low sound, increasing volume of the wordless melody until she had the attention of everyone in the enormous inn. Then, giving herself only a fraction of a moment to reset, the princess launched into her tale.

"*Once upon a time!*"

The crowd of people sitting throughout the room let out a deep gasp as the illusions hiding her identity faded away, revealing the runaway princess in their midst. Several stood, many took steps toward her, but none came closer as she pushed forward, unconcerned with their reactions. As her story continued, the confused citizens retook their seats, though there was a low murmuring through the entirety of her narration.

"-they lived happily ever after, never again allowing such evil to take root in their kingdom!" Snow finally finished, her words bouncing back to her in the pin-drop-silence of the room.

After taking a bow and a single step, a question shattered the stillness.

"Where's your captor, Princess Snow?"

"My *what* now?" The absolute bloodlust in that voice stopped Snow dead, and she looked around in confusion at the hostile gazes directed her way. "No one captured me. I fled the castle when it became clear that—*ahem*. When it became clear that the queen did not have the best of intentions for my people. Now I am on the run in my own kingdom, hoping to tell people the truth of what is happening."

"It's just as they said..." someone muttered, and dozens of heads bobbed along in understanding. "She doesn't even realize she was abducted! Listen, Princess, come with me. I'll help you get back home-"

"No, *I* will!"

"You're just after the land and title the queen promised to whoever saved her daughter!" another roared, throwing his seat to the ground as he stood up. "*I'm* man enough to say that's why I want to help her!"

Immediately, the crowd of passive listeners turned into a huge mob of unruly people. Blood began to flow nearly immediately as fists proved not persuasive enough, and those with combat skills drew weapons and tried to cut their way to the princess. Snow yelped and backed away as the crowd surged to the stage... only to fight with all their might to grab a cloak someone had thrown onto the wooden surface.

"The illusion I put on that will keep them busy for a while." A gentle hand closed around her elbow, and the princess was guided off stage a moment later, her wide eyes locked on Bashful's mask as he threaded the mob without allowing even a single person to bump into them. "Now you know what you're up against, Princess."

"How?" was all Snow could get out, gesturing behind her with a panicked expression on her face.

"What? How did I convince them that the cloak was you?" Bashful snorted, a too-wide smile stretching his lips beyond the bounds of his head. "I'm well past being only a *Master* Illusionist. This is what I *do*. By the way, this was Zed's idea. It's always fun to see my student become the master. We call this 'Nero's Gambit', by the way. Throw something into the fire and see how quickly it burns, while getting the actual fuel, in this case you, out of there safely. This allows us to gauge the reactions of the crowd without putting ourselves in, well, in *much* danger."

"Where are the others? Snow frantically looked around for her friends at Bashful's casual mention of Zed, but couldn't see them anywhere. She deflated slightly, partly in relief, but mostly sadness, when she didn't spot them in the room. "They're already gone, aren't they?"

"Indeed they are." Bashful confirmed in a conciliatory tone. "But they've taught you what you needed. Abyss, you've even developed quite the knack for showmanship. Going forward, always remember to use your props to your advantage, and speak from the heart. Now, it's time for you to move on to learning the next way to spread your influence. Here, take this sack and this missive. On that *note*, heh, I recommend taking a peek at your skills as we walk along. I've been hearing oh-so-many people spreading your story during my travels."

Snow's eyes went wide as they dropped to her left arm. She had long since fallen out of the habit of regularly checking her influence, as it accrued so slowly that there seemed to be no point to it. Running her index finger along the inseam, her lips parted slightly in surprise at the numbers waiting for her.

Influential Aura: Level 6/10.

Influential Aura subtly yet powerfully affects those around you, [Rudimentarily] influencing their thoughts in a positive or negative manner using Influence as a currency. You are able to [Rudimentarily] sway opinions, inspire action, and guide decisions with a variable cost. Influencing people in ways contrary to their desires will cost additional Influence, while moving them in ways aligned with their own goals will give an Influence discount of [30%], increasing to a maximum of a 100% discount. Use caution, as leading others toward goals not in their best interests will slowly push you toward darker powers.

Your Influence is gained at a rate of ([3]*total followers/10) per day with a minimum of 1.)
Current followers: 2,900
Influence: 3,400/5,036

Requirement to advance to level 4: Collect and maintain a minimum of 5,036 influence for 24 hours. 0/1.

"I'm already level six with this skill? When did that happen?" Snow didn't get an answer. Instead, Bashful let go of the sack he'd been trying to push into her hands, and she stumbled and nearly dropped the heavy burden in shock. "By the *system*, what is this, rocks?"

"It's a large amount of gold, silver, and copper, intended to be used to pay for the next portion of your training," Bashful explained cheerfully. "Happy sends his regards. It should be explained in the note."

Having left the chaos of the large inn well behind them, Snow turned incredulous eyes to the scrap of paper the man was insistently pushing at her.

Greetings, our rebel queen!

Our efforts persist in the background, just as we realize yours are ongoing. However, we've decided you are in need of a bit of, shall we say, reinforcement. Your tutors have told us that you have learned as much as possible under their instruction. We have come to the consensus that it is time for you to explore new avenues for reaching your full potential.

We are going to start with learning to exert external influence, now that you have learned how to rely on yourself to grow it the old-fashioned way. First, you get to practice my favorite form of influence, which I find works rather well when one has the means to attempt it: bribery.
Never forget, money makes the world go round and works better than oil for allowing you to slip into exclusive, new, and exciting places! I know you likely have never had this much coin on your person at once before, so I'm sending a second sack with twice as much to meet you at your destination. Just go out there and have fun with it! You deserve to be-

-Happy.

"I hope you enjoyed your time under our tutelage, Princess." Bashful's voice tickled her ear, and Snow glanced up, then frantically around when she didn't see the man anywhere. "Go to the markets and gear up. Travel clothes, food, and other such. Don't forget what you've learned with us; I'm looking forward to seeing the queen you will eventually become."

"Bashful? Bashful! Where am I supposed to go after that?" The princess frantically questioned the empty air, but no response was forthcoming. After a minor panic attack over having been left alone in a strange area, she decided she had no choice other than to do what the guild leader had instructed, hoping it would be enough to earn additional instructions.

Shivering the entire time she walked through the city, Snow barely realized how bright it was until she stepped into the market square and saw the sun in the sky above her. "It's already late morning? Where... where did the night go? Did Bashful somehow put me to sleep?"

Unfortunately, there was no one she could ask these questions to, as anyone in the market could be an agent of the queen. Buying a cloak and scarf from the first vendor she found, Snow began drifting from stall to stall, finding it strangely uncomfortable to shop while spending someone else's money for herself. After securing hardy travel clothes and a stout knife, she turned her eyes to the window of a dress store. Her feet moved almost of their own accord, and soon she was looking at the reflection in the window, her face hovering above a blue and yellow dress and topaz-studded necklace combination.

Snow's hesitation vanished as she stepped inside, trying on the dress and purchasing accessories to go along with it. Even if the garments *didn't* have self-repair, self-cleaning, and anti-wrinkle magic gently imbued into them, she still would've bought them. From her time as a princess, she knew the gown had many applications in different parts of society she had yet to attempt to influence, and her travels with the bards had impressed upon her the power of a costume in the right situation.

After carefully packing the new garments away, then changing back into her travel gear, she stepped into the market, feeling far more confident than when she'd first arrived.

"About time, Princess," a gruff voice reached her ears, the voice low enough to make her bones vibrate. "All done spending your entire budget? What am I saying… of course you aren't. I know what he sent along, and no matter what else might be true, you're no wastrel."

"While I admit I'm relieved to see you," turning to look at the huge, muscly, absolute *mountain* of a man waiting next to the door, Snow gulped and bobbed her head. "You don't appear to be happy."

"I'm not." Grumpy pointed at his own mask. "I'm Grumpy. As you should know by now, statistically speaking, six out of seven of us *aren't* Happy."

CHAPTER
FIFTEEN

"What is physical influence, Princess?" Grumpy's uncompromising voice pulled Snow out of her dead sleep. Startled awake, she shifted to a seated position, only to let out a deep groan as every inch of her body ached from the previous day's rigorous drills.

"Grumpy! No! Please, I swear my blisters have blisters inside them, in places blisters aren't supposed to appear." Her abdomen spasmed, and Snow dropped flat on her bed, trying to take deep, calm breaths as her muscles writhed.

"An excellent opportunity for me to educate you." Grumpy's eyes glittered beneath his mask as he impatiently waited for her to start moving. "At the end of every argument, at the heart of every empire, power sharpens itself to a single truth: all influence begins and ends at the tip of a blade."

He waited another moment for Snow to get up, and when she didn't, he slowly uncoiled his arms and let them drop to his side. "In other words, Princess… every law passed by the kingdom is enforced by *force*. If you put out a tax, and people don't pay it, very strong people that work for me or you directly will go and haul them off to prison or cut them down if they try to fight. Every theft, destruction of property, every little social spat we have. At the end of the day, if you don't have the might required to impose your will… you have no true influence at all."

"On that note," he continued after a heartbeat. "My job is to train you. If you don't want to be trained, then be strong enough that I have no choice but to let you sleep in. Otherwise, you can either get yourself up or be *dragged* to the training yard. Which is it going to be?"

"I'm up! I'm up," Snow grumbled as every part of her body angrily protested her movements. The last several weeks had been spent traveling off-road, carrying everything she had purchased, and all remaining monies given her by Happy, as she alternated between jogging and sprinting in a strange form of torture Grumpy called 'conditioning'. Only the long months with the bards allowed her to survive even the first day, as somehow Grumpy was able to perfectly judge whether she had truly expended all of her energy or not.

"Good. As you can see, I've successfully exerted my influence." Grumpy stepped out of the way, allowing her to step out into the open area around his house in the hidden village they had traveled to as rapidly as she could manage. "Tell me, Princess. Why is this form of influence kept in the background?"

"Because it's what that Witch queen does?" Snow tried to keep the annoyance out of her voice, but it was hard to focus on anything other than her own discomfort.

"Indeed, it is what she does," Grumpy stated approvingly, and Snow blinked rapidly as she realized she may have gotten a question correct. "As far as we can tell, she's been putting every bent copper she can collect into buying massive quantities of alchemical reagents from across the lands. Now, obviously she has a specific goal, but we don't know if she'll ever achieve it. We don't want her to, as it will likely mean a qualitative shift in the amount of power she can bring to bear. Why is what she's doing an issue?"

"She's destroying the kingdom around her in an attempt to fund her projects." Snow warmed up to the conversation, her anger toward her father's wife allowing her to push past the creakiness in her joints and start to warm up. "Eventually, it doesn't matter how much she demands of the people, they will either not be able to give her anything or will actively rebel."

"Precisely." Grumpy pointed at a small table set up next to an open pasture. "Breakfast is over there. Take care of any other necessities behind those trees; there's a small creek that goes back underground. The cold water will be good for your sore muscles."

As Snow sat to break her fast, Grumpy studied her for a long minute before waxing eloquent on physical influence. "The best way to use this type of power is to gain an initial foothold in a hostile area. After that, allowing it to remain a background thought instead of a major factor in running your operations allows you to begin building trust and goodwill through *less* violent influences. Creating a stable, prosperous land is the best end result for everyone involved."

"But the kingdom already exists. You have so many fighters ready to go against the queen, why do I need to-" Snow backpedaled as Grumpy glowered at her. "I'm not trying to complain! I'm just saying, I don't have a combat class. I'll never be as proficient with a weapon as someone who has class skills already focused on those areas. Being able to be of service is important, but taking care of myself is as well. Right now, I feel weaker than I ever have before."

"No. You are sore and hurt. You're not *injured*. There's a major difference." Grumpy began pacing, glancing at her food to see how close she was to being done. "You can get over being *hurt*. Soreness is an indicator that your body will heal stronger than before. What the queen did to you? Any longer, and you would've been permanently injured, crippled and shrunken from malnourishment. Pliable, even easier to bend to her will. Being able to fight and choosing not to is strength.

Saying you won't fight because you are physically unable simply means you're weak. We are here to give you *options*."

The first hint of dawn's light peaked over the horizon, and Grumpy grimaced at it. "Abyss, we're already behind schedule. Get ready, my battle daughters will be here momentarily to begin putting you through your paces."

Quickly finishing her food, followed by a dip in the creek —which felt more like dunking herself in a frozen lake—Snow returned to the pasture, shivering and dripping from putting her clothes back on while soaked. A familiar trio awaited her, several young women wearing lesser-embellished versions of Grumpy's mask.

"What a lovely day to be alive, Princess!" the first of them called out in the middle of performing a warm-up routine. Snow watched Ida move through weapon katas with a fluid grace which left the princess wishing she'd spent another year or two practicing tumbling and acrobatics with her bard friends. "Our battle father says you've shown minimal proficiency with the dagger. High praise for someone who hasn't trained with the blade their entire life."

Thunk.

A knife sank into the tree trunk the princess had just walked past, and she turned to look at Clara with a hint of caution in her eyes. The blonde battle sister had seemed to have it out for Snow since she arrived, an outsider in their midst. "Whoops! Was that one too close for comfort? Don't worry, I'll get you so comfortable with thrown weapons that you'll never shy away from them. Battle daddy's orders."

"Battle *father*, Clara." The third, Adele, spoke directly into Clara's ear, having disappeared entirely, only to reappear behind the blonde, masked woman. "You ask much of someone who did not grow up in our ways, while not adhering to the rules yourself. Remember, we lead from the front. If the tip of the spear is dull, the rest of the weapon is all but useless."

Clara didn't seem to mind the admonishment, though she did leap back in concern as her dagger sailed through the air only to stick into the ground a few feet in front of where she'd been standing. Snow simply shrugged when she was glared at. "Abyss, looks like you're right. I'm not good with flying daggers yet. Just trying to get some early-morning practice in."

"A dagger is your weapon of last resort, Snow." Grumpy suddenly sat up from where he'd been completely hidden in a small scruff of grass that should have never been enough to conceal him. All of the ladies flinched away, and the small portion of Clara's face that could be seen went bright red. "If you don't have proper bodyguards when you're on the throne, we've done something quite wrong. Even though I wish to give you proper training, the short few months I have with you won't be nearly enough time. As you said yourself, when faced with someone with actual system-granted skills, it'll never be enough."

"But didn't you-"

Grumpy interrupted her with a partially raised hand, "Worry not. While speed and strength are not, and never will be your forte… stealth is something we can certainly work with. It's not my preferred method, but I've plenty of knowledge to offer. Typically, I'd have someone with your skillset working on building up their aura to *exude* all of their willpower, emotions, and *bloodlust*."

For an instant that seemed to last an eternity, Grumpy's eyes flared bright red, and the air around him twisted and warped into the shape of a terrifying monster—then Snow blinked, and the intense feeling was gone. Examining her memories, she realized that he hadn't altered in the slightest; her mind had simply played tricks on her when it felt an apex predator staring her down. The princess let out a small cough, which seemed to be enough for Grumpy to continue his lecture.

"Good, that didn't paralyze your lungs." He turned to let

his eyes shift between each of his battle daughters—a term Snow had realized meant any lady he personally trained in the village, while the men were his 'battle sons' while training. They would remain as such until they'd tasted true combat together, at which point each of them would become battle brothers or sisters. "Instead, we're going to work on the opposite version of this influence. Stealth, as I mentioned, in a sense. You'll be doing your best to influence us to not notice you or not want to hurt you. Feel free to choose whichever you think will be most likely to succeed."

When Grumpy didn't speak any further, Snow raised a hesitant question, "How do I, um… wait. I couldn't look away from you when you had pushed out your emotions and blood-lust, so would this be basically the opposite? Absolutely hiding all of my intent and emotion?"

"That, and controlling your facial expressions and body language." Grumpy offered a mirthless smirk, according to the shift in his neck muscles. "You should've been getting some training from Bashful's people about that, though they tend to focus on being *more* expressive. Think you can handle swapping it around?"

"Do I have a choice?"

"Not if you want to live."

"Then yes, I can absolutely make it happen," Snow grumbled even as the battle daughters chuckled at the banter flowing between them. Well, Ida and Adele laughed—Clara just gripped her daggers tighter. "How do we start? Should we move into the woods, or…?"

"No, a nice open field like this is perfect." Grumpy pointed to where he had just been hiding. "A battlefield isn't going to offer you such conveniences as a thick hedge or a handy forest to duck into. Before you start pointing out semantics—ooh, Mr. Grumpy, when will *I* ever be on a battle-field—just stop. How many hiding spots do you think the hall-ways of your castle are going to have? Right now, you're going to start learning how to blend in with your environment. That starts by being really *bad* at it, then practicing until you don't suck *as* much."

Adele appeared to Snow's left, tossing her a rough linen scarf. "Wrap this around your head to obscure your face. A flash of skin *that* pale is going to catch the eye day or night. For the rest, you'll have to rely on instinct, timing, distractions, and your system-granted skills—*influence* us to ignore you."

"If you can," Clara clarified with a humorless grin, eyes locked on the already tired and sore princess.

Ida walked over, handing Snow a satchel with a set of small wooden balls filling it. "You need to practice disappearing, like our battle father did. When one of us catches sight of you, toss one of these in an attempt to create a distraction, then move to a new location. Understood?"

"By the way, when we see you, we're going to throw *our* balls at you." Clara held up a bag filled with bright yellow balls. "That way, you can practice dodging at the same time."

Snow nodded, unsure how she was going to manage, but willing to try. Feeling like an imposter as she faced the battle daughters, Snow tied the scarf tight around her face, barely leaving room for her eyes to peek out. Grumpy didn't give her even a moment more to ready herself, simply staring her down and barking...

"*Go!*"

SIXTEEN

"ALL YOU NEED to do is get close enough to stab us with that wooden dagger, Snow," Clara taunted the princess, who was rubbing at a freshly forming welt. "Get close enough without us seeing you and without getting hit. Come on, this should be easy! Didn't battle father Grumpy even commission a special tool just for you?"

Snow glanced down at the wrist brace she had taken to wearing at all times which had a special mechanism which would flick the—currently wooden—dagger out of its hidden position and into her hand. Grumpy had tossed it at her, calling out that this was hidden, accessible, and stealthy; the weight and handle should be correct for her small hands. Overall, it was exactly what he had promised: a weapon of last resort. The princess let out a sharp *hiss* of pain as a wooden ball drew a line along the side of her head, painfully battering her ear before falling to the ground.

Looking up at Clara, who was staring back without any hint of trying to play innocent, Snow took a single, threatening step forward... only for another ball to *whiz* toward her from another direction. As the princess dropped to the ground and rolled, Adele called over, "She's actively trying to distract you, Snow. Are you going to let her? In combat, are *you* going to stop and allow your enemies to re-arm themselves? They certainly will not give you the same courtesy."

"Hidden, accessible, and stealthy." Snow repeated her new mantra under her breath as she grit her teeth and glared at Clara, who had gone out of her way over the last few weeks to target the most painful spots possible when throwing wooden balls at her. The battle daughter clearly had some form of system-enhanced ability with throwing weapons and had never missed a single throw, even when Snow was certain she had managed to dive out of the way. "I'm not any of those. *Yet.*"

"That's right!" Clara called back, and Snow's face fell when she realized she had been speaking loudly enough to be overheard. "More like easy to spot, slow to react, and too overly emotional to suppress your aura in the slightest. Why don't you just give up on this and accept permanent protection from our clan?"

"Only if you specifically work directly for me," Snow called back, feeling a smidgen of gratification as the young woman taunting her pulled a disgusted face. "Yeah... I can see that. You standing next to me, watching out for my best interests, at least half the day, *every* day. We'll be best friends. Of course, that would mean you wouldn't have any opportunity to pursue your *Battle Daddy-*"

Snow dropped to the ground and covered her head as three wooden balls *whizzed* through the air toward her, barely ahead of Clara's shriek of impotent fury. They struck the princess, and she grimaced as she felt soft flesh give painfully under the impacts, but she accepted it happily. "Totally worth it."

"I don't need to suppress *my* emotions, Snow!" Clara shouted at her, "only cowards and assassins need to *hide*. What does that make *you*?"

For a moment, the princess froze up, but the answer

quickly coalesced in her mind, and she stood to her full height. "Until I take the throne, I suppose I'm an *assassin*. If it means saving my family, keeping my loved ones safe, and rescuing the kingdom? Yeah… if learning this means I get close enough to that Witch of a queen to put a dagger in her heart, that's what I'm going to do."

"Abyss. You're *twisted*." Though the words were rough, there was a surprising amount of respect coming from the blonde battle daughter.

Taking the moment of respite, the princess settled into a crouch behind a sparse bush offering little in the way of actual cover. Another ball flew toward her, this time from Ida's direction, and Snow forced herself to stay perfectly still as it struck her on the shoulder with a sharp **thwack**. Focusing on exhaling slowly, she allowed her tension, stress, and fear to flow away. "That's right. All of this is a means to an end. The *end* of the Witch. It doesn't matter if I'm in pain, or sore, or even if I'm broken at the end of it. I need to scrub it *all* away."

Focusing on her singular goal with the majority of her mind, the peripheries of her thoughts worked on visualizing her influential aura and pulling it in, or at least dimming it. "Until I've freed my sister, my existence is just…"

"…background noise."

"By the system, I think she's got it."

Adele's words nearly broke Snow out of the half-trance she had sunken into, but at the last moment, the princess managed to let the intrusion go. Moving ever so slowly, she crept away from the bush, her gaze lazily roving across the pasture—

Thwack!

"We can still see you!" Clara called out, though there was much less angst in her tone than there had been at any point in the last few weeks. Then, surprisingly, the battle daughter offered *advice* for the first time. "Your shoulders are too rigid. Relax your limbs, keep your core strong as you move along.

You need to blend in with the movement of the leaves and grass as the wind blows. Know who's a great assassin? Snakes. Lethal, hard to find before they strike, yet they're practically *everywhere*."

Snow shivered as she looked around nervously, wondering where the snakes were. Ida let out an annoyed **harrumph**. "Clara!"

"It's not my fault she can't hold it yet!" the blonde shouted back defensively. Then she whipped a ball at the princess in agitation, driving home the point that they could still see her. Snow dove into a bush, hidden from view and therefore any further strikes.

"Relax… but stay ready. Breathe." Snow unclenched her groaning muscles one by one, pushing the pain of welts, thorny grasses, and the scratching branches of the bush out of her mind. Moving carefully this time, she crept out of the foliage and began slinking along the pasture, remaining pressed to the grass as she moved along.

It might have been her imagination, but the world around her felt… muted. As if she usually was walking along with her hands to the side, catching the wind, but now was tightly cocooned in an overcoat. Halfway to Ida's last known location, Snow found herself staring blankly at a thin noodle of a reptile, which looked back at her uncomprehendingly. She had no presence at the moment, so the easily startled creature simply remained where it was—waiting for easy prey.

The snake being mere inches from her face broke Snow out of her meditative cycle, and she threw herself away while letting out a harsh, shrill shriek. An instant later, she heard the telltale **whiz** of a wooden ball flying through the air, then she knew no more.

"Get up." Snow let out a pitiful groan as Grumpy nudged her with his foot, rousing her from… not sleep. Unconsciousness? "How many fingers am I holding up?"

"Ugh. I don't know, three? How many are you hiding

behind your back?" Snow's answer earned her a sharp nod of approval, and the enormous D'wharve showed his other hand, where two fingers were extended. "Excellent. No brain damage—probably—if you're waking up and thinking tactically. Clara sends her apologies; she threw the ball too hard when you screamed."

"Is *that* what happened?" Snow blinked several times, trying to recall the last few moments she had been awake. "How do I return the favor?"

"Get good." Grumpy shook his head as if to admonish her. "You're not going to land a hit on her if she knows you're coming. She's likely the most talented untested warrior in the clan. Now-"

"Bet she'd *love* to hear you say that to her." Snow teased the huge man, who simply continued speaking as if he hadn't been interrupted.

"-today you're taking the day off of this type of training and coming into the village." The huge man started walking toward the door. "My battle brothers and sisters, and all of our battle sons and daughters, are going to be competing in a grappling and wrestling match in the town center. It will be a good learning opportunity for you."

"I'm not much for wrestling, Grumpy." Snow flexed her arms at him, clearly defined with muscle only because she had barely any energy stores whatsoever. "Pretty sure if someone manages to grab onto me, there's nothing I'm going to be able to do about it."

"It's a different kind of learning opportunity for you. You won't be wrestling, but you will be competing." Grumpy stepped out of the room, closing the door to give her some privacy. "I highly recommend wearing clothes which fit tightly against your body, but it's your choice to follow my recommendation or not."

Snow quickly got dressed, following his advice to the letter by wearing a set of white robes he had provided for training purposes. When she stepped out of the room, and saw the surprise in his body language, she rolled her eyes at him. "What? Who *wouldn't* listen to you when you give them a recommendation? I don't even know what I'm going to be doing, so why would I set myself up for failure?"

"To test yourself against me," Grumpy calmly asserted, as though it were a common occurrence. "To push the boundaries of your own freedom and see where that leads you."

"Would that work well for me?"

"*Abyss* no." Grumpy huffed through his nose, the closest he ever got to outright laughing. "Doesn't stop most people. Someday, when I'm not in charge of you, we should have a drink, and I'll tell you stories of how many people try to fight me to impress the lady they are courting. Again, situations that don't work well for other people."

"I can imagine," Snow replied dryly, though there was a bright smile on her face thanks to the dangerous man opening up to her even this much. As they walked down the path through the pasture, her gaze landed on Adele, Ida, and Clara, who were clearly waiting for them. "Good morning, all. Isn't it a *great* day not to be throwing things at me? Makes me want to sing."

"Please don't." Even as Clara grumbled, she looked anywhere but at Snow, refusing to meet her eyes. "Last time you did that, I had to eat rabbit, squirrel, and pheasant for *days*. Do you want that on your shoulders again? Actually, you know what? Go ahead. They're going to follow you around and give away your position. Make yourself an even *easier* target for me."

"Maybe I'll just hum." Snow stuck her tongue out at the blonde as she strolled past her, earning soft snickers from the other girls for her immature response. "Grumpy, what can you tell me about this village? I understand you want some of it to be, you know, secret, but-"

"This town is home to the finest warriors in the kingdom."

Grumpy began explaining in an even, measured tone. "I do not say that casually. Whenever someone from the kingdom's armies distinguishes themselves and decides to leave the service of the crown, they are offered a home here. Beyond that, talented people are recruited from everywhere, so long as they can align themselves with the mission and goal of the clan. Every child raised within our territory is taught to fight from the time they can hold a weapon, no matter what class or skills they are granted by the system."

"You haven't had any trouble from the queen?" Snow quietly wondered as they moved from dirt to stone roads, entering the village proper. "You call this place a secret, but... it doesn't seem like it really is. I kind of doubt *those* people come from here, right?"

She nodded toward various wagons packed with goods, with moon-faced merchants happily pulling their horses along. Grumpy glanced at the wagons, but returned his gaze to the path ahead. "They have deep ties to the other guildmasters, but yes, you are correct in thinking the crown knows our location. They also know better than to try to send their Huntsmen into our borders. The queen has been seeking out weak towns, with weak citizens, exploiting the corruption and people seeking *easy* paths to power. Look around. Do you see *weakness* here?"

"Only the merchants," Snow replied after carefully assessing the people they were passing, "and myself, I suppose."

"Choosing the easy option every time eventually makes for a hard life. Choosing to do the hard thing *eventually* allows for an easier life. What Happy calls 'compound interest', I call 'productive use of time'." Grumpy glanced at her, hoping to drive his point home. "Believe it or not, sometimes I am envious of people who can find joy in monotony. Truly, both paths are hard. Here, we simply choose which version of hard we wish to live."

"Hard muscles." Snow bobbed her head in understanding, causing Grumpy to bite off what he was just about to say.

"That's not... no, while it might be a byproduct of-" Snow laughed as the battle daughters stared at Grumpy with shocked expressions, having never seen him without a ready retort or a pithy saying at the tip of his tongue. "Enough of this! Your task for the day is to maintain situational awareness. Attentiveness is key today, in all things. At the end of each match, I will be quizzing you on who did well, where the loser failed, and where the victor took advantage."

Before Snow could ask clarifying questions, her current mentor turned to a man who was writing down bets, pulling out coins and tossing a few over. As he called out his guess at who would win, a sharp bell rang out, and two enormous brutes threw themselves at each other, clashing with a meaty *thwap* that made the princess's jaw drop.

"Abyss... good thing I don't need to wrestle. That impact *alone* would have snapped my spine."

SEVENTEEN

THE MATCH WAS MESMERIZING, a brutal dance of strength, strategy, and sheer willpower. Sitting on the edge of her seat, the princess's eyes darted between combatants as they twisted and strained against each other. Clearly both men were Masters at this sport, shown by their calculated and purposeful movements. Though wrestling had never been a form of entertainment she had partaken of, now she couldn't help but be drawn in.

One of the competitors, a barrel-chested man with broad shoulders and a neck studded with vine-thick veins, was leaning nearly his entire weight against his opponent, trying to leverage his bulk into tiring out the leaner, more agile man. The large man maneuvered for a grip that would pin his opponent, yet the wiry fighter twisted and countered, wiggling out of his grasp over and again.

"The way he turned just now," Snow murmured to Grumpy, who sat next to her, glaring at the wrestling men with his arms crossed, looking for all the world like he wanted nothing more than to fight both of them at the same time. "How did the smaller one manage to throw that big guy just there? From his position, he shouldn't have had any leverage. Was that a system skill?"

"Turned his momentum against him," Grumpy grunted, eyes never leaving the ring. "Sometimes stopping something outright takes far more effort than *increasing* its speed a little bit. When someone is unprepared for their arm to suddenly speed up, the rest of their body moves with it. Look closer. Watch his feet, how he's driving his shin up into his opponent's knee. If he didn't have that *exact* positioning, he'd already be flat on his back."

Snow's gaze traveled lower. What had been impressive to her only moments ago—huge muscles shoving against each other, white-knuckled grips on forearms, and two faces pressed against each other while bellowing—suddenly paled in comparison to the constant shifting of their feet, the delicate balance of the opponents. Even a shift in how their toes were aligned suddenly seemed... *intense.* Compared to the loud, highly visible fight going on above, down below was a deliberate, quiet, strategic battle complementing the struggling of their upper bodies.

She gasped in excitement as the larger man's foot swung to the side, disrupting the wiry fighter's stance and allowing him to bodily throw the smaller man to the ground. Snow jumped to her feet as the dust settled, jaw going slack in shock when she saw the agile man wiggle free and twist, reversing the larger man's position in an instant. "*How?*"

The crowd began to cheer, and she found herself joining along, then turned to Grumpy with shining eyes. "They're *really* throwing everything they have against each other. Look at the *sweat* pouring off of them! Normally I'd find that disgusting, but right now? It's just proof of their efforts."

"I'm glad you approve," Grumpy replied as he nodded at the fighters, then casually waved his left hand at the crowd. "The clan understands what they're seeing. It's not like the castle or an arena meant for show, where half the audience pretends that they know the difference between good technique and brute force. Even *those* are better than the other half, who don't even *pretend* to know. They just want to see people get hurt. Here, the warriors get to perform for peers. Warriors who know the craft. They're going to use maximum effort, because when people here judge them, it is an *accurate* assessment."

"Is that the real reason I'm here? To learn the difference between expert fighters and those who can only put on a good show?" Snow wondered aloud as she returned her full attention to the competition. Just then, the match reached its climax as the wiry man locked his legs around his opponent's neck, swinging him to the side and driving him into the ground with enough force to kill a bull. A roar of approval swept from the crowd as the huge man realized his helpless position and finally tapped out.

Both of them hopped to their feet, shaking hands and smiling as though they *hadn't* just tried to break each other in half. Snow clapped as enthusiastically as anyone in the crowd, and as the applause began to die out, she turned to give her thoughts on the match when movement just behind Grumpy caught her eye.

An older man, covered in scars and grizzled with age, suddenly spun to the side, caught a young boy's wrist, then hauled the man into the air and tossed him to the ground with casual ease. The boy, barely a teenager, landed hard but quickly scrambled to his feet, trying to catch his breath after the wind was knocked out of him. He lifted his hands, showing off a small, strange-looking dagger with an uneven blade.

"I'll get you yet, old man!" After delivering his threat, the boy spun and darted into the crowd, his posture sinking as the old man bellowed out a hearty laugh.

"Not this year, Wilbur!" The man's voice carried easily

over the crowd. "Maybe next year, after you've had plenty of time to practice. Actually… make that two years; I've seen how much effort you put in! You crash about like a pig in a truffle patch, and that lunge was about as graceful as a hog spotting an extra fluffy mushroom and trying to claim it for himself. You're welcome to try again, any time!"

Before Snow could decide on how to react to the attempted murder, another boy rushed out of the crowd, another dagger clumsily held forward as he practically tripped over his own feet trying to ram it into the older man's back. She sucked in a harsh breath, but before she could call a warning, the old man swung around and slapped the weapon out of his hand with the same effortless movements he had used against Wilbur.

"Walden! You didn't really think you'd be able to catch me unaware, did you? Where Wilbur goes, I always expect you to be near." The older man's tone was lighthearted, an absolute *shock* for the princess after two attempts on his life, no matter how clumsy they may have been. "It would have been more surprising if you *hadn't* tried to take advantage of this situation. Maybe next time *don't*. That'd make me all sorts of paranoid."

The second boy muttered something as he bent to grab his fallen dagger, only for the old man to give him a gentle kick and send him scampering after Wilbur. It was clear now to Snow that something had just happened she simply had no context for. Perhaps some sort of training, or maybe just a lesson in humility for hot-blooded young teens.

When the people spectating the brief interaction only laughed and turned their attention back to the ring, Snow gestured subtly toward the older figure. "Grumpy, who is that, and what just happened?"

"Benson just took a fist to the face, that's why he's bleeding so badly. Split his lip something fierce." Grumpy snorted as he swatted at the air in front of him. "Vance got a cheap shot in.

Going to cost him a few points on that technicality, but look at how he's already sweating. He's practically dripping, and the match just started! Want to run my bet over before they get too far in to place-"

"Not them, that old man!" Snow pointedly indicated the grizzled veteran in the crowd. "Two kids just tried to stab him, and he only tossed them around a little bit and made fun of them. He even invited them to try again! What if they had managed to hurt him? Would they have... I don't know, at least gotten in trouble? Or is that acceptable behavior in this town?"

"Old man Magnus?" Grumpy replied in an exasperated tone, clearly wanting to focus on the fight in front of him. "He's been around since even *I* was a small lad and knows every trick in the book. He's worth triple points, which is why everyone's always trying to land a strike on him. Almost never manage it, though."

"Points?" Snow's ears perked up as she remembered the odd shape of the daggers. "So it's a game?"

"Yeah, it's just something the children of the village play. For example," Grumpy's hand shot out, wrapping around a small wrist and pulling a tiny waif of a girl into sight. Her huge eyes immediately welled up, and Snow's heart melted. The warrior scoffed at the sight, slapping the 'dagger' out of her hand. As it hit the ground, the blade broke and revealed itself to be colored chalk. The child's face scrunched up as she growled at the huge man like a feral beast, only for him to spin her around and send her on her way. "You're ten years too early to try marking *me*!"

"Is this... can anyone play this? Grumpy, you might call this a children's game, but isn't this exact situation what you've been trying to teach me? Stealth skills?" Snow excitedly inquired. "Besides the whole getting thrown around thing, it even seems kind of, I don't know, fun?"

"You want to *play*? Sure, go play around instead of doing

what I told you to do." Grumpy shook his head at her uncomprehending expression. "What did I tell you when we got here? Attentiveness is key today. Wherever there's a crowd, they'll try to mark people up. Anyone with any kind of awareness can catch them quickly and quietly, sending them on their way without a fuss. How about you, *princess*?"

"What do you…" With a sudden feeling of dread, Snow twisted around and looked at her back, horrified when she saw how many chalk marks had been drawn across her back and legs. "They were marking *me*?"

"You were an *easy* mark, I'm disappointed to see." Grumpy's tone was scathing as he took in the myriad marks across her clothing. "I even specifically tried to help you feel them marking you by getting you to wear a close-fitting outfit. Magnus hasn't gotten a mark on him for over two years. Be like him."

"Look, anyone can play, right?" Snow brushed past his grumbling and tried to remain focused on the core of her question. Grumpy nodded sharply, likely realizing she was going to insist on joining in. "I think this is exactly what I need. A change in pace for a little bit. I understand it's just for today-"

"Tomorrow also. We have honor duels to settle," her mentor chimed in.

"Excellent!" Snow clapped a single time, eyes widening slightly as she saw his pupils momentarily shift to the side. Whipping around, she caught the outstretched arm of a child, who looked up at her with a gap-tooth smile as he snapped his fingers. "Look, I'm getting better already. Off you go!"

She bent down and scooped up the makeshift chalk dagger, then twisted to look at her back. "Do the colors mean something? Should I go wash this off before I participate?"

"That would be unfair to those who marked you. At the end of each day, the marks are tallied up, and a prize is given to whoever gets the most 'kills'." Grumpy rolled his shoulders, part of his attention locked up in the fights which had just begun anew. "Also, you were told to be attentive, so now you must wear your shame for all to see. As for the colors, yes, purple chalk is given to the *youngest* of the children."

Snow's back was nearly covered in purple chalk, and she blushed slightly as she realized what he was insinuating—even a child was able to sneak up and 'kill her' at this stage of her training. Not a princess's *favorite* thing to hear. Cheeks burning from having been embarrassed like this in front of the highly respected warrior, she forced determination into her voice, "This is going to help me improve, so I'm going to do it. Do you have any objections?"

"Not in the slightest," Grumpy informed her with the first hint of a smile that she had ever seen, even if it was only at the outer reaches of his lips. "We've been beating you up for weeks, waiting for you to take an active interest in determining the path you want to walk along. Why would I slow you down when you are finally making that choice? When you mark someone, remember what they looked like. Everything is tallied on the honor system; make sure you keep yours intact."

Snow took a sharp breath as she realized what he was saying, holding it for a moment, but ultimately deflating as she rubbed the back of her head and offered a sheepish grin. "I suppose making my own choices in life is still a new thing for me. Thanks for helping me get here, I guess?"

"No thanks needed. You've already paid the price in pain and bruising." Grumpy turned back to the fight, where Benson had just successfully grabbed his opponent and *hucked* him out of the ring. Seeing an opportunity, Snow lifted her chalk dagger and stepped forward, swiping down at his unguarded back.

Even without looking, Grumpy gently swayed to the side, avoiding the strike with ease. "Nice try. You're not going to get me; I'm far too good at this game. Remember how I said the last time old man Magnus got marked was two years ago?

That's when I retired from the game to give everyone else a chance."

"Worth a shot." Snow stepped back, slipping into the crowd while keeping an eye on Grumpy to make sure he didn't try to retaliate. Holding her chalk dagger close to make it less obvious what she was doing, the princess slowly strolled around the bustling square. "You can do this, Snow. All you need to do is sneak up behind someone you have never met and mark the back of their shirt with chalk. That's not strange for an adult to do, definitely not."

Her first attempt was a predictable disaster.

Eyes locked on a group of adults chatting about the wrestling match, Snow allowed her dagger to drop down into her hand as she got close to her target—a man nearly as large as Grumpy himself—hoping he wouldn't be able to feel what she *hoped* would be a feather-light pull on his shirt. Now directly behind him, she raised her hand, swung-

Whap!

Snow let out a yelp of pain as a firm slap on her wrist sent her dagger flying. The man she had been trying to mark didn't even bother to look at her, and it was the lady standing next to him, likely his wife, who had smacked the 'weapon' out of her hand. Glowering at her petulantly, Snow accepted the fallen dagger the woman had caught.

"Don't look at me like that, you're the one who was far too obvious," the lady chided her with a hint of amusement hidden not-quite-well-enough in her voice, "You think I'm going to let some random person attack my husband? Certainly not. Your steps are too heavy, and you were staring at him for the last half minute before trying your luck. If you're trying to be sneaky, perhaps don't rumble towards someone like a cart full of cabbages."

Snow murmured her thanks for the pointers and immediately retreated into the crowd, hoping to never lay eyes on that particular group of people ever again. "Well, that didn't work."

Calming her racing heart, the princess loosened her muscles, relaxed her posture, and started moving through the crowd with a *deliberate* lack of purpose. "I'm not here to make anything happen. No intent. No excitement. If I mark some-one, it's going to be all but an accident."

CHAPTER
EIGHTEEN

HER NEXT FEW attempts were better but still ended in failure. Each person in the crowd easily swatted her hand away, few offering any advice, most just smirking at having thwarted her attempts. Finally, in desperation, her eyes locked on a merchant hawking his wares in the distance, and she began weaving through the crowd nonchalantly.

Even better, as Snow got close, he began haggling excitedly with a customer. Drifting closer, she remained relaxed, exuding non-threatening body language until she was nearly behind the merchant. Raising her dagger-

"Merchants are off limits." Adele came out of literally nowhere, having either phased or teleported to block her attempt. "Anyone who isn't from the town or getting training here doesn't get to play. It causes too much... concern."

Snow tutted softly, staring longingly at the unmarked back of the unaware merchant. "But he's just, you know... so wide open."

"He also has actual guards who might consider you a *real* threat." The battle daughter shifted her chin to the side, and Snow followed the movement, coming face to face with a man in leather armor showing an inch of steel before pushing the sword back in its sheath. "There's a reason our games have rules. We don't want anyone to get actually hurt, at least not permanently. Find someone else."

"Any other rules to be aware of?" Snow questioned archly, frowning ever so slightly as Adele nodded at her.

"Yes. Anyone you try to mark and fail is off limits to you for the next hour." The battle daughter smiled softly, breathing out one last comment before vanishing. "Don't cheat, or you'll ruin the experience and training intent for everyone."

Snow was forced to retreat yet again, doing her best to ignore the frustration bubbling beneath her skin. She swept her gaze around the market once more, eyes briefly landing on Grumpy, who was still attentively watching the matches going on. "As much as I want to mark him up, he's probably out of my skill level for now."

Continuing her scan, Snow eventually found all of the battle daughters she had been training with staring at her from different positions. For a moment she was annoyed, as their close scrutiny had impacted her attempts, but that thought quickly passed as she realized they were likely acting as bodyguards. Even in a town as close-knit as this, she felt comforted knowing they weren't willing to risk her well-being by allowing her to roam freely. In fact, it was that realization which allowed her heartbeat to level out.

Focusing on her breathing, allowing her steps to be casual yet silent, she approached a woman carrying a heavy container while keeping her own expressions neutral; gaze soft and unfocused, lips parted slightly as if contemplating some distant memory. As she passed the women's side, Snow flicked her wrist out and brushed the chalk along a dangling sleeve.

"Success!" Snow cheerfully whispered to herself after she was a few steps away from the unsuspecting woman, who went about her day as though nothing had happened. Then, out of nowhere, a blur of movement in her periphery caused Snow to react instinctively. She ducked low and twisted to the side, tumbling across the ground and coming to her feet with her impromptu dagger held out. The princess was back in position just in time to see the child who had darted toward her—tiny hand clutching purple chalk just like her own—reentering the crowd as though nothing had happened.

"You little sneaky-sneak!" Snow couldn't help but admire the failed attacker. "How long was she following me, I wonder? What a *fantastic* idea to use the moment I attack to launch her own."

Thwap. Snow let out a pained, quickly cut off yelp as a wooden ball smacked into her elbow, sending her nerves tingling as her funny bone was impacted. Clara's voice reached her ears at that moment, and the princess was absolutely certain she was smirking under her mask. "Stay on task! You got one, you dodged one, that doesn't mean you're done!"

The next few hours proved just as grueling as each of her previous days of training, even if thankfully less painful. Time slipped away unnoticed in a series of near misses, awkward failures, and only the occasional success when she managed to find someone who was simply too focused on what they were doing to pay attention. Ever so slowly, but with increasing frequency, she began to adapt and succeed.

Taking her would-be-attackers' plan as her own, Snow started targeting the youngsters holding their chalk a little too obviously, flitting past them as they lunged at their prey, leaving a purple mark along their backs before slipping away. She also found a surprising aspect of her skills she had never noticed or explored before, quickly learning how to read the flow of the crowd to anticipate movements and distractions. Finally, she stepped out of the crowd and took a break, relaxing the suppression of her aura and eating a bowl of soup and noodles from a street vendor.

The extra sustenance helped to alleviate the tension headache that had slowly been creeping in, and Snow moved with far more confidence as she practiced becoming a faceless shadow among the crowd of people in the square. Each of the rings where the bouts were taking place were scheduled to end as the sun dipped below the horizon. When they finally did, Snow was exhausted enough to lay down on the stone ground and fall asleep right there. Her arms and legs ached from hours of dodging and twisting, and her shoulders, biceps, and wrists were nearly numb from the sudden bursts of motion she was unfamiliar with.

Glancing at herself in the fading light, Snow grumpily found dozens of chalk smears of every color across her clothes. "I got some of them back, at least. What sweet children they… at least *pretend* to be."

A bell rang out, calling everyone's attention to where Grumpy was now standing atop some table or barrel—Snow couldn't quite make it out from this distance. "Listen up! Today's games are concluded; it's time to give the winners of the head-to-head matches, as well as the stealth games, their prizes! Anyone marked by chalk, please line up over here so we can get an accurate tally."

Snow joined the line, only to find that it was filtered by how many marks someone had, and she quickly found herself at the very front, staring at an unamused Grumpy while the others in the crowd openly laughed at her rainbow palette of a shirt. "That's a lot of marks. You have anything to say for yourself?"

"Well…" Snow shrugged nervously as she looked around, deciding to play to the crowd a bit. "Yeah. I guess today probably *wasn't* the best day to wear a white outfit?"

The soft chuckling turned into a roar of laughter, and the condescending glances turned to approval as she took the admonishment without complaint. A voice behind Snow called out, "I'm counting fifty-two different marks. The strength and coloration indicate that five people marked her four times, three people got her thrice, eight got her twice, and the rest allowed her to go with only a single mark. Anyone who managed to mark this lovely lady, please step forward to be accounted for!"

A gaggle of children stepped forward, immediately bringing the dying embers of laughter back to a full-throated roar. Amusingly, one adult also joined the group, a sheepish grin on her face when she realized she was the only one who had gone after such an easy target. Grumpy rubbed his chin, nodding toward the woman quizzically, "Brynn? Why would you…"

"To be fair, I was the *first* to mark her," the battle sister named Brynn called out. "I thought *you* would be protecting her today, like she was a visiting merchant. Frankly, I was playing under the assumption that I had gotten one over on *you*, not her."

"Understandable, if ultimately incorrect," Grumpy replied, casually crushing the tentative smile that had appeared on Brynn's face. "As you are the only adult to have marked her, you get half the points, while the children split the remainder."

"*Booo*!" A chorus of childish voices rang out, and Brynn hid her face in her hands as the adults in the crowd chuckled at her shame. Snow felt bad for her at first, only to realize the shaking of the battle sister's shoulders was *laughing*, not crying.

"Of course…" Grumpy continued slowly, drawing out to the moment, "if someone manages to mark you in turn, they can lay claim to the points you collected."

Dozens of children turned as one, launching themselves at the woman, chalk held straight out as they did their best to swipe her. Snow wasn't sure how Brynn managed, but the battle sister avoided every single attempt, eventually making her way up to Grumpy and showing her pristine, clean back. "Not today! Those points are mine, brats!"

She shook her fist dramatically, taking any sting out of her words as she played to the kids. Finally, Grumpy decided enough was enough, and they moved on to the next person in line. At the end of the accounting, Snow had gathered what she considered a respectable twenty points, only to lose all but five of them to those who had marked her in turn. The final winners were chosen from each color of chalk, purple for the youngest, blues, greens, all the way up to a bright red indicating an adult familiar with the points playing the game. Each of them was given a small sack of copper coins, more a token of success than a real prize.

Then came the winners of the grappling and wrestling, and before she knew it, Snow was walking along the path back to Grumpy's house along with his trio of battle daughters. "That was surprisingly fun."

"All joy in *any* career comes from mastery-" Grumpy began to say more, only to be cut off by an unexpected raspberry being blown by Ida.

"Oh, give her some real praise!" The battle daughter nudged Grumpy, her elbow stopping dead against his muscled flesh as though she were trying to press on a granite block. "She managed to improve more today than in the last *week*."

"I lost track of her. Twice." Adele murmured under her breath, not looking at the others as she admitted her failure. "Something about the way she walked, combined with the hypnotic myriad of colors on her back made me fall into a trance or something."

"Seriously?" Snow asked with wide eyes, already trying to figure out how she would adjust her wardrobe in the future.

"No, not really." Adele patted her on the shoulder, "I did lose you twice, but it's because you were just suddenly so easy to overlook. It didn't actually have anything to do with your clothing."

"Oh. That's… that's *better*!" Snow smiled brightly, nodding at the battle daughters' version of high praise. Turning back to Grumpy, she spoke even as she blinked extremely heavy eyelids. "Can we do this again tomorrow?"

"No," Grumpy roughly replied. "You *will* do this tomorrow. You don't have a choice."

"Same thing as just saying 'yes', isn't it?" Snow waved him off, using her other hand to cover a massive yawn. "I'm looking forward to it."

CHAPTER
NINETEEN

WAKING up feeling more refreshed than she had in months, Snow quickly made herself a meat-heavy breakfast in the tiny kitchen of Grumpy's house. Not long after she had finished, the door swung open with a bang, and the D'wharve himself stood framed in the entryway, a hint of surprise clearly showing.

"You're awake already."

"Something about not going to bed after being pushed to the absolute limits of my endurance will do that." Snow smiled at him innocently, though Grumpy ignored the expression with his usual *harrumph*. Seeing that she had already finished her food, the enormous warrior gestured for her to follow him, and soon they were walking through the pasture enjoying the cool morning and scent of plants beginning to open up for the day.

As they walked, Snow sent side-long, calculative glances his way. After the previous day's fun, and confirmation that she should be trying new things even without instruction, she had woken up in what Grumpy would call a 'strategic mind-set'. Already, she had a burgeoning plan she was just *itching* to put in place. As the rhythmic thumping of their walk shifted to heavy thudding against the stone roads of the town, she prepared to slip away to find a new chalk dagger, only to freeze and reluctantly continue along with her guardian as he began speaking.

"Today is somewhat different than yesterday's games. Instead of fun in the sun, it is time for our monthly duels." She glanced at him, noticing how the morning sunlight catching the hard edge of his jaw was ever-so-slightly distorted by the illusion magic woven into his mask. Instead of the wavy light softening his appearance, the distortion made him look increasingly imposing. When he spoke again, Snow snapped out of her thoughts, nearly flinching but managing to remain calm and placid thanks to the training she had been undergoing.

"There will be six duels in total today, as those with grievances against each other fight to first blood." A muscle in his jaw worked subtly, and he turned to look directly at her before finishing with, "I expect you to learn much today, and that you will not embarrass me again. Even if you are not my battle daughter, I *am* still teaching you. Failure twice in a row will reflect *poorly* on me."

She nodded solemnly, her internal determination hardening as she suppressed a grin. "Don't worry about that; I *guarantee* I won't."

Studying her for another moment, Grumpy narrowed his eyes but could only bob his head in acknowledgment as they approached the square. Even at this early hour, the area was buzzing with activity by the time they arrived. Snow followed Grumpy toward the edge of the rings, actively working to appear even more relaxed than she had been the day before. As soon as she could do so without appearing overly suspicious, she separated from her current mentor and collected one of the many chalk daggers hanging on posts throughout the square.

Then she walked back into the bustling crowd, keeping

her eyes straight ahead even though she was acutely aware of the wide-eyed children, their small hands clutching chunks of chalk, lying in wait for her. Carefully gauging the expressions of the people around her, Snow waited until she saw a spark of mirth appear, then spun around and deftly caught one of those small hands. A young boy, no older than seven, yet already having a surprising amount of muscle definition, blinked up at her in shock.

Dropping into a crouch, she smiled at him and winked. "Tell me, how much is the prize for the most marks?"

"Um. Half a silver, for the purples," his voice wavered slightly, though he knew he wasn't in any real trouble. "Can you let me go now? You're not supposed to keep me unless you're offering advice on how to do this better, and... I saw how you did yesterday. I don't want to learn from you."

"Yes, I don't have much to offer you in the form of *combat* advice." Using a trick she had learned on the road with her bard friends, she lifted her hands, twisted her fingers, and a silver coin appeared between them. Leaning in slightly, she spoke in an overly loud, conspiratorial tone. "How about I give you this, right now, as payment for spreading a message for me?"

The boy's eyes widened, and he nodded vigorously, "Sure thing, lady! You say the word, and I'll repeat it all *day* if I need to."

"Here's the deal..." Snow continued speaking loud enough for each of the others creeping toward them to hear. "If I remain unmarked the whole day, I'll *double* the prize for *each* of the colors. On top of your actual winnings."

"Ooh." A sly grin appeared on his face, and Snow shook her head as she wondered what sort of future citizens this town was creating. "It's just that, I don't know if bribery like this is allowed?"

"It's not bribery. It's a bonus from your princess for keeping her safe." Snow winked at him once more, his grin

and nod proving to her what she had already suspected—
everyone here already knew who she was. There was only one
person who could have told them... Snow felt as though the
sun was suddenly shining on her as an idea popped into her
head while thinking about the huge man. "Wait! There's
more. Grumpy sure does seem certain no one is going to be
able to mark him. I think he's been getting complacent, don't
you? Add this to the message. *Anyone* who marks him gets a full
silver from me. Every. Single. Person."

"Awesome." The kid ran off, and the others who had been
listening in scattered back into the crowd. Feeling as though
she were flying, Snow decided to hold off on joining in on the
fun, and returned to the edge of the arena, happily joining
Grumpy just in time for the first of the duels to begin.

"Young Conrad has challenged Vince to a duel over what
he claims were disparaging remarks toward his late father," a
man announced solemnly to the crowd, standing in the middle
of the wide circle between the two men preparing to fight.
"Vince claims it was a misunderstanding, but Conrad has
claimed the need to fight for his family's honor. Let the match
begin."

Conrad rushed forward, axe hefted in preparation of
starting the round with a battle-ending blow. His opponent
met the attack with his sword, causing a thunderous clang of
steel on steel to set Snow's ears ringing. The young man swung
again and again, his strikes quick and technical, clearly
someone who had been trained from a young age along a
specific path. Unfortunately for him, it was clear that the grizzled veteran was unimpressed with his energy.

Snow leaned forward, eyes darting between the flashing
metal and the feathers for feet the men seemed to have as they
danced around each other. "Conrad has already lost, hasn't
he? He just doesn't know it yet."

Grumpy raised a brow in approval of her observation, the
fuzzy line appearing at the top of his mask for a brief moment

before the warrior suddenly twisted, massive hand shooting out to slap away a chalk dagger aimed at his side. "Brazen brat! That's the fourth time I've been targeted in the last ten minutes; what's going on here?"

An instant later, his hand swatted out, pulverizing a chunk of green chalk zipping toward the back of his head. Somehow the back of his hand deflected it, sending the projectile into the open area in front of him before it puffed into powder. Snow watched in awe as he did it twice more, with the practiced precision of someone used to swatting away arrows in actual combat. "Since when do they throw these things like flying daggers? Has Clara been training them in secret?"

Keeping her face carefully neutral, Snow shifted her focus back to the duel just as Conrad made a desperate, reckless lunge. Vince smoothly sidestepped, slashing a shallow *snick* at the point where shoulder met collarbone. Blood immediately welled and began dripping down Conrad's chest—a superficial wound just enough to sting his pride more than his body. For a long, tense heartbeat, the young man stiffened up, and Snow was nearly certain he was going to ignore the rules of the duel and throw himself at the older man once more.

Instead, he dropped his axe to his side and stiffly bowed at his opponent, exposing the back of his neck. "It was a... match. No, I shan't belittle your skill... it was a *good* match. I accept the resolution."

"Good man," Vince stated calmly as he put his weapon away and extended a hand. "For what it's worth, I liked ya da'. I hope this drives home my point; a person can be a good man and still have faults."

"I'll try to take your words to heart." Conrad managed to grind out around his clenched jaw, clearly containing himself only due to the sheer weight of the crowd's stares piling on top of him. Without another word, he turned and jerkily began walking off with his head held high. Each person in the audience began to clap, and Snow couldn't help but appreciate the deep traditions of the town that must have led to this point.

"What a fantastic way to arbitrate things," she murmured quietly as she considered what she had just witnessed. "I can only assume this is only a viable method for civil issues, and only in this village because of the sheer number of combatants. Still, it makes me wonder how I might be able to apply this at a broader scale for less combat focused people in my kingdom-"

"Abyssal-!" Grumpy bellowed, fending off yet another sneak attack aimed at his back. "Why is this happening?"

No matter how much she tried, Snow failed to hold in a soft snort of mirth, expression shifting to project only curiosity as Grumpy spun to stare at her with suspicion causing his eyes to narrow. Voice filled with honeyed sweetness, Snow blinked several times and carefully maintained her Aura of Innocence. "Is this a strange occurrence? I'm not too familiar with how this game works, having only played it once."

"Is that so?" Grumpy's hand shot out, wrapping around the wrist of a youth who had been lurking behind Snow. The boy was in his early teens, but as Grumpy lifted his hand, he revealed a dagger-filled with bright red chalk. "What's this? *Red* chalk? So you want to play at being an adult? Or are you just greedy for the sheer number of points you'd get for marking me as one? Answer me, why am I being targeted? Don't look at her, she's not going to save you. Look at *me!*"

The crowd began to take notice of the exchange, murmurs rippling through the area as the young man failed to speak, frozen like a rabbit caught in a snare. Finally, he managed to squeak out, "*Targeted?* We're all just playing as usual-"

"Ohh, ho-*ho*, is that so?" Grumpy started walking toward the recently vacated open fighting area. "Since you decided to strike me as an adult, I have every right to duel you in order to get to the truth of the matter. Is that what needs to happen? Well? Out with it! Why can't I get a moment's peace today?"

"Easy, Battle Lord Grumpy, *easy!*" The young man's voice was shrill as he dug his feet in, trying to slow Grumpy's relentless yanking. Snow cocked her head to the side in interest—she had never heard that title being applied to the warrior before. "No need for all that! It's not anything other than fun, I can swear it!"

"Then why me?"

The boy grimaced apologetically at Snow, who only smiled at him in return, knowing that this had been a likely outcome. "It's just, there's a price on your head. A full silver bounty for anyone who manages to leave a mark."

"Who has that kind of…" Grumpy's gaze flew to Snow, whose face was burning as bright red as the boy's chalk even while an uncontrollable grin spread across her face. "*You!*"

By now, the drama had everyone's attention, and so Snow shrugged expressly, allowing herself to enjoy the moment and bask in the attention—not to mention working to project her voice to every corner of the square as she replied. "Look at these arms, *Battle Lord* Grumpy. I'm not a warrior, and unless I spend the next couple decades utterly dedicated to learning, I never will be. But, there's one thing I'm fantastic at. Adapting. You were the one who encouraged me to find my own path. Well, here it is. I'm using every bit of what I've learned so far."

For a long moment, the square stood silent. Then Grumpy let out a shout and spun on his heel, dancing back with his jaw dropping open. His movement revealed a small child with a massive, gap-tooth grin… and a bright purple streak across Grumpy's legs. There was a collective inhale of shock, then a lady standing near Snow began to giggle, quickly followed by another person, and soon the entire crowd was laughing as Grumpy collapsed to his knees and threw his hands in the air.

"My record! Noo!" Grumpy's howls only fueled the

laughter further. "Five years without being marked, and she ruins it in less than a *day*!"

Then a sound escaped him, a deep snort which usually preceded someone bursting into laughter. But Grumpy was anything but usual when it came to humor. He stopped any involuntary sounds, standing up and offering his hand to the boy who had managed to mark him with purple child's chalk. "That was impressive, I admit it."

Snow felt a deep tingling on her left arm and glanced at it excitedly as the system informed her of an increase to her power.

Skill increase! Aura of Innocence [Level 8 (Extensive) → Level 9 (Master)]!
Requirement to advance to level 10: Turn a would-be assassin into an ally.

"That counted as redirecting the efforts of the combatants attacking me back on their leader?" Snow's whispered voice was filled with wonder. "I *definitely* thought I wouldn't be able to increase this further until I fought against the queen directly! Also... I'll probably reach Perfection with this sooner rather than later, won't I? Whenever I leave here, I'm certain there will be no end to the number of people out to stop me when I start spreading the truth about the queen."

As the drama came to an end, Grumpy returned to his spot next to the dueling ring, casting deep glowers at Snow every once in a while, muttering under his breath when he did so. She made a quick motion at him, and he flinched away, acutely aware of the chalk she held in her hand. Deciding enough was enough, she smirked at him and slipped away into the crowds, determined to bolster her own skills.

The hours passed quickly, and the duels concluded honorably from start to finish. As the day wound down, Snow felt flushed with quiet satisfaction. She had participated, observed, learned, and put into practice all the things she was supposed to be learning from the D'wharves she had been training under—even managing a bribe that would have left Happy clapping in delight. Best of all, she hadn't embarrassed herself or her mentor.

When it finally came time to tally the chalk marks, she stood proudly among those who had participated for the day and were fully unmarked by any streak of color. In comparison, Grumpy was near the end of the line of those who had gotten marked, turning to show the crowd three vibrant streaks across his body, one purple, one green, one red. To the delight of the crowd, Snow paid out the bounty then and there, genuine warmth spreading through her as the townsfolk cheered her on and sent knowing looks at the fallen champion of the game.

As she walked back to her temporary home alongside the D'wharve, he clapped her on the shoulder—gently for him, but still enough to cause her to stumble. "Not bad, Princess. Not bad at all."

"Thanks, Grumpy." Snow smiled at him slyly. "Tomorrow I'll be even better."

"Tomorrow?" He nodded solemnly. "Yes, you'll have to be. Today you set my expectations. Tomorrow I expect them to be exceeded."

CHAPTER
TWENTY

PRINCESS SNOW REMAINED in the hidden village, training her ability to sneak and stab with precision until spring officially came again. To her great delight, something about the location of the village kept the area warmer than expected and *mostly* dry throughout the cold season. The days it had been cold and wet had not gotten her out of training, simply shifting it to be even more unpleasant.

Now, once again, she was faced with giving up on her newly ingrained routine and moving on to her next trainer.

"—she's been controlling him, and us, for years! Snow… she's a *Witch*!"

As Snow jolted awake on the day she was meant to leave, her sister's words once more echoing in her mind, she remained in bed a little later than Grumpy would normally allow, though she spent the extra time staring at the ceiling for over an hour. Her thoughts and emotions were churning and roiling, as she had come to find this village to be pleasant and exciting. Even her memories of the intensive training she had gone through over the last long few months now had a tinge of nostalgia coloring them.

Eventually, her body, now well-used to her routine, forced

her out of bed. When Grumpy opened the door to the small cabin, he found a simple meal waiting for him and his charge gesturing at a seat across from her. "Care to join me, Grumpy?"

"Not particularly. You look like you're hoping for some sort of emotional closure. I don't really do that." For the first time, Snow got to see the utterly stoic man shift in discomfort. "You've got an hour before your carriage arrives; want to get some training in?"

"No, I understand this isn't your favorite thing to do." Snow pointed more sharply at the chair. "Please, sit with me."

Reluctantly, he moved over, pulled out the chair obviously too small for him, and sat down with his knees nearly reaching his chest. "I don't often sit in these houses meant for my battle sons and daughters. I'm a bit too tall. I'm glad you got some proper training while you were here. Not that you're any good at fighting. Or using a dagger. You know, when I mentioned those were supposed to be your last resort, I didn't think you would be content being terrible at both of those permanently. Still, I recommend you don't stop practicing. Hey, I'm trying to give you a compliment here. Don't look at me like that."

Snow's smile faltered as he continued, seemingly doing anything to avoid the awkwardness of the situation she had put him in. "What truly impressed me was how you altered the parameters of your training to fit the skills you had already gained, adding them to your arsenal like a true professional in the field. I didn't expect it to work, yet you did it so easily, and I think in the future you will thrive because of it-"

As the man rambled ever onward, Snow blinked in surprise at how easily he had been persuaded to sit down and join her. Not to mention, now he was speaking more than she had heard him ever do in a single day, and she hadn't even felt any of the strange drain that came with using her power actively.

"People were convinced to do stuff for others all the time

even without such an ability, weren't they?" Murmuring to herself as she swiped a finger along her left arm, Snow studied the changes that had occurred and the influence she had accrued over the last few months.

Basic Class: Darling Princess
Basic Skill: Precocious Command: Level 10/10.
Advanced Skill: Aura of Innocence: Level 9/10.
Breakthrough Skill: Permanently locked.

Advanced Class: Influencer
Basic Skill: Influential Aura: Level 7/10.
Current followers: 3,480
Influence: 10,150/13,181

Requirement to advance to level 4: Collect and maintain a minimum of 13,181 influence for 24 hours. 0/1.

"How's it going?" Only then did Snow realize Grumpy had been silent for nearly half a minute, and she offered him a sheepish grin as she looked up at him. "Without needing to invest in influencing the people around you to ignore you for the next few days, you should be reaching the next level in your skill by the time you arrive at your destination, no?"

"Probably." Snow quickly did the math, as laid out by the skill. "I should gain a thousand and forty-four *Influence* each day, unless I do something to gain or lose some people. Three days, at the most, to reach *Extensive* in the skill."

"Quite impressive," Grumpy replied succinctly, seemingly back to his normal self. "Did you have something you wanted to speak with me about? Just seems strange you would use this time to stare at your arms, when you'll have nothing better to do than play with the numbers as you sit for the next few days. Time management is an-"

"Essential pillar of a highly functional person?" Snow

finished the sentence for him, now long used to his seemingly endless pithy advice. "I'm going to miss the talks we have. I always walk away from them feeling like I have something to think about for the next few days."

"Good. It is a failing society that separates its warriors and its scholars."

"You just can't help yourself, can you?" Seeing that the guildmaster wasn't going to touch the thinly cut steak and eggs she had prepared, Snow decided not to keep him in an uncomfortable position any longer.

Getting to her feet, she grabbed her travel pack, filled with all of the fine garments she had purchased in Thalfanghein and never worn, as well as new additions, such as throwing daggers from Clara and a leather vambrace from Adele. The weighted straps from Ida were already tied in place around her ankles, guaranteeing she would be improving her level of conditioning simply by moving around. "I'm as ready as I'm going to be."

"No need to sound so sad. Each of us has to go out and…" Grumpy trailed off as Snow raised an eyebrow and shook her head. "That is… I believe you will also be missed around town. Never before has the ruler of the kingdom graced us with their presence. When you take the crown, know you will have a loyal clan you can always visit when things seem too easy, and you need to work harder for a while."

"…yeah." Snow giggled lightly, her intended chortle being usurped and altered by Aura of Innocence to sound more playful than intended. "Or I can just come back to see all of the friends I made while I was here. I think I would prefer that."

"Haa…" Grumpy shook his head slightly, which she knew was him acting dramatic. "Power over other people is going to send you right back to being lazy, isn't it?"

"Absolutely," Snow agreed instantly, keeping her eyes wide

and sincere. "Realistically, it should take no effort at all to right the wrongs the queen has imposed on my people. You know, undoing the massive tax burdens, setting up logistics to repair villages and recapture hearts and minds. I'll finish that in the first week, then lounge around for a while."

"Sounds like a plan to me." Grumpy extended his hand, and Snow waited patiently for a weapon to appear in it, or for him to curl his fingers into a fist and launch a surprise attack. Instead, he simply held it there, and it took her an embarrassingly long time to realize he was trying to shake her hand. She reached out, and he wrapped his massive paw around her dainty limb, the interaction looking like nothing more than an adult shaking hands with a toddler. "You have impressed me. I look forward to putting my people under your command in the near future."

"I'm looking forward to your help getting rid of Queen Kat, the Witch who has usurped my kingdom," Snow formally responded. They released each other and were just about to step outside when Grumpy launched himself forward and slammed the door. "*Wha-*"

"Sit down! Do your best not to move a muscle, and try to appear completely relaxed and unaware of what is happening!" Grumpy reached up to his mask, tapping on it with three fingers, alternating from side, to side, then bottom and top. Snow felt a strange tingle of energy which seemed like a far lesser version of what the system could command, and blinked in discomfort...

Only to open her eyes and find herself in an opulent chair as seven short men with massive beards swung oversized pickaxes at a wall absolutely *stuffed* with enormous gemstones. They appeared to be whistling as they worked, breaking out into song just as the sensation of what Snow realized must be magic began washing over her from a new direction. Out of the peripherals of her vision, she watched as a distortion in the air appeared, swirling and growing larger until she could see a silver, mirrored... *something* hanging in the air above her.

Exactly as she had been instructed, she scrubbed her aura of any emotion and did her best to exude relaxation and nonchalance in her position on the oversized throne she found herself sitting on. The hanging distortion persisted for a long few seconds, turning from side to side, before becoming covered in cracks and shattering into motes of light that swiftly vanished. As the last bit dissolved into nothingness, the illusion snow had been trapped in began to streak like painting which had gotten water poured over it.

In the next few moments, the colors swirled and receded into Grumpy's mask, as though it was drinking them in. The man himself took a deep breath, glancing at Snow with concern before explaining himself. "I didn't think that would come in quite so handy this quickly."

"Do I need to *ask* you to explain, or...?"

"It's the magic mirror, Snow," Grumpy informed her in a heavy tone. "When a certain person is attempting to use that magical object, and her name is spoken, that will act as a focus for her scrying efforts. All I can say is that it's your bad luck that she was using that object as you spoke about her. While I'm certain she suspected, and has heard reports to this effect, now she knows for a fact that you are alive and well."

"Okay." Snow took a breath, swallowing down the odd lump that had formed in her throat. "This doesn't change anything though, right? Not for me at least."

"Well... now she may begin more active methods of seeking you out," the guildmaster slowly spoke his thoughts. "Other than that, nothing will change on your end, besides a necessary increase in your constant vigilance. Hopefully you will keep up with your training and not be caught by surprise in the future."

Snow simply remained quiet for a few heartbeats,

processing the information, then looked at Grumpy's mask with intense curiosity. "What was that… illusion?"

"Oh that?" The man let out a snort from his nose. "That's Bashful's idea. We're trying to throw any suspicion off of us by showing that you have found a group of friendly magical beings that are funding your war efforts. He thinks it's hilarious that we are the D'wharves, and went through various beast companions until he found a type of non-hostile ascended beast that takes on a humanoid form. They tend to live underground, which is why you saw a cavern."

"I'm guessing it's practically impossible to find them normally?" Snow questioned hopefully. "There's a lot of layers to this decoy… I'm impressed. He must have needed to do an immense amount of work to put all of that together."

"An Illusionist with Perfected standard skills and a high-ranking Breakthrough Skill can do incredible things, I admit." Just then, the sound of a rumbling wagon reached their ears, and the duo looked at each other, one steadily, one holding back tears as yet another chapter in her life came to a close. "Time to go. Remember to keep the queen's name off your tongue, and describe her only in the most vague of terms, and only then when you *must* do so."

"Thank you for all the things you have taught me, Grumpy. Please pass on my well wishes to your battle daughters, and… maybe, when your training with them is done, you should have a different sort of conversation with Clara. I think you might get along even better than you might assume. Both of you are *grumpy*, after all."

"I appreciate your kindness," the immense warrior replied neutrally. "I will pass your thoughts on, though I'm certain they got the message during your tearful goodbyes last night."

"Yes, well, some of us aren't made of stone." Snow breath hitched briefly before she forced it out, gripping the door handle as she stepped into the open air, pack following with a practiced swing. It settled into place easily, and she barely noticed its weight—enough to bring her to her knees, panting in exhaustion, only half a year previously. "Until we meet again, Grumpy."

"Yup." He remained in the building, closing the door between them to preemptively cut off any further conversation. With no other options in front of her, Snow got into the wagon and settled into her seat, preparing for the long ride ahead of her.

SHE WAS LOOKING FORWARD to learning under Doc and focused on that excitement as the days passed with the constant, low rumble of the carriage's wheels as her only companion. The solitude allowed Snow to fully relax for the first time in far too long, and she was asleep more than she was awake for the first few days. Her body took the opportunity for a break to accrue as much rest as possible, recovering and removing the inflammation in her muscles she had become all too familiar with.

Then, as she settled into this routine of forced stagnation, the princess started to become antsy. Snow's thoughts often circled back to Rose, hoping she wasn't being treated too poorly, and about her father, wondering after his health and well-being now that—as far as she was aware—no one had heard directly from him since she escaped the palace. For hours and hours, her thoughts spiraled, until a tingle in her arm announced she had reached a new level with her skill. Desperate for any distraction, she quickly swiped her arm and read over the entirety of the information available.

Basic Skill: Influential Aura: Level 7 → 8/10.

Influential Aura subtly yet powerfully affects those around you, [Extensively] influencing their thoughts in a positive or negative manner using Influence as a currency. You are able to [Extensively] sway opinions, inspire action, and guide decisions with a variable cost. Influencing people in ways contrary to their desires will cost additional Influence, while moving them in ways aligned with their own goals will give an influence discount of [80%], increasing to a maximum of a 100% discount. Use caution, as leading others toward goals not in their best interests will slowly push you toward darker powers.

Your Influence is gained at a rate of ([8]*total followers/10) per day with a minimum of 1)
Current followers: 14
*Influence: **13,282/20,672***

Requirement to advance to level 9: Collect and maintain a minimum of 20,672 influence for 24 hours. 0/1.

"If nothing else changes, I'll reach *Perfection* in less than a week." A satisfied smile curled Snow's lips, and for just a moment she basked in the excitement of having reached a new height in her power.

Then the horses let out a terrified, shrieking *neigh*, and the cart bounced dangerously as it rapidly decelerated and came to a halt. "Driver? What's happened?"

"Princess Snow," a distorted voice called out, sending her heart into her throat. "Come out of that wagon at once."

Heart in her throat, Snow slowly pushed the door open, peeking around the corner and nearly becoming sick to her stomach as she saw the Huntsman waiting in the center of the road, hand on the hilt of his standard-issue sword.

"Well… abyss."

CHAPTER
TWENTY-ONE

STEPPING down from the carriage and closing the door with deliberate gentleness, Snow began slowly walking toward the queen's impatient experiment. As she moved past the front, her gaze flicked to the side, meeting the terrified eyes of the driver. Giving him a small nod to affirm his decision to stop, she saw a bit of the turmoil in his eyes fade, clear relief showing when she didn't judge him for not trying to run the Huntsman down.

Quite frankly, she was glad he had stopped: there was no reason for *both* of them to die.

"May I ask what all this is about? I have places to be, sirrah," Snow called evenly, keeping her voice level through sheer force of will. Holding herself to maintain a careful appearance of as non-threatening and nonchalant as possible, she approached the cloaked and masked figure. She was trying to determine whether she could influence him to walk away, and failing that, didn't want to give him the satisfaction of seeing how terrified she truly was. Who knew if he was the sort of person to enjoy inflicting pain and fear?

"I'm certain you already know. By order of the queen consort, surrender yourself to my care immediately." The

Huntsman was now holding his sword lightly to his front, its edge catching the sun at just the right angle to send its light into her eyes and make her wince. The careless way he brandished it showed his confidence in himself, as if knowing the weapon was overkill and he could casually overpower her without it.

It irked her deeply how true that probably was.

"Please, there's no need for violence," Snow quietly and demurely stated, pushing Aura of Innocence to its maximum capacity to tug at his heartstrings—if whatever alchemy the queen had infused the man with allowed for such emotions to remain. To her surprise, he did sheathe his sword, though he then raised a hand and made an impatient 'come hither' gesture. She stepped into his reach, and the man put a firm hand on her shoulder, turning to lead her away.

That was the moment she struck.

Halfway through an abrupt twisting motion, the dagger in her wrist guard sprang into her hand, and her fingers clenched tightly around the hilt. Just as the tip of the blade was about to drive into the Huntsman's eye, her wrist was suddenly stopped from behind; her attack ended before managing to land even a single blow.

Snow spun around, and for a long, uncomprehending moment, stared at the second attacker she hadn't even heard approaching. The moment she realized she was standing face-to-face with the carriage driver, Snow gasped out the only word her numb mind could latch onto, "*Traitor!*"

Behind her, the Huntsman snorted. Strangely enough, the odd, androgynous tone each of the Huntsman shared when wearing their masks shifted into a familiar cadence as he began speaking. "You pass. You might have even had me, were I not the one to train you."

The princess's jaw dropped as her arms were released, and she spun to face the Huntsman, revealed as Grumpy now that the illusion began fading away. "You! What? What is this? Are you being *cruel* just to-"

"Simply a final test, Princess." Grumpy let out a satisfied grunt. "I'm surprised you didn't say anything about not having an escort sooner. I'm not sure if you think so poorly of us that we would let you go to your destination unguarded, or if you were just that confident in your own abilities. Well, I'm pleased to say you *are* feistier than I had anticipated. It's one thing to have training in something and an entirely different thing altogether to actually follow through when the time comes. I am *very* impressed."

"I… thank you? I need a minute, I think." Snow swayed on her feet as the torrent of adrenaline flowing through her body found no outlet. "I almost killed you, Grumpy."

"You did good…" Grumpy agreed flatly, clearly unconcerned with that potential outcome. "But you're not a miracle worker."

Snow looked at the bulky man with deep annoyance in her eyes, but if he noticed, he didn't let on as he spoke. "To be taken by a Huntsman means this kingdom will be left to whatever your father's wife has planned. The fact that you would put your training to good use on your own behalf is excellent. Remember, what's good for you is good for *all* of us. Don't worry about the death of a single person, especially one of the Huntsmen. Frankly, they barely qualify as people anymore. I've seen what they truly are beneath their cloaks and masks. Twisted, vile mimicry of what they once were."

Grumpy lifted his hand, throwing a handful of shockingly blue powder into the air where it drifted like smoke for a long few moments before fading away. Shortly afterward, the telltale rumbling of wagons drawing near reached Snow's ears, and in only a few minutes, there was a full caravan surrounding her wagon.

"I thought I was supposed to travel *inconspicuously*?" Snow finally managed to say after she had finished wrestling with her personal doubts.

"You think a single wagon going through bandit territory is inconspicuous?" Grumpy clearly wasn't looking for an answer, as he simply pressed on, "Pretty sure the only people comfortable doing something like that are Huntsmen, myself, or that one high-strung merchant-Fairy that makes her way around the continent at least once a decade. Bobbles, or something like that. When all's said and done… I can see why she shuns an escort. Never seen a merchant wield magic like she does."

"Bibbidi?" Snow inquired as they walked back to her carriage. "She can't be real, right? My father told me stories of her travels from when *he* was a boy."

"She's quite real, in fact." Grumpy helped the princess into her carriage, gently closing the door behind her. "I've met her twice. She doesn't seem to age like the rest of us. Anyway, I hope you don't mind company."

Snow turned away from the door, finding the three battle daughters she had been training with for the last several months already seated. Swallowing the thick knot of emotion that had suddenly appeared in her throat, she joined them as the wheels began turning once more.

The next weeks of her journey were far more happy, as she had people to converse with, train with in the mornings and evenings while the horses rested, and sup with at meal times. Still, all things pass, and eventually the caravan rumbled into the port city of Emdenvale, a small but thriving city far to the south of Deckbett.

After yet another tearful farewell to the battle daughters and a casual 'see ya later' in return, Snow took her pack and walked into the house of healing she had been dropped off at. Behind her, the caravan had started on to their final destination before she even reached the door. Happily, the thin barrier swung open well ahead of her, revealing a pangolin-masked man whose overjoyed smile showed that he was truly pleased to see her.

"Welcome, *welcome!*" The door bounced off the wall as he hurried out to greet her, flinging aside the stained apron he had been wearing over his clothes and swinging his arms wide to wrap her in an embrace. Snow leaned back, for a fraction of a second leery of the warm greeting. Blinking at the realization of how she had become *perhaps* a bit jaded after living in the warrior's society for the last few months, she stepped forward and belatedly accepted the hug.

Only as she felt the gentle grip around her was she struck with the awareness of how starved she had been for human contact and effortless companionship. The battle daughters had been efficient and competent, but not exactly warm. Grumpy? Well, he was... Grumpy. "Thank you. It's... it's good to be here. I'm looking forward to what you have planned to teach me."

"Yes!" Doc waited until Snow released him from the hug then stepped back casually to give her some room. "Well, so you have no surprises, what I intend to teach you is something I call 'positional power', though you can think of it as 'borrowed influence' for your purposes."

"That sounds intriguing." Snow's voice carried a hint of apprehension as she followed him into the house of healing, her attention lingering for a moment on the distant caravan. "I'm looking forward to hearing what you have to say."

"Yes, well, let me give you a better description." Doc brought them to a small, cozy office where several chairs faced each other. Easing into one of them, the elderly man waved to the other, and Snow sat. She immediately regretted it, as she was reminded that she had been sitting for most of each day over the last week. Noticing her discomfort, he tilted his head to the side, "Please, do what's most comfortable for you. Sit, stand, *dance* if you so wish."

Snow popped to her feet, stretching side to side in relief.

The healer continued to watch her with a gentle gaze. "That was actually a decent example of what I mean to teach you. Let me point out the three factors which led to you sitting down, though you clearly did not want to do so. First, I'm going to be someone who's training you, and your previous mentor demanded strict adherence to his words. Some of that will certainly carry over. Second, I clearly *appear* to be an elderly man, and you don't wish to disrespect me. Thirdly, I'm a healer, and therefore you have been taught from a young age to listen to any reasonable requests by someone in my *position*."

"Ha!" Snow's laugh was somewhat out of place, and Doc patiently waited for her to voice her thoughts. "I definitely thought you were going to say that you were sitting, so my mind told me to sit with you. Positional influence. More... literally, I suppose."

"That is certainly something to consider, but that was already clearly explained and instructed by Bashful and his people, correct?" The princess paused for a moment, blinking as she grasped how even sitting down could and did fall under the auspices of body language. Doc didn't let her fall too deeply into her thoughts. "No, what I mean is, the influence someone is able to generate simply by the factors of their position, title, and traditions."

Seeing that he had her full attention, Doc launched into a quick explanation. "The fact is, you can *not* like a person, yet still respect the *position* they hold, gained not by their personal abilities perhaps, but by the position itself. People might not respect me or my people as individuals—rare, but it happens —but they *will* listen, because I'm a healer. My role grants me influence that I can use to save lives and sometimes even keep the peace. As an example, even the highest authority in the land needs to follow the words of the person ensuring their health. While a convoluted topic, that is *positional* influence in a nutshell."

"But why do you call it 'borrowed influence', as well?"

Snow's pertinent question was rewarded by Doc reaching over to his side table and pulling the lid off a plate. Swiping a cookie from underneath, he handed it over with what she was certain was a smile under his mask.

"It *is* borrowed influence, power, or authority, however you want to think of it," Doc explained as she took a tentative bite of what turned out to be a *delicious* treat. "The influence is borrowed from the position and must be repaid by performing quality work. Each time someone abuses the power their position provides them, it permanently spends some of the trust and influence everyone else in that position can wield in the future. Part of the reason we as guildmasters exist is to police our own members and ensure the highest standards are held. Else, too many bad actors within our groups can and will reverse our influence, making people actively avoid us."

"Like the Qu-" Snow bit her lip as she remembered how the queen had managed to peek at her the last time she had been spoken of. Trying again, she carefully picked her words. "Like when someone in charge of the entire kingdom is doing things no reasonable person would approve of, they still have the power and authority to do so. Until... that trust is eroded far enough, and the people rebel?"

"Exactly." Doc inclined his head sagely. "When you retake the throne, you will have an uphill battle in restoring trust among your people. Yet, it seems the system itself has already been preparing you for that eventuality. I speak of course of your very first skill, Precocious Command. This ability to gauge moods and personalities will allow you to surround yourself with people who will not act against you, while still holding firm to their own beliefs and doing their best to get you to do the right thing."

He let out a soft sigh. "Convincing courtiers to support your initiatives, inspiring your subjects with your dedication, the system itself was warning that someday you wouldn't just 'be adept' at navigating complex social dynamics... having that skill would be an utterly necessary capability you *must* possess. My hope is to teach you how to leverage your position without damaging the foundation it is built on. Of all of the D'wharves… I firmly believe only I can give you a true understanding of what this entails."

"The key to this is understanding that your borrowed influence is not something you personally have earned, therefore it will be ever fragile. Misuse it, and it will crumble. Yet using it wisely will allow you to accomplish things you never could have on your own. Like using tools to build your house, instead of punching trees and hoping they fall correctly, turn into planks, join themselves, and provide you shelter." Doc saw how the princess's eyes were starting to glaze, though she was doing her best to pay attention. "Now, let's put this aside for a moment. You've just arrived, and I don't mean to be a poor host by speaking your ear off."

Hopping to his feet with surprising spryness, he moved to the door and motioned for her to follow him. "I was going to set you up in a room to get some rest and relaxation, but by the look of you… solitude and patient, quiet waiting is not what would serve you best at the moment. I have a gift for you!"

Seeing his words matched by an energy she hadn't expected from someone so clearly elderly, Snow hurried to keep up, her pack jostling slightly as she half-jogged to follow along behind him. "Doc, if it's not rude to ask, how are you so…"

"Healthy for my age?" Doc glanced back at her, clear mischief glinting in his eyes as he knocked on his chest with a closed fist. "I'm a healer! That's what I do! Remember, it's what's *inside* that counts."

Pushing open a door, Doc waited until she had stepped inside, then pulled the key out of the lock and handed it over. "This will be your space, and no one will be allowed to enter without your permission. I figure after… oh, what, more than half a year of close contact and low levels of privacy, you may appreciate-"

He trailed off as Snow's eyes locked on the gift he had put in the room for her: a travel-sized portrait of her captured sister, Rose. It was a copy of the portrait the king and queen had commissioned years ago, so it showed her a bit younger than she truly was, but it was still unmistakably the person the princess missed most in the world. "It's small, but I thought that, after all this time, you might be a bit homesick. Before I left the capital, I had this recreated. I hope you don't mind—*oof!*"

Doc huffed as the air was knocked out of him from the force of Snow's sudden hug. Though her words were slightly muffled, that didn't stop her from pouring out her gratitude. "I don't know what to say. This might be the nicest thing someone has ever done for me. Not that I don't appreciate the gifts other people have given me, but... there's a difference between a bangle with a hidden dagger and a portrait of my other half."

"Nothing *needs* to be said, Princess." Doc patted her on the back gently. "I'm just glad you like it. Ahh, there, there. Don't look so mortified. Let it all out. Never be sorry for how you feel; you're allowed to be human."

"I'm a princess, and I've been training to be able to control myself." Snow stepped back, dashing tears from the corners of her eyes.

"Stop *that* immediately." Though the words were firm, there was no condemnation in them. "As I stated, you are a *person* before anything else. We are born crying. Never apologize for something like this, which comes naturally. These are not tears meant to manipulate or control; they are an outpouring of what you feel in your very soul."

He let her quietly sob for a few moments, then spoke in a hushed tone, "I believe the body is at its healthiest when the mind is as well. During our time together, feel free to ask me anything whatsoever, talk to me about whatever you need, and I will hold your fears, doubts, and secrets without ever sharing them. At least, not without your express request. To this I swear. I cross my heart, and hope to die, should this oath become a lie."

As Doc finished speaking, the attention of the system descended upon them. Energy flooded into the room, swirling around the guildmaster of healers until it coalesced into a nearly blindingly bright golden 'X' which hovered above his chest for a bare moment before sinking to his skin, then fading through it. Snow let out a slow, controlled breath as she watched the most permanent, dangerous oath anyone could utter being so... so *casually* offered to her.

"But why would you do something like that? What if you simply misspeak sometime in the future?" She shook her head in horrified confusion. "The system would slice your heart apart!"

"Better losing mine than breaking yours, Princess." Doc gently placed his hand on her arm and began to pull her out of the room. "There is no better way to earn and keep your trust than having you know I will be *held* to it. Besides, with how many oaths I've made, by now I'd *better* have a heart of gold. Someday, I might even find if there's an upper limit to what the system will allow!"

"You've... made oaths like this before?" Snow glanced at his chest, then up to his face, where any system marks were hidden behind the pangolin mask he wore.

"Like I told you before, Snow," the man knocked on his chest once more. "It's what's *inside* that counts."

CHAPTER
TWENTY-TWO

AFTER THEIR CONVERSATION and getting a tour of the house of healing, which would be her base of operations for the next few months, Snow found herself far more tired than she expected. Doc had a way of raising poignant questions which lanced to the heart of the loneliness, self-doubt, and other such issues that had been festering beneath the surface. Beyond the warmth he had as a person, which would have made her trust him over time, knowing his life would be forfeit should he betray her had allowed her to open up to the man instantly.

Even so, confronting all of the issues she had been avoiding for the majority of the year had caused multiple emotional moments, and by the time he had suggested getting some rest, Snow had practically felt hollowed out. Simply agreeing with him took effort, and after locking the door behind her and taking a few minutes to appreciate *her* room… she had slept soundly, without any of the troubled dreams that had been plaguing her for months.

The following morning, she awoke feeling more rested and *aware*. After going through the exercises taught to her by both Grumpy and Bashful's people, she cleaned up, got dressed, and strode out into the house of healing to find Doc. Though it was still an early hour, the sun cresting the horizon only a short while before, the surprisingly spry old man was already hard at work. Snow hurried over when she saw half a dozen people suddenly piling into the building, but the healer waved her back.

"It seems you may have come at an inauspicious moment," he called over to her calmly, as other healers seemed to come out of the woodwork to begin tending to the clearly sickly people. "There's been outbreaks in towns along the coast, especially among those who have been... shall we say, repeating a certain story the bards have been telling?"

Snow's smile faltered as she realized this new development might be due to her actions. Before she could begin blaming herself, Doc came closer, allowing his staff to partition off the sickly people in individual rooms. "This is clearly an unnatural disease, and I've been briefed on this for weeks... but it arriving here so quickly does not bode well."

"What makes you so sure this is something malicious, instead of just an illness you haven't encountered before?" Snow edged closer to the door as yet another person stepped in, and Doc didn't stop her from studying the man who was barely on his feet after getting himself there.

"Essentially, the first clear sign is the pinpointed nature of the outbreak," Doc explained in a tone that was just as calm as it was firm, as though he were teaching any other person who had arrived with a healing class from the system and needed instruction. "Next is the black sweat these patients exude. It's clear to each of my healers who have studied this illness that it is no ordinary affliction. We've even gone so far as to consult with *Dopey*, if you'd believe it, and all tests have shown that the sweat's color and consistency are caused by alchemical reagents entering the body through ingestion."

"You mean," Snow's stomach twisted as she grimaced, having been warned off of eating food from unknown sources since she was a child, "this is something that they are *eating*? Someone is intentionally poisoning them? What sort of monster..."

A trace of grim amusement flashed in Doc's eyes as Snow trailed off, realizing *exactly* what sort of monster would do this. "I would say, perhaps someone not overly concerned with morality. Thankfully, *subtlety* doesn't appear to be among the list of her strong suits, or she could have employed harder-to-detect reagents."

"What does this do to them?" Snow tracked the man who had entered until an assistant healer scooted him over to another room. "If it gets in their system because of something they ate, I'm guessing it's not terribly contagious?"

"So long as people are making sure the ooze is not getting into their food or drink, and carefully keeping soiled areas away from orifices, no one else has become sickly." On that note, Doc motioned for her to follow him and set her up with a healer's apron, the standardized pangolin mask all healers in his organization seemed to wear, and thick white gloves that would show any filth they gathered. "Drop any garments that need cleaned in here, and take a fresh set from that room. Please don't confuse the two."

"As for the symptoms..." Doc thought for a moment as Snow pulled the garb over her own daily wear. "Malaise and fatigue. Those afflicted lack the energy to perform even the simplest tasks once the illness has taken root. Now, were someone plotting to suppress rebellion in areas already showing an interest in doing so, this is a clever strategy. After all, how can people rise against tyranny if they can't even rise out of their beds?"

"But it's not fatal? Have you found a treatment?" Snow let out a relieved sigh, only to freeze as Doc clicked his tongue sharply.

"Not *yet*." For the first time, she saw true anger in his eyes. "But we don't know what effects this will eventually have.

Imagine, if you will, this compound settling into her subjects, seeming to eventually fade away, only for her to release a second dose of this—or something else—which exacerbates the effects beyond the sum of their parts."

"What can we do? What medicines or techniques should I start to learn to help you treat this?" Snow took a deep, shuddering breath, resolving herself to do whatever it took to keep her people healthy or at least *return* them to good health.

"In fact, I think your specific skill set would make you better suited to another task I need completed." Doc lifted both hands in front of his chest as he took a deep breath, lowering them and seeming to intentionally shove away the dark feelings he had been allowing to build. "Come, walk with me. There are many people I'd like for you to speak with."

Doc's long strides forced Snow to hurry to keep pace with him, though she felt a long, lingering tingle of concern. "I don't know what you've heard about me, but I'm not sure what I can do to help here. I can't influence someone into *not* being sick, that's just not how my skills work."

"Have you ever *tried?*" Seeing her thunderstruck expression, Doc let out a wheeze of laughter and shook his hand at her. "I'm only teasing! No, I've seen your skills, and that would be quite an extreme stretch, even for the system. However, what I believe you would be best at doing is helping us uncover crucial information from those afflicted with this ailment. Many of the patients are too lethargic to answer the questions, but some are simply unwilling."

The elderly man grumbled softly, deep in his chest as he looked at a particular room. "This points toward them doing something they *shouldn't* have been doing, and they are worried about what we will do when we learn. If you can coax out the details of what they were doing before becoming sick, we might very well uncover the source of the contamination."

Gesturing toward the door, he stepped aside and allowed Snow to walk ahead of him. "Leslie has no family to care for her, and her neighbors brought her in after finding her collapsed in her front yard. We've managed to get her to eat and drink, but she won't talk to us. Why don't you see what you can accomplish? I'll leave you to it."

With that, he stepped back, not leaving the area entirely, but clearly attempting to allow the patient some form of privacy, no matter how minimal it truly was. To Snow, the room was stiflingly warm, and her heart sank at the sight of the elderly woman lying listlessly on the bed. Leslie's too-pale skin was slick with the unnatural black, oily sheen, and she breathed as though each inhale would be her last.

Casting around for a starting point, Snow's eyes landed on a cloth in a bowl of hot water resting on the nightstand. Picking it up felt strange behind the thick gloves she was wearing, and the princess had to be extra careful to keep her movements gentle as she wiped the woman's face.

Without the sheen of the unnatural sweat on her face, Leslie looked far more peaceful, natural, though still frail, as if her body would fail at any moment. When her efforts didn't get the lady to react, Snow softly tried speaking to her, "Leslie? My name is Snow, and I'd like to speak with you. I'm sure you have a story worth hearing."

She could tell that the woman was awake, but simply couldn't, or didn't want to, use her scant remaining energy to speak. Even so, now that the slick was off her face, Leslie's eyelids fluttered open, and she cast about with an unfocused gaze. Encouraged by earning a reaction, Snow began to quietly tell stories, falling back on those from her childhood, while combining her training with the bards with her best mimicry of Doc's calm energy.

When an assistant brought in a tray of brothy soups, Snow offered to feed the fallen woman herself, but was quickly rebuffed. Hoping the patient would have more energy after eating, Snow waited patiently until the woman had taken in as much as she could manage, then tapped Leslie's arm. "I've done so much speaking… I know it won't be fun for you, but could you tell me a story? Perhaps a story about what you were doing just before coming here? I might be able to figure out a way to help you get better."

Leslie's eyes slowly closed, cracking open only after Snow tapped her on the arm insistently. "Eh… tired…"

"I understand it's hard, but this is important." Snow took Leslie's hand in hers, hoping her body heat would help show her sincerity. Focusing on her need to gather information, she urged her skill to activate, trying to insist as gently as possible to make this lady speak to her. "Let us help you."

She thought she failed, as Leslie's lips pressed closed, shallow breathing resuming, only to moisten her lips and whisper, "Truffle… hunting."

As though those two words had taken every ounce of energy she had, Leslie immediately fell into a fitful slumber. Snow didn't mind, gently placing her hand down, tucking her in, and hurrying out of the room to find Doc. He hadn't gone far and was simply scribbling notes on a clipboard as she hurried over to him. Before she could say anything, he held up a hand and pointed at her gloves. "Straight into sanitation with those."

Snow glanced down, shocked to see dozens of lines and droplets of the thick black gunk on her gloves. She peeled them off with extra caution, dropping them in the bucket Doc indicated and returning to him.

"Now you see why the masks are important as well. It helps us not accidentally touch our faces with sickness-coated fingertips." He pulled her mask off, showing her where her fingers had unconsciously touched over her mouth and below her eyes. After tossing the mask in the bucket as well and grabbing her another, he inclined his head, patiently waiting for her report. She quickly filled him in, and though the information was scarce, his eyes lit up when he heard what had been said. "Well done, Snow! I'm certain that's going to be crucial as a clue."

"Then, you think the truffles were poisonous? Or perhaps they simply soaked up the reagent better than other things?" Snow reached for the ties of her apron, ready to toss it off and rush to the town square. "We need to warn everyone not to eat any truffles from this area!"

"Wait, *wait.*" To her surprise, Doc only chuckled at her urgency. "One patient doing something fairly normal does *not* a trend make. Let's not go putting the mushroom sellers of Emdenvale out of business just yet. This is promising progress, but we need more before putting together an initial guess. Try the next room."

A tickle on Snow's arm grabbed her attention, and she swiped her arm and read over the change before putting on the clean pair of thick white gloves.

Skill increase! Influential Aura: [Level 8 (Extensive) → Level 9 (Master)]!

Requirement to advance to level 10: Collect and maintain a minimum of 50,000 influence for 240 consecutive hours. 0/1.

"What kind of ridiculous jump in requirement is *that*?" She gasped in shock at the unfairness of the incredible leap. Half-focused on her increased skill, and at the same time far more confident now that she had managed some initial success, Snow moved into the next patient's room, where an assistant introduced the young man as 'Leo'.

Visually inspecting him, Snow realized he was perhaps even worse off than Leslie had been, so she didn't waste time introducing herself—going straight for the data she needed. "Tell me, before you got sick, how many truffles did you eat?"

His distant gaze drifted toward her, but the young man remained silent and simply blinked at her. Leaning closer, she tried again, voice insistent as she pushed on him with her

Class Skills. "Please, Leo. This is very important. Talk to me."

She sucked in a sharp breath as influence poured out of her like a sieve trying to hold water and cut off the skill before it canceled out all of the hard work and saving of influence she had done over the last few months. Even though the man's eyes had suddenly shot wide, there was still no response. Frustrated and unsure of what to do, she stepped out of the room and walked up to Doc. "I can't get him to talk to me."

"Oh? Is *that* what just happened?" There was a glint in his eye that chilled Snow, "It seems to me that you attempted to *force* him to speak about something he doesn't want to talk about, and that failed. A healer who doesn't care for their subject won't hold their *position* long."

"That's…" Snow hesitated and tried to find a justification for what she was doing. "This is for his own good, isn't it? I'm trying to help him get better!"

"Many are the kingdoms that have fallen because rulers have suddenly decided *they* know what is good for everyone else." Doc lifted an eyebrow. "Is that who you want to be? Someone who forces someone else to see things her way because she's 'in charge'? Or would you rather treat your position with respect and leverage it to your benefit?"

"I don't understand, Doc." Snow huffed in frustration. "This is my first time doing anything like this. I had hoped for instruction, not guessing games. People's lives are on the line."

"Hmm." Doc bobbed his head agreeably. "I can see why you would move straight toward attempting to skip to the end of your conversation, as this is what Grumpy was no doubt teaching you to do. I'm sure he explained to you that all power is derived from the threat of force, but… tell me, Snow. What happens when someone refuses to abide by the rules? If they have enough power to resist the threat of incarceration and enough allies to fight back so they cannot be slain for their insubordination?"

"I…" Snow's mind went blank. "I guess I've never thought about it?"

"A perfectly *fine* answer, and never let anyone tell you differently," Doc commended the princess, once more warming toward her. "When you don't know something, pretending you *do* is almost always worse than simply asking for help to learn it. On the scale of kingdoms, typically what that situation would mean is the birth of a new nation. Kingdoms rise *and* fall. Land is one of the few resources there is no more of when it is gone. So, when a situation like this arises, you must either clash until one side is completely defeated, or negotiate until both sides are willing to get along and make concessions."

He wiggled his hands, calling Snow's attention to the clipboard he was carrying. "What I have here is all of the patient information on Leo that we have collected over the years of treating him. I'll show this to you, as you are currently in the position of my direct apprentice, and therefore any of the actions you take fall on me as my responsibility. Do not use this information to bring harm to him, or *I* will suffer for it."

Snow solemnly accepted the clipboard and the thick stack of paper it held. Paging through the documents, her brow furrowed as she found page after page of incomprehensible information, and certainly nothing she could use to either clash with Leo, or… "Negotiation, huh? Do *all* of your patients' records list their favorite meals?"

"They don't," Doc remarked in an easy tone, clearly trying not to laugh at the frank glance she sent his way. "However, I had hoped that this would be pertinent information."

"It seems I must speak to the chef." The princess slipped away, hurrying to the kitchen and enlisting the cook's help in preparing dakota kuchen, a type of dessert Snow herself was rather fond of. Soon she was carrying the rich custard dessert with steaming apricots poured into a sweet crust back to the patient's room, casting a glance at Doc as she passed him, only to get a nod of approval.

Waving the pastry slowly back and forth in front of Leo's face caused his eyes to flutter open. Past the unnatural lethargy, Snow was certain she saw a flicker of longing. Enlisting the help of the assistant to help the patient sit up, Snow carefully fed him a small bite, ensuring it was mostly gooey fruit that would enter his system with minimal chewing. A faint smile crossed his lips, enough to make Snow's heart pound with excitement.

"Between bites, could you please tell me how many truffles you ate before coming here?" Snow kept her tone light and conversational this time around, continuing to move slowly to give the ailing young man time to swallow his food. "We're trying to find what is doing this to you and your fellow citizens. Right now, I'm thinking it's the mushrooms, am I right?"

"Allergic…" Leo gasped out, voice weak but clear. "Never ate any. Ever."

Snow took a long inhale through her nose, closing her eyes in frustration, yet unwilling to show it to the sick man. "Then what were you doing before you got sick?"

Leo slowly smacked his lips, as though his mouth was suddenly as dry as a desert. Taking another bite of his dessert seemed to give him enough energy to answer, and he took a deep breath, speaking as he exhaled to minimize energy usage. "Fishing."

"Well, that's just… *great*." Snow turned the grumble into a compliment at the last second, remembering that *she* wasn't the sick one in the room. Belatedly, she added, "…for you. Do you like fishing? Or do you do that for work?"

Any attempts to further rouse him failed, as Snow realized he had fallen asleep sitting up. Setting the dakota kuchen next to his bed, she stood and went to report to Doc.

TWENTY-THREE

"I GUESS that pretty much throws out my truffle theory," Snow dejectedly stated as she relayed Leo's answer. Yet, Doc didn't seem disheartened or surprised in the slightest. Instead, he appeared only to become intrigued.

"Fishing, you say? That's… new. I wonder if he changed careers recently; from what I remember, his daily life kept him far from the water."

"You *knew*." Snow crossed her arms, and Doc had the decency not to pretend he didn't know what she was saying. "If you already knew the truffles weren't the cause, why did you let me think they were? I suppose I should thank you for stopping me from rushing off to spread the word, at the least."

Doc rubbed at the back of his neck in discomfort, but his words remained as even as usual. "Princess, I am not here to make you do things my way, but to help you think critically. To use your talents in ways you haven't before. You are so close to achieving level ten, Perfection, with your newest skill, yet you've barely tapped into the possibilities it has to offer. I know you don't understand exactly how much, but your progress today has already been *incredible*. Did you know not even a single healer has managed to get their patients to speak directly to them once they arrived?"

Snow brightened considerably at the intended praise, but didn't allow herself to be distracted, "What about Leo? Why let me put him through the round of questioning about truffles if you already had the information?"

"Because, I didn't have *all* the information." Doc stressed his words, draining the last vestiges of her annoyance away. "Fishing is not at all what I had expected to hear, coming from Leo. That's an entirely new data point and helps us get a picture about what he was doing, where he was, and to what he may have been exposed. Every detail matters in a new case like this, Snow. For instance…"

Despite herself, Snow leaned in to make sure she captured every nuance.

"Fishing. We are in a port city, are we not? So the immediate conjecture would be that he was down on a boat, or perhaps on a pier. But Leo has a history of fearing deep waters after his father's ship went down when he was a child. There are also two rivers which run through the area, less than half a day's walk north and south of the city gate. That means there are three potential sources we will have to look into. *But-*"

His last word was stated sharply, as Snow had slumped dejectedly as he laid out his thoughts, "Only having three places to check means we have narrowed the possibilities nearly *infinitely*. You're doing good work, my dear. Tomorrow, I'm certain you'll uncover even more of the missing pieces. For now, it's time for you to do other things. You have nice clothes, good training, and a sack full of coins. Go into the city and learn what sort of activities make you happy."

"Sorry to say it, Doc. I just don't know if that's possible." Seeing his concerned glance, she could barely keep her face straight as she finished, "Statistically, there can only ever be *one* Happy, and I'm not him."

196 DAKOTA KROUT

"Bah!" Doc shooed her away, though she was certain she had seen him holding back a laugh. "That sounds like the sort of dry humor I would expect from someone who has been hit in the head a few too many times. Go! Be young, play games, meet people. All work and no joy will make you a bitter, jaded person. Also…"

He hesitated, some of his mirth fading as Snow slowed down, "Just to be safe… perhaps avoid the seafood dishes wherever you end up."

She didn't go far that night, unfamiliar as she was with city life, but at Doc's urging, her days swiftly turned into a satisfying routine.

Each morning, she would wake up and practice her exercises, both physical and with her voice, to ensure she didn't backslide. The days were filled with speaking with an ever-increasing number of patients, each one adding another fragment to the puzzle. Some mentioned specific foods, others she managed to convince to speak on habits, work, or the leisure activity they had been partaking in. Yet every evening, Doc demanded she stop everything else and focus on going out and about, pushing her to learn more about herself than others for the rest of the day.

Over the course of the next month, patterns began to emerge, but nothing pointed at a single, definitive source for the disease. Beyond simply speaking with people, Snow was taught about all sorts of various common maladies and remedies, as well as how to identify issues that required intense intervention, whether it be from a skilled surgeon or magical source. She took meticulous notes, and every few nights even snuck them out with her so she could study while enjoying a hot cup of hibiscus tea whilst overlooking the ocean. Still, she couldn't shake the feeling that there was something critical they were missing.

It wasn't until she met an irritable old man that the pieces finally started falling into place.

Arnfried was a gnarled old man with knuckles so swollen they looked like they hadn't been able to bend in years. She tried her usual routine of cajoling questions, offers of treats, and all manner of other tricks she had picked up during her tenure at the house of healing. No matter what she did, he at most only grunted, absolutely uninterested in speaking to her.

"Are you secretly *mute*, Arnfried?" Snow questioned him suspiciously one day, only to feel her jaw slacking as she saw a glint of mischief in his eyes—the first new reaction she had ever earned with this particular patient. "You old *codger*! What, were you just enjoying the attention of a pretty young lady coming and speaking to you every day?"

"Heh." His grunt this time certainly sounded like a laugh, and Snow began to pick up on how much he enjoyed her indignation.

Instead of trying to hide it, she allowed her emotions to flow out, exaggerating them beyond anything she truly felt. The more she overacted, the more he seemed to come back to himself, until finally the princess judged the moment was right. "You're not going to just tease me like that without giving me anything in return, are you? You're a *funny* guy, not a mean one, I can tell. Go on then, what were you doing before you started coming down with the dark sweats?"

As the disease had begun impacting more people, the slang name for it had stuck, and now everyone knew to be careful to get anyone with the foul excretion to the house of healing as soon as possible. Arnfried's hint of a smile slipped, but he managed to weakly gesture toward the far side of the room. Snow immediately went to check what he was pointing out, only to find his personal effects stored in a box. One by one she pulled them out, lifting them until she got to a small, wooden carving of a bear, and Arnfried reacted.

"Did you make this? Blink once for yes, twice for no." He blinked, then stared at her, and the princess knew she was on the right track. "It's well made... you must be very good at this. Did it take you a while to make?"

Two blinks.

"You made this all in one go? Right after that you got sick?"

One blink.

Snow felt the wood, noting how, even through her gloves, she could tell how soft the actual material was. She started speaking out loud, keeping her eyes on Arnfried the entire time. "This is driftwood, yes? Good. Did you pull it from a river, or-yes, a river. The north one? No? Interesting. Were there any landmarks or features near where you got this? Yes..."

At that moment, Snow was stymied, as she had no idea what sort of landmarks to ask about. However, before she could try to figure something else out, Doc suddenly stepped into the room and took over. He went through several rounds of questions, using her same system, and managed to narrow down where to look before the gnarled old man drifted away, too tired to keep going.

"The southern river, somewhere around the third bend to the right of the city gates." Doc swept out of the room, seemingly forgetting Snow's presence as he hurried away.

Unwilling to be left behind, she dumped her gloves in the 'sanitize' bucket and hurried after him, managing to enter a large conference room she hadn't been in before just as the door closed. She looked around in shock at the dozens of people surrounding the large table that took up the majority of the room, each of them rapidly speaking to each other while shifting through different papers. As soon as Doc began talking, all other noise and motion stopped.

"We have a lead on a possible source of the contamination. Somebody get me a map." Questions and replies flew rapid-fire as a detailed drawing was flipped casually across the room to the guildmaster, who caught it with a practiced ease and held it out to the light. "Third bend, to the right of... have we commissioned anyone to look into the caves situated between the river and the bog?"

"Checking..." one man called out from across the table, flipping through papers rapidly, clearly knowing exactly where the information would be found. "Got it. Yes, we had someone look into that near the start of all this, as stagnant water buildup was a primary point of concern for pouring back into the city water supply. A qualified inspector was sent out and reported no backflow from the bog."

"A *kingdom* inspector, or one of ours?" Doc questioned darkly, a resounding silence being his answer. "At least we know how we overlooked this. They wouldn't have lied to us; they physically can't. Tell me, does it specifically say it is not a backflow of water *from the bog*, or that there is nothing there that might be causing this?"

"Backflow," the man replied as he read from the report to double-check.

"Get someone out there, right now." Doc turned and glanced at Snow, a hard light in his eyes. "The only reason we found out about this is thanks to our guest and her dogged persistence in seeking out the facts. Finally, a leader who leads from the front."

The room erupted into applause, and for some reason, Snow felt her eyes moisten as the masked group of people stood and clapped at *her*. Ducking her head, she quietly thanked them before following the guildmaster out of the room in the next moment. Once they were alone, she tried to shake off the bizarre feeling by getting back to work. "When do we go look at this?"

"Absolutely not," Doc immediately responded, already halfway out the door. "We have people trained for this, not to mention how to properly use all the protections, mundane and magical, that they will be using. If you went directly to the source and got a full dose of whatever this is, there's no guarantee you would be able to take a single step away. The most likely outcome would be immediately passing into a coma and then just *passing*. I'll be busy for the next few days; I'll see you soon."

Before she could argue further, he was gone. As she wandered down the hall after him, an intense, pearlescent light suddenly blazed from her left arm, filling the room with splendor and iridescence as the system's power collected on her, then erupted outward in a thin nova that passed through everything around her without damaging it or even causing dust to lift off the surface.

CHAPTER
TWENTY-FOUR

ONLY ONE OTHER time had she experienced something like that—when achieving Perfection in a skill. All other thoughts fled her mind as she looked to her arm to confirm what she already knew.

Congratulations! Influential Aura Has achieved level 10, Perfection!

Influential Aura subtly yet powerfully affects those around you, [Perfectly] influencing their thoughts in a positive or negative manner using Influence as a currency. You are able to [Perfectly] sway opinions, inspire action, and guide decisions with a variable cost. Influencing people in ways contrary to their desires will cost additional Influence, while moving them in ways aligned with their own goals will give an influence discount of [100%]. Use caution, as leading others toward goals not in their best interests will slowly push you toward darker powers.

Your Influence is gained at a rate of (total people influenced) per day, with a minimum of 1.)
Current followers: 5,281.
Influence: 71,313.

Somehow, just by being around so many people regularly, she had managed to nearly double the number of those influenced by her. She could only attribute that growth to the sheer number of people packed into the city compared to the tiny towns and villages she had been visiting before now. Yet, if achieving Perfection in her skill hadn't been enough cause to celebrate, the new skill she had gained in her Advanced Class certainly was.

Advanced Skill gained: Brand Ambassador: Level 1/10

At the cost of 5000 influence - 250*[skill level], you can choose a person to generate followers on your behalf by [Minimally] imparting one of your skills on them. The same skill cannot be imparted to the same person while it is currently imbued, but other skills can be put on the same person at the cost of an additional 25-[2.5*skill level]% influence per skill. Upon choosing to activate the imparted skill(s), they will be able to act with your granted skills for [2*skill level] days before the skill(s) fade. While using the skill(s), every [skill level] in ten new followers will count as influenced by you.

You are able to stipulate conditions for granting your skills and are able to remove the applied skill at any distance.

Requirement to advance to level 2: gain 100 followers through the efforts of your Brand Ambassadors. 0/100.

"I did it!" She breathed the words softly, as if speaking aloud might make the new skill vanish like a soap bubble popping. "I gained a *Legendary* skill."

She celebrated that night and the next, treating a dozen people to dinner and fine tea, a relaxing habit she had fallen in love with.

Though Snow was frustrated by her inability to seek out the source of the illness, especially as she had been the one to find the anomaly, it was only two days later that a report came in. As she started work that morning, the princess was called back to the conference room, where she found several people in tiny-mouthed masks amongst the healers who were hidden behind the comforting pangolin shape. "What's going on?"

Doc came to a stop next to her, nodding at a person patiently standing by the oversized table. "A member of Sneezy's guild has brought us information."

"Sneezy's?" Snow didn't try to hide her confusion. "I thought Bashful and his subordinates were the ones who gathered information?"

"Yes and no," Doc responded, stepping closer to keep their conversation volume as minimal as possible. "Bashful's people are far more concerned with the goings on within settlements. Towns, villages, cities, and the like. Sneezy is... well, they work as scouts and sentries. Usually, what that means is being within cities and providing warnings when guards are coming or clandestine meetings are happening which require someone keeping an eye out to ensure they are not interrupted. On the other side of the coin are the scouts who go into the wilderness and assess various threats."

"Rangers?" The princess hazarded a guess. "Aren't those directly under the employee of the kingdom?"

"Typically, they start that way." Doc lowered his chin, allowing his eyes to bore into hers. "Eventually, they do tend to retire. Retired people still need coin to live. Not to mention, in recent years, ever more have been flocking to Sneezy's banner for training in the first place."

"I see," Snow responded quietly, fractionally more burdened by this knowledge. It seemed that, each time she learned about a new profession, she was only finding more people disillusioned with the kingdom, people she would need to eventually coax back into her employ—likely at a significant cost. Already having plenty to think about, the princess turned to listen as the details of the find were explained.

"Reporting!" A rough voice called from behind a lacquer mask, much less elaborate than Sneezy's own, though still containing the exaggerated features of a tiny mouth with puffy cheeks, as well as huge black eyes with a panda smudge of red paint. "Near the area indicated by your initial supposition, we found a large cave mouth which was clearly intentionally hidden by human intervention. Even with our skillsets, we would have missed it, had there not been a carpet of strange black flowers spreading along the bank where the water exiting the cave mouth sprayed up onto the grass."

The tiny mouth of the mask made a whistling sound as the man inhaled deeply, "For reference, the flowers had red, spiny thorns along a thick stem and black petals with a red center. They had a particularly concerning... *call* to them. As though they were practically begging to be sniffed and admired."

He trailed off, his body language telling Snow that he was looking into the distance longingly, though she couldn't see his face. Doc coughed into his hand, and the man shook off whatever daydream he had been caught in. "Right! Upon entering the cave, being careful not to touch the water—which had a thin layer of iridescence over it—we found a section of the cave which seemed to all but repel both the sunlight as well as the non-flaming light sources we took with us. Because of this effect, it was not until we were nearly on top of them that we discovered three oversized barrels. Not small versions, but large enough to store several hundred gallons of fluids on their own."

The man gestured, and one of his subordinates carefully walked over with a sample of a dark liquid held within a glass flask, which itself was sealed in a larger glass canister. "As you can see, we managed to gain a sample of the contents of the barrels. To the best of our knowledge, each of the barrels contained the same reagent. They were clearly not left there by accident, as there was piping connecting each of the three barrels. Only one was releasing this into the water supply, and it did so at a constant, slow drip. That is the end of my report."

"I will conduct my tests." Doc motioned for someone to accept the canister then glance back at Sneezy's man. "Do we have someone delivering a second sample of this to Dopey so we can get a confirmation on its makeup?"

"Indeed," the scout reported easily, having expected this question. "We are sending the secondary sample via minor teleportation, the spell's magical signature diffused as demanded by Dopey's safety protocols."

Snow could see the relief in Doc's shoulders as the man took a deep breath, "Fantastic! Between the two of us, we'll have an understanding of what this is by tomorrow, and will be working on a cure within the next handful of days. All of you... I cannot say how impressed and proud I am of your hard work and dedication. We are saving lives with this, perhaps even entire cities over the next few years. As I'm sure you are all aware, this is not the only occurrence of this strange 'dark sweat' disease. Keep up the good work."

As he finished speaking, everyone in the room stood to their feet and inclined their heads slightly in a show of respect before returning to what they had been doing. Doc turned to Snow and gestured for her to follow after him. "Are you up for a lesson in preventative gear, followed by a discussion on how to discern the various components of poisons such as this? If not, this will likely be a large part of what you are learning at your next destination, and you can wait until then to get a full explanation."

"I'd love to see this through, if I won't be slowing you down," Snow returned quickly. "The most important thing is finding a cure and getting it out."

"You... are correct." Doc winced slightly. "If you wouldn't mind, I think doing this myself would be the most efficacious way."

The princess blinked rapidly in surprise, smiling self-deprecatingly at the awareness that she had gotten exactly what she had asked for. "For some reason, I was sure you would have me join you. But I'm glad; please don't slow down the process of healing others just to make me feel more important. Might I walk with you for a few moments? I achieved *Perfection* in my influence skill and wanted to speak with you on the best way to train my new Advanced Skill."

"Oh? Congratulations, and do tell!" Doc never slowed down, winding through the building and down several flights of stairs as Snow laid out her newest skill. "Quite intriguing indeed... essentially, you are able to make an investment of your influence, in hopes that the return will be greater over time. I wonder... no, I'm sure-"

"What?" Snow started to nudge him, only to pull back at the last moment as she realized how gingerly he was holding the glass container. "You can't just start saying something, then not finish! I'll lose my mind wondering."

"It's just that... the timing of gaining this skill is quite *interesting*," Doc explained as he approached a large door *glowing* with the magical protections woven over it. "I've been trying to teach you about the pitfalls and triumphs you can achieve using positional influence, then the system hands you a *Legendary* skill based on the same principles. This just goes to show how important dependable, high-level training is in order to achieve higher heights with the system."

The princess considered his words for a few moments as Doc pulled what appeared to be nothing more than cut gemstones out of his pocket, touching them to different parts of the door in sequence. After the fifth such poke with what appeared to be clear quartz, the dangerous, warning glow over the door faded away. "Wait, we never talked about how I should use this skill!"

"As an interesting point of conversation... I've taught you all I can about positional influence. Not that there was much for me to do; you were already far closer to *Perfection* than I had ever hoped you would be." Turning to her, the elderly man smiled gently, his change in expression shown only by the shifting wrinkles around his eyes.

"I only had one final lesson to offer on this subject, but it seems the system has decided to make it more *official*. When you reach the height of your position, you need to learn how to delegate. Learning who to trust, to whom you *should* grant your authority, are not easy lessons to learn. Luckily, it seems your skill comes with the ability to immediately stop them from using your gifts further when misdeeds come to light."

Completely stumped on how to respond to his words, Snow could only awkwardly accept both his praise and clear instruction. Doc pulled on the handle of the door, and the massive slab of metal swung out smoothly. It was so weighty that even though it moved without resistance, its momentum kept it from moving more than a few inches per second. When there was just enough space for him to slip through, Doc pushed against the door, grunting with the effort it took to halt it.

He hesitated only a moment before stepping through. "Without the proper protective gear, you are not allowed past here. But, as food for thought, when you next go to a Class Shrine, mayhaps you ask the system what considerations went into earning this skill? I'm certain it will at *least* give you a breakdown of the merits applied. Usually, people only see those merits during a breakthrough or class advancement, but as it turns out, simply *asking* is usually enough to get the answer you've been looking for."

"What should I do now?" Snow was nervous about his answer, as she felt she had many, many things to learn under his tutelage. Unfortunately for her, Doc answered exactly as she had feared.

"Frankly, my dear... I don't have much else to teach you, unless you want to leave behind all claims of being a princess and join us in the houses of healing." Doc heaved on the door, and it ever so slowly began to swing closed. "As much as I enjoy your work ethic, can-do attitude, and genuinely just being around you, it is already time for you to move on. I called for an escort, and they should be arriving in the next few days to bring you to train under your next D'wharven guildmaster."

"Who is it this time?" Snow tried not to let herself sound too despondent—she was a princess, not a toddler. Even so, when she didn't get an answer, she raised an eyebrow and studied Doc. To her great surprise, the man seemed to be holding himself carefully... as though to not say disparaging things about someone he held... contempt for? "What's the matter?"

"I think it would be best for you to go into your next training with... caution," Doc stated as the door slipped ever closer to being shut. "I don't know where you are going, or how long it will take to get there, but I do know that anyone closely affiliated with Dopey quickly begins to become a worse version of themselves. You came here to learn to heal, to learn how to wield influence in the light. With him..."

As his voice trailed off, Snow grimaced and belted out a question, "What guild does he run?"

Doc had just enough time to answer her before the door clicked shut, and the darkened lines of magic sprang back to their full brilliance.

"Dopey runs the *Night's Heart Exchange*."

TWENTY-FIVE

Barely a week had passed since the sample of the contaminating reagent had been delivered to the house of healing, but to Snow, it felt like a month. Many things had happened extremely quickly: first, Doc had managed to synthesize a cure for the poisoning, and within a day, a crate of the cure had appeared, mass produced by Dopey and his people.

Second, the cure had been applied, and those suffering from the dark sweat had almost entirely recovered, those who still remained doing so only because they needed some small natural rest to fully get back on their feet. Third, the cleanup efforts of the alchemical reagents had been completed, including the ripping out and careful destruction of the strange flowers that had bloomed because of it.

Lastly, familiar faces had arrived at the house of healing.

Ted and Zed had been waiting for Snow when she woke up, a mere seven days since Doc had warned the princess that she would be moving on soon. The sting of having to get back in motion was somewhat reduced by the joy of seeing her friends once more, but even so... the princess was yet again walking away from a place she had quickly grown to love. Literally walking, in this instance.

The port city vanished as they crested the first hill, as the entire population center was designed to run along the coast near sea level. Watching the last vestiges of it disappear was a disconcerting sensation for her. "Seeing it go away is like... I don't know, it makes it feel like my entire time there was nothing more than a dream."

"You know, I feel like that fairly often as well," Zed answered in a more contemplative tone than Snow had ever heard from him. "Sometimes I feel like I'm just one small chunk of a larger overall Zed hivemind, out exploring the various universes and learning as much as I can before reporting back. I don't think I'd have much to say about this place, though. Great people, but I bet you there are worlds out there with *far* more advanced magics."

"Yeah?" She chuckled softly, though he only offered a wan smile at her mirth. "I suppose that's one way of putting it. I'm with you. Having all these experiences certainly doesn't feel like *real life*, you know?"

"What would be real life, then?" Ted joined the conversation, casting a glance at his still-contemplating contemporary.

"You know... being at the palace." Snow shrugged her shoulders, easily bouncing the over-stuffed pack on her back. "Working on various trade deals, negotiations, logistics for taxes, food, planning which sections of road need to be fixed-"

"Ick," Ted said as he looked at Zed, who seemed lost in his own head. "Sometimes I forget that there is more to being a princess than wearing pretty dresses and going to midnight soirees. I'll just focus on putting a smile on people's faces and catching a few coins in my hat. There's a freedom in just going out there and performing, you know?"

"I do." Snow was suddenly struck by an idea. "Hey! Would you two like to help me test my new skill? I'm able to give you one of my skills, though for now just a minimal version of it. If you are going out there and speaking on my behalf, it would really help *me* out as well!"

"Ooh!" Ted perked up immediately, and even Zed shifted, showing some signs of acting like his usual self once more. "I want the one that lets me read body language."

"I want to seem extra innocent." Zed laughed as the others looked at him and rolled their eyes. "No, really! I'm the one that drums up business by juggling and tumbling for half the day—it would be a lot easier if I was able to exude a child-like wonder like you do, Snow."

"Mhm." The princess focused on the duo, activating her newest skill for the first time. Immediately, a voice resounded in her mind, the words it spoke appearing in the air—though, going by how the others didn't react, only she could see them.

Target selected as a Brand Ambassador. Please select a skill to package for your target.

1. *Precocious Command. Package contains: [Minimally] understand the body language of others around the target who are not using skills or magical effects to adjust their appearance. [Minimally] persuade people to fulfill their requests. [Minimally] enhance their ability to gauge moods and personalities. Makes the target [Minimally] adept at navigating complex social dynamics.*

2. *Aura of Innocence. Package contains: bestows a level of enchanting presence, making the target exude an air of purity, kindness, and sincerity, [Minimally] amplifying their natural charm. When speaking in a heartfelt manner, the target's true thoughts will be [Minimally] felt by those they are speaking with. If their words and meaning are in alignment, the resistance of those around them will soften, making them [Minimally] more receptive to their words. Gentle creatures find [Minimal] comfort in the target's*

presence, often gathering around them in a serene display of trust and affection.

3. *Influential Aura. Package contains: Subtly yet powerfully affect those around the target, [Minimally] influencing their thoughts in a positive or negative manner using your Influence as a currency. Target will be able to [Minimally] sway opinions, inspire action, and guide decisions with a variable cost.*

4. *Brand Ambassador: Not available.*

CAREFULLY READING OVER THE OFFERINGS, Snow realized that for both of her Basic Class skills, it seemed that the entirety of the skill's power was copied over. Yet, with her Influential Aura, she noticed there was no mention of discounts, nor gaining of influence. "Abyss, that likely means he'll be using my influence as his own currency…"

Happy to be able to test how that worked at another time, she started with Ted, giving him the Precocious Command package and sucking in a deep breath as five thousand points of her influence flowed out of her. Feeling light-headed and dizzy, she paused and put her hands on her knees, breathing deeply. Ted was at her side in an instant, "Snow! What happened? Are you okay? This… there's a notification telling me I can open a 'package'? Should I-"

"No!" She gasped out. "As soon as you open it, the skill will only last for two days. Please try to do your best to only use it when you have a huge crowd… otherwise, it's going to be *really* difficult for me to gain levels in this skill. Hang on, let me do Zed's. Might as well get all the icky feelings out of the way in one go."

Selecting the other bard, she gave him a minimal version of her Aura of Innocence, and just like that, she had lost ten days' worth of her accumulated influence. "Oof… good thing

I already reached *Perfection*, or Influential Aura would be stagnant forever from now on."

"Interesting. Kind of distracting, isn't it?" Zed murmured to Ted, who nodded an agreement. "Right, Snow, since you can't see this, there's a little... I don't know, a present in the corner of my vision? It's a tiny glowing dot of golden light, unless I focus on it, then it gets bigger and asks if I want to open it. I... we need to get to a town soon. I don't know how long I can resist."

"Each time I use that, it costs me five days' worth of building up my resources," Snow stated while staring Zed down. The man wilted slightly, but his smile remained shining with full force. "I don't expect you'll make me regret it."

"Of course not!" Zed happily replied, quickly followed by Ted doing the same. The princess could only narrow her eyes and look between the two of them—both wearing innocent expressions... *too* innocent.

"You already opened it." She rubbed her forehead but found she couldn't stay mad at him. *Physically* could not stay mad. "That's so bizarre. Is this how you feel around me all the time?"

"No," Ted answered on their behalf, looking between his traveling companion and the princess. "It's a *far* more powerful effect coming from you. I want to go out of my way to help you, but the skill on *him*? It just makes his face a *little* less punchable."

"Be nice," she admonished him reflexively. "Zed's a good person. You're both just rather... theatrical."

"Dramatic." Zed agreed, nodding over at Ted.

"I prefer 'I know how good I am'." Ted tossed his mane of hair, striking a pose as he did so.

Snow chortled at their antics, sobering slightly as she was suddenly struck by how short their time together was going to be. "Can I ask... how long are we going to be on the road?"

"Sadly, not long," Ted replied kindly, picking up on her

quiet distress. "As soon as we get to the next city over, we are going to get you to a hidden entrance to the Night's Heart Exchange. Before you ask, it is not *there*. The entrance is a single-person teleportation circle."

"Can you tell me more about what that is?" Snow felt a surge of dread as the two bards glanced at each other. "That's the same expression Doc had under his mask, I'm sure of it. What's going on?"

"After Happy," Ted started slowly, "Dopey is *easily* the most wealthy of the guildmasters. There are arguments to say he is even richer than Happy, but his funds are tied up internationally, whereas Happy is exclusively here. That allows him to use more of his wealth than Dopey can bring to bear."

"Beyond that, he is also arguably the most *powerful* of them—even if he does only control their forces in this kingdom." Zed interjected, his voice quiet as they crunched along a gravel section of road. "The Night's Heart Exchange is an international crime syndicate. Think of it as the black market, but… everywhere. If you want something not just illegal, but deadly, they are who you go to. They don't have fighters like Grumpy. They have *assassins*. They don't have healers like Doc, they have poisoners and dark alchemists. In fact, Doc and Dopey are almost always at odds."

"Why would the rest of the guildmasters even be *associated* with someone like that?" Snow had to resist the urge to stop in her tracks and turn around. "Is it wise for me to put myself in his power?"

"Oh, yeah, you'll be fine." Ted nonchalantly shrugged off her worries. "Before anything else, when it comes to selling their services, they are *neutral*. The only reason they're even going to help you in the first place is that the… err… *current tyrant* has been attacking them and having her Huntsmen take their shipments."

"Shipments?" Snow snapped her fingers before he could

explain. "Alchemical reagents. Poisons. I see... things are starting to make more sense."

"Also, Happy has a *great* relationship with him," Zed offered another tidbit. "There's only so many experiences someone can have before they lose interest, unless they are properly *addicted* to them."

"Ehh." Snow tried to form a proper response, but could only manage to articulate the sick feeling she had in her stomach hearing that those two powerhouses were working together. "Is there anyone out there who can regulate them, at least... somewhat?"

As an answer, the two men simply stared back at her until she realized what they meant. "Ah. It's me, isn't it? It's the duty of the crown to make sure they aren't overstepping. But, that means I would need to allow at least a portion of what they do to be legally acceptable."

"You *may* find," Ted carefully began, "that the crown has more use for poisoners and assassins than you ever hoped would be true."

Seeing Snow's face crumple, Zed patted her on the shoulder and tried to cheer her up. "Don't worry! With that sweet, innocent face you have? No one will ever suspect *you* of using their services. You'll be able to get away with *way* more —*oof!*"

The bard bent over, clutching his gut where Ted had sharply elbowed him. "Buffoon, she's not worried about getting away with it! Who wants to employ that sort of person?"

"I mean... who wants to say they want them, compared to who actually does?" Zed straightened up, glaring at his companion resolutely. "There's a reason they are a massive syndicate and likely the most wealthy single powerhouse on the planet. They would probably even give the *dragons* a run for their money, at least in terms of sheer volume of gold and precious materials."

"Really... I'd rather not talk about this anymore." Snow shook her head, pressing on only due to the knowledge that *Doc* was the one who sent her. Were it anyone else, and she was in possession of this knowledge, the princess would have simply refused. But since it was him... Snow's jaw dropped, her eyes going wide.

"Positional Influence. By the system, he used exactly what he was trying to teach me to get me to follow through with this."

"Yep." Zed agreed happily. "He certainly didn't get where he is by accident, I'll tell you that much."

"Brilliant master strategist, that one." Ted's voice held nothing but respect as he bobbed his head.

Snow continued putting one foot in front of the other, not for the first time rethinking her decision to collaborate with such powerful, influential, and now apparently perhaps even *dark* organizations.

"I suppose... I can only hope I haven't struck a deal that'll lead to a worse fate for the kingdom than whatever that Witch has planned."

CHAPTER

TWENTY-SIX

Bang, bang, bang!

Snow's eyelids fluttered open, and for a long moment, she lay on the uncomfortable bed staring up at an unfamiliar ceiling. A flickering candle in the corner of the room barely reached the weathered plaster above, yet it still drew her eyes along the cracked patterns forming bizarre constellations shifting in the weak light. Her focus wavered as the pounding came once more, an indecipherable voice calling out afterward. Her head throbbed in dull waves, her limbs felt heavy, and lifting her head felt like a monumental effort, as though she were trying to push against ropes lightly tying specifically her head to the pillow she lay on.

"Coming?" she croaked out, her voice a dry rasp as she forced herself upright. The room swayed around her as though she were out at sea. For all she knew, she was. "Where am I?"

The last thing she remembered was, "Ted and Zed were there, and we walked into the city. They were going to bring me... somewhere?"

Bang, bang, bang!

"Ugh... sto~op." Snow lurched toward the door, slowly

piecing together the fragments of her memories, which felt like shattered glass scattered along a foggy ditch. Ignoring her command, the banging continued, insistent and impatient. She staggered forward, feet unsure beneath her as she reached for the handle. Twisting it, the ball-shaped handle released a *click* as it unlocked, and the door swung open in the same motion.

Dopey stood in the threshold, shifting from foot to foot, hand raised in the air as though to beat on the door once again. She glared at him, his watery eyes sharp and assessing over his monkey-faced half mask as he scanned her. When he spoke again, she realized why his voice had been indistinguishable behind the door; it was muffled both by the barrier and the mask hiding his lips. "Moving *forvard*... if you could be ready by ziz hour, it would be much appreciated, my rebel queen. Ve can't risk losing ze limited time we have togezah. I need you to be as *discreet* as you are *prepared*. You can do zis, yes-yes?"

There was a smile in his eyes, but the simple lack of emotion she could distinguish made Snow shiver, as though he wore something that *resembled* a smile but had been borrowed from someone else. "Yes. I am a light sleeper, usually. What happened to me? Did you-"

"Before making any wild accuzaaay~tions," Dopey put his hands behind his back and leaned forward, glaring at the young woman still swaying on her feet. "Please be aware that I would never give you any elixirs or potions-"

"I appreciate that-"

"-for free." Dopey finished his thought, turning around and beginning to very slowly walk away. "Follow as you are able. What you are feeling right now has a simple explanation. Zees is your first teleportation, and you traveled a great distance. Both of zose are factors zat weigh in on your speedy recovery. In case you had any questions as to why kingdoms do not simply teleport armies onto the battlefield, you are currently feeling the effects zat keep such fantastic tactics out of reach. For now."

"Side effects of teleportation include…" As the man began to ramble on, his voice slowly faded into the distance, Snow did her best to find her shoes, wincing at the sharp ache in her temples as she bent to retrieve them. By the time she managed to set foot out the door, the monkey-masked man was nearly at the end of the hall, and she had to rush to catch up—nearly losing the contents of her stomach as she did so.

The stairs they walked down *creaked* beneath their feet as they descended farther into the shadows. Only as they reached the landing did Snow begin feeling well enough to start looking around and taking in her surroundings. Beyond the lantern she only now realized Dopey was carrying, every other light source in view was on the move. "Are we… underground?"

"Do not *concern* yourself with where we *are*." The more he spoke with Snow, the less of an accent he seemed to have, as though he were adjusting to her speech patterns incredibly rapidly. "You only need to have a thinky-think about what we are *doing*."

"Which is what?" Snow inquired sharply, feeling rather prickly over her current situation.

"False. What is what. Which is which. Do not do the strange, tricksy-mixy wordplay of your home kingdom and think you can tomfool me."

The headache she had hoped was gone twinged through her mind as Snow took a long, deep breath. "What I mean to say is, what sort of influence are you trying to teach me?"

"Ahh… yes." Dopey rolled his shoulders, twitching spasmodically as though he were preparing to ingest a particularly delicious treat. "Yes, that. It is so *cutesy-cute* how the others in our little group keep teaching you *low-impact* influence. How to speak to a room. *Mmmyes*. How to stand just right to draw attention. Oh, how do I get people to *like* me and *respect* what I do for a living?"

The surprisingly vicious little man barked out a condescending laugh. "No, here you will be learning *higher-order* influence. If I had to reduce the incredibly potent concepts to a single overarching term, I suppose *subversive* influence would be the best way to describe it. While you are here, I will be teaching you how to undermine a person's ability to *resist* your influence. We will not be inspiring people through positions or happy-slappy examples. No… here you will achieve compliance through manipulation or incapacitation. A *guarantee*, not a wishy-washy wishy-wish."

"I… I don't want to learn this," Snow directly stated, signifying her absolute refusal by not taking another step even as Dopey continued moving forward. "I *won't* learn this."

"No?" Dopey had a strange lilt to his voice as he turned to regard her almost pityingly. "You *vo~on't*? Fine. If you don't even understand what is being done to *you*, you will never resist it. When you leave my halls, without learning what I have to teach, proud little Princess Snow will never hear from me again. Not because I will avoid you, no. It is because you will have no hope in withstanding the subtle machinations of *Queen Kat.*"

He barked those words loudly, and Snow gasped in shock as there was an immediate tingle on her skin—what she'd come to recognize as powerful magic washing over her. Dopey looked up, where a bright spot of light was shining above them, the powerful scrying magic Queen Kat had at her fingertips punching a hole through the distance between them so she could peek through.

"Oh, yes, look at that. So very nice, powerful, magical…" Dopey lifted his hand and snapped his finger, and the mirror forming in the air shattered and vanished as though it had never existed. "Yet ultimately useless. A child's plaything, useful in this little kingdom only because you are so far behind the curve. Just as you will be, should you make these angry-baby tantrums and refuse the teaching keeping you alive and in control of your own faculties."

"Can you…" Snow grit her teeth and balled up her fists as she tried to contain her rapidly changing emotions. "Can you teach me how to stay in control, without having to learn how to do those things to other people?"

"Can you paint me an orange, without knowing the color palette description of the fruit?" Dopey scoffed at her naivete. "How would you choose what to use? Its shape? How would you know you are about to eat one, if you never knew its citrusy scenty-smell in the first place? That's right… you would need to rely on someone else telling you at all times. Princess, you cannot afford to hire me to safeguard you at all times. Frankly, even if you could, it would be a step down for me. Getting tossed out would make me an Ov-verzeer. Understand? Perhaps? Your language lacks, mmm, complexity."

He turned and began his slow walk, the soft glow of his lantern swaying back and forth as he shuffled along. "As I was saying, subversive influence has… mmmyes, let's list each of the lower-order influences within them. Alchemical pacifying influence to dull the senses and remove resistance from your more *rebellious* subjects. Insidious influence, something your queen is currently proving quite adept at. It's a slow-acting, creeping type that takes a long time to establish. But once it's there… *ooooh*-hoo-hoo-hoo. It's nearly impossible to remove without eliminating the sourcey-source."

"Erosion of will…" Dopey turned to glance at Snow, who was ever so reluctantly trailing along behind him. "Even the *strongest* eventually fall in line, don't they?"

Snow was glad for the first time of the ever-present darkness, as her angry flush was harder to see in the flickering lamp light. Not having anything pleasant to say to the man, she simply held her tongue and waited. The guildmaster grunted approvingly, and to her surprise, bent down, pulling on a ring and motioning for her to step closer.

"Downward, *ever* downward from here, my rebel queen."

Snow peered into the hole left behind by the trapdoor, but there was nothing to see but a pit of inky blackness. A damp odor wafted up, not quite foul, but certainly on the edge of it. Snow crouched and felt around until she found the first cold metal rung driven into the side of the hole, slowly beginning her descent. As her head dropped below the surface, the darkness swallowed her whole, making each step down slightly more terrifying than the next.

Only when Dopey sidled into the hole as well, his lantern lighting up the carved space, did she allow herself to breathe a sigh of relief. Reaching the bottom, she carefully tested her footing, making sure she wasn't on a platform and about to fall. Snow stepped aside to allow Dopey to land next to her, his boots splashing a thin spray of water from where he stood.

"Onward, zen."

The tunnel soon opened into a vast chamber, and Snow's eyes went wide as she took in the sight of a vaulted ceiling arching high above, a single orb shimmering with magical light floating in the center. The huge sphere cast a pale glow over what was no less than an entire underground city—and a full city it was. Even from where they stood, the princess could see people moving through the space in a quiet frenzy, visiting booths selling all manner of items.

"Here are the rules," Dopey's words were barely above a whisper. "Never speak louder than a calm conversational tone. There are *things* in the darkness that react *poorly* to loud noises. Speak to no one unless they are selling goods you wish to know more about. Anonymity is part of the service we offer here. Lastly, wear this mask at all times, unless given permission to take it off. It will not only protect you from some of the, hmm, *potions* I will be teaching you about, but will also mark you as one of my people. Wearing that, you will have no trouble from *anyone*. Not here."

Snow took the monkey half-mask with nerveless fingers, not saying a word as she lifted it to her face. It glowed with a subtle green light before adhering to her skin perfectly without need for straps or attachments. "What am I looking at, Dopey?"

"The only place in the world where you can purchase everything from unicorn and qilin horns, phoenix feathers, dragon scales, all the way to crocodile tears and puppy dog tails," Dopey explained with intense pride.

"Things no one should possess, pulled from the most innocent or powerful beings. Things no one should trade," Snow responded in a low tone, her stomach twisting as she witnessed secret after secret she didn't want to hold in her mind.

"Exactly that, and so much more, my rebel queen." When Dopey looked at her again, the light in his eyes sent a deep chill through her heart. "We have everything your dark little heart could ever wish for… for a price."

"Welcome… to the *Night's Heart Exchange.*"

CHAPTER
TWENTY-SEVEN

Snow followed Dopey through the dimly lit city, keeping an eye on anyone they passed, only to feel a mounting frustration when she realized each of them wore some kind of mask or disguise. "I'm surprised more people aren't carrying lanterns like you are. Even with the glow from the crystal above us, it's still pretty dark in here."

"Wearing a lantern makes you a *guide*," Dopey told her without actually explaining anything. "It is not a service most people are willing to pay for. Only the most wealthy or the weakest will ever do so. So far, at least fourteen people have not attacked you for whatever you might carry, as you not only are with me, but are wearing the mask of a trainee *guide*."

Snow decided to hold any further questions, and their journey progressed without speaking to anyone else. Dopey offered a few nods to shadowy figures standing in archways, but he never stopped moving. He threaded through the warren of roads with the ease of someone who belonged there, who'd come into their own on these darkened streets. Even with his bobbing lantern highlighting his position, Snow struggled to keep up, as her eyes were drawn to every stall, every whispered transaction.

"I want to memorize it all… who are these people circumventing the king's justice? Then again… are we even in my kingdom right now?" The details she managed to capture blurred together, painted in a monochrome coloration, thanks to the minimal light in the area.

"You are indeed within the borders of your own kingdom," Dopey replied to her after she'd hurried to catch up as he rounded a corner. She stumbled backward, trying not to run into the stationary man suddenly facing her. "Were you to try to escape the borders of your lands, the ward structure would act to 'protect' you. The queen would be alerted to your location, and you would be deposited in a 'safe' house by the magic, waiting for the royal guard to collect you. Even worse would be attempting to teleport you away, as you would be dropped into the center of the palace, no matter what you had as your original destination."

Even with all the information he was lavishing on her, Snow could only focus on a single question, "How did you hear me? I was all the way back there, and I barely *whispered* my thoughts."

"The walls that can hear your whispers are the first to betray you. Good thinky-reminder for when you are back in'za palace." Dopey tapped on the wall as he spoke, and it shimmered with a soft light, outlining a doorway that swung open silently. They stepped into a building, the room beyond the door smaller than she'd expected, though that may have been because of the ornate table sitting in the center taking much of the space.

It was carved from stone, the tabletop as smooth as cut glass, and its legs carved with golden swans fighting against each other—the clearest depiction of the swan wars she had ever seen outside of paintings. Snow's gaze trapped around the room, finding shelves lining the walls that were packed with the vials, jars, and bottles waiting to be filled. The scent in the air hit her next, bitter and cloying, chemicals and cleaners in one. Most concerning to Snow was that, as she tried to catalog the potions, she found she didn't recognize a single one of them.

"I'm surprised I didn't see anything like this in Doc's offices. He has to be working on a way to cure… I'm assuming these are all poisons?"

Dopey's face twisted with disdain, and he looked like he would've spit were it not for the mask blocking his mouth, his words falling from his lips hot and angry. "Now *zer* is a man who's wasted his talents. Ah, don't look at me like that. A man can know many things, but if he willfully ignores all the tools at his disposal, what can a peer have for him but *frustration*? Look at this… these concoctions would make Doc's job simple, yet he refuses out of a misplaced sense of 'right-eousness'. You are fighting a Witch in a fortified location. Tell me, my rebel queen, does *not* ze ends justify ze means?"

Snow opened her mouth to answer, but apparently the question had been rhetorical, shown by Dopey strolling through the room, opening a small door containing a spiral staircase descending even further into the ground. "Zis is *your* room-"

"I hope you mean at the bottom of the stairs." Snow couldn't think of any other way to show her displeasure with the situation than sniping at Dopey anytime she had the opportunity, but her barbed words seemed to bounce off him without being acknowledged in the slightest.

"Here you will spend your days until I am confident in your ability to remember each and every poison, potion, and dangerous substance that might be used to weaken your will when you fight against the queen." Dopey stepped out of the way, gesturing at the stairs with a flourish. "Consider this my gift to you, as I will not even charge you for my time or a safe place to sleep within the exchange."

Deciding against pressing her luck further, as she had no idea how she would manage to pay for whatever services he decided to charge for—let alone how to escape this place without his help—Snow simply nodded and got onto the stairs, descending to take a glance at the tiny space where she was expected to live, sleep, and learn. There was a cot tucked against the far wall, a flimsy thing with a straw-filled mattress. There was a small basin for washing and a single candle in a sconce fused to the wall.

The room smelled of bitterness and sharp chemicals, a cloying scent of decay; whereas the same smell in the house of healing had inspired feelings of hope and cleanliness. Moving back up the stairs, she found Dopey waiting for her with a large book filled with tiny writing. "Each page gives the name of one of these substances, its characteristics, as well as its effects. Normally, our *valued customers* would be using this book as a catalog to make purchases, but it will serve equally well as a primer for your education."

Dopey moved to a well-lit corner of the room, hung his lantern from a hook in the ceiling to brighten it even further, and pulled on a rung built into the wall. A small table and chair folded out, forming into a desk as it landed on the ground. "Let us not waste any time, like you did shaking off your simple motion sickness this morning. Inform me when you have memorized the book, and we will move on to the next step. This will be your study space; use it well."

"I'm meant to stay here and do nothing but read?" Only a year or so ago, that would've been a delightful invitation. But after so long spent on the road, working her body into the best state it had ever been, the thought of sitting potentially weeks on end sounded terrible.

"Not just read, *memorize*. What is this looky-look? Why do you sigh and wring your hands like a widow hoping for a pension?" Snow could see that the man was genuinely confused by her reaction, only then understanding how few normal people he must interact with in his daily life.

"I need movement, or I will backslide with my health,"

Snow explained succinctly, seeing the light of understanding appearing in Dopey's eyes.

"Yes! Very good. I forgot you are not accustomed to our ways. Here…" Dopey moved over to a shelf, carefully selecting three bottles, looking at a fourth but ultimately reluctantly putting it away before grabbing a different one. "Infusion of Bodily Stasis. Take one of these each day, and your body will be unable to grow or wither. Your muscles will not get sore. They will not lose strength, but any attempts at growing stronger will also fail."

He set the next bottle down. "These are known as fasting pills. They go along with the first, but must be taken at *least* an hour after. If you are uncertain, wait longer. Do *not* take them too close together. This will supply your body with everything it needs to maintain itself *exactly* as it is now and nothing more. This one here is a… simple stimulant, which will increase your focus and remove much of your need for sleep."

"Lastly, and I am giving this to you now as a sign of my good intentions… this is a *cleansing tablet*. There are no side effects to the first pills, none that you should be concerned with at least, but upon absorbing little washy-washy here, it will scrub the interior of your body from head to toe." Leaning forward, he locked eyes with her. "Do *not* take it unless you are alone. A Duchy couldn't afford this casually. I recommend being near a large water source like a river to quickly cleanse yourself as any remnant impurities are flushed out of your pores."

"Is there any reason, other than greed, why I shouldn't have other people around when I take it? Wouldn't it be-"

"Trust me when I say, they would never look at you the same way again." Dopey stepped away, moving back to the counter where he had set down a bottle he originally intended to hand over. "At the end of your time here, you will be taking this solution. It is an alchemically engineered concoction that will selectively remove some of your memories. You will not remember anything about how to get here, the features of anyone you've seen, or how to navigate the exchange. Standard procedure for those who do not *appreciate* the services we provide."

Snow's nose twitched as she tried to maintain a straight face, her quiet plan of finding and destroying this den of darkness hitting its second roadblock. "What about the things I learn here? Will any of that be affected?"

Dopey shook his head carelessly. "Certainly not. What would be the point of teaching you, only to take it away? Plus, this will serve as a way for you to learn what is possible when you reach out to us in the future to use our services. We certainly wouldn't want to put a barrier to entry in front of a returning customer."

The D'wharve walked away without another word, going directly to the table and twitching his hands, somehow summoning dozens of bottles off the shelves. He started working immediately, combining powders, liquids, then chopping what seemed to be nothing more than a common onion into fine slices. Snow wasn't certain if he was making a potion or his dinner, but either way, she had work to do.

Before anything else, she took one of the 'Bodily Stasis' pills and looked around for something to drink with it, only for a glass of water to fly across the room and slide across her desk, only saved from going over the edge by her quick reflexes.

"Apologies, I wasn't paying much attention to you." Dopey's distracted murmur came from across the room. "The water is perfectly pure at this stage in your training."

"That doesn't inspire confidence, Dopey." Snow sighed when her words elicited no response. Tossing back the first pill, she began her task immediately, hoping to get out of this terrible place as quickly as she could.

On the first page of the book was a vial filled with a golden liquid, the details done so perfectly it looked like it was laying on the desk in front of her. The liquid inside of the specifically shaped glass was a gold so deep it looked like nothing more than molten amber. She whispered the name out loud, working to commit it to memory. "*Stiller Tropfen*. Potent medicinal scent, wilted herbs, and burnt sugar. Effect, a single drop dulls the senses completely. Pain, fear, pleasure, all smoothed into nothingness. Perfect for moving soldiers into a combat situation that seems hopeless, to avoid a mutiny. By the *system*…"

There was an antidote listed, just in case someone took too much of the potion. Snow studied the page carefully but couldn't find an explanation for what happened if someone did take too much of it—something she assumed could very well happen when the person taking it had no fear of consequences.

"It's not written down?" The princess shook her head sadly. "I'm sure they know, they probably just don't *care*. Abyss, day *one*, and I already miss Doc terribly."

TWENTY-EIGHT

SHE QUICKLY FELL into an endless routine. Days blurred together... or perhaps weeks? Snow couldn't be sure, as the dimness of the underground city never changed. The lantern above her never went out, and the candles in the room never seemed to be needing replacement. The only way the princess was able to mark time was by the cycles of exhaustion that pushed past the stimulant she'd been given, giving her just enough time to get to her room and collapse onto the straw caught before being yanked into a fitful slumber.

Even in her dreams, the names, effects, and descriptions of the myriad poisons and potions haunted her.

"*Stechen.*" Snow whispered in her sleep, dreaming of the vivid pink powders with particles as fine as pollen that could be thrown in the air to affect dozens at a time. A single grain on the skin would bring hours of burning pain and painful welts. The antidote, *Entlastung*, was a murky yellow salve that caused the entirety of the hours-long pain to be felt in under a minute, but it *did* expunge the poison at the end. Some considered the cure worse than the disease, but for those who could endure one long minute without breaking, it was an effective option.

She shifted on her cot, dream shifting into a nightmare as she relived her experience with *Der Seufzer*, the sigh of surrender. Dopey had taken her out of the small room for the first time when she had gotten to that page, on what he called a 'field trip for good behavior'.

"Der Seufzer is a wonderful thing for those who need it. It is a releasing of heavy-sad breath one does not want to hold. A laying down of burdens they have carried too long." Dopey had brought her into a large room, where dozens of chaise lounge chairs were set up. The room had been eerily silent, even though every single one of the chairs had someone laying on them. "When mixed with water and set to a gentle boil, *the sigh* can be absorbed over hours instead of minutes."

Snow's eyes had grown used to the dark, allowing her to notice a detail Dopey had been glossing over. "Are... are they *all* missing their pinkies?"

The sight made Snow recoil away, as the lowest form of a binding system oath was a pinky promise. When someone broke that oath, the system would literally cause them to lose the digit—making a missing pinky the number one indicator of an untrustworthy person, someone who was willing to make a severe, extremely serious promise, then break it, even while knowing the consequences.

"Perhaps they told someone they would not spend their time here. It is not my fault they possess a... weak will." Dopey shrugged off her horrified glare. "Don't think I haven't been useful to you. The queen has been throwing her efforts behind poisoning the people rallying behind you in your kingdom, and my people have been hard at work countering her efforts with our own. For instance, there have been many who are quite, *quite* loud-outspoken about you and your efforts. Some had been all but leading the charge to convince their friends to join your stepmother's ranks as Huntsmen. After a good *sigh* of relief, they no longer worry about things above their station."

"Tell me there's an antidote for this." Snow managed to spit out what she thought of as a reasonable question, holding her stomach so she didn't vomit from what she was seeing.

Yet, Dopey only appeared perplexed at her disgust with him. "Why would one need an antidote for joy? Does someone need a balm to stop skipping, laughing? Look at how relaxed they are. This is what they want."

"This isn't real. They aren't themselves." Snow leveled her finger at the D'wharve, not for the first time lamenting that he'd taken her hidden dagger while she was recovering from teleportation sickness, citing a no-weapons policy when she asked after it. "You say you are fighting the queen by using things like this? You will never again do such a thing in my kingdom. Certainly not in my name."

"As you wish, Snow Weiss. Not in your name, not on your behalf," Dopey's voice didn't raise, his tone didn't fluctuate, yet still Snow shivered as he finished, "but never again? To that, I cannot promise. I have a business to run, and if I want to move higher up the ranks, to oversee more than one little kingdom? You must understand, I need to show winning success beyond that of my competitors."

The memory faded away as Snow rolled over in her cot, teeth grinding in fury as she roused herself enough to break out of the memory, only to sink back into a deeper sleep, thinking over the litany of poisons and tonics in her mind.

Each day started the same, all the way until she could verbatim explain the effects of each of the items shown in the catalog. Then Dopey increased the difficulty, pulling out the actual vials and uncorking them, at least when the smell alone wasn't enough to cause her harm.

"What is zis?"

"*Gleitender Schlaf*," Snow would answer through gritted teeth. "A sleep draught. Instant, dreamless. The antidote is *Weckruf*, a sharp-smelling powder that stings the sinuses."

"Güd."

So went her training, day after day. To her, the worst part was how her senses adapted. At first, each new item was an assault, acrid scents, burning sensations, cloying tastes as he began slipping poisons into her drink. Snow was forced to recognize which poison had been given to her, then quickly find the antidote among the shelves. When she was unable to do so, she almost invariably passed out, only to wake up an unknown amount of time later, sick from the aftereffects of the belated application of the restorative Dopey would have forced down her throat.

But over time, they became just another afterthought, a lingering taste she would recognize as something she needed to remove from her system. Her understanding of how to keep herself alive grew exponentially, as did the relaxed way she searched and managed to restore herself over time.

Once she had gotten a handle on even this version of what the guildmaster had to teach her, he began adding in lectures on how they could be used, ways that she could turn each of these horrors into power for herself as an influencer and eventual queen. His voice was always a constant, patient drone, as if teaching history or arithmetic to a bored group of school children.

"Remember! The true power of poisons is not in lethality, but in their promise." To emphasize this point, he held up a vial of dark blue liquid. "*Kalter Griff.* It makes the limbs go cold and numb. This is not fatal, but is instead a promise of what could come next. A hint of what you are willing to do is often more powerful than the act itself. After all… if you were able to poison them once without them noticing, with this, you are informing them that you could do it again, even if they were wary from then on."

Snow couldn't deny the logic of his words, though each day she swore to herself that she would only ever use this knowledge to keep herself and other people alive and safe from these magical concoctions. For now, she would keep her

mouth shut while clenching her fists, the weight of her responsibility to her people pressing down on her.

Finally, she reached her breaking point. Snow didn't even
realize how much she'd been learning, and how dark the
knowledge truly was, until the system itself sent her a message.
Her left arm *burned*, drawing a gasp out of her as she looked
down at the *green* words scrawling out across her flesh.

New optional modifier unlocked for skill: Influential Aura!

*Boost the power and efficacy of your aura by [1000%] by combining
your influence with alchemical means. Your followers will never abandon
you, unto death. You will never have a dissenting opinion nor need to
worry about another person's point of view. Would you like to add this to
your current skill, increasing the number of modifiers to five and
upgrading it to a Legendary skill?*

"-this, my rebel queen, is why you should allow us to
openly sell this-"

"No." Snow's voice was firm, resolute as she shut down his
wheedling sales pitch while at the same time refusing the boost
in power offered by the system. She had finally been shaken
out of her complacency by being offered a skill clearly
designed to eventually make her a full-blown Witch, and she
wasn't about to be lured back into it. "*Never.*"

"But so many of your people lose their cute little pinkies
over it," he told her with feigned sadness, hard eyes boring
into her. "Don't you care about how they will *suffer?*"

"I do." Snow slowly stood up from the table, swallowing
hard as she faced the man who wielded a vague yet immense
amount of power. "But I will help them by following that trail
of lost pinkies and destroying those who are peddling these
wares."

"Now, now-"

Snow cut off his condescending words before he could get

more of them out, "You are a parasite in my kingdom, creating ever more parasites. I don't care that you're running a market for which there will always be a demand. I understand that there will always be people who want this, but I will *always* fight against it. If I have any opportunity to do so, I will run this entire organization out of my kingdom or *burn it* to the ground."

"Ah. You are angry with me." The guildmaster watched her carefully. "But I am merely providing a service. If it were not me, someone else would. At least *I* keep things controlled, regulated. *I* give help where I can, and make sure those who start along this path understand what they are getting into. That is, I make sure they are told in no uncertain terms. You see, *child*, life has a way of pushing people-"

"Then they need allies who will stand with them against the storm." Snow put her hands on her side, stance resolute and unwilling to back down from her proclamation. "Every bent copper I can rip away from the Night's Heart Exchange, I will devote to the houses of healing to undo the harm you have done to my people."

"Big words... *Princess*." Dopey seethed in return, finally rising to her inflammatory remarks. "Yet how are you-"

"This I swear. Cross my-"

"*No!*" The D'wharve stepped forward and slapped her hands out of the air, forcing his palm over her mouth before she could make the most serious oath to the system possible. "No... Princess. I feel your conviction. But do not make an oath against me. Not here. Not in a place where doing so would turn thousands of people against you in an instant. There are some things even *I* cannot protect you from... and invoking the system in this place would bring them *all* down upon you. A compromise, please."

Snow trembled in rage as he pulled his hand away slowly, clearly ready to slap it back over the red mark already forming if she tried to finish her vow. "What sort of compromise would you possibly think I would be willing to make, Dopey?"

"Exile."

Snow blinked uncomprehendingly as the guildmaster stepped back, giving her some space to think.

He clarified after a moment, "You have seen, tasted, and smelled the immense amount of effort that goes into training my *guides*. Let us make an accord. I will continue to supply what is needed, what you will allow, to your kingdom and your houses of healing. I understand you eventually will try to—*heh* —sorry, it's just funny that you think you will be *able*... *ahem*. You will *try* to come after us. Scary-fear I feel in my heart. As payment for my services, once you've *left this place*, you will swear to *exile* any of my people from your borders you manage to catch."

"What would stop them-"

"In return, as I said, I will continue funding the supplies. I will also swear that they will be transferred to a separate group, not only unable to return to your kingdom, but unable to do any work that would send deadly poisons or other such back here." Dopey locked eyes with her. "Iz a good deal, no? Manage to catch enough, and all who remain are those who are working to supply restoratives to your people! Yup-yup, we shake on it?"

Snow breathed hard for a few moments, doing her best to push her own emotion out of the negotiation and think of the best outcome for her kingdom. "Getting rid of them from here only makes them someone else's problem-"

"Exactly! We'll just let someone *else* deal with it." Dopey's words were sharp, filled with warning. "I will not offer you a better deal than this."

Snow took a deep breath, thinking furiously, but slowly began to nod. "So long as I have your oath in return, then I can accept this outcome. You have a deal."

"Iz a lovely thing to have. I *love* deals." Dopey instantly relaxed, a small smile on his face as he stepped back to his position at the table. He turned as Snow's footsteps rang through the area, quickly coming up behind him. Spinning around, he dropped into a defensive position, only for the speed-walking princess to move past him and pluck a bottle off the shelf. "What are you doing? That is-"

"I can't stand being here another minute, Dopey." The princess popped the bottle open, having a perfect under-standing of what dosage to imbibe. "I will honor the terms of our deal, so long as you do the same. This is goodbye, and I hope to never lay eyes on you again, unless it's to watch with great relief as you're being thrown out of my kingdom... never to return."

Before she could change her mind or allow her current instructor to protest, she downed the contents of the bottle.

The world went dark, accompanied by the sensation of falling a great distance... only to begin floating to rise above it.

CHAPTER
TWENTY-NINE

"—SHE's been controlling him, and us, for years! Snow… she's a *Witch!*"

As Snow woke up, now used to the nightmare—even happy to have it just to hear her sister's voice once more—she was in a place she didn't recognize… again. By the sounds of life outside the thin walls, she could only assume she was back in a city. Whether it was simply the above-ground version of the Night's Heart Exchange, or a different one completely, she wasn't sure.

In fact, she wasn't sure she even cared. Hopping out of bed, Snow was able to mostly ignore the intense motion sickness, as she had definitely suffered worse in the last few… months?

The princess shook off her trepidation, throwing the window open and leaning back in delight as sunlight streamed over her for the first time in who *knew* how long. After basking in the warmth for a protracted pause, she turned to inspect the room in which she had awoken. There were simple items on a table, such as her missing hidden blade cuff—she immediately strapped it to her wrist— a long cloak, and rations enough to last her the day. Her hefty sack of coin made itself known as she pulled the chair out, falling to the floor with a ringing **clink**, leaving only one item of note.

In fact, *a* note.

Your task, should you choose to accept, is to play a game of tag with me. Hide and seek is not enough of a game for me, you see. I say 'choose' to accept, only because Dopey has already informed all of us how you refused further training under him.

Doc was ecstatic.

Any-hachoo~

I'll be at one of these three locations, keeping it nice and easy. Love, Sneezy.

Snow flipped over the note, finding the name of three businesses she had to assume were some kind of taverns or public buildings, along with a name to give when she got there. "Sneezy, huh? This is an interesting method of training, I suppose… maybe I've got them all worried I'll start wars with them if they reveal too much of their business to me?"

Even if that were the case, the princess couldn't find it within her to feel any remorse for how she'd handled the situation with Dopey. In fact, if she were to do it all over again, she would have left immediately after learning what he was doing to her citizens. As she took some time to relax and recover, thinking over the last few months, she found herself idly looking at her arm, wondering if anything had changed in her status.

Advanced Skill gained: Brand Ambassador: Level 1/10
Requirement to advance to level 2: gain 100 followers through the efforts of your Brand Ambassadors. 31/100.

"Huh." Snow was suddenly struck by a concerning thought. "How long was I down in the darkness? I didn't look at my status that entire time… that 'stimulant' Dopey gave me must have had more going on than he explained. But my bard friends got me thirty-one followers in less than the two days that they had the skill package active. I knew they'd be a good choice."

Having ordered her thoughts, centering herself, she found that she was pleased with the decisions she had made about the person she wanted to be, Snow reached for a pack of food, only to displace a small, delicately wrapped package that clattered to the table. Picking it up carefully and unwrapping it, she was glad she had started there. Inside was the cleansing tablet, as well as a short written statement informing her that it was recommended not to ingest it within twelve hours of the last time she'd eaten food.

Deciding to get as clean as possible, hopefully ridding herself of every last bit of filth Dopey had convinced her was necessary, Snow grabbed a few coins out of her bag. "Find a river, or failing that, pay for a bathhouse. Only *after* that will I move on to my next tasks."

After hiding the sack of coins under a loose floorboard and shifting some furniture around to make its location less obvious, Snow stepped out of the building she had woken up in, finding herself in the heart of a city she didn't recognize. Shrugging her shoulders, she murmured to herself and started her search. "Bathhouse it is. If the result is as bad as Dopey alluded, I'll have to make sure to leave a generous tip for whoever has to clean up after me."

As she walked along the bustling street, the sunlight bathed her in a type of warmth she hadn't quite realized how badly she had missed. It was a stark contrast to the cold, shadowy underworld she had just left behind, and she loved every *moment* of it. The cobbled streets were alive with people going about their days, the sharp calls of merchants, the clatter of hooves, and the indecipherable roar of people, *hundreds* of people, speaking at the same time. "No bizarre monsters hiding in the darkness waiting to pounce on anyone who gets too loud. What a strange thing to *get* to be happy about."

As she walked, she allowed her instincts to guide her, using the skills she had honed with her teachers over the last long... months? Had it been a year yet? More? Eyes flicking from one passerby to another, the princess noted the subtle shifts in posture, tension, and shoulders, and the stares that lingered just a moment too long. As Ned had once told her, everyone was telling a story, if you knew how to read it—and she did.

An older man with a stiff gait was looking for something he had lost. No... someone who was late without an excuse. His daughter out past the agreed end time of a date? He didn't seem concerned, only annoyed, which helped Snow keep her smile strong. A group of women leaned close together as they shopped, conversation animated but furtive— clearly they were passing along gossip, or perhaps something a bit more concerning, by the way just a *bit* too much of the whites of their eyes were showing.

A child darted through the crowd, hand brushing lightly against belts—a pickpocket, young but skilled. He had been having a profitable day, going by the way he kept his expression carefully neutral, yet the corner of his lips kept twitching upward. She checked her own pouch, keeping a careful eye on the crowd as she absorbed every detail, anchoring herself more firmly in the moment, all the while reminding herself that she belonged out here in the world and not hidden away in darkness.

Deciding she needed to ask some questions if she was going to get anything done, Snow stopped at a small tea shop tucked into a quiet alcove, choosing one of the small tables on the patio and ordering a deep green tea. The scent of spices and herbs wafted around her, yet another change between yesterday and today. Calming, pleasant smells, instead of astringent, harsh ones. Soon a cup releasing a spicy, minty fragrance was set on her table, and she lifted it to her nose, breathing in deeply.

Frankly, she wasn't certain Dopey had truly left her alone yet. As Snow remembered how Grumpy had tested her well after she thought she was done with him, she made sure to pick apart the combination of smells, pour a bit of the liquid out on the table and inspect its clarity, and even requested a fresh cup when she noticed a stain on the ceramic of the mug itself. Finally taking a sip, her lips pressed into a firm line as she lamented the fact that she would likely never be able to fully trust her food and drink again—not after what she'd witnessed in the Night's Heart Exchange.

Allowing the mug to warm her hands, and the hot beverage to fill her gut with heat, she allowed her gaze to drift over the patrons of the tea shop, catching snippets of conversation. As she had learned from Zed, the trick to remaining invisible to others was to seem relaxed, perhaps even bored, even while every *fiber* of her attention was focused on her surroundings.

"-fishing boats didn't come back today. Harbormaster is absolutely beside himself-"

"-patrols increased again? They're claiming it's some kind of rebel activity, but who'd be foolish enough to-"

"-market's been bustling! That ship that came in was filled with all sorts of rare-"

"Did you hear?" Snow's ears twitched as she focused on the conversation spoken in a soft voice a few tables over. "Wolf Warband was spotted to the south of the kingdom. Barbarians, raiders this close to our shores, and what's being done about it?"

"I heard they were for hire these days. Pirates or some such. Apparently their leader got himself hitched to someone who's keen to make some coin."

"Mercenaries then," the first spat as he replied. "Probably being sent to soften us up for invasion. We've got the Huntsmen snagging people in the night, rebels fomenting issues in the countryside, and enemies of the kingdom on every side. This is *just* what we need."

The duo went quiet, clearly contemplating the future of the kingdom, before tossing coins to the table and parting ways. Still, from everything going on around her, Snow had managed to learn everything she needed about where she was. "We're still on the coast, so we must be in Magdenburg. We're as far south as we can be while still being within the borders of the kingdom, which means, when I leave here, the only way out is moving closer to the capital. Did they set my route in this way by design?"

As the server came around, all smiles and chipper attitude as she collected Snow's dishes, the princess smiled despite the grim news. She went to leave a handful of copper to show her appreciation, but paused and instead pulled out a large silver coin, laying it on the table but keeping a finger pressed on it as she locked eyes with the lady. "Can I ask a couple of questions? Take a seat."

The server's smile faltered slightly, but between Snow's gentle appearance and the silver coin, she simply nodded and slid into the seat across from the princess. "What can I help you with?"

"Nothing too exotic; I'm just new in town and hoping to get the lay of the land." At Snow's words, the smile returned in full force. "First off, I've been traveling, and I'd rather not say how long it's been since I've had a proper bath. Could you direct me to not the nearest bathhouse, but the *best* one in the area?"

"Oh! Certainly. You don't need to pay me for that, silly." The young woman gave Snow detailed directions, and the princess was pleased to find that she was only a few blocks away. "Anything else I can help you with?"

"Yeah…" Snow steeled herself, "I've been hearing some concerning rumors about Princess Snow. Something about how she was captured?"

"Ah…" the woman fiddled with her apron, taking a deep breath and looking up with a strong gaze. "I've been hearing *different* things. Apparently she fled the castle and is out among the people, trying to build support for her cause. The rumors are *quite* detailed, and I've been making sure anyone supporting her is getting extra honey in their tea."

Snow felt a warmth in her stomach that had nothing to do with her finished beverage. "I'd like to give you a small gift to help you out over the next couple of days. Something that should get people to leave a bit extra for you, to help deal with the outsized taxes I'm sure you've been paying recently. Would you mind if I used a skill on you real quick?"

"Er…" the server leaned away, uncertain what to say. Snow fully understood, as skills that could be used externally were almost always some kind of combat or bizarre ability given by the system. "What does it do?"

"It will just make you seem nicer, friendlier, and overall more pleasant." Snow selected the server as a target, choosing her as a brand ambassador and passing along Aura of Innocence. "After you choose to activate this, it will only last a couple of days. But if you keep up with what you're doing, and you like its effects, I'll make sure to reactivate it the next time I see you."

The server was quiet for a few moments, clearly reading the information the system gave her about the skill package. In the next moment, the air around the young woman shifted, and when she blinked, it was like seeing a sweet baby calf do the same. "Ooh. This feels *interesting*. Unless it has some strange side effect, I don't mind at all."

By the time the server looked away from the words of the system, Snow had caught her breath and moved past the momentary weakness she always felt after investing so much influence. "Wonderful. Thanks again for the information."

As she walked toward the bathhouse, Snow tried to decide if what she had done was wise. But, a glance at the influence she'd been accruing while underground consoled her: the investment was barely a fraction of what she had available to her, her total collected influence still comfortably above a hundred thousand. Now she just had to find out if her hare-brained idea would be worthwhile or not.

When she got to the bathhouse, a low, wide building built from dark stone matching the exposed bedrock near the base of every other building she'd seen, Snow had to hold herself from rubbing her hands together in anticipation. Steam was curling invitingly out from small vents in the roof, and the promise of sinking into a hot bath, cleansing herself inside and out—not to mention following the treatment by eating proper food in who *knew* how long—proved almost too much for the princess. She rushed into the building, only to be greeted by an attendant who choked off whatever he'd been about to say as she pressed a gold coin into his palm.

"I want a private room, the largest tub you have. Not the largest *single-person* tub you have, the *largest* tub in the bathhouse." Seemingly unable to muster any words, the attendant barely managed to tear his eyes off the golden coin long enough to lead her down a hallway lined with wooden doors. He stopped at one which seemed slightly grander than the others, pushing it open to reveal a thick cloud of fog that poured out into the hallway, clearing just enough to reveal a sprawling room.

In the center was a massive, sunken tub clearly carved from the natural stone of the area, easily large enough for ten people. The water shimmered invitingly as it reflected the flickering light of oil lamps set around the room. Snow needed no instructions, simply stepping in and gently closing the door behind her, making the attendant rapidly step back as she firmly latched it and threw the bolt to ensure her privacy.

Shedding her garments, she held the cleansing tablet out of the water as she eased in, sighing in delight as the warmth seeped into her muscles—muscles that had been held in stasis through alchemical means. While she wanted to relax, simply take time to let go of the tension that had been building up in her, Snow decided that would have to happen another time.

She unwrapped the tablet once more, hesitating for a heartbeat as the large, unassuming pill reacted to the humidity in the air. "Whatever is about to happen... if even *Dopey* warned me, it's definitely going to be far from pleasant. He spoke in positive terms about *Stechen*, and that can cause agony for *days*."

Only the thought of taking this and being done with Dopey, finished with any lingering taint he had allowed to accrue in her body, convinced Snow to grit her teeth and pop the tablet into her mouth. She swallowed, grossed out for a moment that she needed to drink a mouthful of bath water to get it down, but reminded herself that anything in it would be cleansed away momentarily.

A slow, creeping squeeze began to build in her stomach. It rapidly spread outward, causing her muscles to tighten as though she were clenching in preparation of running from a bear or some other terrifying creature. She shifted uncomfortably in the water as her clenching muscles heated up, and a sweat that had nothing to do with the hot water broke out along her brow.

The heat turned to fire. Her skin prickled like a thousand *thousand* needles had pierced every inch of it at once. Snow's vision blurred as the chemical process reached her eyes, tears rolling as she blinked in a vain attempt to clear them. Wiping them away, she gasped in horror at the black streaks left on the back of her hands. "I've contracted *the dark sweat*! I need to get to a healer..."

Halfway through trying to launch herself out of the tub, the savage heat caused her legs to clench and spasm. A sudden acrid smell filled her nostrils, like a combination of burning metal and spoiled herbs. A black, oily substance began floating to the surface of the water, and she looked on in disgust as the pristine bath rapidly darkened, inky plumes swirling around until even the farthest reaches were tainted. Her heart hammered rapidly, adrenaline pumping through her from the combination of fear and pain as the tablet cleansed deeper, reaching into every cell in her body, passing through and leaving every iota of her feeling scoured, scraped raw.

Her vision swam, and she lost a few moments, coming to consciousness floating on the surface of the water as the interior of her head was swept through.

The concoction went ever deeper. Sharp pain faded away, replaced with deep aches as impurities were dragged kicking and screaming from her bones, blood, and even her thoughts, going by how she kept *waking up* on the surface of the black water. A final wave of heat surged through, less intense, but just as thorough—as though the tablet had finished cleaning and now was simply polishing a silver chalice.

Then it was done.

Snow reached for the edge of the tub, feeling hollow, emptied out. But as she drew a deep breath, then another, the emptiness shifted. Slowly she was filled with clarity, lightness… the princess pulled herself out of the rancid tub, finding her way over to a mirror hidden around a bend. She gasped at her appearance: practically *bleached* white-jade skin, radiant in a way she had never seen before. Her hair seemed three shades darker black, and her lips were luscious red, like a seashell pulled from the depths of the ocean.

Flexing her fingers, she marveled at the strength strumming beneath the surface. The fog of exhaustion, lingering residue of poisons, and mental weight of her recent troubles —all of it was gone.

"So this is how Dopey tries to buy back my favor? That had to have been at least a Legendary-grade alchemical creation." Wonder tinging her voice, the princess begrudgingly admitted, "I've certainly never felt better in my entire life."

Unable to think of anything *other* than nice things to say about Dopey, Snow instead decided to keep her mouth firmly closed until she had a chance to consider how she would respond to this gift. Glancing in the mirror one last time, she dressed in her dirty clothes before gathering her things and rushing away…

…as it was probably best to be *well* away from the bathhouse before anyone came to check on the state of the tub.

CHAPTER

THIRTY

WAKING UP TO A BRIGHT MORNING, with birds singing and people chattering, put a bright smile on Snow's face as she lazily stretched on the comfortable bed. "Sunshine, laughter, and a bed that isn't a ragged cot in a dark hole. Awesome."

She hopped to her feet, practically flying off the bed, thanks to her muscles seemingly being able to put out more effort with less energy required. She stretched from side to side, skin practically glowing in the sunlight. There was an undeniable lightness to her step as she readied herself for the day, looking forward to meeting her current mentor, Sneezy, for only the second time ever. Just before she stepped into the bustling streets, she glanced at the note once more, rereading the teasing message.

"A game of tag… at least he's fun."

Taking a deep breath, she powered onward, a spring in her step as she walked along with the confidence of someone who'd grown up in the city. But her eyes, trained by four different masters of their crafts, alighted on everything and everyone with practiced precision. "Who among you is going to be the best guide for my day?"

It wasn't long before Snow's gaze landed on a scrawny boy

all but pressing his nose to the glass of a bakery window. He was a picture of hunger, ribs practically visible through his shirt, wearing an innocent, wistful stare that may or may not have been the reason she decided to hire him for the day. Approaching the young man with a warm smile, she crouched slightly to be at his level, lifting the hood of her cloak just enough that he could see her eyes.

"Do you know where the *Green Light Tavern* is?" The boy stared at her, startled that she would speak to him. His eyes crinkled slightly as he took in her shapeless garments, the cloth half-mask of her cloak covering up to her nose, and the makeup she had applied to what little skin was showing to make her appear weathered and somewhat grizzled. The only thing she couldn't easily alter was her voice, though she did her best to make it sound deeper than normal.

He blinked at her a few times, then slowly began to nod. She smiled under her facial covering, making sure it reached her eyes. "How about the *White Snake*? The *Singing Bone*?"

The boy nodded twice more, the confusion in his eyes growing with each subsequent question. As soon as she had confirmation, Snow extended her hand, shifting to pointing at the bakery when he simply ignored the outstretched limb. "I have a deal for you. If you help me find my way around to those places, I'll let you pick out any four things from this bakery. One to eat right away, and one after each stop. What do you think? Sound like a plan?"

His eyebrows flew up, and his mouth dropped slightly. Instead of saying a word, he instead grabbed her outstretched hand and dragged her, laughing, into the bakery. Snow tried to keep up with him, but nearly slipped and fell, thanks to her crouched position as he yanked on her enthusiastically. Inside, the warm aroma of crusty, freshly baked bread and pastries wrapped around them, and Snow couldn't help but inhale deeply as her stomach rumbled to remind her she was past due for filling it.

Wasting no time at all, the boy surprised Snow by pointing out thick loaves of bread rather than sweet pastries. Only the fourth item was different: a large, savory strudel filled with cheese and bits of sausage. Snow got one of those for herself as well, and on impulse, grabbed an extra for the boy.

After paying and stepping out into the street once more, the princess pulled away the layers of thin parchment to pull out the hot treat, handing it over to him as promised. Despite her quiet warning about not burning his mouth, the youth devoured the strudel in seconds as Snow looked on with great concern. As he was finishing the last bite, she tilted her head to the side. "Tell me, what's your name?"

"Joringel." The response came as a whisper, his eyes darting to the road, back to her, then sliding back to stare fixedly into the distance.

"Well, Joringel, I'm sure you're going to be the best guide I could have ever hoped for!" Snow cheerfully called as they began walking down the road. "Do your friends call you Joe? Can I be your friend?"

As he shrugged non-committedly, Snow decided to just go with it and hope it didn't bother him more than he was letting on. "Well, Joe, which one are we going to first?"

"The nearest one is going to be the White Snake," Joe responded, still in a soft, low voice. "Can I ask you questions, as well?"

"You just did!" Snow replied chipperly, though she nodded and motioned for him to keep doing so. "What's on your mind?"

Joe hesitated, sweeping his eyes over Snow once more. "I'm just wondering… why's a lady like you dressed in a disguise and going to a gambling hall? You don't seem like a bad person, and you've got all your fingers, so it's just not making sense to me."

Snow stopped dead, thinking over all of the extra details she'd added to her disguise. Joe flinched away as he realized she was staring at him, snapping her out of her mounting frustration. "Well, I would certainly prefer you speak your mind with me. Could I ask how you know I am not a man?"

"There's a certain *sway* when you walk…" Joe mumbled, going quiet as Snow let out a long-suffering sigh and let her head drop back.

"I learned how to make my disguise from some of the finest bards in the land, learned to walk, and hold different positions with masters of combat. I've studied medicine and poisons under the respective masters of their craft." Snow dropped her face into her hands, slowly shaking her head side to side. "Yet somehow I haven't been able to throw off my habits from the time before all that?"

"Well… there's more than just that." Snow's head shot up from her hands, eyes peeking over the tips of her fingers as she stared at the youngster. Joe pointed at his face. "The system gave me a skill that lets me see a person for who they are."

Snow froze in place as Joe shrugged as though he hadn't just revealed that he had an amazing talent. "Does that mean you can see through any disguise, even illusions? What are the limitations of-"

"No, I mean, I still see your makeup and stuff. But I see you for who you are. At your core. Deep down, most people aren't… pretty." Joe's eyes shyly drifted over to her, then away in an instant. Snow felt herself melt as he spoke, barely able to hold in a soft 'aww' as he continued speaking, not wanting to interrupt the young man who was already clearly nervous about doing so. "It's just that, when people pretend to be someone they're not… I've almost never seen them also be *good* people."

"Oh." That made far too much sense to the princess, and she made a mental note to personally hire this young man to be her advisor when she made it back to the palace. "You see, this disguise is something I need in order to walk around and stay safe. Right now I'm… let's say playing a game of sorts with an acquaintance of mine. I have to find him, and he gave me a few places he is staying to look for him. I'm not going to hurt anyone, and there shouldn't be anyone upset that they can't see through my disguise."

"That last part was a lie, even if you didn't know it," Joe informed her immediately, turning away as her jaw dropped. "The rest of it was true, though, so… let's keep going."

It took everything she had not to immediately start the process of hiring this child and bringing him away with her— a person who could see the hearts of others and know immediately if they were lying? It was far too valuable of a skill not to acquire, and also… Snow winced as she realized the immense burden it must be on someone so young to constantly know each time they were being lied to. Adults lied to children all the time, even if they were doing it for their own good. Suddenly, his thin appearance and ragged state started to make sense.

It was unlikely that many people enjoyed having their falsehoods pointed out so casually.

After leading the princess through a maze of winding streets, Joe stepped aside and gestured casually at a building with a sign carved in a looping pattern. The White Snake was a modest tavern, though its shutters were closed, and its sign was slightly askew. Pushing on the door only caused it to rattle, clearly the building was empty, or at least out of use. Still, she called out, voice echoing slightly as it came back. "Hello? Anyone in there?"

"Sounds pretty empty to me." Joe offered carefully, still not certain how to treat the person he'd been wandering the city with. "Should we go to the next one? The Green Light is closest to here."

Another hour of navigating the twisting maze of streets finally brought them to a tavern that was as bustling as the White Snake had been empty. Snow entered the building, glancing at the full-to-capacity tables occupied by various patrons playing cards or dice games. Most of them were far too occupied to pay the intruding duo any mind, which Snow greatly appreciated. Winding around to the back, where the bar was set up, she approached the bartender, a middle-aged man who greeted her as casually as he would any other customer.

"What's your pleasure, young man?" For a moment, the proprietor's face darkened. "Just so you know, we've got people with the skills to know if you've brought your own cards or weighted dice. We don't take kindly to cheating, but all *I'll* ever do is point it out. The people you're playing with might take a limb or two."

Then he leaned away, breaking back into a wide smile. "But you don't seem like the sort to get into that kind of trouble! I see you've brought your... little brother? If you're here for the wrestling match, you're too early. Seems a bit young to-"

"I'm looking for..." Snow froze in place as her words echoed out. She'd been so focused on deepening her voice to maintain her facade that she hadn't realized that she was practically shouting. Even in the cacophonous establishment, her loud words had drawn some attention. Feeling rather sheepish, she quieted down and asked after the final name that had been on the back of her note. "I'm looking for... Ortrun?"

"Are you asking me or telling me?" The bartender replied with a snort of amusement. "Yeah, he's come and gone already. In fact, you just missed him."

Snow *tsked* in annoyance, wondering how she was supposed to know what Sneezy's schedule looked like. "Any chance you know when he'll be back? Should I... is he a regular? Should I wait for him?"

"Oh, yeah, he's irregular, all right." The bartender chuckled to himself as Snow turned back to check on Joe. When she shifted around again to ask more questions, she found the man looking at her with a perplexed expression. "Hey, you've got something on your cloak."

Snow twisted, pulling on the fabric of her outerwear, blanching as she found a bright purple slash of chalk along the back of it. She gasped in outrage, "A *child's* color? He marked me with-!"

Unable to get another word out, she simply clenched her fists and took a few deep breaths. The bartender, witnessing her fury, tapped on the countertop and reached for something out of sight. "Must be you, then. In fact, Ortrun left a note for someone; told me I'd know who to give it to when I saw them. Purple chalk, purple chalk. Yep, must be you."

The outside of the folded note had a mark the exact shade as the slash across Snow's back, and she felt her face burn as her humiliation was doubled. "Not only did he manage to mark me without me noticing, he *knew* he would be able to do it."

Grabbing the note, she stormed out of the tavern with Joe hot on her heels, waiting until she was outside in the sunlight to open it.

Strolling in blind, what was your plan? No guise can conceal an unready… man?

Snow took a deep breath, having to close her eyes for a few long moments before reading the rest of the note.

I appear to have my work cut out for me-zie! Try again tomorrow; you failed far too easy.
-Love, Sneezy.

THIRTY-ONE

WAKING up to a bright morning with birds singing and people chattering caused an annoyed scowl to paint itself across on Snow's face. She stretched on the comfortable bed, but found no pleasure in the motion. Letting herself be slightly sarcastic, she breathed, "Sunshine, laughter, and a bed that isn't a ragged cot in a dark hole… awesome."

She rolled out of bed, her movements brisk and sharp, landing on her feet and immediately going through her exercise routines. Her muscles still worked with an ease she was unaccustomed to after a full month, the increased efficiency mocking her by making every motion just a *tiny* bit too wide, every attempt at being gentle thwarted as delicate objects were crushed unintentionally. Stretching from side to side, her skin caught the sunlight and reflected onto her cloak, where yet another purple mark was waiting to be washed away, just like every day since the first.

Once she was fully ready for the day, she glanced over at the crumpled paper on the table, faded from having been handled so much as she searched for any sort of clue as to what she was supposed to be doing. She shook her head and scoffed, wrapping her cloak around her tightly before rushing into the bustling streets.

"A game of tag... yeah. Real fun."

Outside of the house she'd begun to call 'hers', the city streets greeted her with familiar chaos. Snow took a calming breath, doing her best to embrace the vibrancy of life around her, instead of letting it feed the frustration she had woken up with. One bright spot was that, near the corner of the street, a familiar figure leaned against the wall, serious eyes scanning the people moving along the street. Joe's gaze flicked over to her, a bright smile breaking through his otherwise somber face.

"Morning, Joe," Snow managed to get out, doing her best to shake off her dissatisfaction with the situation she'd found herself in. He responded with a simple nod, pulling open his pack to reveal a still-warm strudel as well as a rare treat—fresh apples. "Thanks, as per usual. It's still strange to me that you're the one bringing me food now."

"Eh. You're the one who pays for it." Joe shifted uncomfortably as a smile began to grow on Snow's face, as ingesting the food swiftly put her in better spirits. "Where are we going to start today? Green Light? White Snake? Singing Bone?"

"I..." Snow slowly shook her head at the thought of yet again rushing over to one of the possible locations, only to earn herself a purple mark and be sent home in disgrace. "Actually, I was thinking today we could do our *alternative* work."

"To the tea shop, it is," Joe agreed without kicking up a fuss. Why would he? It wasn't often that Snow *didn't* throw herself into whatever task she'd been given, and a day of making pleasant conversation with random people, sipping tea? It would be a nice break for both of their feet. He led the way through the labyrinthian streets, Snow trusting his sense of direction implicitly.

Once more, she thanked the system that she had run into

this youngster. Even now, a month after arriving in the city, Snow found herself getting lost when she ventured on her own into the shockingly inefficient paths consisting of alleyways, arches, and switchbacks they called *roads*. His guidance was the only thing that kept her from tearing out her hair in frustration. After their first day together, she had happily paid him well for his time—hoping to instill in him the knowledge that she was a generous benefactor.

Though she'd never discussed her plans of bringing him back to the palace, it remained her plan for this young man. As they made their way to the tea shop, a place Snow usually only visited every few days instead of making it her main destination, she glanced down at her arm to track the progress of her efforts gifting skills to her server friend, Chrysanthemum. For obvious reasons, she preferred to be called Chrissy.

Skill increase! Brand Ambassador [Level 1 (Minimal) → Level 2 (Limited)]!

Requirement to advance to level 3: gain 350 followers through the efforts of your Brand Ambassadors. 101/350.

"It leveled!" Snow gasped out loud, hopping in place in excitement. "It cost seventy-five thousand influence, but I finally *leveled*! Let's see… oh, it looks like the skill is following the same progression path as the Basic Skill. Thank the system it counts my previous progress toward the next level. When did that happen? I didn't notice, so it must have been while I was asleep."

"Congratulations on the 'ding'." Joe spoke quietly, making Snow realize exactly how large of a scene she was making at that moment. She glanced around but found only smiling faces as other people looked on fondly at her excitement—likely caught up in memories of doing the same.

"Snow, Joe!" Chrissy waved from the patio as the duo walked over. Seeing her face lit up with genuine happiness over seeing them, Snow felt the last vestiges of her dark mood get blasted into non-existence. After waving back, they settled into the nearest unoccupied table, only for the server to appear only moments later, plopping a pot of fragrant mint tea onto the table with a knowing look. "You look like you've had a rough morning. Is it getting better?"

The princess deflated slightly, reaching for the steaming pot with a long, frustrated sigh. "It's been a rough *month*."

Joe tilted his head to the side, a glimmer of a grin showing on his lips. "If I'm being honest, this has been a *fantastic* month. Sorry to hear it's not the same for you."

"Well, meeting the two of you has definitely been a high point." Snow pushed the first cup of tea over to her helper, quickly pouring another cup and breathing in the dense scent.

"It's just that I'm supposed to be *training*. You know… I just feel like Sneezy isn't taking this seriously. So many lives are at stake, and he's having me play hide and seek, only to tell me how badly I failed each day. I just can't see the purpose in all of this." She sipped at the tea, closing her eyes and basking in the delightful flavor. When she opened them, she found both Chrissy and Joe looking at her with slight disappointment. "What?"

"Snow, my sweet friend, if anything… this is on you." Chrissy offered a conciliatory smile as she explained herself. "From what I can see, *you're* the one not taking this process seriously."

Stunned into momentary silence, Snow eventually managed to cough out, "Excuse me? I've never *not* thrown absolutely everything I have into completing my tasks. Every time I have a purple mark put on me and am told to go home… Chrissy, it's devastating. I want to learn, I just don't know what to do. I'm not getting the instruction I need."

"We've talked a lot over the last month, Snow." Chrissy didn't back down even after Snow explained herself as clearly and heartfeltly as she could. "I'm glad you've trusted us with so much, but one thing I've noticed is that, while you are fantastic at completing tasks—even going out of your way to make them happen even if it's terribly inconvenient for yourself—one of the things you're not great at is working with incomplete information."

"Which is exactly what Sneezy's guild is all about, right?" Joe interjected, getting a clap on the shoulder from Chrissy as he sussed out what she was trying to say. "They do scouting, lookout duty, and information gathering."

Chrissy wagged her finger at Snow as she walked away to help another table, "He's right, you know. Maybe instead of throwing yourself at those locations Sneezy is having you go to, you should start making a plan to act with intention. Find a way to expand your talents beyond what you're used to, beyond what's comfortable. What does that look like to you?"

Snow opened her mouth to respond, but Chrissy was already away, making small talk while pouring tea. Closing her mouth before flies could zip in, she looked down and frowned into her teacup. "I'm not trying to be comfortable. I'm *trying* to get better. I just don't know where to go from here."

A soft rustle caught her attention, and she glanced to the side as an object zipped through the air toward her head. Letting out a yelp of surprise, she ducked under the projectile, only for it to twist and come to a rest on her table, bumping against a pastry plate Chrissy head left in preparation of them ordering a treat before leaving. Joe reached forward, picking up the object and revealing it as a folded paper glider. "Looks like you've got mail."

Snow took the paper, unfurling it and smoothing it out as she read over the words written in smudged purple chalk. As soon as she'd gone through it once, her head whipped up, and she began scanning the streets for any sign of the man who was supposed to be her mentor.

"Nothing." Feeling deeply dissatisfied at the knowledge she was likely under constant surveillance, but couldn't spy the

D'wharve in return, she read over the looping handwriting once more, a spark of hope igniting as she did so.

Talking with friends is a good place to start.
You figured out pieces, but not every part.
You're caught in the habit of all or none,
Remember to be a thread, not a drum.
Everyone feels you coming their way,
Influence just <u>one</u>, or you'll catch <u>none</u> every day.

The note wasn't signed, except for a splatter of fluid she assumed had come from someone sneezing. She dropped the paper in disgust, but her mind was already churning with ways she could interpret the hints. "Be a thread, not a drum? What does that mean? I'm already good at influencing people; what is he on about?"

"I think he's trying to teach you how to be quiet." Joe's words drew her gaze, and he wilted slightly under the intensity of her stare. "Not, you know, speaking. More like… you know how everyone always knows exactly where you are when you're in the area?"

"Oh, for-" Snow grumbled as she shifted her mindset, pulling her auras in to enter her version of stealth.

Joe reeled back as if he'd been slapped, almost falling out of his chair as he stared at Snow, rubbing his eyes and doing a double take as the princess shamefacedly admitted, "Yeah, I learned how to pull in my auras a long time ago. I just didn't think it would be necessary in a place like this."

"Snowy! Are you okay?" Chrissy came over at a run, sliding to a stop and looking at the princess with immense concern. "I just… I suddenly felt like something was wrong with you?"

"Well, that at least explains a part of why I've been having such a hard time. I haven't just been failing, I've been failing *loudly*. All I did was close off my aura, Chrissy."

"Wow…" She shook her head in wonder. "I didn't know you could do something like that. Can you still use your skills when you're closed off?"

"Of course I…" Snow thought back to her training, where she'd needed to slip past highly trained warriors, and nodded firmly. "I definitely can."

"A thread…" Joe murmured, causing the other two to glance at him. "Oh, sorry, I was just… you can use your skills like this, but can you *thread* it out? I mean, can you influence just *one* person?"

Certain she had the ability to do so, she demonstrated by glancing at Chrissy and actively attempting to influence the server to look anywhere but at *her*. It worked, but Snow gasped in shock as influence absolutely flooded out of her, a torrential stream of power reminiscent of granting someone a skill via Brand Ambassador. Cutting off her skill, she looked around with wide eyes and realized everyone in the area was… looking anywhere but at her.

"Abyss."

"I'll take that as a no?" Chrissy murmured as Snow's softly spoken curse drew her attention.

"I can't believe this." Snow was practically in shock as the realization hit her. "I've only ever tried to get people to do a single thing at a time, and I was always trying to get *all* of them to do the same thing. How did I never notice before now?"

"Well… at least you now have an idea of the path forward?" Joe tried to offer a silver lining, but Snow was already entirely focused on trying to reach out and convince just one person to ask for a refill of their tea.

Immediately, dozens of voices began clamoring for Chrissy to bring a new teapot, and dozens more rushed onto the patio and into the store, suddenly desperate to get a taste of the flavorful hot beverage. The server glanced at Snow in horror before rushing off to try and accommodate her guests, whining a soft, "*Sto~op!*"

"Whoops." Snow ruefully grinned. "At least I know how to make a large-scale distraction if I ever need to in the future. I'll just blast out a deep desire for tea."

Joe was noisily sucking down the remnants in his cup, feverishly reaching for the pot as soon as it was empty. Snow had to physically stop him, though he struggled for a moment before snapping out of his unnatural urge to drink it. "Wha...? Oh. That was you? I didn't even notice at first. Did you know your influence lingers even after you actively sending it?"

"I..." Snow blushed as she realized that nearly every other time she'd been attempting to influence someone actively, she had been doing something they opposed. Therefore, they would usually go right back to doing that thing. In all other instances, she'd been trying to influence a crowd of people to act in a certain way, so it had seemed natural that they then listened more intently or clapped vigorously. "I can't honestly say I've really tested it before."

"Hm." Joe refilled his cup, though at a more sedate pace this time. "Maybe this is what Sneezy was trying to tell you. There are still plenty of things you don't know about your own abilities. I'm happy to help you test them, if you'd like."

"Yeah..." Snow took a deep breath and shoved her embarrassment to the side. "That would help a lot."

Snow and Joe spent the rest of the day hanging around the tea shop, observing customers, staff, and passersby on the street. She had narrowed her goal to a simple objective: extend her influence to a single person and spend the absolute minimum influence to give them a subtle *nudge*. No groups, no fanfare. One person who did not look like they planned to stop at the shop, only to be influenced to come in and have some tea.

She even planned to pay for them, just so it didn't feel

quite so wrong to extend her influence like this. Selecting a middle-aged woman walking along the street, Snow focused carefully and called up her influential aura, picturing it as a long, thin tendril weaving through the crowd and extending like a hand to gently pull the lady into the shop.

Almost immediately, her target's head swung to the side, eyes brightening with interest as she looked at the tea shop and adjusted her path. Snow's heart leapt at the triumph, only to drop back into its usual position when she noticed dozens of other people making their way to the entrance at the same time.

"Abyss... training this skill is going to be expensive, isn't it?"

THIRTY-TWO

WAKING UP TO A BRIGHT MORNING, Snow cataloged the birds singing and people chattering, rather than enjoying or becoming frustrated over the repetitive start. "Another day, another chance to succeed."

Her voice was calm as she acknowledged the bed's comfort, not indulging in it as she hopped to her feet. As Grumpy had once told her, comfort bred complacency. That was no way to live when she was hunting the best scout and lookout in the kingdom.

Her body, honed over now nearly two years of disciplined effort, moved with quiet strength without wasting energy. Having long since gotten used to the increased output the cleansing tablet had provided, she moved through her forms with clockwork reliability. The sunlight caught on her pale skin, but no longer did she focus on how she was looking, at least not while alone in her room.

Even so, as had become her routine, she glanced at the cloak still bearing the chalk mark from the previous day, yet another reminder of expectations going unmet. Happily, she'd long since graduated from a purple child's mark. Three months of practice containing her skills had allowed her to infiltrate the taverns in such a way that earned her a blue youngster's mark, and five grueling months of effort, planning, and investment later, she'd been given what she could only call a *begrudging* green mark.

"The mark of a teen…" Well, Snow had her own plans for revenge. Each day that she planned to go out and hunt for Sneezy, she had pocketed her own chunk of chalk, ready to give the guildmaster a mark of his own when she finally found him. After cleaning up, getting ready for the day at the same time as beating the chalk off of her cloak, she prepared to throw the door open and walk out onto the bustling streets.

An aged piece of paper on the table caught her eye, the original note given to her by a Sneezy having been kept this entire time.

"Just a game of tag? Watch out, Sneezy. I'm ready for it."

Stepping out into the lively streets with the air of someone who belonged there, Snow quickly collected Joe—who had grown several inches, and filled out rather well over the three quarters of a year she'd been feeding him actual food, not to mention a solid salary—and began their usual walk around the city. Her hood was drawn low enough to conceal her features without becoming overly suspicious, and the opening was perfectly shaped to catch the wind, delivering the scent of baked bread, drying herbs, and even a hint of brine from the not-too-distant harbor.

There was another freshness in the air that had nothing to do with the shops and vendors and everything to do with how Snow had been working her way around the city, weaving her influence throughout the population as she made a patchwork quilt of brand ambassadors. After months of work, and massive investment of time and literal skill, she'd managed to raise her skill all the way to *Extensive*, level eight.

She hadn't set out to use her abilities the way she had, but after several days of practicing her control at the tea shop had resulted in Chrissy being nearly ready to drop. The young lady had been terribly overworked, running from one customer to another. At first, it had been a pleasant, profitable experience. But as the hours went by with no end to the new, demanding customers, the strain had become clear. By the third day, she was nearly in tears as she begged Snow to give her some respite.

Obviously, Snow hadn't intended to put her friend in a bad position and had immediately chosen a new place, far distant from the tea shop, to begin frequenting. As per usual, she had quickly made friends, and by day's end, had started investing in the nicest people, those who'd proven themselves already kind-hearted and sympathetic to her cause. Now at level eight in the skill, the effects of a single investment lasted sixteen days, allowing her to extend the overall number of brand ambassadors, as well as the area they affected, over a huge area.

The effect was palpable. In recent weeks, she'd noticed that people smiled more easily, standing with far less tension in their shoulders as they went about their days. There were fewer arguments in the area her skills held sway, especially since each skill package now imbued the recipient with an *Extensive* aura of their own for the duration. People who once haggled in heated tones now bartered with good-natured cheer, and this entire section of the city felt happier, lighter… more innocent.

As they reached an intersection, she closed her eyes and focused.

A subtle brushing in the air told her she was now actively standing within range of one of her brand ambassadors. It was only after she had begun withholding her own aura that she'd started to feel the magic around her. The thought of having given herself away by allowing them free rein still put a blush on her cheeks when she thought about her previous obliviousness. The aura flowing toward her felt like a soothing breeze against her skin. To her, it was a gentle reassurance that she was surrounded by allies—even if the vast majority of them didn't know her true identity.

"You're not going to be here much longer, are you?" Joe spoke quietly, not looking at her as his sharp eyes swept across the bustling crowds. "I can feel it. You've put a lot of power into this city, and I know you have a plan."

"I really want to tell you about it, but…" Snow bit her lip as she held back from comforting him. "It's not that I don't trust you, it's just that Sneezy's people will absolutely report back whatever I say. I'm just so *sure* I'm under constant observation."

"Don't worry, I get it. Ready for another day of chasing after shadows?" Joe's words caused Snow's lips to curl into a half smile, a combination of happiness at the faith he was showing in her and frustration at her own inability to guarantee she would be succeeding soon.

They began walking through the streets, though the city's layout was no longer the bewildering puzzle it had once been to the princess. Truthfully, she didn't even need Joe's help to navigate anymore, but she certainly wasn't going to willingly give up his company. She knew which paths led to cul-de-sacs where only residents could go farther, which shortcuts could save them precious minutes, and even the quickest paths to her favorite restaurants and ocean overlook spaces.

While Snow had ostensibly agreed with her companion, today's plan was *not* to chase after the ever elusive D'wharve. Instead, she intended to put her final game plan into effect. As they walked near the three possible tavern locations, she began creating brand ambassadors in each of them, long since familiar with the bartenders, servers, and even the people who regularly frequented the spaces. Each of them were gifted with an Aura of Innocence, a strange find in places that relied on heavy imbibement and careful gambling.

One of the men playing cards that she'd given the aura to quickly began racking up wins, his usual tells when bluffing hidden behind the faux innocence he exuded. All in all, no one was unhappy to receive the skill package, though there was certainly some grumbling from those who noticed the strange effect cropping up all over the place. As she moved between each of the buildings—two of them bustling with people, the final one still boarded up after the majority of a year had passed—Snow looked around with satisfaction.

"Now these taverns are not only safer and more welcoming, they are also going to be easier for me to move within completely unnoticed." At this point, Snow didn't mind if someone else heard her words; it was already too late for them to intervene. After someone had activated the skill package she passed them, only she could deactivate it. At least, until the time ran out.

Things started to come to a head as she walked around the *Singing Bone* tavern.

After entering the building farthest from her temporary home, she put her plan into action by closing her eyes and focusing on spreading her own aura out with a feather-light touch. Her own gentle, yet more powerful aura swept through the crowd as her original skill, Precocious Command, allowed her to pick out each of the individuals whose body language indicated that they were watching her in return. She took a sharp breath through her nose as one of them suddenly darted forward, spinning and lashing out with a palm strike.

Paf!

A cloud of purple chalk dust floated into the air where her assailant's chalk dagger had landed, cleanly smacked out of his hand without leaving a mark on her. Snow's eyes narrowed as she looked at the man wearing the most rudimentary version of Sneezy's mask she'd ever seen. "Has it been you with the purple the whole time?"

"Only the last month. They cycle us out as we get better at

this." The unknown person shrugged nonchalantly. "It's pretty good pay to simply put a little paint on someone."

He stepped away, fading into the crowd and quickly getting lost among those milling about. Snow kept her attention on the others who'd been watching her, the sweeping aura filling the room trembling to her magical sense each time they moved even slightly. She began moving, walking around the room as quickly as she could while maintaining the tenuous grasp she had on her focused aura. Time after time, she presented openings, and finally, one of them took the bait.

He casually moved past her, a blue chunk of chalk whisking out, only for his hand to be stopped dead as her strengthened grip wrapped around his wrist. She raised an eyebrow at him, part of the only skin she was showing, and gently slapped the back of his hand to force him to drop his chalk dagger. "You all done?"

"Yep. Now I'm out of a job. Thanks for that." The man grumbled softly, but didn't truly seem too upset that he'd been caught. As he stepped away, Snow took in his more advanced mask, realizing that this had likely been training for Sneezy's own guild members as well.

"Why *not* sharpen two blades with one whetstone?" She had to admit it was an impressive play, all the more so for its subtlety. Bashful and Grumpy had both done the same, advancing the training of their own students by having them train her. "I'll have to remember that trick when I'm working on my own people in the future."

Even though she hung around a bit longer, no one in the tavern made another move, and during her walking, she had double and triple checked to ensure Sneezy wasn't there. Walking to the door, she took one last look back, nodding solemnly before collecting Joe and beginning her journey to the next. "One down, two to go. Hey... I don't have any chalk on me, do I?"

"No." Joe informed her after a quick, searching glance.

"Then I haven't failed yet. Since he's not here, he *has* to be in one of the other two." They hurried along to the Green Light, where each person in the establishment had already had a couple hours at this point to get used to the near-suffocating blanket of innocence she'd pumped this place full of.

She entered with quiet and measured steps, immediately taking a hard right and walking along the wall as she opened her senses and began sweeping the crowd with her focused aura. The bartender saw her and waved vigorously, calling more attention than she wished for, but she wasn't someone who would grumble about others being happy to see her, even if it made her life harder in the moment. "Matthias... it's good to see you."

"Ah yes, my most edgy yet *frequent* return customer," the bearded man called out pleasantly. "Isn't today just a *lovely* day? Everyone seems so happy and amiable, almost as though you've been hanging out here all day instead of gallivanting around the city like I figured you must be."

"Glad to know I can light up a room for you, Matthias." Even as she spoke, her eyes remaining focused on the bartender, she'd been carefully threading her influence around. As she passed an empty table, she could only be impressed as the person hiding in the shadow of a chair under the table managed to snake their arm out and swipe at her with a green chunk of chalk. At the last moment, she danced away, kicking up and landing a blow on the outstretched hand, sending the green facsimile-weapon to break against the low ceiling.

"I'm disappointed." Snow finally decided what to say as an ornately masked man came out from under the chair. She turned and looked at the bartender as she finished her thought. "How many times have you distracted me so he could land that?"

"Only a few..." The bartender hesitated before admitting, "...*dozen* or so times."

"Hmm." Snow extended her hand and shook with the person she had managed to not only block, but catch for the first time ever.

"How long have you been able to pick us out of a crowd? Find us even when we're hidden?" The masked man's voice wasn't playful, instead, this was someone searching for data points so they could achieve more with their own skills.

"I would be happy to let you know," Snow smiled as he leaned forward excitedly, "in the final report Sneezy will no doubt write up for you."

The scout blinked as if waking from a trance, his stern face softening before taking a deep breath and walking to the bar, raising a mug in silent toast to the princess. A few people who had stopped to watch the drama clinked mugs together, laughter bubbling up around the establishment. All that mattered to Snow, as she finished her careful circling of the tavern, was that Sneezy was not there.

"Only one last place to search, huh?" Snow's nose twitched as she ground her teeth in frustration. "The White Snake, 'closed' for the last few seasons."

She stomped toward the final establishment, managing only at the last moment to collect herself and scrub her aura out of existence as she and Joe approached it. Now sensitive to outside energies, she felt the faint ripple of her gifted auras as the residents in the surrounding buildings moved around, going about their daily business. Where the boundaries of the auras touched, the rippling chaos smoothed and shifted into a greater whole. "Mm, I'll need to make sure I do frequent tours of my kingdom in the future. What will a large-scale effect of twenty days of innocence, warmth, and good will do to these cities? I can only imagine it will be *good*."

Instead of going to the door and trying to bash it in, or something equally noticeable, Snow instead carefully and quietly circled the standing structure, looking for each place someone might slip out of, as those could just as easily be entrances for her. Eventually, she chose a window that had slipped its frame from the months of lost maintenance, fully devoting herself to stealth as she slipped into the building, tumbling soundlessly across the dusty floor in the interior and coming up with her chalk dagger at the ready.

The building was empty.

CHAPTER
THIRTY-THREE

HER LIPS TWITCHED IN AGITATION, but Snow wasn't ready to give up just yet. Now that she was inside and had a clear line of sight across the space, she allowed her auras to flow out, extending further, stretching, growing, until they connected seamlessly with the ring of aura built up around the location. Tapping into Precocious Command, she simply watched, and waited, until the faintest of movements—someone breathing—became noticeable.

Moving with the utmost care and precision, she slunk through the empty, wide-open tavern. There were no walls for someone to hide behind, and all the chairs and benches had been flipped over and placed atop the tables. Except one. The table in the exact center of the room had piles of papers, ledgers, reports, and all sorts of other articles of business which perfectly aligned with what a scout would be producing strewn across them. Snow walked over to them, chalk slipping from her cuff as she inched closer…

Only to spin around and slash a bright red line of chalk against a wooden beam which had been directly behind her. Dust exploded outward, and the illusion Sneezy had been hiding in popped like a soap bubble.

"Pretty good," he told her, voice raspy as though he hadn't spoken to anyone else the entire time Snow had been searching for him. "Well done, Snow Weiss, you've impressed me so. Getting to me without the skills *I* know?"

She opened her mouth to respond, but he wasn't done. "True, you got this close 'cause I *let* you near, but my pride as a guildmaster means I'm sincere. Your talents have grown; you've even learned to sneak. I believe you'll face *her* strong, no longer so weak. The inevitable draws nigh, and here we stand. Ready to fight with you, hand in hand. But... before we plan where this path shall progress, are there any requests you'd like to address?"

The princess waited to make sure no other rhyming statements or questions were going to be following along on the first, then let out a satisfied sigh as she allowed her hands to drop to her sides. "I have two questions and one request. First, how long have you been planning out that little speech? It was pretty good, but you obviously rehearsed it a lot."

"That question falls below my standard for receiving an answer." Sneezy glanced to the side involuntarily, and Snow followed his twitch over to where scores of papers were crumpled and thrown into a heap. "Hey, eyes on *me*."

"Mmhmm..." She couldn't help but laugh at the tiny tinge of color that crept up his neck. "I appreciate your dedication to theatrics, at least. Second question then: was this the entirety of your training?"

"Yes," he responded simply. "You did a good job, even learning a few things about your own power that caught me *extremely* off guard. Frankly, the fact that you ended this trial by swiping me with red chalk? It was absolutely poetic. A perfect way for you to signify your transition from being a child to grasping your destiny as an adult with both hands. Actually, being an adult is part of the conversation we need to have. You *are* nearly nineteen..."

Snow leaned back as he lavished praise on her, praise she

wasn't certain she deserved, and uncertain what he meant by his leading words. "Okay, now I have a third question… *what?*"

"Your Full Class, Princess." Sneezy explained as he gestured at her left arm. "With the Class Shrines having been abruptly co-opted by the crown, with at least four Huntsmen on duty at each of them no matter the time of day, we've had no opportunities to sneak you into one to help you attain your Full Class. As I'm sure you know, most people don't consider you an adult until you've taken your Full Class. This is part of why it's also called your 'adult class', exactly as your Basic Class is referred to as a 'child class'."

Seeing that she didn't quite catch his point, he elaborated further, "Unless you have your Full Class by the time you're at the head of your forces, leading them to the palace, there will be many people who refuse to follow you, stating that they cannot put their trust in someone who isn't considered by the system to be an adult yet. I don't have a solution for this yet, but… we'll burn that bridge when we get to it."

"I see." It was a complication Snow hadn't ever considered, focused as she'd been on growing her current skillset and finagling new ways to express them in interesting and useful ways. "I'll make my request then, unless you have some other pressing information?"

"Please. I'm looking forward to seeing what I can offer you that I haven't done already." Sneezy chuckled behind his mask. "I've been an *amazing* instructor, if I do say so myself."

"Sure. As to what I am hoping to take away from here…" Snow squared her shoulders. "Sneezy, I would like to ask you in an official capacity to allow me to hire Joringel as my personal advisor for when I am—*ack*, when I'm in charge of the kingdom."

She had almost called out the title of the queen, which she was certain would call the tyrant's scrying upon herself. There'd been a *whole* lot of motion within the kingdom in the last few months, as the queen ramped up her efforts to quench the surge of resentment Snow's people were fanning into flames.

"Um?" The guildmaster tilted his head at her in confusion. "Why would I have any reason to say no to that? Truly, I'm not sure why you'd think to ask *me* in the first place."

"Seriously? Sneezy, it can't be any more obvious that Joe is your son."

Snow paused as the guildmaster reeled away, then tapped at her face as she slowly pressed on, "You have the *exact* same eyes. Both of you see *way* too much."

Watching his jaw work, yet hearing no sounds come out, it was the princess's turn to become confused. "Are you being serious? You didn't know? I thought he was someone you had planted in my path to keep an eye on me. *Your* eyes."

"Stop saying that!" The man gasped out, turning and rushing to the door, which he directly kicked open instead of using the handy crowbar to pull the nailed-down board out of the way. There he came face to face with Joe, and dropped to a knee, looking over the somber young man. "Abyss. She's right."

"Daddy. It's me. Your son," Joringel blandly stated, nearly knocking Sneezy flat on his back, while Snow began laughing so hard she started wheezing for air.

"Are you *messing* with me?" The guildmaster only managed to make a few choked noises, hand lifting, then dropping, over and over, as if he wanted to poke the boy to make sure he was real. "Because… as far as I can tell…?"

"No, truly, he is! At least, going by everything I can tell. I'm sure you could go to a house of healing and confirm," Snow managed to choke out. "It's just… Joe, what was *that*? Did you seriously just call him *daddy*?"

"I could hear you speaking to him, and… I thought it would be funny. Also," the young man had turned to look at

Snow, a hint of hurt clear in his eyes, "You thought I was working for him?"

"No," Snow assured him as soon as she could catch a lungful of air. "I thought he got you into place, and you were working for him without knowing it. I would have noticed a discrepancy in your body language if you had known what was going on."

Joe finally broke, a huge smile crossing his face as Snow broke down in a fit of laughter once more. "Sir, my name is Joringel. My friend calls me Joe. You can do the same. My mother is-"

"*Ahh!*" Snow let out a sharp gasp as her arm tickled fiercely. She slapped the notification from the system away, not wanting to miss out on the unexpected reunion between the duo.

When she returned to the conversation, Sneezy was babbling, both hands on his head as he tried to make sense of the situation. "The apothecary who sells us smelling salts and restoratives? I haven't seen her in person in-"

"Probably about fourteen years?" Joe offered with a ghost of a smile. "She's not, you know, around anymore. I looked for you in the past, but... you're a hard person to find. I didn't know you were the elusive *Sneezy*, so at least I feel a little better about it."

"Yeah, that..." Sneezy deflated, hands coming out to land on the lad's shoulders. "Abyss. How am I going to make this up to you? We'll start with spending time together. Do you like training? I can give you the *best* training. Gear? Opportunity to see the kingdom! I'll-"

Joe cut off the deluge of words. "How about we try a cup of tea and get to know each other? I know a pretty good shop where the owner likes us a lot."

Sneezy looked over at Snow, clearly dazed and in shock at her having noticed something directly under his nose that he hadn't, especially as both of them must have been under close scrutiny for nearly a year. "Yeah. Let's do that. Princess... let's have that conversation soon. First, I..."

"Hey, far be it from me to keep you from meeting your son." She held up her hands in a gesture of surrender. "Meet me back at my place later, so we can have a private conversation about the next stage of my training?"

"There's no more training, Princess." Sneezy's voice became slightly more firm. "The next step is gathering our forces and marching on the capital. Somewhere in there, we'll get you to a Class Shrine, unless someone managed to secure an Awakening Artifact for you. They've been searching for nearly a year without any luck, so... we'll probably have to overrun one of the shrines. Prepare yourself. We won't remain here for any length of time."

"We'll talk about that later. Go." Snow shooed the duo away, trying not to think about the pit that had formed in her stomach at his words. No more training? Was it finally time to pit herself directly against her father's wife, and... what would Rose think of her? The Witch had likely been working at breaking her will for the last two years, while Snow had been throwing herself into ever more rigorous or skillful training.

Slowly walking back to her house, Snow contemplated how strange life had become, how she and her sister's roles had essentially reversed. Where Rose had been the one to throw herself into training, while Snow did her best to avoid thinking about it too much... now she had to wonder if her vibrant sister could even *think* at all. "Back when I was under her thumb, how long had I drifted in a fugue state? I wonder... will she even notice I've been gone? How much time has passed?"

Though she had finally completed her training with flying colors—particularly red—she had to let out a deep sigh as she realized it meant once more leaving behind the place she'd come to call home, and the people who had been good friends to her. "He told me to get ready to go... I've never met a

D'wharve who would beat around the bush, so that must mean I should get back to my house and pack up. Abyss, I'd probably already be on the road if I hadn't introduced him to Joe."

Determined not to vanish from the lives of the people she'd become a part of, she set out from the empty establishment, determined to visit each one and bid them farewell. Backtracking all the way to the Singing Bone, Snow stopped at each bakery, tea house, restaurant, bookstore, and curio shop she had made friends in. Unable to give them a reason for her departure, she wished them well and gained many well wishes in return.

Finally, she got to the last stop of the night, having to swallow the lump in her throat as she walked onto the patio where Chrissy was hustling around refilling cups. The familiar aroma of tea brewing wafted over her as she got closer, and as her friends' eyes lit up when they landed on her, Snow nearly lost her composure.

"There you are! I was wondering if you were going to… what's the matter?"

Snow lowered the mask of her cloak, her return smile tinged with sadness as Chrissy hurried over while wiping her hands dry on the apron tied around her waist. "I just wanted to thank you for your kindness. This tea shop has been… so much to me. Even more than that, your company-"

"You're leaving, huh?" Without another word, Chrissy pulled her into a tight hug. "I knew you were probably near the end of whatever your training ended up being, but I didn't think it would be the end of… you know. Your stay in our fair city. This place is so much better for having had you, and, while it kind of sucks for me, wherever you go next will be lucky to have you."

After a few more words, the two of them parted, Snow pulling up her face mask and taking her leave. From there, she rushed back to her house, unable to bear any more nostalgic reminiscing with others on this night.

Upon returning, Snow morphed into a whirlwind of activity, loading up her travel pack with everything she had brought. Then, she looked around sheepishly at the myriad of small items she'd accumulated over her lengthy stay in the city. "Whoops. What am I going to do with all of this?"

Eventually, the princess decided she'd simply have to ask Sneezy to have it packed up and sent to her someday in the hopefully not-too-distant future. Then… she waited. As she usually did when needing something to do to pass the time, she trailed a finger along her arm and looked at her skills.

Basic Class: Darling Princess
Basic Skill: Precocious Command: Level 10/10.
Advanced Skill: Aura of Innocence: Level 9/10.
Breakthrough Skill: Permanently locked.

Advanced Class: Influencer
Basic Skill: Influential Aura: Level 10/10.
Current followers: 18,697
Influence: 181,379
Advanced Skill: Brand Ambassador: Level 8 → 9/10.

Requirement to advance to level 10: Gain 50,000 followers through the efforts of your Brand Ambassadors. **13,921/50,000**

"Bleh. It's a ridiculous jump in requirement again." Snow flopped onto the bed as she looked at the glowing, five-digit number she needed to achieve by delegating to other people and getting them to get even *more* people to work on her behalf. "To be fair, I'm already shocked at the number of followers I got in this way. Still, that was my efforts over the course of almost a year in a densely populated city. I think there's only a few hundred thousand people in the entire *kingdom*! That means I need to get a huge percentage of my people behind me."

Snow didn't lament her situation too much. Even though it was a difficult requirement, she had heard all too many stories of people who had extremely abstract requirements for leveling instead of something concrete and easily understandable. "At least I have a clear path forward."

Thump.

If she hadn't been listening for it, the princess would've likely missed the gentle knocking on her door. Peeking out the shutters, she saw Sneezy, surrounded by dozens of people she didn't recognize waiting for her. Throwing the door open, she stepped out, swinging her pack up over her shoulders. "Are we leaving immediately?"

"Are you *ready*?" Snow's eyes shifted to a glare at the surprised tone filling Sneezy's voice. "I mean, yeah, let's get going."

She was led to a sturdy wagon, third from the front of a group of seven of them, and offered a hand to help her up. Snow climbed in and settled on the bench as her pack was stowed away for her, enjoying the cool evening air carrying the distant sounds of the city's nightlife moving into full swing.

As the wagon lurched forward, wheels clattering over the cobblestone, Snow looked back at the heart of the city—a city she was now more familiar with than anywhere else in the world, barring the palace itself.

"It's not farewell forever, only for now," Snow reminded herself, trying to steel herself for the next challenge: going against the queen herself. "Soon it will be my kingdom, and I can visit them whenever I want."

As they reached the edge of the city, she looked back, silently vowing to herself that she *absolutely* would return.

But only after her people were safe once more.

THIRTY-FOUR

HER JOURNEY NORTH was immediately eventful. As they crisscrossed the land, attempting to stop at every small town and village they could manage along their way, she would stand in the town square, on a stage for visiting bards if they had one, and make a speech. Every one of her speeches was accompanied by the faint scent of *aufgeschlossen* blossoms that her escort burned to make the townspeople slightly more receptive to hearing her out.

The princess refused to use anything stronger, going so far as to threaten Dopey's people among her escort when they tried to force the issue. She wanted her citizens to make their own decisions, even if it meant her marching on the palace with a smaller army. Walking into the most recent town square, her eyes swept over the boisterous crowd, who quickly quieted as they turned their rapt attention on to her.

She wanted them to be watching her with this much interest because of her message; but frankly, she couldn't be certain it wasn't the simple curiosity of those who'd never seen royalty, anger toward the queen, or if something else had been slipped into the thick smoke sweetening the air of the town. "Good people, I am Princess Snow Weiss. Today, I am here to appeal to your better nature and ask you to stand with me against the wicked Witch who has imprisoned the king, my father, and my twin sister, Princess Rose."

Immediately, there was an outburst of noise as looks of alarm appeared on every face. Snow pressed on, having already gone through this eight times in as many days. By now, such a reaction was simply part of the new routine. "While I would happily accept anyone who wants to fight, I also need people who can cook, help with the wounded, and even the elderly among you who have become trusted figures in your community to reach out to other towns in this area on my behalf. Truly, I want to tell you everything is going to be alright, but until we topple her tyrannic grip on the kingdom… I just can't make any promises."

At this point, her bard friends stepped in, calling out to the nervous crowd and directing them to different areas, based on their skill sets and ability. From there, the only group Snow personally interacted with was the elders of the village. After a careful discussion to ensure they truly stood with her, she would make each of them her Brand Ambassadors, giving every one of them all three of her giftable skills and sending them to reach out to others.

As soon as they were done, they loaded up their wagons and moved on once more. But this wasn't a silent, contemplative ride like her previous journeys. No, now the princess had taken on the mantle of a contender for the throne and was treated as such.

"Happy's people are moving ahead of us, greasing the palms of gate guards and patrolmen to look the other way when you speak." A lady was reading off a scroll rapid-fire as the wagons trundled along. "We're canceling your engagement at the next village; they've been shown to be sympathizers to the Witch. Instead, a hefty bribe has been paid to open a path into the next city over-"

"Every population center is a risk," a burly guard in a

Grumpy mask growled at the woman wearing a lesser Bashful half mask. "Putting her in a city with unknown affiliation? It's like guiding a mouse into a cage and telling it there might be cheese when it arrives."

"We need every able-bodied person on our side if we're going to push through the Huntsmen blockade," the lady replied so quickly Snow almost expected to hear a whip crack punctuating her words. "By the time we reach Thalfanghein, we need a force superior to the standing army and the alchemically twisted minions of the king's consort."

As her assigned assistants figured back and forth, Snow could only shake her head, impressed by how many variations of the word queen they'd managed to come up with to avoid coming under scrying scrutiny. "I'm in no rush to get to a Class Shrine just yet."

Snow's frank statement caught the duo off guard, and they looked at her with growing concern until she explained herself. "I'm at level nine in my Advanced skill, and my power is growing there by the day. In case you're wondering, for every ten people influenced by a Brand Ambassador of mine, I gain nine of them as followers. The more towns we go through, the faster I will increase in power. I hope to achieve Perfection and earn a Breakthrough Skill at the same time as gaining my Full Class."

"A worthy goal," the burly head of her security detachment nodded at her words. "Glad to hear you're only looking to postpone your power-up to have an even more firm foundation to grow from. I was worried you were chickening out in the final hour."

Luckily for him, Snow had long since grown used to the direct way in which Grumpy's people spoke—but her logistical support looked absolutely shocked, even more so when taking the perpetually surprised eyes of her mask into account. Before she could explode at her counterpart, smoke in the distance resolved into a village they were moving toward at speed. "Enough, you two. I have to prepare to speak once more."

Less than a half hour later, she was once more shouting from a stage, doing her best to rally her people to action. "-and if you cannot walk away now, join me at the castle in exactly three months' time! We will throw off the shackles of tyranny, excise the rot that has infected our kingdom with despair and corruption!"

As she stepped off stage, her left arm lit with pearlescent light. A quick glance made the blood drain from her face— Aura of Innocence had reached Perfection.

Someone among the crowd had been an assassin.

Though the system itself all but guaranteed they had been swayed to her side, Dopey had always warned her that, where there was one assassin, there was another to ensure the job got done. She moved quickly to get amongst her security detail as several of her people looked at her with quizzical expressions. Snow shook her head, hissing at them, "Not here!"

They quickly bundled her away, and her security head stepped close, clearly more than aware of the situation. In a low voice, he spoke to only Snow and her direct advisors. "You heard them, too?"

"Heard who?" her logistic support inquired just as softly.

"Not who, *what*. The sneezes. There were several of them, too many to put off as coincidence, each at the same perfectly pitched note. Sneezy's people spotted trouble. We need to get out of here." At the muscled man's words, the group surrounding Snow shifted into a half jog, conferring amongst themselves in rapid shorthand.

"Was our intelligence incorrect?"

"-I've got confirmation that the original destination was a crown sympathizer, but this place was supposed-"

"Man, purple robes, black hair," came a deep mutter from Snow's right, quickly followed by another member of the Shield and Truncheon Association calling from the left.

"Green frock with lilies hemmed on the sleeves, red-headed woman. Blonde man in all brown coming up quickly, he and the dog both have vacant stares."

"We've got subjugated attackers incoming!" The last was from her head of security, who had put together the information and quickly made a determination. The group spun to a halt, weapons coming out as they closed in on Snow, practically squishing her as from the outside they shifted into a bristling, hedgehog-esque formation as he roared, *"Huntsman spotted!"*

"In this tiny little town?" Snow yelped as a half-dozen people drew weapons and rushed the formation, heedless of their own safety. Rapidly coming up behind them was a man hidden in a black, tattered cloak, moving with an unnatural grace and gait. In each hand he held a dagger, and even though he had started far behind the others, he was the first to arrive to test the formation.

Even as they were set upon from all sides, more than eight of the twelve guards around Snow were required to break off just to engage the Huntsman as he flew among them, striking with unnatural strength to disrupt their defensive position. The others easily managed to fend off the townspeople who were swinging their weapons with little skill, faces expressionless as they threw themselves against the skilled guards.

Grumpy's people from SATA did their best to push them back without grievous injury, but even when the man walking his dog had his knee inverted, he simply crawled at them while urging his animal to attack.

Snow stepped past the protection, focusing on the civilians who were clearly being forced into attacking, extending her Aura of Influence around them and allowing her collected influence to pour out. *"Stop this. Go to sleep."*

Her collected power dropped, but not nearly as much as she'd been expecting. Instead, each of the people simply halted what they were doing, let out what sounded like nothing other than a sigh of relief, and collapsed where they stood. Turning to her people, the princess barked out, "Somebody bind their wounds and tend to them. I can confirm they weren't acting under their own power."

"Got him!" came a guttural roar from the other side of the group, where the eight defenders wearing Grumpy masks had pulled the Huntsman to the ground and were in the process of hacking him apart. "Don't let those pieces touch each other; I've seen them pull back together. Good... you'll know it's dead when it starts to melt. Someone go get a shovel and a bucket. A barrel, if you can manage."

He turned, catching the horrified expression on Snow's face, and shook his hands, absolutely misinterpreting her disgusted expression. "No, don't worry! After they start to melt, they won't pull themselves back together."

"No wonder we need to go against them with an overwhelming numbers advantage," Snow murmured as she looked at the somehow-still-raging fight. When the Huntsman's arm had been sliced off, the limb hadn't stopped fighting, instead lashing out at anything that moved near it—like a snake that had been beheaded, yet would still strike anything that brushed past. "This is going to be all but impossible, even without taking the Witch and her own power into consideration, isn't it?"

"There's a reason they didn't let you rush back, Princess." The words of her Bashful attaché came as a squeak as she hid behind Snow, while dark fluids gushed from the Huntsman's wounds. "They had to be absolutely sure you had better than even odds against her. No matter how..."

"How slim that advantage might be?" Snow finished grimly as the words her companion clearly hadn't meant to utter trailed off. "I'm beginning to understand. Don't worry, I'm going into this with open eyes. I might not succeed, but at this point, I am willing to die trying."

Turning to her assistant, she smiled brightly. "Though I'd rather we all live through this. Sound like a plan to you?"

Eyes nearly as wide as her mask's painted version, the woman nodded, hiding the lower half of her face behind the clipboard she carried everywhere like a security blanket. Just then, there was a pained gurgle, which turned into a liquid bubbling Snow didn't care to see the source of. Taking a deep breath, she held her head high and marched back toward her wagon as a part of her guard forces cleaned up after themselves.

When everyone had settled into their positions, Snow nodded at the wagon drivers, trying to hide the sadness she felt toward the citizens who'd been twisted by her father's wife. "What's the nearest, largest population center?"

"Emdenvale, my rebel queen." The reply came from one of Dopey's people, making her wonder if the man had given them specific instructions on how to refer to her.

"Emdenvale? Lovely." Taking a deep breath, she leaned on her bardic training to hide her sadness, resolved to only show a stern front of confidence and strength. "What's the holdup? Let's get moving; we've got a city to capture."

"*For Princess Snow!*"

The cry went out, quickly echoed by everyone in the small caravan then the townspeople who had lined up to see them off. Snow took deep breaths as her heart clenched, but she waved and smiled all the same, until the last of her people had faded into the distance behind them.

THIRTY-FIVE

LONG WEEKS of travel had taken their toll on Snow and her entourage. The endless clattering and creaking of her wagon as it rolled along their current worn dirt road suddenly shifted, allowing her a few long moments of relief from the jarring noises as it squished through a path muddied by an endless stream of boots, hooves, and wheels that had preceded her caravan. Opening her eyes as her wagon slipped sideways slightly on the slick surface, she glanced behind her conveyance and shook her head.

"This is only going to get worse. Look at all of them." Snow was deeply touched by how many people had taken up her call, as what had started as a small band of loyalists now stretched beyond what the eye could see. Following along after her wagon were a tide of determined, angry citizens. Farmers, bakers, smiths, healers, people from every walk of life surged in her wake—even older children with boundless energy, certain they could get a job running messages and materials between different groups. "Is there anything we could do? Maybe find some people with earth-shaping skills to toughen up the road?"

"They're churning up the countryside." Her logistic-assistant murmured as she crossed something off of her checklist. "There are too many of them to fit on the road, so even turning it to stone wouldn't have much of an effect."

Snow felt a thick sense of guilt as she saw hungry people pressing onward behind them, and her shoulders slumped from the weight of responsibility. " I'm not sure if I should feel proud that they support me or terrified about how we're going to take care of them. So many people are…"

"Likely to die, yes," the head of her security detail interjected as she hesitated. "That's what they're signing up for. As Battle Lord Grumpy would say, the only time wrongs are righted is when the pain of change finally becomes more than the pain of staying the same. Clearly, allowing things to stay as they are is completely untenable to your people."

"We could probably import a few hundred thousand tons of grains and fruits from our allies across the southern sea." The muttered words tickled Snow's ears as her logistic assistant quickly scribbled her thoughts down. "This will absolutely impact the harvest."

Snow tuned out the ceaseless murmuring, thinking over the last few weeks. They'd seen the number of their *literal* followers rise with each town, village, and hamlet they passed through. Now that number had grown to thousands of people winding across the countryside like a river of humanity. On top of that, her *figurative*, system-recognized followers had been growing exponentially as well, though she did her best to make that number increase based on her Brand Ambassadors.

"We should be arriving at camp shortly," the wagoneer driving them called over his shoulder, drawing Snow to shift and face forward once more. The scent of hundreds of cook fires had reached them hours ago, enough smoke filling the air that she was worried a forest had caught on fire.

As they crested the hill, Snow's jaw dropped as her eyes took in an enormous encampment sprawled across the vast plain only a few miles south of Emdenvale. Tents of all sizes peppered the landscape, canvas walls fluttering in the stiff easterly breeze. A thin haze of smoke hovered over the area, somewhat trapped by the rolling hills around the plain. The sounds hit her first, hundreds of people streaming in from all directions, converging into what she had to assume was the main camp of the rebellion. Feet squelched in mud, metal ringing on metal as weapons and armor were churned out in preparation of battle, and horses let out high-pitched whinnies that echoed across the area.

"All of this…" Snow's voice trembled as they began their descent into the camp, "They're here to support me? I never imagined what the scale of this battle would look like."

"Don't get too terribly weepy," her guard snorted as he started pointing out different sections of the camp. "Probably only a tenth of the total number of people here are going to end up being fighters. The sheer amount of resources necessary to keep them strong, healthy, and ready for battle accounts for the other ninety percent. You need to feed the people, those who are *feeding* the people, the animals… you get the idea. Then there's water and shelter to take into consideration, not to mention training and mobilizing the actual forces. Abyss, there's probably a couple hundred people here whose only job is to set up and tear down *tents*."

Snow was amazed by the quick recounting, as she hadn't ever thought of what that portion of things would look like. The sheer detail work that had to have gone into this? The fact that her D'wharves must have been purchasing and moving supplies since the day she announced her commitment to fighting the queen? It was only at this moment that she realized how much her decisions had already been impacting her people. Powerhouses must have been talking about her, negotiating on her behalf, betting on her success. Yet, if she failed…

Luckily, her logistic assistant chose that moment to speak up, breaking Snow out of her thoughts before she could sink into a downward spiral. "What sort of measures do we have in place to root out spies? With so many people flooding in, I can't imagine the princess would be very secure here."

"We've got people from the house of healing offering mandatory free exams and are using that as an opportunity to search for any of the noticeable side effects found in people *Queen Kat* has altered," a man in a Bashful mask, of fairly high quality, answered as he fell into step beside their rolling wagon. "My group is out there telling tales and keeping people entertained, which is helping to mitigate fears and tensions, and also helps us find those who are showing muted reactions—yet another tell. There's even dopers from the Night's Heart Exchange circulating and testing random people and items with strange swabs."

"Not enough," Snow's SATA security head rumbled.

"Well, then get her out of here." The bard rolled his eyes and gestured helplessly. "There's only so much we can do. We're *all* taking risks here."

"You called out the title of the tyrant…" Snow quietly interjected, the others falling silent as she spoke up. "I'm guessing there's just no hiding what we're doing here?"

"Exactly that, Princess. If we can all use her name and title as often as possible, we are hoping it'll interfere with her scrying capabilities when smaller groups begin moving out to work on delicate missions," the bard informed her warmly. "Also, I'm supposed to pass on Ned's greetings. You should be seeing him shortly, if you are on your way to the command tent. His exact words were, 'look to the north to find me'."

"Let's get that out of the way before we settle in," Snow replied with gentle determination. Her advisors continued to speak to each other, but the princess focused on the camp as they wound through it, waving as they were greeted with exhilarated, enthusiastic cheering.

As they approached the heart of the camp, rolling along as little more than a parade at this point, they seemed to pass over an invisible demarcation. Anyone who was following along after them out of excitement was forced to stop as various guards posted about the area waved them away. That didn't stop the noise from increasing ever louder, whistles, clapping, and banging of metal on metal as the citizens welcomed their princess. Snow took it all in, hoping she'd be able to live up to the hopes they were pouring out onto her.

They stopped in front of a massive structure, a command tent that was half canvas, half temporary wooden structure. Six large structures surrounded it, each of them flying banners marked with the sigils of the various D'wharve factions. A gentle green and blue showing the mark of the Houses of Healing, a black flag with a blood-red heart indicating the Night's Heart Exchange, a red and green banner with the sword and shield of SATA. Next was a fanciful burnt orange flag with the official mark of the bardic organization, kabuki masks showing happy and sad faces set behind a harp.

Wanting to pay her respects to each of them, Snow allowed her gaze to drift along, picking out the others. "A bow and… what is that on the green and brown banner? Over Sneezy's organization, I'd assume?"

"It's a pepper grinder." Her guard grunted with a roll of his eyes. "Sneezy is the original founder of the group, and… it shows. It's called 'The Achoo Collective'."

"You're *joking.*"

"I wish."

Shaking her head in astonishment at how such a serious, professional group could allow themselves to be known by such a silly name, she moved over to the last of the structures, a full-blown brick building that had been lavishly decorated. Its banner was gold and purple, a bottle and sack with the symbol of the kingdom's currency decorating it. "Happy's group, yes?"

"Yes… and *we're* not too happy that he built it up there," the bard who had joined them interjected with some hesitance in his voice. "He wanted to know why he needed a building specifically for planning, when there was a command tent right *there*. So instead, he built a gambling and drinking hall."

"Of course he did. Let me guess, for 'troop morale'?" Snow sighed as her guide nodded, then she looked around for any representation of the final D'wharve. "Where is Sleepy's group?"

"He doesn't have a group. Sleepy's not what he does, it's who he *is*." The cryptic reply from the high-ranking member of the bardic organization earned him a squint from the princess, but he didn't choose to elaborate further.

"Great. Let's meet the generals." Stepping out of the wagon, Snow was greeted by two guards who saluted her then reached to the sides and pulled back the tent flaps to allow her ingress.

The temperature inside was easily ten degrees warmer, and only then did Snow realize exactly how chilly it truly was. "Mm… we need to push on soon, or we are going to be trying to march against the palace as snow starts flying."

"You can fly?" The teasing voice put a wide smile on her face, and the princess rushed forward to throw her arms around Ned. "*Oof!* Yes, it's good to see you as well, my soon-to-be queen."

Stepping back, Snow composed herself, though she allowed her bright smile to remain. Looking around the room, she nodded at the assembled collection of men and women, each of them who appeared as though they'd been chiseled from stone to represent the peak form of humanity. Whether they wore a Grumpy mask, all the way over to being a healer, she could see at a glance how each of them was as disciplined in their own lives as they likely demanded of their people.

"Princess Snow." A woman in a weathered Bashful mask stepped to the table. "We're ready to receive your orders."

Straightening her back, Snow stepped to the table each of the generals were standing around. Turning her head slowly, she locked eyes with each of them in turn, nodding in approval at what she saw. "Please, take your seats. Now, I've seen what you've all done out there. In short, incredible work."

Taking a breath, she thought back to the prepared speeches she'd been spouting about how she had grown... and pushed all that to the side so she could speak from her heart. "Now we need to get everyone ready to fight. Every farmer who picked up a pitchfork, every healer who is preparing bandages in preparation of the upcoming battles. The non-combatants who will be carefully packing supplies for the scouts who are going to risk their lives to bring us information. While I might be your princess, we are all threads in the same tapestry. Only together can we weave a future free of the tyranny Queen Kat has created."

Taking a momentary pause, she looked down, steeling herself, before glancing up with hard eyes. "I am not going to stand on the sidelines. I'm here to lead my people to victory. Not just for me, but all of us. We are outmatched, in terms of sheer combat power. All of us know this, as we've all at least heard the stories of what the Huntsmen are capable of. The only way we're going to break through and topple the queen is by remaining unified, disciplined, but more than that... having hope. We are fighting for a better life, for all of us. Thank you for trusting me. I will not let you down."

A thick tension passed through the room as the generals looked at her with shifting expressions beneath their masks. Snow could tell that each of them held their own reservations; they'd been sent here by their guildmasters to be their voices in the operations of the army they were raising. Most of them were used to being all but the final say within their own orga-nizations, but Snow had pushed each of her abilities to the maximum—Precocious Command allowed her to speak in such a way that she was able to navigate their complex social dynamics, not pulling away their agency as leaders, but instead offering to enhance it.

Aura of Innocence softened any of the hard edges she might have otherwise exuded, allowing them to feel her immense sincerity on this subject. Her Influential Aura had been put into play, ever so subtly helping to sway the last variables of their opinions on her. Finally, it was time to add in a gift to seal the deal—a calculated gesture that would've made Happy cry tears of joy. "I'm going to give each of you a portion of my power, and I hope you'll go out among your people and advocate for the vision I have shared with you. Remember, I'm here for you, you're here for me, and all of us must be there for *all* of us."

She targeted each of them in turn, passing the full suite of her skills along as quickly as she could, wincing only slightly as the mystical energy of influence that she had collected drained out of her in large chunks. Each of the generals became Brand Ambassadors moments after she applied the skills, opening the 'gift' almost immediately upon receiving it, even if they had done so out of curiosity more than anything.

The air itself shimmered, turbulent for a brief moment as twelve intense auras activated one after another, two auras per person. Many of them gasped as information flooded into their minds while looking at each other. They were suddenly able to *Masterfully* understand the meaning behind a subtle cant of the head, the uncomfortable shifting of those who thought Snow's words had been somewhat cheesy, and the intense faith Ned had in the princess by the way he stood in an open position, face unclouded as he nodded along at what she had to say.

"This…" the representative General of Happy breathed, "I'm going to be able to find every single person who tries to cheat."

"The applications for *training* alone," the general representing Grumpy grumbled softly as he stroked his beard. "I'll be able to know who's giving it their all and who's sandbagging."

Even without checking her status, Snow was nearly positive she'd just gained six more steadfast followers.

"I'm going to go settle in now, unless there's anything pressing that requires my attention." Snow looked around, but each of them shook their heads in the negative. "Lovely. Now please, go and lead my people to the best of your abilities, so I can send every single one of them home to their families when this is over."

THIRTY-SIX

Brand Ambassador: Level 9/10.
Requirement to advance to level 10: gain 50,000 followers through the efforts of your Brand Ambassadors. 38,438/50,000.

SNOW STARED down at her arm long enough that someone gently nudged her, and the princess flinched and looked around wildly. "What's next?"

"Next, I think… is some sleep, Your Highness. You've done enough for now," her assistant stated gently, and Snow was so tired she could only nod in agreement as they adjusted their path.

The last several days blended together in a swirl of speeches, endless meetings, and constant, deliberate usage of her influence across the encampment. She had stopped to speak with people from all corners of the kingdom, finding those among them she deemed to be key figures—lieutenants, quartermasters, and people with a natural tendency toward leadership who had been working to help others get settled. To each of these, she had gifted a skill, making dozens, then scores of new Brand Ambassadors across the entirety of the fledgling army.

Now the entirety of the plain was all but *humming* with her auric infusion. Ever so slowly, as she invested additional power, the chaotic mess of thousands of lives crammed into a temporary city began to shift into one, massive, thriving community. Just as she'd tested back in Magdenburg, people had begun moving with purpose and intent, arguments that once flared into fights now smoldered before they could catch. Orders were given and obeyed with swift efficiency as the people settled into place with a sense of calm readiness.

Well over a hundred thousand influence had been poured into creating the sweeping slate of energy, and only the knowledge that it would come back quickly, and the gifted skill would last the remainder of the month, let her spend her carefully collected power so freely. She took a deep breath as her own aura extended outward, all but clicking into place with the others. "It has to have been worth it. There is no other choice."

They took a detour through a quiet section of the camp, guards spread in a delta formation behind her at a close yet respectful distance. Snow took a moment to appreciate everything that was happening... so, so fast. "Soon we will be marching on Emdenvale, and they will either join us, or we will lock them in place with oaths not to hamper our progress. I would far rather be able to use Doc's teachings, or perhaps Bashful's, than Grumpy's... I can only hope they will see reason and understand our cause."

A shout rang out behind her, sharp and urgent, followed by a blood-curdling scream. Snow spun around, already looking at the backs of her guards as they drew their weapons and close ranks around her. "What's happening?"

"Stay back, Princess," one of the guards growled, glancing over at her head of security and nodding. "There's a disturbance; you need to get out of here."

"I can stop it-" Snow tried to push past them, only to be

body blocked as they sent her level stares. "Someone over there needs help! I can order you-"

"Then order us." The Grumpy-masked man spoke in a cool tone. "Snow. I completely understand you want to help. At the same time, if you try to handle everything on your own, you will die of exhaustion long before that Witch manages to get her talons into you. Trust us, we've dealt with far more than whatever is going on over there."

The noises and clamoring had continued increasing in intensity, and now a thick column of oily smoke was rising into the sky not too far from them. Biting her lip and clenching her fists in frustration, Snow finally acquiesced, "Fine! But someone do *something*!"

"We'll handle it. Let's get you back to your tent." As her guard spoke in a soothing tone, Snow wearily bobbed her head, turning and walking along the path. As she turned the corner, the sounds of the camp didn't simply *fade* away, they cut off as though someone had slammed a door between them.

Glancing over her shoulder, Snow did a double take when she saw her escort had vanished. "Guards? Where did…"

"*Sssnowww.*" The soft whisper echoing through the air could have been a figment of her imagination, perhaps the whisper of the falling leaves being caught in the autumn wind, were it not for the dark shadow approaching the princess from the underbrush of a small copse of trees the camp had set up around.

"*Guards!*" Snow shouted as she backpedaled, the shape resolving itself into an extremely tall man, made slightly shorter due to the way he hunched forward as he walked toward her. "Where are you?"

Light glinted off a cold steel mask as the Huntsman stepped into the light, movements fluid as he approached her. The princess opened her mouth to scream, and the Huntsman flashed across the distance in an instant, as though he had teleported through the intervening space. He lifted a finger up to the horizontal mouth slit of his mask as his offhand clamped over her lips. Snow thrashed, but his grip was as solid as the metal he wore over his face.

"*Shh…*" Every sound he made echoed as though it were coming from a deep well. "I am not here to harm you, Sssnowww. It's me. Ssssleepyyyy."

Though she was all but hyperventilating, the fact that the Huntsman hadn't simply put an end to her once he had her in his grasp made her take a closer look. Indeed, his mask was ever so slightly different than a standard Huntsman's, eye slits horizontal instead of vertical, with a slightly wider hole for his mouth for air to pass through. Seeing her calm down enough to listen, his hand was removed from her mouth.

Even still, she took a step back, working her jaw as she tried to think of how to respond to this sudden… meeting. "I suppose you're the only one who hasn't yet offered me training. Is this…?"

"No. I am here to issue a warning, as well as to test your resolve." Sleepy told her, the space where his eyes should have been glinting through the holes instead a deep, dark pit as though she were staring into the abyss itself. "*Shhhheee* has seen your army and is gathering her own in response. Your people are fleeing Deckbett in droves. Few make it past the queen's forces, and those who try are pulled into the castle to bolster the ranks of her Huntsmen. Each day you delay, her forces grow stronger."

"I understand." Snow's heart sank as her concern for her people grew, but her chin lifted higher as she responded, "I hadn't planned to delay, and now I will actively push for us to move faster. We had planned to take Emdenvale next week; I will ride to the gates at dawn. Do you have any word on my sister? Has the queen… *twisted* her?"

Sleepy shook his head back and forth, ever so slowly, as though his neck was a chunk of rusted metal that had not been oiled in far too long. "*She* needs your twin healthy and *unchanged*. Although she has been working to subvert the wards of the kingdom, she has not yet succeeded. If she fails with your father, she needs another of royal blood to make another attempt."

"Thank the system." It was the best news she'd heard about her sister in nearly two full years, and Snow felt both relief and increased pressure to push harder.

"You will not find your journey north to be as easy as it has been to this point," Sleepy warned her darkly. "The queen has been spreading rumors, her propaganda painting you as the most twisted, vile of monsters. She says you've been destroying everything in your path as you march on the palace."

"Tell me more," Snow hurriedly demanded. "If I know what she is saying, I can craft narratives to counter her words far more easily."

Sleepy seemed to glance at her with a hint of admiration, something Snow could only tell because of the minute shift in his posture. "She says your disappearance from the palace two years previously… was because you died."

"Well, that's clearly false and easy to disprove." Snow shrugged and gestured at herself, "clearly I'm here."

"Yes. You *are*." Sleepy shifted ever so slightly. "That is exactly why she has been adjusting their minds to see you the way she wants them to see you. Skin as white as your namesake, paler than is humanly possible without intervention by the system."

The princess glanced down at her hands, where her jade-white skin still practically glowed with the after-effects of the cleansing tablet Dopey had provided her. "That one is fair, I'll give her that."

"She says you have enthralled a group of monstrous dwarves to serve you, and the beasts of the forest flock to you and do as you command." Sleepy paused, allowing her to start building up an image in her mind of what the queen was attempting to insinuate. "Your apparent death two years ago, followed by you living in a coffin, then coming back to life... living for long periods of time without eating any solid foods..."

"By the system... are you trying to tell me she's going around claiming I'm an abyssal *vampire*?" Snow huffed and puffed, not sure how to react to this information in the slightest. "But *why*? Something like that hasn't been seen in my lifetime."

"She's claiming that everything she is doing is her attempt to save the kingdom from having an undying, eternal *Monster* take the throne." Sleepy lifted his shoulders ever so slightly, as though to agree that it was far-fetched. "Believe it or not, far too many people believe her lies, especially when the people spreading them are those who have been bewitched by her music."

"Ugh... I had all but forgotten about that part of her power," Snow muttered, kicking at a stone and sending it skittering across the ground. "I've been so focused on her recent alchemical exploits, it slipped my mind."

"Our time runs short, Snow. I have nothing else to warn you about. Just... don't let yourself break under *her dark influence*."

"Runs short?" Snow jerked her gaze back to the enormous faux-Huntsman. "I feel like there's a lot of information you could pass on-"

"I cannot. I have reached my limit." His body language sang with confusion, then understanding. "Oh. I see. You have not yet realized."

"What do you mean?" Snow looked around nervously at the stiflingly silent camp around them.

"Princess... you're asleep. *Wake up*."

Snow's eyes flew open, and she sucked in a huge gasp of air.

Sitting bolt upright, she glanced around rapidly, taking in the myriad of concerned aides rushing around, though everyone came to a standstill and let out a sigh of relief as she woke up. The Bashful-masked assistant let out a cry of relief, wrapping an arm under her back and pulling her into a standing position. "She's awake! Get her to the healers' tent right this instant! Clearly she's worked herself into a state of exhaustion, I want to see food, clean water, and-"

"I'm fine!" Snow interjected, though her words were ignored as her people tried to pull her along. "No, I'm *fine*! I just came under the effect of someone's skill. Some kind of long distance communication."

Only firm denial met her statement, and the assistant simply pushed harder. "I'm sorry to say, no one has that kind of power-"

"It was Sleepy." Those words were enough to cause those around her to pause, some even recoiling slightly in distaste.

"Oh." The firm pressure vanished as the people around her reconsidered the events of the last few minutes, eventually giving in as Snow gently demanded to be allowed back to her actual tent.

"Before I go to bed, I need to speak with Bashful's main representatives," Snow informed her entourage. "Sleepy gave me some important information. We have some serious rumors to quell. The queen's propaganda is… potent."

"Anything else, Princess?" her logistical assistant inquired as she rapidly scribbled across her clipboarded paper.

"Yes…" Snow inhaled a deep, controlled breath, like a bow string being drawn taut. When she spoke, her words were released with the same finality as an arrow flying to strike a distant heart—there was no way to pull them back after being released.

"Have our people prepare. We ride to conquer Emdenvale at dawn."

CHAPTER
THIRTY-SEVEN

EVEN AS THE first rays of dawn broke over the horizon, painting the sky in hues of gold and rose, the plain to the south of Emdenvale was awash in movement. Banners fluttered in the crisp morning breeze, the sound of armor clinking and cold leather creaking filling the misty air. Thousands of feet shuffled toward the distant city, a sea of faces filled with resolute determination... though many barely concealed fear.

At the tip of the formation, atop a midnight-black stallion, sat Snow Weiss—doing everything she could to look natural as she rode along.

While she wasn't afraid of heights, she certainly wasn't used to being so far off the ground while moving, not to mention the constant shifting of the horse, its coarse hair grating against her armor as the creature twitched individual muscles. Each time, the princess winced, though happily, her expression was hidden behind the faceplate of her helmet.

The polished silver breastplate etched with swirling patterns and inlaid with fine pearls was undeniably stunning, but it was also cumbersome, certainly more ornament than protection. Snow felt awkwardly restricted as the horse moved, as if she were about to be thrown with every step.

Still… all of this was *necessary*. Appearances mattered, especially during a first impression, and today, she needed to look every *inch* a princess.

"Ready for your grand debut?" Ned called to her, feeling no need to keep his voice down among the immense amount of noise already causing the air to tremble. "If we're lucky, this will go quick. Oh… if you needed a little pick-me-up, Ted and Zed should be joining us sometime soon from the south or the east, but both should arrive near the same time. They sent a dove ahead; apparently they don't want to miss history in the making."

Snow didn't bother to hide how happy that information made her, though when she nodded at him, the chin of her helmet bounced off her pauldron, nearly knocking her off her horse. The princess immediately decided not to do so again. She allowed her horse to trot forward at a sedate pace for the next hour, until the walls of the city began to loom large above them.

Even from their position far closer to the ground, Snow could see the guards scrambling, rushing to and fro as horns blared. Amplified voices, bolstered by skills or magical items, shouted warnings meant for both the defenders and perhaps the rebel army as well.

"Bar the gates! Archers at the ready!"

As the first implicit threat rang out, the tension in the air rapidly began to ramp up. Doing her best not to show the agitation she felt, Snow instead focused on her breathing, scanning herself with her own skills to ensure she was still projecting confidence. "A fearful leader sows doubt among her people, and the harvest of that crop is a poison we can't afford."

"Well said, My Queen," her stalwart guardian bellowed at her, his voice echoing much farther than she would have expected in the quiet morning air as his mask activated a hidden feature. His next words were far quieter, clearly meant only for the small group around her. "We should halt and allow our forces to form up. Only a few dozen more yards before we're in longbow range, and I'd rather be able to calmly pull you away from an accidental loose from a too-eager town guard than have to dodge a coordinated barrage."

Instead of answering, Snow simply slowed her horse and allowed the forces trailing behind her to spread out, falling into easy formations in a massive half circle around the city. She was certain people were fleeing into the ocean on the other side and only hoped she hadn't caused too much mayhem by marching on them unannounced. As things settled, yet before Snow could turn to ask her advisors their opinion on what to do next, a figure appeared atop the closed city gates.

Not only was he wearing armor of a far higher quality than the others around him, but his posture was the rigid, powerful, straight-back alignment she had come to associate with those used to being in command of others. Nothing about him betrayed even a hint of doubt as he raised an item to his mouth, but that didn't stop Snow's skills from high-lighting dozens of points that betrayed his true uncertainty.

"Invaders, turn back now." His voice was confident and strong, hiding the signs of what must have been quite the stressful morning after his people noticed the army on the move. "No army shall breach these walls; the city of Emden-vale stands loyal to the crown!"

"There it is." Snow whispered as his voice cracked ever so slightly on his last word. Ned reached over and flicked the side of her helmet, winking and gesturing for her to reply to the mouthpiece of the city. "I can feel your commitment to your people from here! Do I have the honor of speaking to the governor of the city?"

"If you know who I am, you'll know that I have never

once gone back on my word!" The response came quickly. Too quickly, a sign of someone used to reading from scripts and living in a careful routine. "We have fought back bandits and pirates, and though you are more numerous than they, we will defeat you all the same should you test yourself against us!"

"Governor." Snow's voice was clear and rang with an authority that only came from long years spent in negotiation and refining her skills—system granted or otherwise. "I guarantee I have enough power to break into the city and take it by force if it becomes *absolutely necessary* to do so. But you do not need to fear. I am not here to sack your city. I do not come with ill intent. I only wish to speak to your people, take volunteers who wish to join us, and ensure we do not leave a threat at our back as we ride away."

There were a long few moments as those on top of the wall conferred with each other, but eventually the governor shook his head and replied, "your words are merely wind. At best, I can only thank you for filling the sails of our ships as they carry our children to safety. At worst, well… the wind is fickle and can turn on you when you least expect it."

"You say you are loyal to the crown." As Snow spoke, she could see Ned mouthing her words alongside her, the kinks in her script having been worked out together the night before. "If that is so, you are not going back on your honor by opening the gates for my people. I am Princess Snow Weiss, and I have raised this army to go forward and remove the tyrant from the throne: *Witch Queen Kat.*"

Only silence followed her announcement, which she had known was a distinct possibility. Taking a deep breath, she pushed her Aura of Innocence out to its maximum, even knowing it wouldn't reach across the distance between them. Yet, it *would* affect her own people, making all of them appear more humble, innocent, and sincere. No matter who among her army the guards were watching, at least around her, they would only see righteous indignation at worst. Only then did she speak out once more.

"I will offer you an oath, Governor." At her words, Snow's own army shifted in discomfort, knowing the consequences she was opening herself up to. "I am here to speak to the people of this city and try to convince them to join my cause. I will not force them nor coerce them. Only those who *wish* to come with me will do so. More than that, I will personally guarantee that I have truthfully and honestly ordered each of my people to exit the city before nightfall, if you allow us entrance in short order."

"What I ask in return is simple." Here, she allowed her tone to become slightly more strong, hinting at untold consequences if the governor threw her generosity in her face. "Each city leader who remains behind must swear an oath not to attempt to hinder us as we move against the palace and the Witch who has taken it for her own. All of these oaths, yours and mine, shall be binding until I have either defeated the queen or have been defeated in turn. Will you accept these terms?"

In under fifteen minutes, far more quickly than she'd expected, the governor returned with his answer. It was with great relief that he replied to her, "So long as you swear you will not harm my people unless they try to harm you, I will agree to these terms."

"In that case," Snow lifted her right hand in the air, "so long as my people are not done wrong as we enter the city, during our time there, or as we leave, I hereby swear by the system that I will uphold the terms we have agreed on. Cross my heart… and hope to die."

As she finished her oath, she brought her hand down and made a large 'X' over her chest. Lightning struck across the clear sky, clouds boiling into existence as the air trembled with the weight of the binding oath she'd just made. Golden light shone down on her from above, collecting along the path she had drawn before slowly sinking through her cuirass and wrapping around her heart. Her breath hitched as the system constricted her heart for a fraction of a fraction of a second, acknowledging the oath had been made and how swiftly it would cut her down, should she fail to follow through.

Even with the system itself acknowledging her words, the governor hesitated, leaning forward across the edge of the battlement as he searched the princess for any sign of deceit. She knew he would not find any, and so he soon had no choice but to swallow his fears and stand upright. "We... Princess, I truly hope we are doing the right thing. I will allow you and your people to enter, but know this. Any treachery, sanctioned by you or not, and we will not hesitate to fight to the last."

"That is fair and completely understandable. My ambassadors will not give you any cause for alarm."

The governor took a moment to digest the princess's promise, then turned and waved his hand; shouting orders compelling those sworn to the defense of Emdenvale to remove the bars and stoppers behind the massive gates. Soon, the groan of ancient hinges filled the air with squealing as the barrier swung open. Chains rattled as the portcullis was hoisted... and a sharp voice called to Snow as she began to urge her horse forward.

"Wait. Your Highness," Ned gently pulled back on her horse's reins. "I think you should stay here."

"Ned. That was *not* the plan, I need to-"

The bard held his hands up in surrender. "I understand! But look around. Look how nervous everyone is. While it is true you have an accord with the *governor*, he does not speak for everyone in the city. If something were to happen to you, half your kingdom would be destroyed in this one battle. Send in my bards and plenty of soldiers to keep them safe. Remain here, easing the tensions of your loyal subjects, and allow those who carry your voice to spread your message throughout the city."

Snow chewed her lip, torn between the desire to lead from the front and the benefits he had laid out. Even as she kicked herself for giving in, her mind began adding on potential benefits Ned wouldn't even know about. Namely, by having her Brand Ambassadors be the ones to go in and try to recruit the people of the city, her skill was certain to increase in power. "Gather the bards."

"Thank you, Princess." Ned sagged in relief as he vigorously nodded. "I truly believe you are making the right choice here."

By the time the gates had fully opened, dozens of Bashful-masked bards were lined up and ready to enter the city to tell the tale of hope and freedom Snow Weiss represented. Snow moved among each of them, ensuring every last one of them had been granted one of her skills. "Go. Show them we are not the monsters the queen makes us out to be. Tell them the truth. We are here to save them from the crushing oppression they have been living under, and likely worse to come."

The bards, with an individual escort of at least three guards each, began marching into the city. Snow returned to her stallion, climbing up and sitting side-saddle as she watched and waited for some sign of success... or, system forbode, failure.

Minutes slipped by like grains of sand falling through her fingers. As the first hour came to an end, the slightest of tickles on her arm made her glance at her follower count, as both it and her skill of progression requirement began to increase.

Requirement to advance to level 10: gain 50,000 followers through the efforts of your Brand Ambassadors. 38,517... 38,520... 38,528/50,000.

As the sun inched upward in the sky, and people on both

sides of the wall began breaking into their lunches, the faintest strains of music drifted out over the city walls. The princess could almost picture the scene, having lived it herself for months at a time: the townspeople, tired of remaining immensely stressed, gathering in town squares and other large spaces to see what was going on. The bards standing on railings, street corners, wrapping one arm around tall statues and leaning out so they could be heard by those as far away as possible.

Bashful's people would be using this moment, when most people were filling the pit of anxiety with a hearty meal and beginning to reach their calmest state of the day, to weave their tales and explain their options. The effect was nearly immediate, as the numbers began climbing too fast to be seen individually.

...38,831... 38,954... 40,210/50,000.

"What if it *Perfects* my skill, but still isn't enough to push the city firmly into my camp?" Snow quietly conversed with her advisors, careful not to allow her doubts to flow beyond her trusted circle.

"Then we take their oaths and move on," a chipper voice chimed in, causing Snow to turn so abruptly that she nearly fell off her horse. She hadn't even realized until Zed spoke out that one, he and Ted had arrived, and two... her legs were completely asleep. "Just like you promised. Too bad you didn't think to bargain for safe passage to a Class Shrine. That would have been helpful."

"Zed, you're here! Also..." Snow had to resist the urge to smack herself in the helmeted head with her gauntleted hand. "How did we forget that?"

There were a few sheepish glances among her advisors, but it was Dopey's general, who had written along with them, who gave her a concise answer. "We forgot."

"Yeah, we've all had our Full Class for so long, it… it didn't cross my mind." Ned replied bashfully.

Snow tried to put it out of her mind, vowing not to make the same mistake twice, as she caught up with her long lost friends. They took her mind off the impending deadline of nightfall, regaling her with their travels across the kingdom, stirring up rebellion everywhere they stepped.

As the afternoon wound down, and the first of her brand ambassadors began making their way out of Emdenvale, Snow felt her heart sink. As the sun fell behind the city wall, not yet night, but close enough to sunset that the thick barrier blocked the light, Snow gasped in excitement as she felt a bottleneck that had been constricting her finally break.

A rush of power swept around the area, so strong her well-trained horse abruptly shifted and began to fret. The princess barely noticed as others stepped forward to calm the animal—the energy had begun collecting along her left arm. It flowed into her fully, and the darkened area blazed with sudden, pearlescent light as Brand Ambassador reached *Perfection*.

Brand Ambassador: Level 10/10.

At the cost of [2500] influence, you can choose a person to generate followers on your behalf by [Perfectly] imparting one of your skills on them. The same skill cannot be imparted while it is currently imbued, but other skills can be put on the same person at the cost of an additional [0]% influence per skill. Upon choosing to activate the imparted skill, they will be able to act with your granted skills for [20] days before the skill fades. While using the skills, every [10] in ten new followers will count as influenced by you.

You are able to stipulate conditions for granting your skills and are able to remove the applied skill at any distance.

You have earned access to your Advanced Class Breakthrough Skill. Touch a Class Shrine to activate it!

"Yeah… access to a Class Shrine would have been a good move." Snow grumbled softly, though she couldn't truly be any kind of upset at the moment.

"Princess Snow," the governor's voice rang out, causing the smile to freeze in position on her face before fading slightly as she looked up at the wall. "Did you just achieve *Perfection* in a skill?"

"I did," she replied, seeing no need to hide the truth. "When I next touch a Class Shrine, I will have an Advanced Class Breakthrough skill, as well as a new, Full Class skill to bring to bear."

A heavy moment passed between them, then the governor let out a low chuckle. "You forced my doors open even without having your adult class? I can't imagine how formidable you will become in the next few months. The crucible of combat truly progresses skills like nothing else. Frankly…"

She could hear his lips smacking as he tried to force himself to speak, and finally he managed to do so. "Princess Snow, as governor of this fair city, I do not wish there to be enmity between myself and… my future queen. On my honor, and by the system, I hereby swear to fulfill my oath to the crown through *you*. From here onward, *Emdenvale stands with Princess Snow Weiss!*"

A cheer erupted from her army, a roar of triumph and relief rolling across the plane. Snow locked eyes with the distant governor, giving him a small nod of acknowledgment as he raised his hand in salute. Though she knew he couldn't hear her, she still whispered, "I won't betray the trust you have shown me, Governor."

"You did it!" Zed clapped her on the shoulder, jumping with joy along with thousands of others outside the city and within. "You captured a city without a drop of blood spilling! *Wololo*, am I right?"

Snow wasn't the only one to give him a confused stare, but

the celebratory atmosphere didn't allow their thoughts to linger on his strange question for long. The princess only heard his sheepish words thanks to him being all but pressed to her side as the crowd surged around them. "What? That's not a thing here?"

CHAPTER
THIRTY-EIGHT

THE LONG TREK north toward Thalfanghein, Drienhurst, then their eventual destination of Deckbett and the palace brought with it a myriad of challenges. Chiefly among them was the waning excitement of their mission, as the reality of life on the road began to settle in. Reaching the capital city was a journey which promised weeks of grueling travel, even if they were to maintain a relentless pace. But, frankly, *relentless* wasn't an option. Not with the army growing larger by the day.

What had begun as a force of five wagons had swelled to hundreds of marching people, quickly turning into thousands, and now tens of thousands as more citizens abandoned the regime and joined the rebellion. With each new fresh face, the pace slowed incrementally. The immense logistical weight of feeding, sheltering, and organizing so many bodies felt like slowly pushing a boulder uphill. One misstep, and their momentum would be lost completely.

The mornings were the hardest, as the camp awoke long before the sun had even considered cresting the horizon, an absolute necessity so the hundreds of workers tasked with dismantling the camp and packing their shelters onto wagons could fulfill their obligations. By the time false dawn had arrived, only the final few canvas enclosures had yet to be pulled down. By then, enormous kettles bubbling with steaming porridge and thick stew would be calling to everyone, enticing them to form into lines and patiently await their turn to eat before joining their formations for the daily forced march:

Easily the worst part of every day.

Being exposed to the elements for so long, especially since the roads they tried to keep to had been churned into mud by passing boots and moistened by the rains of the season—no matter how gentle they may be along the coast—brought a rapid souring of attitudes and added to the hardships. Snow and her Brand Ambassadors had their work cut out for them; keeping people calm was their chief mission throughout the day. Bards rode in open-topped wagons alongside the marching troops, performing from sunup to sundown before collapsing into their own bedrolls at night.

The best among the Brand Ambassadors were tasked with outreach, small groups consisting of people armed with pipes and lutes surrounded by those coated with—and carrying—steel. They spread out to all the villages not along their route, ranging far and wide in an effort to incite the population into rebellion—though they obviously branded it, with perfect honesty, as hope and a desperate yearning for change. Each day, those on the verge of losing their princess-granted skills would return, leading new recruits filled with resolve and excitement.

Each day, the army swelled. Each day, its progress slowed. But never, at least during daylight hours, did it stop.

As for Snow, the princess spent hours each day riding up and down the long columns of people stretching a half-dozen miles at this point. Where she went, tension eased. Doubt flickered and was extinguished like a snuffed candle, replaced by determination as her people found someone who would speak to them personally, listen to their concerns, stories, and fears. With the help of her advisors, she often found helpful solutions for the militia that were simple enough to implement while still on the move—continuously solidifying the people's resolve and helping to tie their hopes and aspirations to their future queen.

Each night brought little rest, at least for Snow. Meetings stretched into the small hours, major decisions being determined by the group of generals and advisors squished into a cramped space to maximize the flickering lamplight. Maps had been created and discarded as Sneezy's people scouted ahead, doing their best to offer the best paths, safest routes, and quickest ways to major population centers while avoiding natural hazards. Snow did her best to absorb every detail, but as the weeks stretched on, and sleep became a luxury outside of her price range, she found herself needing to rely on delegating to others with ever greater frequency.

On the forty-second day after leaving Emdenvale, with half a month to go at this pace before even reaching Thalfanghein, Snow's routine was broken by a rider appearing on the horizon, galloping hard toward them as his clothing flapped in the wind he generated. An alarm was raised as he closed in, his horse heaving for air, its flanks lathered in sweat, only for the call to stand down going out as the forward scout was recognized.

Heart clenching with anticipation and apprehension, Snow waited impatiently as he first went to report to his first line leader, who then brought the pertinent information up the chain of command. As the minutes stretched longer, Snow could only grit her teeth and grumble, "Sometimes I just can't stand bureaucracy."

It was Ned who finally came to explain what had happened. As soon as he spoke, Snow stiffened as she took in the too-formal language. "Your Highness. Our scouts have discovered a town two-day's ride to the east—specifically, a town built around a Class Shrine. They have confirmed its existence, but this means there are guaranteed to be at least a small contingent of Huntsmen guarding the area, as the Witch has decreed they are to be guarded by her abominations at all times."

"What are you wanting to ask, Ned?" Snow gently pressed, hoping to skip the formalities he seemed to be insisting on. "This sounds like the opportunity we've been waiting for. A chance to unlock my Full Class, to begin leveling my Breakthrough Skill and new Basic Skill."

"*Exactly*, Princess Snow." Ned inclined his head at her astuteness. "In other words, it seems… somehow too perfect. The generals have asked for your blessing to put together a strike force composed of our veteran fighters to clear out the Huntsmen and secure the town and shrine for you."

Snow was shaking her head even before he finished his words. "No, Ned. This isn't something I can delegate. No one can unlock my class for me; I have to be there. If we're going to stage an assault-"

"I have been tasked with impressing upon you how bad of an idea that would be." Ned interrupted with a tone that showed he was *attempting* to be tactful. "Your work here is keeping the army together. Once the town has been secured, and a safe route charted, it will be far easier for you to ride there and back at speed."

"If there is combat to be had, especially as this might be our first true test, I need to be there to see it." They stared at each other for a long moment, Ned's mouth tightening with clear frustration as she overruled him. The princess fully understood that he was trying to look out for her and so offered a compromise.

"As you insinuated, there is a strong possibility that this might be an ambush. That is even more reason for me to attend. Instead of a small strike force, just a handful of elite fighters, I want you to go and hand-select a full *dozen* platoons. We will move with a larger force. Small enough to go and return quickly, but large enough to handle whatever might be thrown at us."

"Fine." He exhaled sharply as he all but spat the word, formalities thrown to the side as he allowed his frustration to shine through. "I don't like this, Snow. Every time you risk yourself, every one of the people putting their trust in you is also in danger."

"I'm not trying to be difficult, Ned," Snow informed him quietly, returning to her silent, patient waiting as he did the same. Finally, reluctantly, he bowed his head and turned to go relay her orders.

Though they tried to keep their departure as discreet as possible, there was only so much they could do to hide hundreds of mounted warriors breaking off from the main force, supported by wagons bearing all of the essentials they needed for the multi-day trip. Tents, foodstuffs, clean water, as well as healing supplies. Each rider carried their own personal effects, changes of clothes, and the like. Snow could feel the immediate dip in morale as they thundered away into the distance, though she hoped her ambassadors would keep people calm until she returned.

The ride toward the small town was a terse one, following a path that twisted and turned through the forest beneath a heavy canopy. Happily, the route they took was one clearly not oft-traveled, granting them the dignity of a mud-free journey. Still, the fact they could not spread out as they did on the open plains along the coast the main army was traveling meant that the column of calvary was forced to stretch thin along the route. Only as night fell did the last of the warriors arrive, though they were greatly pleased to see that camp had already been set up for them.

Crash.

Snow glanced across the open glade they had found, casually watching as a falling tree finished its descent. "I would appreciate someone *announcing* what they are taking down. Is that for firewood, or are they just trying to open clear lines of sight?"

"Probably a little bit of both." Ned murmured as he stepped away from her side, offering a proper salute as the princess moved to retire for the evening.

Snow waited a short while before tossing back her tent flaps, taking in the sight of a dozen platoons of disciplined veterans from the Shield and Truncheon Association, various groups of bards who were here to provide support in their own ways, and the dense crowd of healers who had been pressed into joining them to ensure her personal health—with a secondary objective of being there for anyone who took an injury. All of the people there were highly trusted, highly competent, and outfitted with the best gear Happy's investments could buy. Even so, they fell short of being magically enhanced.

Even the wealth of an entire kingdom wasn't enough to outfit an entire army with magical gear.

Snow hummed deeply to herself as she watched them move around the camp, settling around campfires, seeking a bed roll, or standing watch depending on their assigned tasks. Finally, she joined the secondary group, falling into a dreamless slumber nearly as soon as her head hit her rolled-up pack. As they thundered through the woods the next morning, everything seemed much the same.

It was only as they approached the town itself that the trap they had been expecting was sprung. The assault started with a branch snapping in the distance, loud enough to be heard over the pounding hooves of the horses, giving them just enough time to pull their weapons before the underbrush around them erupted with dark forms sprinting from their positions under the trees.

"*Huntsmen!*" Snow's personal guard bellowed into the open air, his voice amplified by his mask. "Ambush! Form up!"

The princess had been riding approximately a third of the

way back from the front line of horsemen and quickly found herself surrounded on all sides as those behind her thundered up and around, creating a massive defensive wall of steel and horseflesh to keep her from harm.

Even with the rapid reaction of the rebels, the Huntsmen didn't slow their charge. They crashed into the thin points of the rider's group, tearing warriors from their saddles, and in some cases, even sending the horses themselves to the ground, crushing those on their backs. Their weapons darted out with more power than precision, digging deep furrows into the metal armor of the rebels or leaving behind enormous rends where they touched flesh. As they went about their grisly work, the twisted once-humans screamed with incoherent rage or laughed maniacally as they swung their weapons to and fro like mad artists.

A chill went down Snow's spine as she froze at the initial clash, other voices calling out the need for spears to fend off the inhumanly strong Huntsmen. The long polearms punched out, only slowing the feral minions of the queen, hampering their movements instead of pinning them in place.

Finally, Snow found her voice and began calling out words of encouragement, urging her auras to bolster her people's courage, *influencing* them to achieve their peak performance as the two sides clashed in a brutal and bloody manner. The clash of steel meeting flesh began sounding out, accompanied by the cries of the wounded—among the rebels only—and howling hatred or maniacal laughter from the attackers, no matter how grievous of wounds the Huntsmen took.

Still, the tide quickly began to shift in favor of the rebels.

Although their opponents fought without fear or hesitation, bodies pulling together after taking fatal wounds that would have caused any normal person to quickly fade, they did so by having traded the entirety of their individual class skills. One Huntsman took a spear through the gut, wrenching it free and jumping back into the fight as the hole in his torso knitted itself closed—only to be met by half a dozen more spear tips as the highly trained warriors coordinated their attacks and pinned the abomination in place.

While her combatants didn't have the seemingly endless regeneration of their opponents, the healers among Snow's troops quickly received the injured and dying, working tirelessly to drag the wounded back and patching them up as quickly as possible. In many cases, they even managed to get the fallen warriors back into the fight. The gear her men wore also proved invaluable, the high-end reinforced armor saving lives that would have been lost beneath the brutal strength of their foe.

Each second of the fight created a crystal-clear memory as everyone's senses hummed, their minds focused fully on the moment as they worked to survive the onslaught. Then: a major shift! A coordinated push splintered off a section of the Huntsmen's ranks, breaking the dark tide of bodies into smaller, more manageable groups. As swords flashed and spears were thrust forward, the bards added their assistance by sending wave after wave of illusory attacks at the Huntsmen, keeping them guessing as real warriors poured into the breach.

"*Forward!*" Snow found herself screaming, voice raw as she worked to be heard above the terrifying clamor. Her words were empowered by a wave of influence rolling off of her, pushing those around her to lurch forward, weapons leading the way as they hacked the Witch's experiments to pieces. Step by bloody step, they advanced as the cohesion of their ambushers began to falter.

Feeling no fear, not a single one of the Huntsmen moved to retreat. Without strategy, they didn't work together to regroup. They simply fought and fought, until they fell. As the horses pushed forward, the Huntsmen began to fall ever faster.

Finally, the last of the abominations crumpled to the

ground, his limbs still rising frantically until sharp weapons with long handles pinned them in place. Already, a massive pyre was being prepared in the distance, the remnants carried away to be set ablaze before they could begin to melt and poison the forest floor. Snow swayed in her saddle, exhaustion from the fear and rage leaving her feeling hollow, the intense draining of her influence to bolster her people leaving her thoughts feeling thick and slow.

But she had more important things to do than worry about herself. Looking around at her advisors, she managed to croak out, "Report?"

Her head of security limped over to her, and Snow blinked in surprise, wondering when he'd gotten off his horse—or, by the look of him, when he'd been thrown off it. His Grumpy mask was cracked, smeared with blood, and sparking with the light of a failing magical item. "It's not good, Your Highness. We lost nearly a quarter of our forces. We're estimating around twenty-two percent. It's not-"

The rest of his words were lost on Snow, as a sharp, ringing sound filled her mind, her eyes going distant as she stared at his head, through his head, spiraling into despair at the horrifying aftermath of the ambush she had all but forced the people relying on her into. Her voice was faint as she whispered, vision beginning to blur as hot tears welled up and trickled down her cheeks. "Twelve platoons... that means I lost *three*? How many people is that? What am I going to tell their families-"

Crack.

Snow gasped as his gauntleted hand shot out, the sharp sound of her cheek getting slapped echoing just loudly enough to drown out her internal despair. As she stared at him with wide eyes, her hand slowly reached up to touch the scalding hot skin where his palm had landed.

Her head of security growled, "I'm so sorry I needed to do that, but you don't *get* to fall into despair. This is combat, and this is what happens. *Listen* to me, Princess. I cannot praise you enough for your demands. I was part of Ned's original planning. This trap was already set, the bait in place. If we had gone in with fewer numbers, as we had planned to do, everyone would have died. *Every last one of them.* Then the Huntsmen would have pulled themselves together and walked away to fight again."

Gently reaching out, he patted her leg comfortingly, looking up to lock eyes with her as she remained seated on her pitch-black stallion. "You saved lives today. That is what matters. They knew the risks; we all did. None of us are greenhorns here, Princess. Fact is, you led us through this, and we're still standing."

Snow's lips trembled, and the tears still flowed, but she nodded at him gratefully as the truth of his word sank in. "What do I do now?"

"Exactly what we planned to do." He stepped away, gesturing down yet another path that had been turned into mud, though this one had been moistened with blood— whether healthy red or tainted black. "We go get you your class and make you a queen."

"See to the wounded. Make sure we all ride together." Snow finally called after chewing on her lip, deep in thought. "I wouldn't want to see a second surge arrive, only to catch our most vulnerable off guard. Not only that, but… gather our dead. They deserve more than being left in a forest for the animals to pick over."

"As you say, Your Highness." He bowed slightly, standing and wincing as he shifted on his injured leg.

"One last thing." Snow's voice took on a slightly incredulous tone as she touched her cheek once more. "Did you really jump and slap me, even with your leg like that? Couldn't you have, I don't know, grabbed my ankle and given me a good shake or something?"

He offered a casual shrug, too tired to express himself

more clearly. "Slaps *work*. Quick and easy way to grab people's attention and force them to focus on the moment."

"Still, I'd rather not get slapped again. Consider that an order."

"Look, if it's a choice between keeping you and our hopes of the future alive, and a little bit of pain, I sure hope you'll forgive my *impertinence*." He bowed again, this time with significant exaggeration.

Snow could only grumble and reluctantly nod at his words. "Fine. In that case, I hope you know I'll be looking for a chance to return the favor."

"Ehh… what?"

CHAPTER
THIRTY-NINE

THE MUCH DEPLETED battalion thundered into the forest town, a place which should have been filled with life and voices. Instead, it was a ghost town. The houses were all dark and empty, the streets silent but for the noise the rebels made. Snow looked over the area, her heart sinking as she realized where all of the Huntsmen they had just fought had come from—the entire population had been taken and converted by the Witch.

Shouts began to ring out behind her, and for a moment, Snow's breath hitched in her chest, her hand falling to the sword at her hip that she barely knew how to wield. Then she realized the voices weren't raised in fear or anger; they were shouted commands as the healers began selecting empty homes to convert into makeshift infirmaries. The warriors went through each and every house ahead of them, making sure there were no traps waiting to be sprung, no further ambushes to reap their lives.

Once the entirety of the area had been secured, the wounded carefully packed away, the other houses were soon filled to capacity with the exhausted rebels. For her part, Snow and her close circle of advisors and guards were walking to the center of town where the class shrine stood.

The small, nondescript white building was why they had come to this place in the first place. Men and women had bled for this, had died so that Snow could step into the shrine and touch the plinth therein. All so she could gain a Full Class and therefore have ever so slightly more credibility when she worked to convert cities to fall under her banner.

Snow understood the reasoning of her advisors, why they had pushed for this so hard, but at the moment... she certainly didn't feel that it had been worth it.

After her guards carefully checked the small space, they stepped back and allowed her to enter on her own, to have some privacy as she interfaced with the system itself. The princess walked forward, heart pounding as she approached the place of power, the first time since her fourteenth birthday, and the solemn ceremony culminating in gaining her Advanced Class.

Reaching out, she placed her palm—trembling with excitement—against the cool stone surface. For a single breath, she simply held her hand in place. Then the plinth pulsed beneath her fingertips, and a surge of energy filled every corner of her being.

Codex Arcane Ledger access requested.

C.A.L. is assessing...
requirements for Breakthrough have been fulfilled!

Checking all system merits.

Basic Class:
-Basic Skill: **10**/*10.*
-Advanced Skill: **10**/*10.*
-Breakthrough Skill: **0**/*10.*

Advanced Class:
-*Basic Skill:* **10**/10.
-*Advanced Skill:* **10**/10.
Total: 40/50.

<u>Bonus points</u>
-*System merit (Rare): Prodigy. Achieve Breakthrough in Advanced Class. +20.*
-*System merit (Rare): Gift of Minor Patience. Achieve Breakthrough in Advanced Class by not advancing your class at 18 years of age. +20.*
-*System merit (Epic): Polymath Prodigy. Achieve system-recognized basic competence in four unique disciplines beyond the scope of your class-granted skills before attaining Breakthrough with your Advanced Class. +30.*
-*System merit (Legendary): Unforsaken Innocence. Achieve Perfection in an Advanced Skill without accepting a Witch-path modifier after being offered one. Please note, by gaining this merit, that path is forever closed to you. +40.*
Total class points to be applied: 150/50.

Generating Advanced Class Breakthrough Skill…
Skill generated!

Breakthrough Skill: Voice of the People. 0/10.
Once per hour, the user of this skill is able to amplify the reach of their voice by [skill level * 100 meters] for 10 minutes, allowing for others to hear them clearly even through cacophonous noise. Each Brand Ambassador within range of the skill will act as an automatic extender of the voice, allowing it to extend outward the [skill level * 10%] further, centered on the Brand Ambassador. Once every [24-skill level] hours, at the cost of [10,000-(2000*skill level)] influence, the user can choose a target area and speak a truth she wholeheartedly believes in, creating a zone of sonic damage lasting [5+(skill level *2)] minutes which will shatter falsehoods, dealing damage to those hidden via illusions, disguises, or anyone who intentionally lies.

Use this zone with caution, as it will also impact the user of this skill.

Requirement to advance to level 1: Use any aspect of this skill for the first time.

Snow found herself standing in the Class Shrine once more, breathing heavily as her mind pulled back from the vast ocean of power and intelligence that was the system. Her hand remained locked on the plinth, and as soon as her mind and body had allowed her new power to settle within her, the system pulled her back in.

C.A.L. is assessing...
Age verification: 19 years. 2 months, 28 days. Conditions for Full Class advancement met.

Assessing skill use and level. Combined skill levels: 40/50. Determination: 86th percentile.

Scanning brain waves to account for knowledge and desires in Full Class selection process. Requirements met for: 8 Full Classes.

Comparing skill use and desires... 86th percentile of skills shows a subconscious desire to continue progressing, with a shift toward specialization in a new area. Waking brain is in alignment with subconscious. Determination made.

Bonus points.

-System Merit (Rare): Rout Averted. Even after losing 20% of your fighting force in a single battle, eliminate your enemy to the last without your troops fleeing. +20.
-System merit (Epic): Conviction Embodied. Maintain unwavering commitment, inspiring others consistently for at least 30 days while being the leader of a rebel army. +30.
-System merit (Epic): Rebel Queen. Unite five distinct factions under your

command while maintaining full authority and refusing to become their leader in name only. +30.

-System merit (Legendary): Benevolent Strategist. Capture a City without spilling a single drop of blood. +40.

Total class points to be applied: 105/50.

Full Class Unlocked!

Full Class: Charismatic Contender for the Throne. (Upgradable)
Basic Skill: Warlord's Presence: Level 1/10.

Warlord's presence is a passive skill which further amplifies the user's auras, infusing them with a [Minimal] sense of authority, causing foes to falter and inspiring allies to action.

When not in combat, the presence of your auras increases the movement speed of your forces by [skill level]%, and reduces the amount of food they require to function at peak performance by [5*skill level]%.

When in combat, the presence of your aura [Minimally] increases the efficacy of the user's words when quelling fears. Thanks to your exacting leadership, any ally under the effect of your aura has a [skill level]% chance to critically strike, dealing system enhanced damage upon landing a blow. These strikes cost 50 influence per success and draw from a pool of influence you may designate specifically to empower this skill, up to a maximum of 100,000.

Requirement to advance: Sustain a 10-hour forced march for the entirety of your army, maximizing the consumption of food while traveling at maximum speed and efficiency.

This class has been deemed **'Upgradable'**. *If you manage to complete your mission, toppling the Witch Queen from the throne, the class will shift into an appropriate analog. Your skills from this class will be replaced, immediately reaching Perfection.*

Conversely, if you fail in your mission, fleeing the kingdom instead of achieving success, your class will be downgraded to an appropriate analog. Your skills from this class will be replaced, losing one level and modifier.

Once again Snow returned to herself, reeling from the immense amount of information, the details and deep contemplations of the system fading away and leaving only the stark information that had written itself out for her to read. The newly christened Warlord leaned on the plinth, breathing heavily as hope and fear intermingled in her heart. "Isn't this a mandate from the system itself? If nothing else, it's increasing my odds against *her*."

Just as she stood back to her full height, breathing finally evening out, one last surge of energy filled her, as the system almost begrudgingly awarded her one final chunk of potential.

*Special modifier applied: You have been granted a modifier '**Damsel of Distress**'.*

Against seemingly insurmountable odds, you transformed a set of skills or circumstances which nearly guaranteed failure or even death into a foundation for success with far-reaching and profound effects. By taking your fate into your own hands, you have broken free of the Codex Arcane Ledger's predicted outcome for your life.

Effect: When in the presence of another 'Damsel of Distress', you will be able to recognize each other as kindred spirits and [Minimally] share the benefits of your skills, if so desired, while in range. This will increase in potency with the skill it was acquired in tandem with.

"That's... thank you?" Snow stepped away and bowed to the shard of the system itself, doing her best to emanate gratitude and hide away every last dreg of confusion. After a moment of hesitation, she stepped forward and touched the potent magical artifact once more, just to be doubly certain there wasn't more it was going to offer her.

An echo of humor swept through her, as though a distant entity were chuckling at her greed. She quickly stepped away, a sheepish grin on her face as she whirled around and walked out of the small building. Her mind was full, clouded with the implications of the new power still settling into her. Her friends, her advisors, as well as her personal security were waiting just beyond the threshold, faces tight with anxiety. As the princess emerged, their eyes brightened with hope.

Ned was of course the first to speak, his words encompassing the unspoken need to hear from her own lips how this leader of the rebellion was going to help them succeed. "You were in there longer than we expected... does that mean the system spoke to you? Did you get some say in what class you unlocked?"

"Not exactly." Snow's words caused visible reactions amongst the assembled people. Deciding that words may not be enough, she intentionally extended her Aura of Influence, watching as those around her faltered slightly under the weight of her new found, system-granted *authority*. "Instead, the system has given me the toolkit I need to lead our army and to fight against the queen's forces. It... well, it also made it all too clear that failure isn't an option."

Though it was slightly uncomfortable to share the exact details, as the interactions between a person and the system were widely considered soul-to-soul and therefore immensely intimate and private, she knew that they needed hope at this moment. She clearly explained not only the names but the effects of each of her skills, even going so far as to spell out the terms of her class itself becoming upgradable. The only thing she kept to herself was the special modifier, *Damsel of Distress*, which she wasn't even certain would be pertinent.

Ned let out a low whistle as she finished, and he wasn't the only one. "That's... yeah, that's potent. I've only ever heard of warlord skills in history books. They died out after the various kingdoms were established and haven't been seen since the collapse of the last empire on this continent, nearly eight hundred years ago."

He glanced around as people looked at him with a hint of question in their eyes, "What? I'm a *bard*. History falls under our purview."

The broad-shouldered, grumpy-masked head of security took over the conversation. "I can't tell you how much our logisticians are going to love the fact that they won't need to panic quite as much over food. As for the percentage increase in movement speed? Perhaps you might discount that, as you didn't linger on it as long as the others, but one percent farther each day would mean *hundreds* of additional miles in a year. We may even be able to reach Thalfanghein before needing to deal with wintery conditions, if we push it."

"What do you think of the critical strike portion?" Snow inquired of him, not certain what to make of it herself. "I've never heard of such a thing before. I assume it will help us fight, but I figure if anyone is going to know more about that, it's going to be you."

Offering a sharp nod, he gathered his thoughts and began, "Often, classes which are focused on death in a single strike, whether it be hunters, rangers, or *especially* assassins, are those who gain an ability like that. Sometimes, with careful planning, and therefore rarely in the heat of battle, a strike can land with more than just force. Hitting with perfect precision, where the blow will be the most devastating, is a critical strike. It turns the slightest vulnerability into a skilled blow, turning a simple attack into a devastating, typically grotesquely coup de gras."

"So it makes people hit harder." Snow shrugged as he sent her an affronted glare. "Am I right, or is there more to it?"

"You are… technically correct, in the *worst* of ways," he ground out through clenched teeth as some of the advisors snorted at the byplay. "It's not just a harder hit. It's a strike that lands in exactly the right place, exactly the right time, at the correct angle, with the proper momentum. Instead of bouncing off armor, it finds the gap between plates. Instead of parting flesh, it pierces arteries, severs tendons, and lops through the joints between bones. The effect is exponential compared to normal attacks, turning what would have been a good blow into a crippling wound, dismemberment, or worse. No, *better*, in this case."

"It's not just blades, though he does a great job at being... visually descriptive." Ned chimed in as Snow absorbed the information. "Imagine a hammer swinging at a Huntsman protected behind the heavy plate armor of your royal guard. Were it to land against his helm, it might dent the steel, ringing the bell of the opponent and perhaps disorienting them. But with a critical strike, the head of the hammer will land where the structure is weakest. The steel instead crumples like a ball of dry dirt, bringing down the enemy without needing to expand further energy on them."

"I see." Snow took a deep breath through her nose, letting it out in a long stream of turbid air. "All of this to say, my initial impression was correct. This is the system doing what it can to give us a fighting chance against *her*."

While everyone else nodded along, Ned looked clearly uncomfortable, leaning back and forth as though unsure if he should speak out. Snow stared him down until he finally gave in to her pressure, "*We~ell...* the system is well known to be unutterably, unalterably *neutral*. While we will certainly craft the *narrative* to show this as direct system intervention, I don't want you to get caught up in your own hype."

Offering a sheepish shrug, he pressed on, "The most likely reason you gained this class in the first place is that you have raised an army and already shown effectiveness in capturing cities, as well as leading in combat. Frankly, if you hadn't had those experiences, you would have probably received a direct upgrade to your Basic and Advanced classes."

"To be fair!" Ned held up his hands and almost shouted before anyone could speak. "That wouldn't have been a terrible thing, either. I'm certain the fact that you are already the princess by birthright also came into effect. None of this would have been possible had you touched the class shrine without earning the merits that you did."

"Yet here I stand, class and skills in place." Snow held her hands out to her sides. "I understand many things had to come together just right to make this happen, Ned. What I care about right now is... what's the best way to leverage this going forward?"

"Oh, I have *ideas*." His eyes sparkled as he began tapping the tips of his fingers together like an evil genius. "The first thing I'm going to do is get together with my contemporaries. We're going to write ourselves a *ballad*!"

CHAPTER
FORTY

THE SALT-TINGED AIR of Thalfanghein stung Snow's wind-chapped lips as she stood by the window of the governor's mansion overlooking the devastated city below. The final light of day was dwindling over the ocean as she dashed away the final tears she would shed for those who had been lost that day. She allowed her gaze to travel along the smoking room of the city center, watching as smoke curled up both from burned buildings, and more distant, from chimneys and the remainder of the city, which stood unchanged from her last visit.

"One month…" she breathed disbelievingly, "One full month since I gained my Full Class, and only a day since Thalfanghein fell."

The coastal jewel of the kingdom, second only to the capital city of Deckbett itself, had been taken with what at first had seemed like an almost insulting ease. Her army had thundered to the gates, arriving faster than anyone had anticipated —especially those who had been tasked with defending the city. Having already raised an army, Snow's new warlord skills had ramped up in power quickly and had attained level five simply by pushing them to maximize their logistics, training, and travel speed while on the open plains.

Now she only had to quell the last of the queen's loyalists in the city in order to achieve level six, then her march on the capitol would proceed even faster. Looking back at the burned section of the city, she grit her teeth and replayed the events of the day in her mind, trying to figure out where things had gone wrong.

They had stayed too far distant for the patrolman on the walls to see them, rushing forward as true night fell, entering the city and forcing the gates to remain open, even as the locals desperately tried to close them. From there, the city had barely managed a token defense. Those few leaders who had refused to swear to her had been rounded up, carefully contained within one small section of the local prison while Snow and her people decided what to do with them. As the sun rose, the locals awoke to find that martial law had been enacted.

It was then, as her forces were spread thin among the city, that the trap had been sprung.

Huntsmen, far more cunning than the mindless husks they had fought in the forest, had been lying in weight deep in the residential sector of the city. Though the surprise of the city guards had been genuine, the lack of preparation had turned out to be a carefully orchestrated display meant to lull the rebel forces into complacency. They revealed themselves in a shower of blood, erupting out of homes in a perfectly synchronized attack, led by some unknown signal to move as one. Hundreds of her warriors, especially those they had recruited in the countryside, died before they could begin mounting a true counter-attack.

But the Huntsmen had made one, terrible mistake—to ensure their secrecy, they had eliminated anyone whose home they had chosen to take over. In order to maintain a cohesive force, they had chosen to infest only one *specific* neighborhood. As soon as the rebels had noticed there was nothing and no one beyond the Huntsmen along that city block... they burned it to the ground.

The vast majority of the ambushing force had been caught in the supernatural flames, burning ever fiercer as Dopey's people added accelerants to the mix to ensure anyone caught by the plasmatic embrace wouldn't have anything to regenerate *from*. It was estimated that thousands of huntsmen had been swept away, a massive win for the rebels and likely a crippling blow to the forces of the Witch queen. Now, as night approached, her forces were combing through the city, scraping out the last dregs of darkness hiding in the woodwork.

As for Snow, the tears she unashamedly allowed to flow were for not only her forces who had died in the surprise attack, but the citizens of her kingdom who had been felled by the Huntsmen in order to launch an attack against her, not to mention those who had been whisked from their homes to bolster the dark forces of the queen.

"You didn't fail them, Warlord Snow." The deep voice behind her caused Snow to freeze for an icy moment, before turning and allowing a thin smile to appear on her face as Grumpy himself entered the building. "It takes time to prepare. If you had walked into this city at the head of this army a year ago, you would not have had the skillset or knowledge required to make the calls you did, decisions that saved many others. You are not the Witch queen. You cannot be held accountable for the horrors she has been inflicting on your people."

A sharp tingle of magical energy washed over Snow at that moment, a silvery pane of light appearing in the air above them. Both she and Grumpy watched as the magical scrying effect of the queen's mirror came into full force. Instead of panicking, or trying to do something to dispel the magic, Warlord Snow simply stared directly into the magical effect, daring the far-distant queen to reveal herself. After a few long moments of tilting back and forth, no doubt giving Queen Kat plenty of opportunity to understand that yet another of her cities had fallen, the magic faded away.

"We don't need to fear her anymore," Snow said aloud, not sure if she were speaking to Grumpy or herself. "From this point forward, all she can do is watch as we come ever closer. Soon we'll be putting her down like the rabid monster she is."

The burly guildmaster of the Shield and Truncheon Association shifted uncomfortably, drawing Snow's eyes to him immediately. She shook her head. "Don't do it, Grumpy. We are going after her as soon as we know the city is ours. It's only a few weeks' march, especially once I'm able to allow our forces to move six percent faster-"

"Look outside. Snow." Grumpy directed her once more to the window she'd been staring through less than a few minutes previously. Only as her searching eyes caught the falling flakes of precipitation did she realize his words had been two distinct sentences. "Winter is here, and with it immense difficulties if you try to march through it. While we are on the coast, and that will help mitigate some of the negatives of attempting to push through, it would be far more prudent to take the season-"

"We just destroyed a *massive* swath of her forces!" Snow pounded her fist on the window, not hard enough to break it, but certainly enough to make it vibrate like a gong. "If we give her the season, all we are truly doing is allowing her enough time to rebuild her entire force! They've never fallen for the same trick twice, Grumpy! We won't be able to contain and destroy them in one fell swoop, not again."

"The most generous estimates show that you would lose thirty percent of your entire force to exposure, exhaustion, disease, and starvation were you to press on." Grumpy firmly overrode the rest of her outburst. "I don't take you for that kind of leader, so let's talk instead about what needs to happen for the next few months."

"Months! *Pah*!" Snow spat as she banged on the window once more, though with far less force this time. She had already lost this argument, and they both knew it.

"Starting in the morning, we will use the city as the anvil we require to forge the foundation of your forces," Grumpy steadily informed her, ignoring any further outbursts. "I've taken care of acquiring and bringing along the best combat trainers I have. There should be plenty of instructors for all skill levels to learn from. For those who are not actively train-ing, I recommend having them work to fortify and rebuild the city. We need to prepare for the long winter settling upon us."

"*Winter*." Snow growled as though it were a dirty word.

Grumpy remained still and silent for a long moment, before finally releasing the pithy statement Snow knew he simply couldn't resist offering. "Patience, My Queen. Victory is not a matter of passion but of preparation. If you fail to prepare, be prepared to fail."

She turned away from the window, taking in his massive form as she accepted his words. "Then what is my role? I'm a warlord, according to the system. A *Contender for the Throne*. How do I spend my time?"

"There will be hardships, which you *specifically* might be able to mitigate." It was clear he was relieved that she had folded so easily. His emotion engendered a slight annoyance within the princess, as she prided herself on being willing to take in new information and put it in place without letting her own desires get in the way. "While staying put is certainly the wisest course, many people will try to use this opportunity to decide they have done enough. Your task will be to ensure that there is a blanket of power over the city, helping people to remain calm, focused, and sane during the close-quarters living of the next few months."

"Beyond that," he spoke on before she could snipe at him that she was being relegated to being a figurehead, "we're currently working under the assumption that your new ability to reduce the nutrition requirements of your people will stay in place even while we are not actively moving around. In order to make it through the winter, we are going to need to empty the city's granaries to feed the swelling army. Every individual mouthful of food we are able to save means lives that will not be lost. If you can make it so your people can survive on less... we should be able to make it through the winter and on the warpath again—allowing the city to survive by a far-too-thin margin."

Immediately, Snow was far more interested in hearing more. "Do you think I can get the entire city under the effects of my aura? The sooner we start, the less likely it is that we will need to implement harsh austerity protocols. Rationing yes, but-"

Under his mask, Grumpy was smiling as Snow immediately took to the suggestion and began issuing orders for new people to be brought under the auspices of her Brand Ambassador skill. By midnight, scores of people bearing newly imparted skills spread to all corners of Thalfanghein. Not only did this have a fast-acting effect on the fears of the citizens, it also pushed the last of the undecided over the edge.

The city officially bent the knee to their new rebel queen.

Skill increase! Influential Aura: [Level 5 (Moderate) → Level 6 (Considerable)]!
Requirement to advance to level 7: Have your forces successfully land 2,000 critical strikes. 0/2,000.

The princess grumbled in frustration as the message appeared on her arm, firmly informing her that stretching her resources and pushing her people would no longer be enough to allow her to quickly rise through the levels—unsurprising, truly. Her skill was called 'Warlord's Presence', not 'Master Logistician' or some such.

So began the long winter of her discontent.

Snow quickly returned to her routines of constant training, followed by moving among her army and city so her
people could get to know her. She ended the day with long
meetings where hard decisions were made about everything
from food to the punishment of crimes committed between
those in her army and the citizens of the city. Each night
stretched into the small hours, and each day started soon after
first light.

One long month stretched, and Snow felt terribly frustrated by the fact that she had marched from taking one city,
taking another in almost the same amount of time, only to
now be locked into position by the world itself. As the second
month came to an end, she found herself once more in her
office, staring at the beautiful, nostalgic view of distant fire-
light as seen through a gentle winter storm.

"You're going to need to replace those floorboards after
you wear them out with all that pacing," Ned called from his
position near the roaring fire, strumming a gentle melody on
his lute in an attempt to help his chosen monarch center
herself. "Why not take a few days and recover? You've been
pushing yourself so hard."

"I can't *rest*, Ned," Snow replied with deep exasperation,
rubbing the bridge of her nose tiredly as she walked toward
the open armchair near the bard. Contrary to her words, she
flopped down and looked over at her friend. "We are so close.
Every day we don't take advantage of our position of strength
makes us weaker and gives her more time to prepare."

"It's not like she's the only one who will have a stronger
army at the end of this," the man reminded her gently. "We
needed this break. Almost everyone among our forces was a
raw recruit. Now they are getting proper training. The
wounded are healed up and have recovered their strength.
Supplies are on the way... even if we are all tightening our
belts these days. You're not the only one itching to move.
Believe me."

A knock at the door interrupted them, and Snow's head of security, who had stoutly refused to give anyone his name—only after months had he allowed himself to be called 'Battle Brother' instead of 'hey you'—pushed into the room without waiting for an answer. "Your Highness. We have a situation. You're needed outside immediately."

Snow exchanged glances with Ned, both of them getting to their feet immediately and following the warrior down the grand hallway, out onto a balcony overlooking the harbor. He gestured into the distance, and for a long few moments, Snow didn't understand what he was so concerned with. "Is there a storm rolling in? The clouds are certainly low to the water, but... *no!*"

Hundreds upon hundreds of ocean-faring ships were sailing closer to the port, their open sails blending in with the falling snow, enough that a casual viewer would have over-looked them. Luckily, a portion of Snow's forces were *professional* viewers.

Battle Brother explained in a grim tone, "Sneezy's people brought the report a few minutes ago. Those aren't just any ships, they fly the flag of Wolf Warband, a warlike people known for invading cities along the coast and making off with every last scrap of food and valuables. Pirates, bandits, whatever you want to call them, they are *powerful.*"

"Why here? Why *now?*" Snow's hands balled up into fists as she took deep breaths. "No... this is good. We've needed a chance to test our forces and blow off some steam. Sound the alarm. If those invaders think they are going to sail in and put my people to the sword..."

"...they've made their last mistake."

CHAPTER
FORTY-ONE

SNOW STOOD JUST beyond the seawall of Thalfanghein, knowing the low-to-the-water ships wouldn't be using the long piers designed for far larger seafaring merchant vessels. What Wolf Warband moved in were certainly seaworthy, but they were sleek, and designed to allow the entirety of those onboard to leap over the edge and quickly come together into a proper fighting formation. They were raiders, not traders, and everything from the snarling wolf motifs carved into their hulls to the crew bristling with weapons showcased this.

As the princess's heart began to race faster with the thought of the impending battle, her breath heated up, becoming ever more visible in the crisp winter air. "Battle Brother, tell me I'm not making a terrible mistake here."

"I think it's the right *decision*," her head of security stated, not directly saying the words of affirmation she so desperately wanted to hear. "Far too many of your forces are untested. While your impressively poignant leadership powers are useful, there's only so much they can do to help if someone is going to crack under the pressure. Better to find out now, while we have a dug-in defensive position, rather than during an attack on Deckbett."

Snow sent him a disgruntled expression, then *spoke* to her people, using her Breakthrough Skill, *Voice of the People*, to issue orders along the defenders. Over the last couple of months of remaining stationary, she had only managed to increase the skill to level three, Rudimentary, by painstakingly finding niche cases which would allow her to fulfill the requirements. It was a potent power, but it was designed for either combat situations, or as a tool of a *queen*—with everything that entailed.

As she had mostly been staying within the bounds of the governor's mansion, not only for training, but to always be easy to find, it had advanced at a crawl.

"Archers at the ready. Spears and shields locked in place." An echo of her words came back to her, bouncing along the enormous relay of Brand Ambassadors and emanating forth as though she were shouting from directly above them. "Prepare to repel invaders!"

She grimaced as the final echoes died away and shouts of acknowledgment went up along the thousands of warriors. "I'm never going to get used to hearing my own voice coming from somewhere else. Do I really sound like that?"

"Yes," Ned casually stated as he came alongside her. "More shrill than you were expecting?"

"I was going to say more *regal*, but…" The princess couldn't help but enjoy his wince as he began to backpedal, though she cut off his smoothly flowing words with a sharp hand motion as a smaller sloop broke off from the main force of the ships. Snow looked across the intervening distance, the falling flakes parting enough in the wind to show that only two people were on board the tiny vessel. "By the system… what's this new malarkey?"

The taller of the two figures, a man with a formidable build, as though he had eaten nothing but thick slabs of beef his entire life, raised his hands in a universal gesture of peace or surrender. As they were still too far out to hear their words, especially with the snowfall dampening what sounds could be heard across the open water, Snow once more spoke her orders, "Hold fire! Let's see what they intend."

"Look at the *arms* on that one. He must follow the precepts of bodily cultivation," Battle Brother murmured, his grip tightening on the hilt of his weapon so hard the creaking of his leather grip became audible. "I wonder what it would be like to exchange pointers with that one. Battle Lord Grumpy could certainly beat him down, but I would pay good coin to be able to have a match with him on my lonesome."

As the small ship came within hailing distance, Snow's mind suddenly flooded with light and information—as though an illusionist who had reached *Perfection* had overlaid the world around her with new colors, along with the understanding of what each of them meant all in one go. One of those new-found colors highlighted the smaller person on the sloop in green, practically singing 'friend, kindred spirit'.

The other light? That one flashed a dark red, nearly black. Immediately she understood there was danger, something with deadly intent moving at her.

Not from the shoreline.

The world seemed to suddenly slow around her, only a flicker of the beginnings of concern starting to appear in Battle Brother's eyes as she spun around, flicking her wrist to activate the function of her cuff, allowing her dagger to pop out into her hand. Even as her fingers closed around the leather-bound hilt, she struck out with a speed and precision she had never managed to achieve before. The blade sliced through the air along a glowing trail only she could see. As the tip of her dagger reached the terminus of her range, it intersected a body shrouded in darkness.

A Huntsman, previously hidden with a combination of darkness and swirling ice crystals, let out a guttural sound as the dagger found its throat. To Snow's great surprise, she was able to watch in slow motion as the entity's eyes widened in shock when her blade struck true. Snow lurched to the side as its momentum continued, having thrown itself from the seawall to try and drive her to the ground and end the threat to its creator.

The cloak-wrapped body hit the icy sand, a moment later followed by a smaller *thump* as its decapitated head landed nearby. Only then did Snow begin to hear the hubbub generated by these actions, as Battle Brother began to let out a stream of curses while pulling out his own weapon and lifting it high, moving as though through a thick honey as he drove his blade through the thrashing body on the ground, pinning it in place before it could seek out its missing pieces and join back together.

"Aaabyyyss-!" His shout finally sounded out as the ringing of steel began shattering the silence around them. Half a dozen more blades slammed into the body, rendering fruitless its attempts to reconstitute itself. Snow watched everything happening with a detached calmness, taking a few moments to carefully block the head of the Huntsman, which was working its jaw and wagging its tongue in an attempt to *row* itself closer to its missing body. Her booted foot came down, kicking it away, which seemed to be the final straw for the failed assassin.

Immediately, its constituent parts began to steam with a black smoke, crumpling and beginning to dissolve onto the shore. Only then did the world suddenly speed back up, as Snow was piled on from all sides by guards ready to protect against a secondary threat. "How did I...?"

"It seems we've arrived at an interesting time." The high-pitched voice came from the smaller of the two representatives of the apparent invaders. Snow looked over, still somewhat in shock at the rapidly evolving situation, and found herself blinking in surprise at the diminutive woman who had spoken.

The woman wasn't even a full five feet tall, barely reaching the height of her companions' chest, yet she walked across the beach with a nonchalance and poise that spoke of someone confident in not being attacked, or handling herself if she were. Long curls flowed behind her, a shocking red against the backdrop of gray and white that was the ocean and clouds behind her. The woman wore brown and green leather armor under her thick red winter cloak and was absolutely *bristling* with weapons. She stopped an appropriate distance away from Snow, after a moment of hesitation sketching out the worst version of a curtsy the princess had ever seen.

"Greetings, Snow Weiss." She stood back to her full height, not that it did much good, and looked the princess straight in the eye. "My name is Lily Redwolf, and we're here at the behest of… Happy? Yes, the person who contracted the services of Wolf Mercenary Company on your behalf is known as Happy. We are here to support your overthrow of the current regime and put you in place as queen of this kingdom. Do you have any questions?"

For a long few moments, the princess simply stared at the lady who had spoken in such frank terms, trying to reconcile her knowledge of the bandit warband with the words this shockingly colorful person was saying. "You're here to… you're a mercenary company now? Look… I'm sorry, I'm not in the best place to receive this information. There was an assassination attempt I thwarted just now, and, frankly, I'm not sure how I did it."

"Have you checked your system notifications?" Lily offered Snow a hint, clearly knowing exactly what was going on. "If I'm not mistaken, I have finally found another *Damsel of Distress*."

"How did you know…?" Snow glanced down at her arm, swiping the inseam and feeling her jaw drop at the notification awaiting her.

Notice! You are within range of a newfound sister, a Damsel of Distress who has, like you, succeeded against seemingly insurmountable odds. Both of you have taken your fate into your own hands and are able to clasp those hands together to push the bounds ever further. As she has not refused to allow you to use her skills, you currently have the following skills available to you at the 'Considerable' rank. Please note, these are not skills you are able to offer out to your Brand Ambassadors.

What followed was a full-blown list of class skills, everything from what Snow could only assume was what Lily had unlocked as a Basic Class, all the way to her Full Class, and even a Conjoined Skill—she had to blush as she read that one, knowing it was meant to be a skill only between a married couple who had had their marriage witnessed by the system itself. Only three of the skills seemed pertinent to what had just occurred, so she focused in on those, forcing herself to push aside the heat rushing through her cheeks at gaining access to such intimate information.

System's Whisper (passive): This is a composite skill which [(Considerably)] enhances your trained skills of navigation, stealth, camouflage, survivalism, archery, and environmental awareness. As you have already honed these personal abilities to an exceptional degree, system guidance will come into effect at all times. The guidance will manifest as a subtle glow [(Considerably)] highlighting any of the actions you are attempting, as well as flashing a warning when the actions are failing or when your attention needs to be drawn to a specific area.

System's Echo (active): is an active skill which allows you to [(Considerably)] yet innately notice life forms as well as rapidly moving objects in a range of [(60)] meters around you for 6 seconds. Cooldown: [2] minutes.

Although these two skills were lacking the grandiose modifiers of her own Legendary skills, the sheer power they offered as direct connections to the system itself made Snow swallow nervously at how close the woman, an unknown threat, had come to her. Finally, as her eyes landed on the final skill, the princess realized not only how she had managed to take down the Huntsman by herself in a single blow, but how terribly outmatched she was if Lily turned hostile.

Constitution of the Red Wolf (passive): Like any other wolf, so long as you have eaten enough food and drank enough water, you are well satisfied and ready to continue. If your body has the resources to support it, your stamina and health will regenerate $100 + [(600)]\%$ faster than your baseline. When your Conjoined partner has chosen a task aligned with your goals and accepted by the system, both of your physical statistics will increase by a multiplier of $[(6)]$.

"I've never seen the system show modifiers with parentheses inside of them; it was an exciting development," Lily stated calmly, clearly pushing herself to speak more verbosely, and with a friendly tone, than she was comfortable with. Snow watched as her body language practically *shouted* how much she disliked having to speak in front of large groups like this, only for the woman to make adjustments on the fly as she reacted to Snow's reactions. "I must say... this Precocious Command skill? I don't think I've ever had such an easy time knowing how to handle myself in public. Thanks."

Snow froze up as a glacial chill swept through her veins. Just like that, another person had gained unfettered access to extremely private details that were meant to be between herself and the system itself. Even so, she choked down her response to her ingrained etiquette lessons before she could make a fool of herself. To the shock of all present, the Warlord bowed deeply to the duo standing across from her.

"Thank you, Lily Redwolf." As Snow came back up, she noted with a hint of amusement that the tiny woman seemed ready to run away, due to all of the intensely questioning stares of the surrounding forces. "Without your timely arrival and gift of your physical empowerment skills, I would have certainly fallen to the queen's assassin. I can't imagine how long that Huntsman must have been lying in wait, waiting for me to leave my command post and the dense security I had around me all this time."

"Did you just say…" the words erupted from Lily's massive companion with a furious, animalistic snarl, causing hundreds of weapons to be yanked back into position around them. "…*Huntsman?*"

Lily lifted a hand and placed it on what must be her husband's arm, clearly trying to get him to calm himself. Snow, along with nearly everyone else nearby, had taken a sharp step away from the enormous man, who looked on the verge of falling into a berserker state. "Drwg… we may have found the source. Give me a moment before you get too excited. Snow-"

"You will address her as-" Now it was Snow's turn to throw out a hand, though hers was done with far less love and care as it *smacked* into position over Battle Brother's mouth to shut him up.

The redhead continued as though she hadn't noticed the interaction, yet Snow knew that was absolutely impossible between the combination of their two skills. "-Pardon my husband's reaction. I hope you will find it understandable. His father was slain by a Huntsman a couple years ago. My grandmother was also brought low by the fell, twisted creatures. Might I examine your attacker, to see if we are speaking of the same type of assailant, or if they simply have similar names?"

"Help yourself." Snow shrugged and stepped aside, gesturing at the melting mass of flesh and alchemical leftovers already working to destroy itself. "They're people who have been twisted by alchemical means. This is what we are fighting against. The queen we're attempting to overthrow has been taking my people from their homes and… and experimenting on them."

Drwg and Lily shared a single glance at the body, then each other, before nodding. The enormous raider stepped forward, going to a knee on the ground before Warlord Snow. Though the situation was clearly extremely serious, Snow had to cough to cover a chuckle that attempted to slip out when she realized that he and his wife were suddenly the same height.

"Princess, my people have sailed through storm and frost, seeking purpose, justice, and vengeance long denied. We are warriors hardened by ice, tempered by battle, and finally our path has led us to you."

As the eloquent words rolled out of the absolute brute of a man, Snow wasn't the only one who glanced at Lily to see if she had cast an illusion over the man and was speaking through him like a puppet. Instead, the princess found that Lily was extremely relieved—she clearly disliked public speaking and was more than happy to have her husband take over for her.

"We arrived as mercenaries, bound only by contract and coin. But it seems that your enemy is our enemy. Your fight, our own. The foul creator of those Huntsmen have left scars upon my kin no time or tide can wash away. So now, I seek not your gold, but retribution and honor. Therefore, hear this." Drwg straightened his back, locking eyes with the princess and refusing to blink. "Wolf Mercenary Company will no longer demand our premium price. We ask only fair wages and to fight alongside you. Treat us well, do not send us to slaughter innocents, do not use us as sacrificial pawns, and grant us the chance to fight the creator of these abominations."

He slammed a fist to his chest, the motion unexpected and brutal—likely enough to kill another man were that fist to fall on them. "So long as these terms are met, we shall stand as loyal subjects for you to command as your own forces, until your campaign has completed its final hour."

As the last echoes of his words faded away, Snow shifted her gaze to those around her, who nodded eagerly. Only a few, like herself, had reservations. Instead of remaining silent on them, Snow turned back to Drwg and voiced them. "I'm sorry… but you are known pirates and raiders. Now you claim to be a mercenary company? You were brought here with the promise of coin. I don't know how I could possibly trust that you will remain true to your word."

She took a deep breath as she prepared to refuse their help, demanding they at the bare minimum remain separate from her people to minimize the damage they might be able to do if they betrayed them, but Drwg spoke before she could unleash her ultimatum.

"I speak no lies." The warrior stood to his full height, proudly reaching up and slashing the lines of a great 'X' over his chest. "As I said, so long as those terms are met, my people will abide by them. I swear this on my own life, to you, and bound by the system itself. I cross my heart, and hope to die."

As the world trembled around them, the system acknowledging its most sacred of oaths, Snow's eyes flicked upward, landing on Drwg's cheek, where pearlescent marks shined with the unmistakable light of the system—marks that were impossible to fake, which showed he had taken and completed such oaths in the past. As golden light flooded into his chest to wrap around his heart and bind him to his words, Snow felt a tickle on her arm, and she glanced down to see a notification that nearly caused her to swoon.

Influence combo! Gain 50,000 or more temporary followers in under five minutes. Influence +50,000!

CHAPTER
FORTY-TWO

Spring had finally broken winter's icy grasp, and with it the rebel army burst from the walls of Thalfanghein like a starved bear exiting hibernation. With a warm breeze at their back, they made for Drienhurst at speed—the final city in their path before reaching the capital.

Wolf Mercenary Company's ships cut through the gentle waves alongside them, the low-slung war vessels keeping pace with the marching troops as they shook off the last dregs of winter's complacency. The princess rode at the front of the army, flanked by her closest advisors as reports came in and orders were sent out, a constant cycle of information that only increased as the first hints of civilization were spotted in the distance.

Snow stared at the walls around the city ahead of them, trying to remain calm as she prepared herself for what might end up as a long siege. "I just want to be past here and on my way. Every *fiber* of my being is straining for action against the tyrant who has been holding my kingdom hostage."

Her frustrated growl was a little more than a whisper, but those who heard her only nodded along, understanding and agreeing with the sentiment. Shifting uncomfortably in her ornamental armor, now scuffed from multiple battles and months of training, she found a target for her over-energetic ire. "Can I get someone to adjust this tonight? The straps need taken in, but I've put on some muscle in my arms and shoulders. It's just-"

"Everything is going to be fine, Princess," Battle Brother broke in, accepting the glare he had earned from interrupting. "The queen can't have *too* many strongholds. Remember, each time she converts someone to a Huntsman, it requires time and a *slew* of alchemical reagents. There's no way that's cheap, and with two-thirds of the kingdom under your control, even with extra time to prepare, she could have only gone through whatever she had stocked up."

Snow blew out a frustrated sigh. "I just want this to be over. No, specifically, I want us to win, *then* have this be over. There's so much work to do with rebuilding and likely negotiation with our neighboring kingdoms, just to survive this next winter."

"It's a good look," Ned murmured, his words coming across clearly though he was also gently strumming on his instrument. "Spring has only just now sprung, your fight has not reached its conclusion, and already you are looking for ways to feed your hungry, enrich your poor, and heal the sick. If I had doubts about who my next queen should be… your casual desire to care for them, for *us*, would assuage them."

"That's not what I'm trying to do, Ned." The princess's shoulders slumped as they continued their quick march. "I just-"

"Which is exactly why it's going to be so *effective*, Snow." Ned bobbed his head at her happily, falling back slightly to make room for the other advisors, now that he had spoken his piece.

As they drew ever closer to the small city, the flat plains of the southern kingdom shifted into rolling hills. The farther they went, the less greenery they saw, as the higher reaches of the land were still reaching the freezing point or below overnight. Where the streams they had passed were trickling merrily along, here they were still frozen over with a thin layer of ice. Even so, Snow felt her heart melting as she looked out at finally familiar territory, especially when they passed some of the villages where she had spent time learning the skills of a bard.

At those, they had one of two reactions, almost *never* somewhere in the middle. Either they were hailed as returning heroes, with villagers coming out to watch, cheer, or even join the passing army… or they were stared at with suspicion, the locals' faces etched with fear and horror at the sight of Snow Weiss—according to the queen being a vampire or some such —marching at the head of an invasion force.

As they finally reached the outskirts of Drienhurst, the head of the army only creeping along in order to allow the trailing forces to spread out in preparation of attacking, the sun was high in the cloudless sky. Before them rose the walls of the city, sturdy stone at the base, topped with wooden fortifications that had been built up over decades. The gates were closed, and hundreds of guards and militia stared out at the encroaching forces with cold expressions. The flag of the kingdom flapped proudly in the breeze, a view Snow would have appreciated in the not-too-distant past. Now…?

Taking yet another step closer, the princess pulled on the reins of her horse, stunned by the sudden change that had overtaken the city. Gone were the hard-eyed defenders, replaced by citizens cheering and waving everything from white banners to flowers as the column of horses and marching troops drew closer. Above the city, the queen's flag no longer flew, having been replaced by those bearing Snow's sigil—a white snowflake with seven points, each shaped as a blade.

The gates had been thrown wide open, an instant transition that had Snow blinking, rubbing her eyes, and checking again. "What's happening here? This is… it's too good to be true, right? Is this some sort of ruse by the queen?"

"I don't think so," Ned called out from somewhere behind her, the delight in his voice one step behind actually laughing out loud, "Something like this? Such a theatrical flair? The only person I know who has enough power to hide an entire city behind an illusion is-"

"Bashful." Snow all but whispered the word, saying it in almost perfect synchronization with her friend. Even as they rode onto the streets of Drienhurst, she couldn't quite believe what her eyes were telling her. She wasn't the only person waiting for this to end up being a trick, an ambush, perhaps a cruel feint by the Witch queen to distract them long enough for her forces to close in.

Instead, they found thousands of cheering citizens lining the streets, their faces flush with joy and relief. Musicians of all skill levels played triumphant tunes, filling the air with fanfare and music. In an instant, larger than life to draw the eye, Bashful himself appeared in the center of the road. His oversized body shrank down once he had captured their attention, and he walked forward with his arms wide to the side, as though to embrace the entire force at once.

"Welcome, Queen Snow, to Drienhurst… *your most loyal city!*" His voice carried across the entire area, magically amplified to reach all corners of the city. In response came a crashing wave of screams and cheers as the population added their voices to his. Bashful stepped closer, eyes twinkling with mischief as he spoke again—this time only to Snow. "Took you long enough to get here!"

Snow leaned back and laughed, the sound a cross between disbelief and sheer joy as the tension that had been hanging over her like a dangling sword vanished as swiftly as his illusion. Gently tapping her heels against her horse's flank, she rode forward and reached down, gripping Bashful's hand in her own, both to show her thanks and appreciation, as well as to confirm he was truly there.

She could only manage one question before being forced to ride forward so more of her army could enter the city. "*How*, Bashful?"

"What can I say, Princess? Your bards did their work well." His voice turned serious. "The people here were ready for change. Not to mention, if there's anywhere her propaganda wouldn't be able to take root, it's in the city of music and art. We have always been loyal to you, and together we made sure she never knew. It's going to be quite the relief to finally let the illusion fade. It's been a long, *painful* winter."

"But that's a discussion for another time." Bashful stepped away, and his voice once more became amplified as he spoke to the city as a whole. "Tonight, we celebrate your impending victory and the installment of a queen who has taken the throne by birthright and the mandate of the people!"

The princess allowed herself to be pulled from her horse, and for the rest of the evening, the entirety of her army was treated to a feast, warm beds, and the finest entertainment that could be found in the entirety of the kingdom.

A WEEK LATER, as the much-expanded rebel army finished marching toward the capital city, the events of that night felt more like a pleasant dream than reality. If she were being honest with herself, Snow couldn't guarantee that Bashful hadn't swept them all up in some grand illusion—but frankly, she couldn't care if that was the truth or not.

The final portion of their march had been the toughest yet, as they pushed through the last dregs of winter, having been caught in a spring blizzard halfway to Deckbett. Only their careful planning and reduced need for supplies had seen them through the storm, which felt like the world's last test of their willpower before allowing them to begin the true fight for the throne: and what a fight it would be.

Snow's breath hitched in her throat as she took in the sheer scale of the defenses around the city. It was clear now why they had run into so little resistance as they swept through the countryside; Queen Kat had focused the entirety of her time and resources reinforcing this area to the exclusion of all else. Any forestry, any grass that had grown too high, had been burned back and away from the city walls. This left miles and miles of dead, empty space, a massive scar across the land which would offer no succor or cover for Snow's forces.

The walls of the city had been reinforced with thick black stone, which glistened with the oil that had been poured across it, and the banners of the Witch queen *snapped* in the air like whips as the wind blew off the sea. Unlike the previous city, the cold glares from those who remained were not some illusion. The reinforced gates were not some false pretense she would find open and inviting if she were to just get close enough.

No, here Huntsmen patrolled the walls with disjointed and unpredictable motions, their limbs extending, stretching jaggedly—which would have indicated terrible fractures in any normal person—only to contract back into place and allow them to lunge across the wall with shocking speed.

"Finally. The creme de la creme of the Witch's creations," Lily murmured from her position alongside Snow. The princess looked at the small woman riding on a horse as her husband walked alongside them, incredibly grateful for her presence both as a source of power as well as a source of feminine friendship she hadn't realized she had been missing so terribly. "I've been looking forward to this for years, Snow. Finally, I'll avenge my grandmother."

"My father." Drwg rumbled in agreement.

Snow chimed in, wanting to be a part of the moment. "My people."

They looked on in companionable silence for a few more minutes, picking apart the defenses with their gazes, especially those added in the last few years. Then Snow's eyes went back to the walls, and a cold knot formed in her stomach. Only as she looked closer did she see that the Huntsmen weren't the only people on the walls.

Instead, regular guards, royal guards in magical armor, and even militia that must have been the population of the city being pressed into service milled about, ready to defend themselves against the invasion to their last breath.

"I was able to create a holdout against the propaganda." Bashful began speaking softly, having noticed the same things Snow had, "Yet here there was nothing I could do to prevent the queen's words, not to mention her mind-altering music, from twisting your people's loyalty into fear and fanaticism. Her power is strong, and she has had *years* to ensure that her grip on them will never fail. As much as I hate to say this… there's a good chance we need to burn the entire city to the ground and rebuild."

"There's got to be good people in there still, Bashful." Snow immediately shoved his gentle prodding to the side. "I'm not willing to give up on them that easily. If nothing else, we can break in and find out if there is anyone who hasn't been altered by her. I can create a zone of power where we can question people quickly."

"I can't recommend-"

"Scorched earth is *not* the only option here." Snow cut him off in a tone that brooked no argument. "I will not ask the army to hold back against those preventing them from capturing the city, but I'm not going to get inside and cut everyone down. That's *not* how I will start my reign."

"On that note," the deep, rumbling voice of Grumpy joined the conversation. "We need to discuss the plan of attack."

Snow looked over her shoulder to find that all of her

generals had gathered, faces grim and eyes hard. Each of the D'wharves, the heads of the various guilds within her kingdom, had arrived that morning, with only Dopey and Sleepy conspicuously absent.

The leader of the Night's Heart Exchange had sent a representative, staying away from the final battle, as he knew the princess would likely turn on him immediately when she became queen. As for Sleepy…? Snow could only assume he was out haunting a dream somewhere in the kingdom.

Swallowing the sharp flavor of bile rising in her throat, the princess firmly repeated herself. "I will *not* allow wholesale slaughter of my citizens on the suspicion that they *might* be loyal to the queen."

"None of us would ever ask that of you." Grumpy raised an eyebrow as Snow shot a sharp look at Bashful, who simply shrugged innocently in response. "No, what we have been discussing is your role in the upcoming fight."

Collecting herself, Snow allowed her confusion to show on her face, glancing around at the flat expressions of her generals. "I don't understand. I lead from the front. That's what I do. We're here. We've come this far, and there's no turning back."

"You've led us to this point," Doc broke in, his warm voice softening the cold steel in his following words. "But this is not a battle for *Deckbett*. This is a war within a war. The city is compromised, and we will likely hold it under siege for the next few weeks or perhaps even *months*. But if there's one thing being a healer and seeing terrible things has taught me, it's that if you cut off the head… the body will fail far faster."

"We've scouted out the best path," Sneezy quickly began to explain, drawing Snow's eyes away from the fortified city and up to the palace sitting like a crown on top of the low mountain far above them. "While the army sieges the city, your generals and brand ambassadors managing the main assault, we need you to lead a strike force against the Witch herself. The sooner she is dethroned, the faster we can spread the news, and the fewer the lives that will be lost."

"She's not…" Snow gestured helplessly at the fortified city behind her, "Somewhere in there? What *possible* reason would she have for remaining up in the palace?"

"If I were to guess," Happy, swaddled under a thick fur blanket called out, voice trembling with cold even within the confined luxury of his ostentatious carriage, "She has faith in the defenses of the palace and likely has some cards to play as of yet. Either she has prepared the entire palace as one enormous trap, or perhaps she *cannot* leave, as it has everything she requires to amplify her dark powers."

"Yeah, attacking a Witch in her designated place of power is always a dicey prospect," Grumpy agreed quietly, speaking with a clear twinge of pain in his voice—one that made Snow wonder if this was not the first time he had led such an assault. "We've already picked out the elites of our forces to join us in this attack. Same goes for your lap dogs here."

The enormous man threw a playful punch at Drwg Mawr, who instantly retaliated with his full strength, trying to catch the D'wharve off guard. They flowed into intense combat, meaty *thuds* ringing out as their fists landed, but as per usual, the fight ended with the co-leader of the mercenary company pinned to the ground, struggling ineffectually against what looked like nothing more than a casual grip on his wrists.

"Maybe in a decade or two, kid." Grumpy released a pleased huff through his nose as he let go and leapt away as Drwg came up swinging.

"Faster than that." Drwg spoke in a pleased growl as he eyed the guildmaster. "Especially if I am able to continue to train against someone of your prowess. How did you reach *Perfection* as a Battle Lord at your young age? How close are you to achieving Battle Lord Ascendancy?"

"There are some things you don't talk about in *public*." To Snow's surprise, there was a hint of something akin to panic in

Grumpy's voice as he shut down the conversation. Turning back to the princess, he tried to get the conversation back on track. "What say you, *Queen* Snow? Do you trust your generals and advisors to run things here without you?"

Snow's first instinct was to argue, to demand to stand with her army. After taking a few deep breaths and casting a long, searching look up to her childhood home, she gave a single, sharp nod.

"Yes. Your logic is undeniable... this isn't about anything other than victory. The sooner we remove her from the throne, the faster we can get to fixing the mess she's made. Assemble the troops. There's no time to waste."

As her people jumped into action, Grumpy, Drwg, and Lily all nodded in silent approval. The redhead stepped closer, throwing one arm around the princess and giving her an awkward half-hug. "You're making the right call."

Snow's eyes didn't leave the palace on the mountain, where dark storm clouds were threatening to drop a blizzard on them.

"I certainly hope so."

CHAPTER
FORTY-THREE

THE WIND BEGAN to pick up as Snow's strike force thundered toward the not-so-distant mountain. As they rushed away from the city walls, the dark forest around the base of the mountain loomed large ahead… then they were under the canopy, the already gray sky further darkened by the twisting branches clawing upward. Thick carpets of snow clung to the roots and underbrush, slowing their progress as they pushed along what had been a well-maintained road only a few years previous.

At the advice of the D'wharves, Snow was in the middle of the column, instead of at its head, as she would prefer. As the sound of battle came from ahead, her jaw clenched tight as she internally berated herself for giving in instead of taking what she thought of as her place as the tip of the spear. "Eyes sharp and weapons sharper! It may not be easy, but it is simple. The time has come to topple a tyrant!"

"*The time has come!*" Her words echoed back to her, re-issued from each of her Brand Ambassadors along the length of the strike force, as well as being taken up by her troops.

They were barely thirty steps into the forest when the first attack came at them, arrows *hissing* through the air from all sides. Grumpy's hand snapped up, easily deflecting the small missiles and sending them spinning into the undergrowth. Lily threw herself off her horse, landing on the ground and vanishing as though she had turned invisible—bright red hair and winter cloak doing *nothing* to highlight her position as she began moving through the forest on foot.

"I *love* that woman!" Drwg roared with laughter as the tiny, effective scout began rapidly countering the hunters and rangers that had been collected by the queen and deposited within the woods. Where the mounted warriors could only press forward, unable to chase their attackers through the thick underbrush, Lily moved like a wraith, the forest seeming to bend over backward to help her.

Sneezy's people joined in on the hunt, leaving their horses to be tended by other members of the strike force as they fanned out and began rapidly reducing the number of attacks coming at the warriors. The main column pressed onward, soon reaching the second line of defenders as the strike force met waves of royal guardsmen head-on in a pitched battle.

The wooded area erupted with the clash of steel on steel, horses screaming in pain, and people grunting with exertion and battle cries. Drwg barreled into the fray, lifting an enormous cudgel that could very well have been a small tree he had uprooted as he began laying low any enemy crossing his path. The war leader of Wolf Mercenary Company went out of his way to target any Huntsmen that skittered into sight, absolutely *pulverizing* them as soon as he could pin them down.

"Those two do well in the woods," Grumpy noted with great interest as he remained steadfastly by Snow's side, refusing to leave her unguarded even as tantalizing targets presented themselves. "It's enough to make me wonder why they live life on the sea."

"They've been hunting the queen, following the trail of

the Huntsmen she has been banishing from the kingdom," Snow informed him as her pitch-black stallion lunged forward along the road, forcing her to split her attention between the battle and staying in the saddle. "They didn't know where their journey would take them, and apparently the stories of Wolf Warband being a group of seafaring pirates is spot on. At least, that used to be the truth. You should hear Lily's story; it's absolutely fascinating. The things she's been able to do with only Uncommon skills? It's astounding. Apparently the island she comes from doesn't have as much of a stigma as the mainland when it comes to modifiers in skills."

"Perhaps another time." Grumpy snorted disbelievingly as he bisected a Huntsman that had thrown itself at them. "I'm a little busy at the moment."

Snow leaned forward, urging her horse to a greater speed as they galloped ever upward. For the first time today, she was thankful for the chill air, as the need to break through the forest to be free of the trees and onto the open slope beyond caused her forces to push their animals to exhaustion. Yet, thanks to the wintry conditions, few if *any* of them overheated.

Sadly, a rapid ascent wasn't meant to be, as the queen's forces became more concentrated and densely packed, rushing down the mountain and getting into position.

The battle quickly became a slog, every foot of progress paid for in blood. The sloped road turned ever slicker with frost and gore, and the muted scent of the forest was overwhelmed by the stench of steel, oil, blood, and death. Snow dumped influence into her skills, pushing for her people to have their fears allayed as they *chopped* their way up the guarded mountain road.

A glance at her arm showed that, thanks to hundreds of attacks being made every second, both here and against the forces far behind them in Deckbett, dozens of critical strikes were siphoning at the pool of influence she had allocated for their use. A quick effort of will topped off the deep well of energy they could tap into, and Snow put the thought of it firmly out of her mind.

Minutes began to slip past rapidly, greased with pain and wounds, but they began to see an end to the troops lined up against them. For just a fraction of a second, she began to hope they had gotten through the worst of it. Then, ever so faint and distant, Snow heard a sound that made her throat close up, and her heart began to pound.

Music, a soft, insidious lullaby carried on the wind from the palace far above.

It slithered into her ears like gossip whispered at a masquerade, trying to wrap into the place it used to occupy in her mind... only to find deep resolve and mental fortitude barring its path and refusing to allow it to find a foothold. Snow let out a sharp gasp as she threw off the mental intrusion, righteous fury filling her as she began to physically tremble with rage.

"Countersong!" Bashful's voice roared above the cacophonous sounds of combat, and moments later, he and his bards began playing their instruments, voices rising as a harmonious wall of sound to clash against the dissonant notes of the queen's song. Immediately, the power it had over the troops cleared, and Snow took a deep, steadying breath. "Keep it up! Only a few miles to go."

Music echoed through the forest, nearly a hundred bards combining forces to push back the queen's magic, amplified as it must have been by the natural acoustics of her position on top of the mountain, as well as the kingdom's treasures normally stored within the vaults. A secondary effect of the Witch's magic made itself known at that moment: feral creatures burst through the underbrush, rushing and lunging at Snow's troops, only to falter, then waver in confusion as the combination of extremely loud noise and the *Perfected* Aura of

Innocence suffusing the invaders halted their advance nearly as effectively as a brick wall.

Bears, wolves, stags with massive antlers, foxes, and even rabbits baring their oversized teeth rushed into view, only to slow and stop at the point where the opposing forces met. Though they wouldn't turn and flee, driven forward by the Queen's insidious demands, they also wouldn't push through the no man's land around Snow's forces that had been created by the overlapping effects of her Brand Ambassadors and the cheerful marching music ringing out. As the strike force passed them, the animals followed along, remaining at a constant distance as they trailed behind, training their eyes on the backs of the troops.

"We're breaking through!" Grumpy roared as he pulverized a hidden Huntsman's skull, casually preventing an attempted ambush of the princess. "*Push!*"

The troops surged forward with renewed vigor, thundering up the slopes as they shoved through the gap they had formed in the queen's forces. Soon, they had left the foot soldiers behind them, the hunters and citizens pressed into the queen's service unable to keep up with the mounted group. Snow's heart soared as they burst through the edge of the forest, hundreds of elite warriors quickly rushing up the winding road toward the palace.

But the closer they got to the palace, the more potent the queen's magic became. They pressed on, one-third of the way, half, getting nearly two-thirds of the way up the slope before the horses began to falter, eyes rolling in fear and confusion, some rearing and bucking while others simply froze.

It was Doc who put everything together. "Her music isn't only affecting the animals of the forest! We have to leave the horses; they can't take this!"

"Dismount!" Snow ordered through *Voice of the People*. "Leave the horses and prepare to move on foot!"

Though some hesitated, each of those on the slope had

been handpicked for their loyalty, and soon the last of them had abandoned their mounts. The horses remained stock-still where they had been left, paralyzed in place by the competing magics filling the air. The soldiers pressed forward, boots crunching through the thin layer of snow blanketing their path as the wind continued to pick up, soon howling around them and chilling them through their winter garments.

Not soon enough, the palace loomed large ahead of them, its spires wreathed in low-hanging clouds. As they drew closer, it seemed that the sharp tips of the towers cut through the storm's membrane, and the blizzard that had been threatening all day finally broke. Snowflakes whipped through the air, driven by freezing wind and seeming to take aim at their exposed flesh. They pushed through, hoping they would find some relief by allowing the palace to take the brunt of the storm, but that hope was dashed as Sneezy called out a desperate warning.

"Shields up! Take cover!" Hot on the heels of his warning was a volley of barbed arrows raining from the walls, swirling flakes obscuring the projectiles as they cut through the air.

As the leaf-tip arrows whizzed through the area, an astringent, unmistakable scent filled Snow's nostrils. "*Tiéfrot?* Poisoned arrows! If you get struck, it won't stop bleeding. We need Dragon Thorn to counteract the blood thinning effect, and distilled Silver Leaf to force a clot. Someone get Doc's people on it! Dopey's people, whoever can help!"

The rebels dove behind what few rocks and outcroppings were available, arrows flooding into the snow and dirt around them as the wind pushed them off course. Dozens were struck, and those who weren't instantly slain were quickly pulled to the back to be tended by either Doc or Dopey's people—*both*, in the worst cases. Lifting her arm to cover her face, the princess wiped away the thin layer of ice accumulating over her eyelashes.

"Good call, Snow." Bashful smacked her arm none-too-gently, "That was fast thinking, you've probably saved some lives."

"Yes, well. I'm glad I knew what those were dosed with, but at the same time, I *despise* that Dopey was the one to teach me." She stared up at the gates, wondering how they could possibly launch their offensive that night. "What's next? How are we getting through that?"

"We're going to have to break it down," Grumpy called over to her, his voice pitched to carry above the howling wind and shouts of pain.

"Are you out of your *mind*?" Bashful responded in a grim tone as he projected the image of rocks in front of them to discourage those on the wall from targeting them. "That's going to take hours! We have no siege weaponry and no mages with artillery spells! How do you propose we *smash* through?"

"We've got axes, don't we?" Grumpy chuckled darkly as he pulled his spare weapon out. "I'll get to work, send some others to join me-"

"Grumpy, that is absolutely foolishness," Happy barked at his peer from his covered wagon, clearly having no fear of the falling arrows. Snow and her fellows paused for a moment as they looked at his conveyance, then turned and ran to get behind it. As soon as they were out of the wind and had a far lesser chance of being struck down by a flitting projectile, the D'wharve expounded on his words. "Even though the gates appear to be a weak point, being made of wood, I can tell you from personal experience-"

The enormous man tapped the back of his fist against his wagon, and a flare of light rose up. Immediately, dozens of arrows slammed into the other side of the carriage, sounding like a gentle rain against the other side as they fell without penetrating. "-It doesn't matter what the material is if you have properly *invested* in it. Traveling is a dangerous proposition, and I doubt we have anything that could smash through even *my* defenses. Now, add on several hundred years of this palace existing, and the fact that it must be directly tied into the ward structure of the kingdom, and you should begin to understand how tough of a nut this is going to be to crack."

"Then we should retreat and... what? Find someone who can start unraveling the protections? Come back with siege weaponry and oversized shields to fend off the attacks from above? There's an Enchanter two week's ride to the East; I can get him here in eighteen days." Grumpy spoke the options rapid-fire, clearly having an encyclopedic knowledge of how to defeat such magical protections.

Doc shuffled into the small protection the carriage offered, clearly having heard most of their conversation. "You're missing an obvious solution! If the palace is tied into the ward structure, and the wards are designed to keep the kingdom and royal family safe, then all we truly need is someone of royal blood to interact with the magic and dispel it."

There was a moment of stillness as the others looked at the ancient man flatly, but he wasn't done. Gently bumping Snow's arm with his fist, he winked at her and leaned closer. "How many times have I told you, it's what's *inside* that counts?"

Snow took a deep breath and turned to Happy. "I need you to roll this wagon closer, provide us cover as we close in on the gates. Bashful, spread the word, get everyone prepared to charge. Grumpy... if this works, I want you to give the order as soon as the gates are out of the way."

Almost immediately, the vehicle began rolling forward, the wood and metal wheels shining with tiny, glowing script as they began moving seemingly of their own accord. Snow kept pace, all but hugging the back wall as the archers above targeted the light shining through the storm. When the wagon came to a halt, she walked directly into it. Rubbing her throbbing forehead and grumbling ever so slightly as she sidled around, the Warlord took a deep breath and rushed forward to be under the front overhang and therefore almost impossible to target from above.

Each time the wind tugged on her cloak, she flinched back, thinking an arrow had managed to find its mark. Moving as quickly as she could, she reached out and pressed the palm of her hand against the ironbound wood, darkened and weathered from time, and extended her aura forward in a thin tendril, just as she would when trying to select a single person to influence from among a crowd. She felt her aura connect with... *something*.

A thrum in the air, a shimmer just beyond sight? Her eyes popped open—she didn't even remember closing them—as the feathery, staticky feeling she had begun associating with magic washed over her. Snow managed to breathe a soft, "There you are."

Then, brilliant bronze light flared beneath her hand, rippling out from her point of contact and spreading across the entirety of the gate, then on to the stone of the palace wall. Threads of magic unfurled like vines, weaving intricate, ancient letters that swirled and shifted, changing in real time as she tried and failed to read them. They pulsed with power, resonating with her own heartbeat as they looked for something in her... and found it.

A ghost of a question emanated from the script, and in any other situation she would have ignored the brief feeling, thinking it nothing more than indigestion. But now? In this moment, Snow understood that the wards were speaking to her, and she needed to answer.

"I need you to open for me," she stated clearly, voice low but firm. Acknowledgment washed over her as the script flared blindingly bright upward and outward, an unmistakable signal for her strike force. There was a deep boom from the other side of the gate as a bar weighing hundreds of pounds was thrown off and away, and the gate began to swing outward.

"What are you all waiting for? More of an invitation than *that?*" Grumpy's voice washed over Snow as she backed away to allow the doors to open. "*Cha~arge!*"

As her troops rushed around the carriage and the princess, Snow shook her head in astonishment.

"I cannot *believe* that worked."

CHAPTER
FORTY-FOUR

HUNDREDS OF COMBATANTS surged forward into the palace grounds, sweeping away the defenders—caught by surprise—in a tide of steel, magic, and enraged vengeance. Far too many of their fellows had been slain on this day for them to pull their blows against anyone who didn't immediately surrender, and their leaders knew better than to chastise them for their fervor. It wasn't easy, but it *was* simple: defeat the Huntsmen lunging from the shadows, the royal guards who had aligned themselves with the queen over the royal blood-line, and interrupt the runners who were bringing crate after crate of arrows up the wall.

Grumpy quickly returned to Snow's side, ready to defend her against any of the grotesque creations of the Witch, while Doc moved forward like a ghost, seeming to be everywhere one of their own had been injured. The elderly man's sharp eyes let him pick out areas he was most needed, and though he walked calmly, he was strangely even faster than many of the warriors sprinting to and fro. His hands, glowing with a green light reminiscent of fresh mint, swooped forward like an eagle snatching a fish from a pond, his triage saving soldiers before death could claim them.

The other D'wharves remained busy in their own way, with Bashful strumming on his guitar like a madman, simultaneously throwing out illusions to create havoc among the enemy. A visage of Grumpy was everywhere, though most vanished like smoke in the wind as the confused defenders swiped through empty air. Far worse for them was when the Battle Lord truly *was* there—they didn't get a second chance after he deflected their blows the first time.

Sneezy pulled flying daggers from a seemingly endless supply on his bandolier, flicking them into the air at the top of the wall. With each quick motion, an archer high above keeled over, often falling over the edge and causing secondary damage to the massed defenders below. When the perceptive man wasn't on the attack, he directed men and resources, somehow keeping the chaos of combat from unraveling into disorder.

"Place your bets here; we've got three to one odds on Snow's strike force sweeping the day! Copper, silver, gold, or time, I accept all as a wager!" Happy called from his carriage, stuck just in front of the gates as the ranks of warriors broke around him like a boulder in a stream as they rushed into the palace courtyard. "Not up for a wager? That's fine! Hot drinks, mulled ale for sale! Cold day to ignore me, soldier."

"I need to *not* be standing near Happy," Snow informed Grumpy, who nodded in understanding. They pushed forward, the princess sending out pulses of influence to bolster her soldiers' reserves as combat dragged on. As they had been able to all but ignore the defenses of the palace, the defenders had no way to break their momentum, and in under an hour, the last of their resistance had been destroyed.

Snow looked around uneasily, waiting for the other shoe to drop. Grumpy noticed her discomfort, and his simple stare was enough for her to begin explaining. "Doesn't this all just seem... too easy?"

"*Easy?*" Grumpy took a deep breath through his nose and

shifted his gaze away from her, "Look around yourself. Hundreds have died getting to the palace alone. Thousands across your kingdom, in combat or because of the starvation, disease, and poverty running rampant. We've been preparing for this blitz across the countryside for *years*, and the Witch has only had a season to mount a defense. The entire time you've been working yourself to the bone, we've been working against her. Celestial feces, *your majesty*. If anything, it's about time we get some abyssal *easy* in our lives."

"I'm sorry, Grumpy, I didn't think of it like that... I suppose you're right." Snow dipped her head at the D'wharve, only for the man to nod at her sharply in reply. He then jerked his chin to the side to pull her attention to where hundreds of people were on their knees with their hands on their heads; having surrendered when they realized their defeat was inevitable. Not a single Huntsman was among them, but that was only to be expected.

"Form up!" Snow's voice echoed through the area, drawing her people down from the walls, swarming from the gatehouse and others rushing from hidden defensive emplacements. A contingent remained to guard the prisoners, who had been stripped of any weapons and armor. The princess was unhappy to see how many of her people bore injuries and winced when she realized a good chunk of her strike force was unable to participate in the next part of the attack.

Whether from injury or worse, she couldn't say for certain, but either way, Snow was forced to push her concerns out of her mind as she focused on the doors of the palace proper. Stepping forward, she placed her hand on the enormous wooden barriers, reaching out with her aura to interact with the wards once more. Taking a deep breath, she sternly commanded, "Open for your princess."

Soft music swelled as she stood there, taking a deep breath in preparation of stepping away, only for the notes to become discordant, as though mocking her. Just then, Snow realized the music was coming from within the walls of the palace, and no magic could be seen coming from the doors themselves. "The Witch wants to play *games*?"

Feeling foolish, she spun around and stepped away from the doors, ignoring the smirks her D'wharves were trying to hide. Rejoining them, she let out a self-deprecating, "I suppose it would have been too much to hope that it would work twice."

Whether it was from the excitement or nerves of the moment, that caused those around her to burst into laughter. It only redoubled as a few muscle-bound men wearing Grumpy masks moved forward and grabbed the ornate handles, hauling back and easily swinging the doors open. Many people sent side-long looks at Snow, but she did her best to ignore them, though she could feel her cheeks turning bright red. Her next words came out more like a rusty hinge squeaking than a proper order: "Forward! Secure the palace!"

Her troops began to march in, spreading out quickly to secure the area. Already, Snow could see contingents of troops down the great hall rushing into position to try and fend them off, and she prepared herself for a long, drawn-out battle of attrition.

It wasn't to be.

Snow felt it in her very being as magical potency rushed through the air. This wasn't the quick inhalation of a spell being slung; it was a long, steady pull on the ambient energies of the world. Deep within the palace, a flare of bronze light appeared; so bright and brilliant that the air itself took on a metallic hue. Every window, doorway, and hallway began to shine with incandescent brilliance, then the pull on the air reversed. It pulsed once, twice, then began expanding toward them, perfectly filling the entirety of the palace from deep within… then rushing *outward*.

The queen's troops were the first to be hit by the silent shockwave of the kingdom's wards activating, as they were tossed like leaves on the wind as the light washed over them. For a moment, it seemed those guarding the palace were suddenly charging at the strike force, as every last one of them was bodily hurled down the hallway. Snow's troops raised their weapons grimly, prepared to fight, only for the power of the wards to catch them up and none-too-gently push them back out into the courtyard.

People were ejected from every orifice of the palace, a tide of bodies pushing out, although those who had been ejected from higher levels were gently deposited on the ground instead of thrown—some safeguard that had been built into the magic generations ago saving their lives.

Snow braced herself as the gentle light crashed over her, but to her astonishment, she remained perfectly rooted in place without being affected in the slightest. She glanced around to see if she was uniquely protected from the light and found that she was not standing alone in the palace, as she had been subconsciously expecting. Each of her D'wharves, as well as Lily and Drwg, remained standing, though none as easily and casually as herself. They seem to be straining against whatever effect was pushing on them, just as someone sturdy and well-braced could temporarily hold out against even hurricane winds.

Clatter.

The strange sound quickly grew louder behind Snow, and she glanced over her shoulder to see what fresh horror was creeping up on her, only to have to blink and check again to make sure she was truly seeing Happy's carriage rolling up the palace steps toward them. "Pardon me! Oh, I do hope I didn't just crush his leg... hello, Princess! This seems *exciting*. An *exclusive* experience I wouldn't miss for the world. Shall we press forward? *Oof!* Oh, my. That is quite the intense sensation. I shall *savor* it as long as possible, but we should... move quickly."

Snow agreed with him silently, and began leading the way

through the palace; as she was the only one among them who had intimate knowledge of how to navigate the absolute maze of corridors and rooms. "Do you think we should first make for the throne room, or should we push to the deeper levels and try to deactivate the wardstone somehow?"

"Throne room," Sneezy grunted as he strained against the unrelenting force of magic pressing against them.

The princess eyed her group, wincing as she saw how their bodies were bowed and trembling, faces etched with discomfort and determination in equal parts. She hated seeing how they were suffering for her, all so they could see her through to the end of this rebellion. Not wanting to spit on their determination by offering to let them stay behind, the *Contender for the Throne* pushed forward, even as the magic pressed against her allies ever harder with each step they took.

Halfway down the final hallway, the clattering carriage came to a stop, and Happy, face pale beneath the blanket wrapped around him, poked his head out of his window and called, "I've done enough. Going any further would risk my health, and I regret to say I can't allow that to happen. You can do this, Princess! I believe in you!"

His carriage clattered backward, stopping after a few long turns of his wheels, and he spoke out once more, "I'll stay right here! After this point, the force of the magic becomes too much, but right here is a nice sweet spot. I'll be ready to rush in and see the results as soon as you cancel whatever magical effect this is. I know it's not the experience I wanted, but it'll still be better than the view the main body of your troops will get!"

"Your motivations are always confusing to me, Happy," Snow called back, the only one among the group who could speak easily. All she gained in return for her words was a happy wave and a fist pump from the enormous man. Shaking her head, she turned her eyes back to her destination, though she did wonder aloud about her situation. "Am I unaffected because this is a failsafe of the kingdom's wards? It would make sense, as they should be attuned to my bloodline, right?"

"Most likely," Doc stated serenely as he walked along beside her, taking the princess off guard by his casual attitude. She looked him over as he walked forward, seeming to do so with relative ease. As her gaze traveled lower, she noticed with a blink of surprise that his boots and socks had been discarded. Looking closer, Snow watched as his bare feet shuffled forward, toes pressing down to grip the cracks between the flagstones like a mountain troll clinging to a cliff.

Even as the light in the air thickened, becoming nearly a liquid they had to pass through, his face remained serene, his breathing even, as though he were taking a gentle stroll rather than fighting a tempest of magic. Snow's head whipped to the side as she heard a muttered, "*Abyss!*"

Eyes on Sneezy, Snow watched as he grit his teeth, clenched his hands into fists, and strained to push one more step forward as his entire body shook like a leaf in the wind. With a strangled gasp, he faltered, losing the battle with the magic and being gently pushed back down the hallway, boots scraping against the floor as he tried to regain his balance. "Sorry, Snow. I'll be with you in spirit, I suppose."

"*Ayy!*" The cheerful shout came a moment later, as Sneezy thumped into the carriage down the hallway, and Happy welcomed his peer with an excited offering of a snack of some kind.

Snow walked ahead, leading the few remaining who still fought against the constant pressure. As the doors of the throne room came almost within reach, the air around Bashful distorted and cracked, his final illusions flickering into nothingness as his concentration splintered under the immense pressure. What remained behind was a masked man, covered in wiry muscle, built like the acrobat he was. He let out a long, frustrated sigh as he offered the princess a sad little wave. "I'm sorry, I can go no further. I'll be here to help you pick up the pieces of your kingdom when you succeed."

Then, he simply relaxed slightly, remaining fully upright as he was pushed back down the hallway, though he leaned forward and grunted once, freezing in place far closer to the throne room than Sneezy and Happy. Snow stepped forward, reaching for the door, but waited as the others struggled closer before opening it. She certainly didn't want to have to face whatever was on the other side on her own.

Drwg and Grumpy were hunched forward, muscles straining visibly as though they were sprinters at the starting line of a race. They looked at each other frequently, eyes burning with a fierce, competitive determination, as though the walk to the room were only a test of strength and willpower. Each time one of them took a step forward, the other pushed himself to take two.

"You're slowing down, old man." Drwg's teeth were bared in a rictus grin as he grunted at his opponent.

For his part, Grumpy only scoffed and moved forward another inch. "'Old man', is it? What if I told you I'm only a year or three older than you? Being a Battle Lord isn't about age, it's about putting in the effort."

"I'll believe it when you take off that mask," Drwg spat in reply, though his eyes had gone wide with concern. Despite the seriousness of the situation, Snow's lips twitched as their stubborn resolve helped her remember why she was doing all of this. Glancing at Lily…

Snow's jaw dropped as the small woman walked through the maelstrom of magic just a touch too slowly for it to be called dancing. Her upper and lower body swayed back and forth, somehow allowing her to weave through the currents of power, slipping between the strongest pressures with precise movements. The redhead met her eye, shooting her a smug smirk as she lifted her hand and tapped her face. "The power flowing out isn't uniform. If I don't try to force my way through it, I can simply avoid the worst of it. Problem is, not everyone sees the world like I do."

"Could you help *them?*" Snow gestured at Drwg and Grumpy, who looked like they were about to pop a blood vessel or three in their foreheads.

Lily looked over and shook her head sadly. "If you think either of them would try to avoid *any* part of this…"

"Got it." Deciding they were close enough, Snow grabbed the handle of the double doors firmly, pulling hard on the barrier and swallowing hard as it opened with a nostalgic **creak**. "Nearly four years, and no one has oiled your hinges yet. I'm finally home."

"But *why?*"

The simple question rang through the throne room, echoing off the hard surfaces as Witch Queen Kat shouted at the people invading her halls. Behind her was a large travel pack, and all manner of items were dumped in piles around the woman. The queen lifted a trembling finger, face flushed with rage as she pointed at Princess Snow.

"You've ruined everything! Why? When you ran. I *let* you leave. You were the weak one. You were supposed to run off and do nothing with your life instead of coming back to bother me. I *hate* that I have to flee from my home *again* because I was kind to another pathetic little girl. You should have stayed *gone!*"

Snow's jaw dropped as the Witch practically threw a tantrum right there in the middle of the throne room.

CHAPTER
FORTY-FIVE

"*I* SHOULD HAVE STAYED GONE?" Snow stepped into the room, pointing at the Witch on the other side of the open area with her dagger. "You invaded my kingdom, using my mother's death as a way to creep your way into the palace and take over! Then you messed with my mind, practically imprisoning me in my room and driving my sister and me apart! It's not that I should have stayed gone, it's that you should have never been here in the *first place*!"

The echoes of Snow's words came back to her, and she and Kat stared at each other for a long, hateful moment. Then the Witch pressed her lips together and bobbed her head back and forth. "Oh, poor *you*, stuck in the lap of luxury. Your mother died? Well, welcome to the club! What about *me*, Snow? You never thought to get close to me, hear my story, did you?"

"You. Are. A. *Witch*," the princess ground out through teeth pressed so hard together she felt they might crack. "Anyone who gets too close to you is going to end up infected by your insanity. Why would I want to hear your story? I don't want to sympathize with someone who has been ripping apart the kingdom she was in charge of, all to earn enough coin to experiment on the people living under her rule."

"You see, Snow," Kat began furiously stuffing piles of magical items, bottles filled with concerning liquids, gems, and *coins* more than anything into the travel pack. Clearly the container itself was a magical item, allowing far more into it than should have ever been possible, especially as she was dumping it in as an unorganized mess. "Only a few years ago, I was living in my mother's house with my older sister and… stepsister. All Mother Matringa asked my stepsister to do was a few chores around the house and to listen to her when she needed her to do things. What do you think happened, Snow?"

"First, I think your story is missing a whole lot of context, and secondly, I think you're about to lie through your rotting *teeth*." Snow chanced a glance behind her, feeling greatly relieved as her companions stepped into the throne room with her, though they were clearly having a hard time being so close to the source of the energy pushing against them. Just their presence alone was enough to bolster her spirits and confidence.

"That's right!" Kat continued speaking in a feverish tone, clearly not listening to Snow's rebuttals. "That bratty stepsister got so upset that she had to be a part of the family that she called a troop of royal guardsmen into our house. Not only were my mother and sister slain, that wench set birds and filthy rodents on me."

For the first time, the queen stopped and looked over at Snow, lifting her hand to her face and pulling a long strip off a thick mask to reveal skin that was pocked and scarred, dozens of small wounds covering every inch. "I was kind to her, Snow! Where my family tried to continue on in the same way, even after they learned that a firm hand wasn't the way to go, I tried to reach out to her. I tried to be her friend! To be nice!"

Practically snarling as she thrust her finger at Snow once again, Kat began shaking her head and nearly laughing at the injustice of it all. "Just like with you... I tried to leave you alone. When you ran, I put you out of my mind, thinking you would end up being just. Like. Me. That you would go somewhere else and make a new life for yourself. But you came *back*? Not only that, but the kingdom rose up with you! Even the palace itself turned against me, when it should have at least bought me some more time to escape. No... a pretty little girl like you comes along, and every door in your path is *literally* opened for you. Why doesn't the world just come on out and spit in my face?"

"I came back because I *love* my home." Snow responded slowly, speaking as if she were talking to a toddler. "I will *fight* for my people. I want to protect them and guide them to a brighter future, not take advantage of and control them. You've done terrible things, Kat. Frankly, I don't care one whit what your reasons are."

"Pah." Kat shook her head and turned back to her task, grabbing another quick armful of items and dumping them into her pack before slapping the flap closed and tightening the drawstring. Grabbing the straps, she swung it up onto her back before replying to the princess. "Now you're here to seek 'justice' for your kingdom, which has been so *terribly* wronged. Look at you, bringing all your little friends to gang up on me. Not relying on your own power, but on the power of friendship or some such nonsense. Isn't that what caused this situation in the first place? Everyone turning against me and tossing me out into the cold?"

"If that really happened, don't you think you should have *learned* from it? Sounds like a simple and easy plan to me." Snow growled at the Witch, beginning to pace toward her carefully. "To live is to grow, and our experiences shape us. You just chose a bad shape to grow into."

"Oh, I've *learned*, alright." Kat let loose an actual witchy cackle, gesturing to either side of the room. "Let me explain. If you take even one more step…"

She trailed off warningly as a door on either side of the throne room was kicked open. A Huntsman walked in from either side, each of them holding a single person with a blade glowing with sickly, greenish-black light held to their necks. Snow froze in place as the queen barked, "…*both* of them will die."

At first, Snow only had eyes for her sister, a pale shadow of her former self with deep bags under her eyes that showed a history of sleepless nights. Even so, there was fire in her eyes, which blazed higher as she stared back at her twin. The smallest of smiles appeared on her lips, and both of them took a deep breath as they tried to hold back tears at finally being reunited—though certainly not in the circumstances either of them had wished for.

Then the princess turned her eyes to the other person, a man she didn't recognize at all. "Who is he, and why are you threatening me with him?"

"You don't know?" The queen's eyes bulged, and she bared her teeth at the young man for a moment before shaking her head. "It matters not. His death would destroy this entire kingdom, either way. Allow me to introduce you to Dwight Charmant, the Duke of Artek. He arrived a few months back on a diplomatic mission seeking your hand. I'm sure he would have been satisfied with Rose, but I needed *you*, didn't I, dear? Especially after your father sadly passed away… making it three times as hard to alter the *ward structure!*"

Her voice rose near the end, practically a scream as she raged against the injustice of the king failing to remain alive long enough for her to fully subvert the protections of the kingdom. She heaved for air, snarling softly as she spread her arms until one of her hands was pointing at each of the hostages. "So… *Princess*… here's what I'm going to do for you. I'm going to leave now, and if anyone comes after me, both of them die. But wait, *wait*... if you leave me enough time to escape, I'll let *you* choose one of them to die. The other will be let go. A little gifty-gift from me to you."

"Choose your sister..." Kat pointed at the starved princess with a cursed blade held to her throat. "And you will be reunited with your twin, ready to take on the world with the last member of your family! Of course, that means you'll have ordered the death of the duke of a foreign kingdom. An extremely *aggressive* kingdom that wars against its neighbors for fun. Imagine what would happen to this kingdom, softened up by civil war, as an invading force crashes into you? Choose him, and you get to live happily ever after... *sans a sister.*"

Finishing her impromptu ultimatum, the queen backed away, scooping up a couple extra bottles as she did so. When she got to the throne, she kicked at a diamond-shaped patch at its base, and the entire, massive chair shivered and groaned as it began moving to the side, stone scraping against stone as a secret escape passage was revealed. "This is the second time in my life I've used a tunnel to escape. It's starting to become quite the little pattern. Ta-*taa*..."

Snow stared helplessly at the Witch as she slunk down into the passage, the last thing she saw being her mouse-nibbled nose and insane, gleaming eyes. Glancing between the two hostages, the princess felt the bile rise in her throat—it was an impossible choice. She softly scoffed, whispering, "I suppose that's the point, isn't it?"

"Oh, I just can't *not* see this." To Snow's great shock, the Witch popped back up out of the passage and marched forward until she was halfway between the Huntsmen and the escape route. "We'll still have *one* hostage, and it will be the one you care about, so I'll still be able to walk away. But I want to see you *suffer*, Snow. I want to see you lose something, after you've made me lose everything all over again. So tell us... who lives, and who dies?"

"Are you kidding me-?" Snow began, only for a rich, deep voice to speak over her.

"Princess Snow, forgive me for arriving too late to help you. My journey... suffered delays," Duke Charmant called out, bringing up memories of Snow's time at her mother's summer cottage, and a man that had been trapped as a bear. "I've owed you my life for far too long. Please, allow me to finally repay my debt. Let me be the one who takes the blade. My father would understand... all you need to do is explain the situation to him."

His humble request made Snow feel numb inside, especially since it was obvious he had already made peace with the situation. But before he had even finished speaking, Rose called out in a weak, scratchy voice, "Snow. You know you can't condemn the kingdom like that. It's going to take decades to rebuild to our former prosperity, and you can't do that if you're fighting a series of endless wars. Listen... you always used to say that I was the strong one, but I never thought so. Prove me right, right now. Never once did you fail to help someone how they *needed* to be helped. You're going to make a great queen, so long as you make at least one more hard choice. For the *kingdom*."

Seeing her sister so frail and weak was utterly shocking to Princess Snow, especially since she had spent the last few years putting everything she had into building muscle and competency. Somehow, her mind had always promised that her twin would have been doing the same, would have somehow managed to become an even better version of herself than Snow could ever hope to be. That-

"I said *choose!*" The queen screamed at her, snapping Snow out of her desperate, spiraling thoughts. "Either you choose, or *I* do! I'll even give you a sneak peek. I want this kingdom to burn for turning its back on me! The duke is my choice for the blade. What do you say? Are we in *agreement?*"

Snow took a deep breath, looking back and forth between

her twin sister and the man who had crossed the world twice to try and win her hand. As she opened her mouth, her eyes widened fractionally as she looked beyond Duke Charmant's shoulder and saw something... out of place. Hoping she wasn't falling into wishful thinking, she slowly made her choice.

"As much as I hate to say it... yes. We are."

FORTY-SIX

"*HOORAY*!" The Witch clapped her hands frantically, the sound like a startled pigeon trying to escape a hayloft. "Huntsman, execute that foreigner!"

The iron grip of the Huntsman tightened further on Dwight's shoulder, and he dragged the duke to the center of the throne room. Slowly, as though savoring the moment, he raised the blade glowing with cursed energy and shifted the point back and forth ever so slightly as he aimed to land a killing blow on the first hit.

Snow and her companions could only look on in horror, unable to lift a finger to help the young man. For his part, Dwight seemed to be completely at peace with the situation, locking eyes with Snow and nodding in approval, a sad but resolute smile on his face.

The princess watched as the Huntsman's grip on his knife tightened, and for one sickening moment, she realized she may have been wrong.

Then the knife dropped down like a guillotine, crunching through bone and unleashing the entire potency of its cursed energy into alchemically twisted flesh. Dwight was tossed to the side, as the Huntsman holding Rose locked up as the power flowed through him, paralyzing him as the curse went into effect. Only a heartbeat later, he began to steam and fall apart as he was destroyed from the inside out.

"Wha...?" Kat's voice trembled as she watched the drama unfolding, staring at the Huntsman who had just betrayed her. "That's... that's impossible! You can't turn on me! I *made* you! You can't do this! It's *literally* supposed to be impossible; I followed the recipe to the letter! You're nothing more than a cursed gingerbread man, you think you can turn on *me*?"

"What's happening?" Rose fell to her knees, too weak to stay upright as she was released. The betrayer shifted his position, swooping down to snatch up the second cursed blade before turning to face the queen, knife held high.

The question was mirrored by the others in the throne room, though Lily ignored the subtleties and just threw herself forward, sprinting at the witch with her blade held high as Grumpy barked out an explanation. "It's not a Huntsman, it's *Sleepy*! Get the Witch!"

Kat screamed with fear as the tiny redhead closed on her, turning and running toward the escape tunnel as quickly as her weighty pack would allow. Unfortunately for her, as the Witch spun around, she came face-to-face with Snow, who smoothly slid into position right in front of her.

Snow had retracted her aura, using the distractions of the moment to flash across the room fully encompassed in stealth; aided by the massive physical boost her fellow *Damsel of Distress* provided.

The Warlord slammed her dagger into the chest of the tyrant queen, who flew back and away, managing to remain airborne for nearly four feet before sliding another five on her pack.

"No blood," Snow noted immediately, holding her dagger up at eye level to confirm.

Kat let out a deep cough, wheezing for air as she tried to struggle to her feet, though she was trapped by her pack for a few moments, like a turtle placed perfectly on its back. "You can't... you can't do this to me! The Grimelias Coven will avenge me, and their wrath will be far worse than anything little ol' me can bring to bear."

"Kat, you have committed terrible crimes against the people of the kingdom you were meant to protect," Snow enunciated in a ringing voice, even going so far as to activate a portion of *Voice of the People* she had never used until now—creating a zone of shattering truth where any falsehoods would be met with immense pain as the air itself shook the liar to pieces. Immediately, the remainder of the mask the deposed queen wore shivered and melted away, revealing her true form for all to see.

Snow felt a deep sense of pity for the woman at that moment—frankly, the damage wasn't all that severe. She had seen plenty of people with worse marks from simple pox, but Kat had focused on the small wounds inflicted on her so much that it had poisoned her heart. "As the princess of this king-dom, by right of blood and mandate of the people, I call on you to answer for your crimes. I'm going to let you have a choice. Either a swift death here and now, sparing yourself further humiliation, or a prison cell where you will live out the remainder of your days in magic-scrambling manacles."

Kat finally rolled forward, managing to make it to her knees before Sleepy stepped forward and grabbed the top of her pack, pressing down and forcing her to remain in her current position. Snow stepped forward, dagger ready as she watched for any sign of returned aggression. What she hadn't prepared for was seeing Kat burst into tears, covering her face as she sobbed.

"I just don't understand-" as she cried her heart out, Snow realized Kat's words must be true, else the air still shimmering with her power would have been punishing her for telling lies, "-why you think I wouldn't take you *with* me!"

The Witch suddenly clapped her hands together over her head, the bottles she had palmed smacking together and shattering into a dense cloud that raced outward. "Hope you like the taste of sour apples, Snow! Now *drown* in a dry room!"

Sleepy reacted instantly, slamming his cursed blade forward, only for the locket dangling around the Witch's neck to suddenly swing around, expanding out into a palm-sized mirror that caught the tip of the blade. Magical and cursed energy mingled, shattering both weapons and sending a shard of combined energetic potency reflecting back at Sleepy. It burst through him, the barest hint of it flying straight through him… and finding a home in Rose's heart.

For her part, Snow tried to leap away, but the potion rushed at her with a malicious will. Just as the wave of alchemical death would have washed over her, a massive furry obstacle interposed itself between the princess and the poison. Snow found herself staring up into the far too intelligent eyes of a massive bear, who began to grunt and glow as his innate magical resistance fought against the deadly potion. Even so, a single drop rolled up over the bear, falling down with an accuracy too perfect to be anything but unnatural: the shimmering droplet avoiding all impediments and sinking straight between Snow's lips.

The taste of granny apples—green, delicious, and just tart enough to pucker her lips—washed throughout Snow's mouth. The taste quickly turned overwhelming, and she felt water generate out of nowhere, flooding her mouth, throat and lungs. She struggled away, trying to cough, to inhale, but couldn't force anything past the sudden wellspring appearing inside her airways. She choked, clutching at her throat, pounding at her chest, as the world around her went dark.

"Get back!" The sound of Dwight's panicked voice reached her through a dusky haze. Snow blinked, finding herself standing in a dark room with the sounds of her friends coming through the edges of the shifting barrier. Looking around, Snow saw another person with her, and nodded at the immensely tall figure as she recognized him.

"Sleepy. Good to see you."

The shadowy shape flickered, his posture one of absolute defeat. "I'm dying, Snow. Actually, my body is already dead. This is my mind reaching out, hoping for some peace in my last moments."

"Thank you," Snow whispered softly, watching as his feet began vanishing into smoke. "I always knew I would lose people during this fight, but thanks to you... I get to have my sister, and at least one war that would otherwise have destroyed us has been averted. You're my hero, Sleepy."

"Ahh..." the Huntsman took a deep breath of satisfaction as her words reached him, comforting him in his final moments. "That's the good stuff. Want to hear something funny?"

"*Anything.*"

"Great book." Sleepy chuckled, though the princess didn't understand the joke. "Haven't read that one yet? I left a copy in the library. You'd love it. No, I was wondering if I could let you in on a tiny secret of mine. Do you know why I chose the name I did?"

"I assume it's because you have some sort of power that lets you walk through people's dreams? When they are asleep?" Snow ventured, knowing she was probably wrong, as otherwise, he wouldn't have wanted to bring it up as some of his final words.

"Nah. That's not it." He pulled off his mask, the steel plate with horizontal eyes and mouth that was ever so slightly different than the other Huntsmen—the mask Snow had recognized as belonging to him in the throne room. His face was revealed: normal brown hair and kind blue eyes... which Snow recognized.

"Sir Upp?" The words were a horrified whisper as she laid eyes on the man who had been her assigned Royal Knight when she was a child.

"What can I say; I had to *stick* around." His torso was gone, faded away, "I'm so glad I have been able to fulfill my duty to you, my Queen. I was always on your side… I was just a… heh, a sleeper agent."

Then he was gone, and Snow was alone in her own mind, the final gift given to her by Sleepy. *No.* Sir Upp. She looked down and found that her own feet and legs had vanished, and knew that death was near.

"Give me room!" Dwight's voice shook the dark space again, and Snow felt her chest being compressed downward. "*Breathe*, abyss blast you!"

Her eyes flew open, the throne room incandescently bright and blurry as her unfocused vision landed on the man locking lips with her as he blew his own breath into her lungs. He moved back, shifting his hands to press down on her chest once more, but she rolled to the side under her own power and released a stream of apple-flavored salt water. Then Snow hauled in a deep lungful of air and began releasing enormous, body-shaking hacks that resulted in handfuls of water at a time being expelled from her lungs.

"There you go," Dwight called soothingly, his tone filled with relief as he gently patted her back in time with her coughs. "Welcome back. Let it all out."

"She was dead! She drowned!" Drwg called in astonishment. "No one ever comes back from drowning. How did you *do* that?"

"Aren't you a seafaring nation? How do you not know this?" Doc's voice came from nearby. "I'll teach you how to pull water from people's lungs another time; it seems like something that would benefit you greatly."

"Why are these wards still active?" Lily called out. "Shouldn't this have ended when the Witch was slain?"

Almost immediately following her words, the bronze light that had been suffusing the room faded away. Snow heaved in a deep breath, practically vomiting out her thoughts. "Grumpy!"

"*What?*" The huge man went silent for a heartbeat, then tried again, "that is… *what*, my Queen?"

"The timing of that… was too good!" Snow spoke around coughs. "She's still alive, controlling the wards!"

Kat let out a screech of rage as she shot to her feet, leaving her pack behind as she sprinted toward the secret passage. "You can't kill me! Don't you know what would happen? My Huntsmen are only contained in this Kingdom by my will! If you do anything to me, they'll spread across the world! Who knows what will happen if one of them stabilizes, or touches a Class Shrine and ascends-"

She didn't make it any farther than that—either through her speech or across the room. Kat was only halfway to the hatch before Dwrg practically materialized beside her, his massive cudgel hoisted into the air. He brought it down with a sickening *crunch*, felling her in an instant.

He didn't stop there, bringing his weapon up and down several more times as he vented his rage over his father's sense-less murder, until Lily arrived at his side and pulled him away from the gory results of the execution.

"We did it." Dwight, who remained entirely stoic at her side, helped Snow into a sitting position.

"The Witch has been slain." The words tumbled from Snow's hoarse throat. "My people are *free*."

"The queen is dead? Then…" Happy called from the doorway of the throne room as his carriage rumbled into position. "Long live the queen! *Long live Queen Snow Weiss!*"

The others in the room echoed the words, all but Doc, who remained at Rose's side, a troubled expression on his face. Before Snow could ask for any further information, a deep power rolled over her as the system took notice of the queen's death.

A huge globule of golden energy appeared in the air above the throne, shifting and twisting until it had formed into a massive 'X'. It spun across the room, hovering in front of Snow's eyes for a long moment. As she stared into the depths of power, she was treated to dozens, hundreds, *thousands* of potential moments in her future. The system showed her a castle, people walking around happily, herself as a benevolent and beloved ruler. It also offered warnings, giving her glimpses as to what would happen should she betray the trust of her people and the directive of the system.

As Snow tried to digest the information that had just been thrust upon her, the mark spiraled down, shrinking and coming to a stop, then branding the right side of her cheek— the mark of a leader of a nation who'd been recognized as the rightful ruler of a kingdom by the system.

She felt tears trickle down her face as a tumult of emotions crashed through her—this was not a mark given to someone simply because they were born or married into the position. It was only granted by the system to those who had shown great acts of heroism and self-sacrifice for their people, and she would forevermore be known as a *system-recognized* queen.

A blessing like this would stay the hands of nations when they thought to wage war on her. No one wanted to bring calamity upon themselves by claiming to their people that they knew better than the system itself. This meant her reign would be filled with peace and prosperity. Gifts and negotiations in her favor would flood into the land from all sides. But it also meant... Rose would never have a chance to claim her own birthright.

Snow looked to her sister, who lay unmoving on the ground. Doc looked up and met her eyes. "She's only asleep, my Queen. Give her time; she's been through a lot."

Letting out a deep sigh of relief that her sister had not

been cut down just as they were reunited, Snow closed her eyes and let the system notifications roll in.

Congratulations! You have been marked by the system as a system-recognized sovereign! May all your people know that the system has seen your benevolence and will help to guide your hand as you lead your kingdom into the future. As a benefit, for the next 10 years, all of the endeavors of your people will result in a 5% higher return.

Growing crops will offer more fruit and vegetables. Animals raised for meat will yield higher cuts. Meals made will be more delicious. Ores pulled from your mines will be of a higher grade. The list is endless.

Requirements for class upgrade have been met!
You have managed to complete your mission, toppling the Witch Queen from the throne. As such, your Full Class will shift into an appropriate analog. Your skills from this class will be replaced, immediately reaching Perfection.

Full Class: Charismatic Contender for the Throne → Sovereign of Unification
Basic Skill: Warlord's Presence → Sovereign's Presence

The presence of a sovereign radiates from a ruler who leads with unmatched charisma, wisdom, and authority, to bind a kingdom together through decisive leadership. Sovereign's presence is a passive skill which further amplifies the user's auras, reducing resource consumption for infrastructure, defense, and trade by [25]%.

When ruling in times of peace, the user's auras carry a [Perfect] sense of system-granted authority, having an outsized effect on the success of diplomatic efforts, negotiations, and public outreach speeches.

When ruling in times of crisis or conflict, the user's auras [Perfectly] calms fears and bolsters morale. Troops and citizens affected by your auras

*have a [100]% increased chance of performing super-human <u>exceptional</u>
acts of courage or efficiency. Doing so will cost 50 influence per success,
drawn from a dedicated pool of up to [1,000,000] influence.*

*You have gained a new skill slot: Monarch's Wards (Prime). This is a
skill granted only to the ruler of each respective nation. Having this skill
slot and the automatically associated skill will allow you to interact with
the kingdom's wards, setting rules and regulations for your people to live
by. Defense, infrastructure, rapid communication, promotions, demotions,
all authority-driven aspects of your kingdom can be managed from this
skill.*

*If you marry, your spouse will automatically gain this skill slot as well,
as Monarch Wards (Consort). You may also assign lesser versions of
ward access to nobles throughout your land, who will be granted authority
to act on the local ward structure in their territory.*

Snow couldn't help herself; she peeked over at Dwight at
that moment, who had remained by her side since she had
woken up. Swallowing hard, she pushed the remainder of the
notifications to the side and got to her feet. The new Queen's
lips trembled as she tried to form a sentence. Her hands,
usually so steady, clenched at her sides as memories of her
sister, of Sleepy, of the father she had only just learned was
already gone, surged like a tide she couldn't hold back.

"There's always going to be work to do… always something to fix, something to rebuild." She let out a shuddering
breath, closing her eyes for a long, necessary moment. "But
grief doesn't stop the world from moving forward, and my
people need me. The war is over… but there's so much to do.
Let's get to it. I need a report on the siege of Deckbett within
the hour."

The D'wharves and others who had started to fill the room
offered her a crisp salute. Lily, on the other hand, was shaking
her head as she looked around and saw the immense amount

of work that had yet to be done. Feeling Snow's eyes on her, the redhead shrugged and spoke her mind. "Just glad I don't have your job right now. Where does someone even start with all this going on?"

"The answer is simple, though I know it may not be easy." Snow showed her friend a soft smile, not bothering to hide the absolute exhaustion she was feeling at the moment.

"...We just do the next right thing."

EPILOGUE

THE BELLS of Deckbett rang clear and triumphant, chiming over the walls that had been rebuilt and the newly restored homes of the capital city. A breeze swirled through the town, carrying the joyful song of hundreds of bards out and about on the bustling streets, where colorful banners fluttered from every rooftop and windowsill.

Snow looked around at the people filling every side street and avenue, cheering and throwing flowers as she and her fiancé rode down the main street. "Quite different from the last time I rode through the city. I've only been here thrice since I turned fourteen, if you would believe it. The first time was when I was attending my mother's funeral; the second time when I was fleeing from the Witch. Third… another funeral, but you were here for my father's final voyage."

"Third time's the charm!" Dwight wrapped his arm around her, pulling his bride-to-be close as they trundled toward the city's Class Shrine. While Snow could directly interface with the system now, under her authority as queen, her advisors had… *advised*… that she make a grand spectacle of the event. While rebuilding was well underway, and her system blessing meant an early and bountiful harvest, allowing other people to have something to celebrate was still important.

The music coming from the massive chorus of bards swelled higher, ending with a triumphant blend of horns and drums that sent shivers down Snow's spine. Together they stepped down from the ornate carriage, walking hand-in-hand into the small, unornamented Class Shrine. She was the vision of simplicity and elegance, wearing only a bright red head-band in her black hair that exactly matched the ruby shade of her lips and a flowing blue silk dress with the symbol of Dwight's home kingdom of Artek: a bear's paw print, created from silvery-white thread.

In response, he wore a simple outfit, a matching blue suit embroidered with a large white snowflake with seven points sharpened into swords—the new royal crest of Snow's king-dom. "Are you ready for this?"

"Are you sure you want to make my problems into *our* problems?" she replied with a teasing glint in her eyes. "So far I've faced down armies, a powerful Witch, and impossible odds... who knows what might be coming next?"

He squeezed her hand, a bright smile on his face. "Exactly! It's going to be so *fun* living here."

Together they reached for the plinth in the center of the small room, Snow activating *Voice of the People* to flood the city with the systems of voice that rang in her head, allowing them to participate in the moment with her.

Codex Arcane Ledger is responding to your request to become married to Dwight Charmant of the Artek Kingdom!

Scanning…. Assessing… you are not being coerced or forced into making this choice. You are at least at the legal age for marriage for your kingdom. No skills or foreign substances are impairing your choices or altering your thoughts. Even so…

Please think through this choice carefully. The effects of a system-witnessed marriage cannot be undone. Who you marry matters greatly, as your highest unlocked skill in your most potent unlocked class will be combined with theirs to make a Conjoined Skill.

You may only ever have a single Conjoined Skill. It will increase in potency in a similar manner to your other skills but will require the presence of your marriage partner to do so, unless they have died in a manner unrelated to you. Killing them or having them killed will forever halt the increase in skill level of your skill.

The system cannot be deceived.

If you choose not to continue this marriage witnessing and feel you may be in danger because of it, you will be instantly transported to a different Class Shrine with your safety guaranteed by the system for 24 hours. With this knowledge, and with a clear understanding of your own thoughts, do you wish to marry Dwight Charmant of the Artek Kingdom?

"I do," she and Dwight stated at the exact same moment, clearly having an experience with the system that mirrored the other's.

Marriage witnessed! Congratulations on this immensely important, irreversible choice! Generating Conjoined Skill.

Snow chose that moment to deactivate her skill, knowing it would be best not to spread around the state secret that was their Conjoined skill. As the system flooded her mind with information and details, applying numerous merits for defeating a Witch and taking her kingdom back, as well as granting her the knowledge on how to actually *activate* her skill, she began to laugh.

Dwight, on the other hand, had a sheepish look of discomfort on his face.

The queen turned to her new king. "Dwight... I can now turn into a... *charismatic bear*."

"There's more to it than *that*, I'm sure!" Seeing that she wasn't upset or angry, he began laughing along with her. "I'm certainly impressed by my skill as well. Not only can I *finally* communicate in my alternate form, people are going to be *Minimally* more likely to listen when I speak... as a bear."

That set the two of them off once more, and they stumbled out of the Class Shrine, being met with a wall of applause as they climbed back up into their carriage, waving at the citizens as they rode away. The celebration followed them as they rode through the city streets, a riot of laughter, dancing, and feasting—all paid for by Happy, who said it was part wedding present, part advertisement of his services. As they rolled through the streets, Snow could only marvel at how quickly the port was recovering.

Not only had the rubble of the war been cleared away, with new buildings rapidly replacing those that had fallen, but the streets had been swept clean, the scars of the tyrant's mishandling of the kingdom already vanishing under the determined efforts of hundreds of people who wanted to nothing more than to clean up their city. Certainly, part of that effect was due to Snow's brand ambassadors being out in force among the population, calming tensions and helping even those who had lost the most to wear a smile on their face.

As the carriage finally left the city and began the long journey back to the palace, Snow leaned into her new husband, putting her head on his broad shoulders while letting out a relieved sigh. "I never thought it would have gone this smoothly. Even the D'wharves are pleased with the outcomes. I think the knowledge that we would have a five percent greater return on everything is the real reason Happy picked up the cost of the wedding for us."

"I think only... Dopey, is it?" Dwight waited until Snow had nodded in acknowledgment, "Yes, Dopey, is the only one who is not happy. A kingdom-wide manhunt and a frankly astonishing price on his head. All so you can *banish* him."

"Well, actually, my sweet husband." Snow looked over at him, reaching her left hand up and poking his nose with her index finger. "Factually speaking, only *one* of them is Happy."

"Married for less than an hour, and she's trying to drive me away already." Dwight pretended to clutch at his heart as Snow laughed and gently swatted him on the arm. "Fine, you have a point. Still, it's nice to see everything falling into place so well. At the end of the day, it's because of you. You did the work, you put in the effort, and it's finally time for you to have the reward."

"*Someone* thinks highly of himself…"

Dwight let his head fall back, groaning at Snow's continued teasing. They lapsed into companionable silence as their carriage and escort wound up the side of the mountain, eventually depositing them at the doors of the palace.

Before the gates closed, Snow looked out over the ocean, watching as the sun slowly dipped toward the horizon, painting the sky in brilliant hues of lavender, rose gold, and gentle greens. Her smile faded slightly, and she turned away from the view to walk back into her home, where the only dark spot in her life remained, laying in a sealed, glass pod, deep in a cursed slumber.

Snow walked to her sister's room, fingers brushing against the medical-grade glass Doc had insisted would help her stay healthy, along with daily applications of the best healing magic and care he could offer. "Rose… the only thing that would have made this day better is if you had been there to celebrate it with me."

Her twin hadn't opened her eyes since the fight against the queen, trapped within her own mind by the combined forces of the cursed dagger and the shattered magic mirror. Snow could only offer silent thanks once more to Sleepy, Sir Upp, who had taken the brunt of the burst of power. Were it not for his sacrifices, over and over, it was probable that both of the women would have lost their lives over the years.

"She's going to wake up, Snow. Hey. Speak to me… there's a type of healing to be had in sharing one's sorrows," Dwight assured her as his hand came to rest gently on her elbow. "We are not going to give up. Neither will Doc. You know that."

"I know…" Snow took a calming breath, turning to meet her husband's eyes. "Still, every day she's trapped in there is another day she isn't getting better. Another day she isn't out and experiencing the life that has been denied her for *years*. When she's better, I want to spare no expense. She'll have anything she wants, training, coins to travel the kingdom, the world. Whatever it is. I owe her *everything*."

Dwight nodded along with her, but as he opened his mouth to respond, the door burst open, revealing Doc, shockingly out of sorts. Barely able to catch his breath, the elderly the man blurted out, "She's here. She's arrived!"

"Who?" Snow inquired before her mind caught up with the situation. Her eyes went wide as she realized who Doc must be referring to—there was only one person who would have made him react like this and rushed to her. "The mind healer you think can guide Rose back to us?"

"Exactly that… it's just…" Doc's eyes darted to the window and he let out a shaky laugh.

"Spit it out, man! What's happening?" Dwight demanded with a deep growl, acting more like a bear than a king at that moment.

"You see… she rode in on a dragon."

The room filled with silence for a long few heartbeats. Dwight blinked rapidly, mouth opening and closing as if searching for words before turning to his new queen with pure excitement shining in his eye.

"A *dragon*? I *knew* marrying you was going to be an adventure, Snow!"

Continue the Damsels of Distress series on Patreon.com/
DakotaKrout - or order on Amazon, geni.us/DamselsSeries.

Red X Wolf
Cinder X Bella
Beauty X Beast
Rob X Punzel

About Dakota Krout

Good. Clean. Fun.

Dakota Krout is a celebrated author known for infusing fantasy novels with fun, punny, and clean humor. With multiple best-selling series—including "Divine Dungeon", "Completionist Chronicles", "Cooking With Disaster", and "Full Murderhobo"—he brings joy and laughter to readers. Dakota's work, renowned for its wit and creativity, earned a place as one of Audible's top 5 fantasy picks in 2017, a top 5 bestseller rank featured on the New York Times, and was chosen by Audible as among "the top 100 fantasy books of all time" in 2024.

Dakota's journey in publishing has been filled with gratefulness, and a deep desire to continue bringing smiles and laughter to the readers. "_I hope you Read Every Book With A Smile!_"

Connect with Dakota:
MountaindalePress.com
Patreon.com/DakotaKrout
Facebook.com/DakotaKrout
Instagram.com/DakotaKrout
Twitter.com/DakotaKrout
Discord.gg/mdp

About Mountaindale Press

Dakota and Danielle Krout, a husband and wife team, strive to create as well as publish excellent fantasy and science fiction novels. Self-publishing *The Divine Dungeon: Dungeon Born* in 2016 transformed their careers from Dakota's military and programming background and Danielle's Ph.D. in pharmacology to President and CEO, respectively, of a small press. Their goal is to share their success with other authors and provide captivating fiction to readers with the purpose of solidifying Mountaindale Press as the place 'Where Fantasy Transforms Reality.'

Connect with Mountaindale Press:
MountaindalePress.com
Facebook.com/MountaindalePress
Twitter.com/_Mountaindale
Instagram.com/MountaindalePress

MOUNTAINDALE PRESS TITLES
GAMELIT AND LITRPG

The Completionist Chronicles,
Cooking with Disaster,
The Divine Dungeon,
Full Murderhobo, and
Year of the Sword by Dakota Krout

Metier Apocalypse by Frank G. Albelo

A Touch of Power by Jay Boyce

Ether Collapse and
Ether Flows by Ryan DeBruyn

Unbound by Nicoli Gonnella

Lion's Lineage by Rohan Hublikar and Dakota Krout

Wolfman Warlock by James Hunter and Dakota Krout

Axe Druid,
Mephisto's Magic Online, and
High Table Hijinks by Christopher Johns

Tower of Jack by Sean Loomer

Dragon Core Chronicles by Lars Machmüller

Pixel Dust and
Necrotic Apocalypse by D. Petrie

Viceroy's Pride and
Tower of Somnus by Cale Plamann

Henchman by Carl Stubblefield

Artorian's Archives by Dennis Vanderkerken and Dakota
Krout